A FAMILIAR DESIRE

Cora paced the perimeter of the room, her need for release growing with every step. Earth drug companies would pay dearly for whatever the hell aphrodisiac the Flock used on her. Only the sense that she was being watched kept her from touching herself and relieving the increasing ache.

What did it matter? At this rate, she'd ravage whatever abomination entered the room.

A subtle *snick* of sound and the enticing aroma of warm male flesh told her she was no longer alone. The fear that wouldn't come to her aid before now blossomed in her. She knew that she should look up, should brace herself for an attack, but she couldn't make herself move. When she found herself quaking like an untried virgin, anger usurped her fear. She sprang up and turned to face whatever the Flock had sent her.

Shock froze her.

"Alexander," she whispered.

STAR CRASH

ELYSA HENDRICKS

LOVE SPELL NEW YORK CITY

To Vern—
You take me to the Stars and never let me Crash.
Love you always and forever.

LOVE SPELL®

December 2007

Published by

Dorchester Publishing Co., Inc.
200 Madison Avenue
New York, NY 10016

ISBN 10: 0-505-52743-X
ISBN 13: 978-0-505-52743-1

The name "Love Spell" and its logo are trademarks of Dorchester Publishing Co., Inc.

Printed in the United States of America.

10 9 8 7 6 5 4 3 2 1

Visit us on the web at www.dorchesterpub.com.

ACKNOWLEDGMENTS

Writing a book is similar to having a baby: it's mostly a solitary endeavor, but every pregnant mother needs and appreciates all the help and encouragement she can get along the way. If not for the following people *Star Crash* would have been stillborn.

Thank you to all my Windy City RWA sisters and brother for their help and support, past, present, and future. Thank you to the Maryland Romance Writers. Their Reveal Your Inner Vixen contest allowed me to check the progress of my growing baby. Thank you to my friends Karen McCullough, Liz Krejcik, Kelle Riley and Anita Baker for being willing to help me change just one more stinky draft and to Barbara Cary for playing midwife and godmother to all my book children. And last but not least, thank you to my editor, Chris Keeslar, for naming and presenting my baby to the world.

STAR CRASH

CHAPTER ONE

Strapped naked and spread-eagle on a table, Cora Daniels squinted against the glare of the white light shining down on her. Cold metal pressed uncomfortably against her backbone. A medicinal smell burned her nostrils. She ran her dry tongue over even drier lips and tried to swallow. Her head throbbed in time with the thump of her accelerating heartbeat. Where was she? What had happened?

The last thing she recalled with clarity was the shriek of her ship's alarm. No; she blinked and groaned. She remembered more. The shrill whine of *Freedom* fighting to pull itself out of the planet's atmosphere. The sudden silence when the engine stalled. The sharp crackle of flames as *Freedom* plummeted downward. Pulling the nose up just before the ship smashed into the ground. Pain rocketing through her, then blackness.

She tugged on the restraints pinning her to the table. Secure and tight, they held her all but motionless. A strap across her forehead kept her from turning.

A form leaned over her. Other than a dark shape surrounded by a nimbus of light, she couldn't see anything.

"Who's there? Where am I? What the hell's going on?" She rasped out the questions through her parched throat.

The translator chip imbedded in her skull attempted to interpret, without success, the sharp whistles and trills the form gave in response: obviously, her rescuer and captor didn't speak any known language.

Something cool and dry touched her belly. She arched her back, trying to jerk away, but could only move a fraction of an inch. The touch became firmer, anchoring her in place. Other hands or things—unable to turn her head, she couldn't tell which—touched her. First they ran over her lightly, from fingertips to toes, as if assessing. She shivered in dread at their impersonal touch. Whoever or whatever handled her ignored her objections and feelings about their invasion of her person.

They held open her eyelids and shone a light into them until she could see nothing but spots. Icy cold things probed her ears and nostrils. Heart racing, Cora struggled to remain calm.

They massaged her breasts, then pinched her nipples until they stood stiff. They massaged and prodded her belly, pushing down until she winced at the uncomfortable pressure. Helpless to resist, she struggled against her rising fear. The examination continued, as did the chirps and trills of her captors.

The light tilted away from her face. She blinked away the spots and tried to focus on the three creatures she could see.

One stood by her head; the other two were situated on either side of her hips. Her alien captors reminded her of a misshapen ostrich-chicken hybrid with arms. Their heads rested on long flexible necks that ended in ovoid bodies. Instead of wings they had arms. They wore white lab-type coats over their multicolored, feathered bodies, and rubber gloves on their hands. Leathery pinkish-gray skin covered their extremities. Aside from having one head, two legs and two arms, there was nothing human about them.

But it wasn't their inhuman appearance that chilled Cora's heart; it was their lack of human expression. Their birdlike facial features seemed frozen. She couldn't read any emotion there. They didn't smile or frown, laugh or cry. The only indication of emotion lay in their vocalizations, but whether a fast, high-pitched trill meant excitement, fear or anger she couldn't tell. She concentrated on accessing her translator chip. The effort caused her head to pound. Had it been damaged in the crash? Or was it incapable of deciphering the language of, as she dubbed them, the Flock?

The biomechanical chip tapped into a person's latent telepathic ability, enabling them to comprehend and speak an alien language. But even with a translator chip, each person's aptitude varied. Some were better at it than others. Maybe the Flock thought processes were just too different from hers or her skill wasn't up to the challenge. She could only hope that as she heard the Flock speak she'd eventually be able to communicate.

Gloved fingers separated her buttocks and something cold and hard brushed the back of her thigh.

"What are you doing? Stop it!"

The creature at her head put a hand on her hair, gave a soft whistle, then nodded to the others.

Cora bit her lip to keep from screaming, more in rage than from pain, as an object was inserted into her anus; she refused to give them the satisfaction of knowing they'd hurt or humiliated her. Instinct made her tighten her muscles, which increased the sting of pulling flesh as the probe sank deep. Beyond the discomfort of having her rectum stretched, it wasn't painful. Still, she couldn't stop herself from trembling in apprehension. Sweat beaded on her body. What next?

One of the creatures moved to stand between her spread legs. Using both hands, he parted the nest of hair at her groin and pulled opened the lips of her labia. Cool air swirled against her dampness. The creature slid two fingers into her, then with his other hand repeated the massage of her belly. The metallic taste of blood filled her mouth.

Though it seemed to last forever, Cora knew the exam took only minutes. In a brisk motion the creature pulled his fingers out of her and removed the probe from her anus. Swollen and throbbing, her vagina felt empty and cold. She couldn't control her trembling. Not even during her pilot training had she been subjected to such an invasive, impersonal physical. Her captors treated her like a mindless lab animal.

The Flock took off his gloves with a snap. Cora glared at the creature, but he took no notice. It chirped, whistled and clicked at the others. They rushed to obey its obvious commands. One gave her a series of injections in her upper arm. By the time that alien finished, Cora felt like a pincushion; her arm swelled and began to ache.

He placed the end of a metal cylinder against the underside of her left wrist. The cylinder began to hum and grow warm. Cora tried to pull away, but the restraints held her. Pain seared up her arm. She shrieked and went rigid as the smell of burning flesh reached her.

After a moment the cylinder was pulled away and the agony eased to a continuous ache. Another Flock smeared a cool salve on her burn. Tears blurred Cora's vision as she memorized the face of each of her tormentors. Someday, somehow, she vowed she'd make them pay for what she suffered here.

CHAPTER TWO

Cora plucked the green-gray slug from the leaf it was happily munching. Though the other women working around her cheerfully popped the disgusting maggots into their mouths, she couldn't bring herself to do so. Instead, she tossed it to the woman next to her and watched the Flock guard. Her plans were in place. Tonight she was going to get off this godforsaken excuse for a planet.

A few days after her capture and the following humiliation, her memory of what had happened subsequent to the crash had returned.

When her ship hit ground, she'd blacked out briefly. Once she regained consciousness, she'd checked *Freedom*'s systems. Though the hull of her ship had taken a beating, the silver metal scorched from reentry and dinged from its impact against the rocky ground, the drive remained intact. With the nav-system out, she couldn't determine where she was or what had caused the malfunction that led to her crash, but with repair *Freedom* would fly again.

Procedure told her she should have made her repairs, taken

off again immediately and contacted Command to send an exploratory team, but a cursory scan of the planet surface revealed an abundance of precious metals, so she'd decided to investigate first. Though her mission didn't include planetary recon, as long as she was on the ground she'd do a preliminary survey for her report and plant her marker. The Consortium paid a bonus to pilots who discovered new planets with usable resources. Now, she realized, confused by the trauma of the crash, greed and not good sense had directed her actions.

So no one and nothing could get into it, she'd programmed *Freedom* to respond only to her voice command, then set out to find the raw materials she needed to implement repairs. Once she fed them into her MAT—matter absorption/transformation unit—repairs shouldn't take long to complete.

A few miles away, while stumbling along what appeared to be some kind of trail, the ground had given way beneath her and she'd found herself trapped in a pit. Despite repeated attempts, she couldn't climb out. All she remembered of her actual capture by the Flock was a sharp sting on her arm and then waking up strapped naked to a table.

She had to escape and find her way back to *Freedom*. She could still get off this godforsaken rock.

For the last ten days she'd played the submissive slave, watching and waiting for her chance. The bundle with the supplies she'd managed to accumulate—some dried fruit and seedpods, a blanket and a skin of water, along with a shard of sharp rock she'd found in the field—was hidden near the edge of the compound. Tonight she'd escape.

When she paused in her work, the guard headed toward her. Though her hands ached from the labor of debugging the field and were scratched from the plant's tiny thorns, she went quickly back to work. Her first day in the fields she'd learned the hard way that slacking off was frowned upon.

The bruise on her shoulder from her first transgression still burned in her memory nearly as brightly as the hate in her soul. And though the brand on her wrist was mending, the scar on her heart would never heal.

For several hours each morning and afternoon she and the other humans were herded out into the fields to pick bugs. Small—none of her fellows matched her own modest height of five feet six inches—and wiry, they were humanoid, but from what Cora could determine, their intelligence level wasn't terribly high. Still, her training was in mechanics and as a pilot, not xeno-anthropology.

Again she wondered if her translator chip had been damaged in the crash. Her attempts to understand the Flock had been unsuccessful. Consortium of Intelligent Life protocol kept her from trying to communicate with them—they strictly controlled first contact with aliens. Violations of their laws, deliberately or by mistake, were severely dealt with. She was in a bad situation: C.O.I.L. considered a few lives expendable if that resulted in a peaceable treaty/trade agreement with a new species. If Cora revealed her intelligence to the Flock, would they believe it; and if they did, how would that affect C.O.I.L.'s subsequent dealings with them? It was a lot to think about. Being an alien captive was bad enough, but C.O.I.L.'s censure looming over her head was even worse.

During the hottest part of the day the guards returned the slaves to the compound. There the women went inside a barnlike structure, curled up and slept in small stalls on a layer of sawdust. In the evening the overseers brought in trays filled with fruit, vegetables and coarse bread. Occasionally there was also a selection of grubs. Cora couldn't force herself to eat the grubs the other women seemed to enjoy, so she existed solely on a diet of bread, vegetables, fruit and water. If she didn't escape soon, she knew she'd have to start eating the grubs for the protein.

The other women went naked, but despite the heat Cora couldn't bring herself to go around unclothed. They regarded her with degrees of curiosity and suspicion. The rectangle of thin cloth she wrapped sarong-style around herself did little for modesty or to protect her previously space-pale skin from the blazing sun. After a few days of a painful sunburn, she was now tanned almost all over to a golden brown.

The sun beat down on her head. Sweat trickled between her breasts. She glanced at the guard. Eyes closed, his head bobbed on his long neck as he dozed under a tree near the edge of the herd. Aside from being firm about where the women could go and making sure they completed their work, this guard wasn't overtly cruel or even unkind. When the field was cleared of its day's worth of bugs, he allowed the women to roam freely and rest in the shade of the trees lining the field.

He opened his eyes as two women wandered to his side and sat down by him. One rubbed her head against his arm. He stroked her hair. She relaxed against him, then stretched out on her back. When he rubbed her chest and belly she squirmed and made little mewing sounds of pleasure. The other woman crowded closer, almost crawling on top of her companion to reach him. The overseer trilled and used his other hand to fondle her.

Sickened by the women's fawning and unable to bear watching them being treated like animals, Cora looked across an open stretch of land toward the river glinting silvery blue in the distance. Trees lined the bank. Off to the left the water gave way to a reed-filled swamp at the base of a cliff. The shade and smell of water called to her, but the Flock refused to allow them near the water. After ten days in the hot dusty compound where she'd been imprisoned without a bath, a dip in the water would feel marvelous. She edged toward the river.

A hoarse shout stopped her. She cringed as the guard jumped up and headed in her direction. The creature took his job seriously. The other women whimpered in fear and edged away from her and the guard. Heart pounding in rage, Cora didn't look up as the overseer stopped next to her. Nor did she react outwardly as he smacked her shoulder with the butt of the long rod he carried and berated her verbally with a series of sharp clicks and whirs. Despite the sting, she refused to give the Flock the satisfaction of making her cry out. She kept her head down and waited.

Finally, with a huff of what sounded like exasperation, he moved off. Only then did she allow herself to glance up. With the threat gone the women went back to their hunting for bugs and edible weeds. A few glared at her as they passed. Their voices filled the air like the sound of a flock of birds. Unlike for the Flock, the translator chip buried in Cora's brain began to interpret the women's simple language.

"Stupid female."

"Get us punished."

"She new. Give time," another voice said.

"Not matter."

"Tonight see—" The word was indecipherable.

Their attention turned from her, they giggled and returned to stuffing bugs into their mouths until they looked like a herd of cows contently chewing their cud. Cora shuddered at the image, and looked away to study the guard.

Like all Flock, whether he was sitting and eating or angry his expression never changed. When he was upset, the feathers on his head stood on end, giving him a comical look. But Cora didn't see anything funny about the result of angering him. She rubbed the bruise on her shoulder.

A horn signaled time to return to the compound. She wiped the sticky residue of grub slime from her fingers and rose. Her muscles groaned in protest. She'd leave tonight, or the stars help her, tomorrow she'd grab the guard's rod and beat him to death.

The women around her laughed and started to babble. They had a language, but beyond communicating necessary information about food and other bodily functions they didn't seem to have much to say.

She fell into line behind them. When she'd first arrived in the compound a week ago, a few of the bolder women had tried to befriend her. Like the Flock, they all found her blond hair, pale skin and blue eyes fascinating, wanted to touch and stroke her. After a few sharp words and slaps they'd backed off. Now Cora held herself apart. They might appear human, but their lack of intelligence and servile manner grated on her nerves. If they were the descendants of a lost colony, in the last four hundred years they'd devolved into a species more like sheep than humans.

Though it went against her nature to run away from a problem, as far as she could see, her best option was to escape, return to Earth, report her findings and let the officials of C.O.I.L. determine if the Flock and these humans were worth contacting. She wished she could to talk to Alex. First contact had been his field of expertise. Even after six years the thought of him brought tears to her eyes.

Alexander had been the xeno-anthropologist. He'd loved all things alien, and had planned on making a career of searching out alien species. Cora on the other hand had a deep-seated—and obviously deserved—dislike of the strange creatures being discovered on distant worlds. Alexander had always teased her about her xenophobia.

They'd had great plans: she'd pilot the spacecraft to new worlds while he made first contact with the inhabitants. That dream had died with Alex.

It surprised her to feel a spark of her old anger. If he hadn't insisted on taking that first assignment, if he'd waited until they could be posted together like she'd asked, then demanded, then begged, he'd still be with her. But for the first time in their relationship he'd denied her something. Up until that point she'd been the one in charge of their affair; she'd called the shots. By accepting a position as a First Contact Agent he'd declared his independence. Afraid of losing him entirely by forcing him to give up his dream, she'd backed off.

He'd even refused to marry her before he left, saying it wouldn't be fair to her because he'd be gone at least six months, if not a year. Finally, at the last moment as they said their goodbyes at the spaceport, he'd agreed to being engaged and accepted the ring she gave him. But it meant nothing now; the past was over. Alexander was dead, disappeared in deep space over six years ago.

Cora blinked away her tears, brought her attention back to the present and followed the other women. The sooner she was off this planet the better. Since Alex had left her, she'd made sure no one controlled her life.

Because her attitude of pride and resistance to their authority tended to anger the guards and bring on punishments, the women gave Cora a wide berth. She preferred it that way. Even if she'd felt the desire to get close to any of them, which she most definitely did not, it made no sense. She'd be gone soon. Besides, she'd given up on relationships of any kind when Alex died. Getting close to someone meant risking losing them.

At the gate, a guard stepped in her path and whistled an incomprehensible command.

"What?" she asked.

Cora was no alien expert. A pilot and a mechanic, she knew engines and machines not people—and on this planet the Flock were the reigning "people." Her translator chip still couldn't decipher the Flock language. The chirps, cackles, whirs, whistles and trills they used as speech sounded like birdsong, but unlike birdsong she didn't find anything pleasing about it. Her one required course on alien contact at the Academy wouldn't do her any good if she couldn't understand or speak their language.

The Flock whistled again. She tried to move around him. He smacked her arm with his rod, then shoved her ahead of him.

"Go where?" she called out to the women.

One woman ran along the inside of the compound fence. "Make young." The answer left a lot to be desired.

"What happen?" Cora asked.

The woman smiled. "Go. Much fun. Good. You like."

"Yeah, sure," Cora muttered. Whatever the Flock had in mind for her, she wasn't interested.

She took the opportunity to look around as the guard herded her deeper into the compound, past the pen she'd occupied since her arrival. They moved down a wide path between a series of pens to where she hadn't yet been. Farther ahead lay some buildings.

It appeared the compound covered several acres, consisting of many pens separated by wooden barriers. The inhabitants of each pen were segregated by age and gender. Her pen held ten women, all in their twenties like her. One pen held girls ranging in age from about five to fifteen. A larger pen held about fifteen women, all with babies and toddlers. In still another pen, fresh wood chips covered the ground, there were tent-covered low benches with soft cushions, and a fountain provided fresh water and cooled the hot, dry air. Six women in varying stages of pregnancy occupied this pen. Cora couldn't help but gape at the women's bulging bellies and swollen breasts. Sweet stars, she was trapped on a breeding farm for humans.

The women paid little attention to her or her guard as they moved through this human chicken coop. She noticed there weren't any pens with grown men. If the women were hens, where was the rooster?

The next pen answered her question. Naked except for

protective cups over their genitals, ten boys ranging in age from four to ten practiced fighting with wooden swords. Her attention shifted from the boys to the adult male who directed their training. Though his back was to her, he appeared as naked as the boys. Forgetting the guard, she paused to watch.

Bronze skin shiny with sweat rippled over powerful muscles as the man instructed the boys in swordplay. With his dark hair and straddle-legged stance, the youngest boy looked like a miniature version of the man. Cora smiled at his clumsy attempts to imitate his elder's fluid movements.

The boy watched the man intently, but his small body, round with baby fat, refused to cooperate. He tripped and sprawled in the dust. His wooden sword slipped from his grip. The other boys' laughter stopped abruptly at the man's sharp command. The man knelt next to the boy, said a few quiet words, then handed him back the wooden sword. The boy rubbed the tears from his cheeks with grubby fists, leaving streaks of dirt. The man's compassion for the boy touched Cora, made these people seem less like animals. More human.

At one time she'd dreamed of someday having a child like this—Alex's child. That dream had died with him. Losing Alex had killed that need inside her. Now she lived to explore. Relationships, love and caring for others were no longer part of her life.

Still, her gaze moved back to the man and traveled from the top of his head, covered with sleek shoulder-length ebony hair, down his broad shoulders to his narrow waist and taut bare buttocks. Her breath caught at the beauty of his form. His unashamed masculinity woke her buried femininity. Her nipples tightened in response. At some primal level her body recognized this man. No one since Alex had stirred her like this. "Turn around," she whispered. "I want to see your face."

Instead, he stepped back from the boys, then lunged forward. Sunlight flashed off the blade of his sword as he whirled. Briefly, before the beauty of his motion recaptured her attention, she wondered why he didn't use his own *real* sword to strike down his captors and seize his freedom. Dark hair obscured his features as his face whipped past. Why did he seem so familiar? She had to see his face. She started forward.

Pain radiated down her arm. Instinctively she turned to confront her attacker—the guard—and ducked the next blow. Acting on rage and adrenaline, she snatched the rod from his hand and cracked it across his neck. Without a sound, he went down and lay motionless.

Their interest diverted by the drama unfolding outside their pen, the boys halted their practice. They yelled, but their words were incomprehensible. The man called out something. She glanced up and for the briefest of moments their eyes met. Though she longed to explore the recognition she felt, necessity required that she return her attention to the fallen guard.

Was he dead? She bent over to check, then stopped. She couldn't stay to find out. She didn't care; she had to flee before other Flock arrived. But where should she go? Her escape route, the hole she'd spent the last ten days laboriously digging under the fence, was back inside her pen.

Crouched close to the ground, she scanned the compound. Several Flock exited a building at the far end; in seconds they'd see her. She darted behind a wooden barrier next to the pen holding the women with babies.

A nursing mother looked up and saw her. The woman started to smile, then noticed the rod in Cora's hand. She glanced at the pathway and saw the guard. Her mouth opened in a shriek. The entire pen exploded in chaos. Women screamed. Babies and toddlers started to bawl. Other pens picked up the cry. Over the racket Cora could hear the whistles of the Flock as they found their fallen companion.

She ran along the wooden wall. It would only block her from the view of the Flock for a few minutes. She had to find a way out of the compound. The wall ended at the back of the pen; a six-foot high fence topped with razor wire trapped her between the wooden barrier and the pen.

She had to get back to her pen. Once through the fence she could lose herself in the surrounding woods.

The only way out was back the way she'd come or through the women's pen. Looping the handle of the rod around her wrist, she climbed the low metal fence into the pen. She landed in the midst of the women. Squawking in fright, they scattered like a flock of chickens. Some grabbed their toddlers as they fled, others left them crying in the dirt as they rushed to safety. The pitiful wail of an abandoned baby made Cora pause. The infant sat helpless in the middle of the stampeding women. Unable to ignore its plight, she turned and snatched up the baby and set it on a bench out of harm's way, then she pushed through the frantic women, ran across the open space and vaulted the opposite fence.

Now she faced another problem: the wooden barriers between the pens. In order to reach her pen she'd have to move around the edge of the barrier into the open pathway. To reach her pen she'd have to expose herself twice.

Through the commotion in the pen she'd just passed through she could see the Flock headed along the pathway toward her position. Did she have enough time before they reached her? What choice did she have? If she stayed put, she'd be trapped.

She darted around the first barrier. A Flock called out. She glanced back and saw them running toward her. The next pen held older women. They didn't scatter like the young mothers; they crowded against the fence, yelling.

Cora couldn't make out their words. Adrenaline interfered with her translator chip. Either they urged her on or they called for the guards. Either way, she couldn't risk climbing the fence and putting herself in their midst. She opted to run straight down the pathway. Lungs straining with effort, bare feet pounding against the hard dirt, she sprinted toward freedom. Her legs were no match for the long stride of the Flock. Once they saw her, they ran her down in seconds. Kicking and screaming, she tumbled into the dirt. Four Flock grabbed her and pinned her to the ground. During the struggle the rod fell off her wrist and her sarong twisted around her shoulders, further hampering her efforts to escape and leaving her exposed. Once more, she was naked and spread-eagle. Panting and sweating, she swore at the Flock but couldn't twist free. Finally, she went still. Let them think she was defeated. Give her one opening and she'd kill them all with her bare hands. She hoped her guard was dead; she was just sorry he'd died so clean and easy.

A shadow passed over her. She looked up into the eyes of the guard she'd hoped she'd killed. The gash on his neck trickled a grayish-pink liquid. On his head his tuft of feathers stood straight up and his black eyes, usually flat and devoid of emotion, glittered with hatred. With deliberate movements he picked up his rod. As if debating where to strike her first, his gaze never left her body. She shuddered.

The end of the rod glowed blue. He touched it to her left breast. Fire licked through her. She choked back her cry and braced herself for more pain.

A sharp whistle checked the downward motion of the rod. The blue glow faded. He waited as another Flock approached.

The new Flock crouched down next to Cora. In the last ten days she'd learned to differentiate between them; despite their lack of facial expressions, like humans each had a unique appearance and personality. She didn't recognize this as one of the guards. Taller and heavier built, the tuft of silvery feathers on his head stood higher and thicker than any of the others. And beneath his chin hung a wattle of crimson skin. Even his clothing looked dissimilar to that of the guards. His long jacket was stylish and elegant, the material finer and more colorful. Pins and ribbons decorated his chest, obviously indicating his station or rank. One insignia on the lapel of his jacket made her pause. It matched the brand on her arm.

"Don't touch me, you overgrown ostrich!"

He ignored her and ran a hand over her body, squeezed her breasts and muscles and poked at her belly. When he probed her crotch with his fingers, she tried without success to wiggle away. The guards held her still for his invasion of her person. Then, as he took her chin in his hand and studied her face, her own musky scent filled her nostrils.

What he saw and felt seemed to please him, because he nodded, then chirped some commands. Wiping his hands against his clothing, he rose over her. A Flock in a white lab coat hurried forward. When she saw the syringe he held, Cora increased her struggles but couldn't break free. A curse escaped her as the Flock plunged the needle into her arm without finesse. Her vision began to blur.

Once she stopped fighting, two guards hauled her to her feet. No longer in control of her body, she sagged between them. The commanding Flock called out more commands. Other guards appeared to quell the continuing commotion in the pens.

As she was towed away, Cora saw a guard pick up a limp, dirt-covered infant from the women's pen. In their panic to get away from her, the women had trampled one of their own. Was it the one she'd tried to save? Guilt made her cringe; then she hardened her heart. Her last conscious thought was that stopping for that baby had cost her freedom.

★ ★ ★

Hours or days later, Cora woke to the sound of singing. Soft warmth cocooned her body. She opened her eyes cautiously and surveyed the change in her situation. She lay on a comfortable pallet in a sparsely furnished but warm room. Next to her sat an older woman whose eyes were closed though she wasn't asleep. She hummed a tune that reminded Cora of a lullaby.

"Wake?" The woman opened her eyes and looked at Cora.

Cora sat up. Her wrap was gone. God, she hated being kept naked all the time. She tugged the bedding up over her bare breasts and glared at the woman. Gray salted the woman's dark hair and wrinkles fanned out around her bright blue eyes. She conveyed a sense of safety and comfort that disarmed Cora in spite of her misgivings.

"Who are you? Where am I now?"

"Matron. Preparation chamber."

Matron? Was that the woman's name or her position? As always, the translator chip did only so much. It translated words. Meanings she had to figure out for herself.

"Preparation for what?"

"No worry. You see."

"That's what I'm afraid of."

"No fear. I care. Come. Bathe."

"Now that's the first order I've had since I got here that I'm happy to comply with," Cora answered in Standard.

The Flock Matron cocked her head to one side. "What?"

"Okay," Cora said.

"Come."

Cora hesitated. Should she try to escape? The room had two doors, but no windows. Which door, if any, led to freedom? Were guards outside just waiting for a chance to grab her again? She knew one guard who'd love to get his hands on her.

Finally she tucked the sheet around her body and followed Matron through a doorway into another chamber. If necessary, she could handle the old woman; she wasn't so sure about the outcome of another encounter with the Flock.

What lay beyond the door melted away Cora's doubts. Steam rose in the air from a large sunken tub filled with swirling, mint-scented hot water. She took a deep breath and let the bedding drop. Her nipples puckered in anticipation.

Matron smiled and motioned her forward. Like a child Cora took her hand and stepped into the water. Bliss washed through her as the heated bath caressed her parched skin and eased her abused muscles.

She sank back until only her face remained above the surface. Water lapped over her lips and eyes. Sound disappeared as she floated in the heavenly liquid.

Too soon memory intruded and pleasure evaporated. How could she let down her guard so easily, leave herself naked and vulnerable? Sputtering, she bolted up. The chamber remained quiet and softly lit. Matron sat on the edge of the tub dangling her feet in the water.

Matron smiled. "Ready?"

"Ready for what?" Cora tensed.

Matron slipped into the water. In her hands she held a tube and a cloth. She came to Cora's side. Without asking permission she squeezed a thick cream onto the cloth and began to wash her. Cora started to resist, but the sensation of the slick cream and rough cloth against her skin felt too good to refuse. Since Alex died she'd forgotten what it felt like to have another person touch her. She stood motionless as Matron scrubbed her from head to toe. What felt like years of dirt and grime sloughed away. The way the mint from the water and the fruity scent of the cream blurred her mind and relaxed her muscles made her wonder if either or both were drugging agents. She didn't care.

The water swirled gently around her, carrying away the dirt and residue of the cream. When she finished, Matron led Cora to the edge of the tub and had Cora sit there while she combed the tangles from her hair.

Relaxed and nearly asleep, Cora didn't object as Matron had her lie down on a mat next to the tub. Eyes closed in contentment, she knew she should put a stop to this; instead she sighed with enjoyment when Matron began to massage her with fragrant oil. Again, the thought that she was being drugged crossed her mind, but again she didn't care. With each stroke energy and vigor suffused her body. The bruises and aches from the beating by the guards and her time in the pen faded from the mind-blurring effect of the water and cream.

As the oil seeped into her skin, heat built between Cora's thighs. A need to fill the emptiness inside her started to grow. She squirmed at the long forgotten sensation. She opened her eyes to fight off the feeling and prepare herself for whatever came next, somehow doubting she was going to enjoy the next chapter as much as this one.

"Come," Matron said.

As much as she wanted to refuse, Cora found she lacked the will to fight. She followed Matron down a narrow corridor into another room.

Matron left, and Cora stood on a well-padded floor of an octagonal room about ten feet across. The walls and ceiling were made of panels of a material that reflected her naked image back at her from all angles. The effect was dizzying and disturbing. But it was the feeling of being watched that made her skin crawl.

She studied her reflection. Tall and well-proportioned, she wasn't ashamed of her body, just not used to parading around naked. Her breasts stood high and proud, her waist was narrow, her hips rounded but not fat. Her nipples were taut with expectation, but of what she didn't know.

Her hair lay soft and damp against her shoulders. Her skin looked and felt smooth from the residue of oil Matron had rubbed on her. She shivered in remembered pleasure;

her nipples grew tighter and moisture slicked her sex. She squeezed her knees together, but that didn't stop the growing ache of emptiness.

Whatever was in that cream or oil had heightened her physical responses, and she didn't want to like it. Letting Matron touch her had been a mistake. It had awakened needs she'd suppressed. For the last six years this hadn't been an issue in her life, but now forbidden memories flared to light. Alexander had enjoyed her body, as she'd enjoyed his, but their time together had been too brief. He was dead, vanished on that deep space exploration, and she'd shut down her libido, closed off her heart and devoted herself to her career. Her colleagues, both male and female, would never believe how the sight of her own naked body was turning Cora on. She barely believed it herself.

What a time to get horny! For all she knew she was about to be fed to whatever passed for lions on this planet, all for the amusement of the Flock. Somehow, she doubted what they had in mind for her would be that easy. The soft lighting and the padded floor, along with the sexually stimulating bath and massage, warned her what was truly coming.

Heaven only knew what kind of creature they intended to mate her with. Against her will, the image of the man from the compound popped into her mind. Her belly tightened. She tried to summon anger. Even fear would work. Instead, all she felt was anticipation.

She paced the perimeter of the room, her need for release growing with every step, with every movement. Her genitals felt swollen and hot, her breasts heavy. The Earth drug companies would pay dearly for whatever the hell the Flock had used on her. Only the sense that she was being watched kept her from touching herself and relieving the increasing ache.

What did it matter? At this rate, as long as it had a hard dick, she'd ravage whatever abomination entered the room. Reason melted away beneath wave after wave of need. Cora sank to her knees and clasped her hands over her bent head. "What are you doing to me?"

A subtle *snick* of sound and the enticing aroma of warm male flesh told her she was no longer alone.

The fear that wouldn't come to her aid before now blossomed in her. She knew that she should look up, should brace herself for an attack, but she couldn't make herself move. When she found herself quaking like an untried virgin, anger usurped her fear. She sprang up and turned to face whatever the Flock had sent her.

Shock froze her.

It wasn't his obvious human form. His rugged good looks. The many scars that marred his muscular bronze body. The fact that he was the man she'd seen in the compound. It wasn't even his impressive male equipment, unhampered by any scrap of clothing.

Her gaze riveted on his face—his familiar, beloved face.

"Alexander," she whispered. And for the first time in her life, she fainted.

CHAPTER THREE

Zan caught the woman as she crumbled. For a moment when their eyes met, he thought he knew her, remembered her. And not just from the glimpse of her he'd seen earlier in the compound as she'd crouched over the fallen guard. Then as now, something passed between then.

The word she spoke sounded familiar. Had he serviced her before? The chance that they'd put the same female with him twice was unlikely; his stud service was in great demand. He studied her face. It stirred something deep in his mind. A familiar throb began behind his temples.

Her skin felt soft and smelled of sex stimulant. In spite of his will, his maleness rose in response. He lowered her to the floor and took a step back. If he held her much longer, he'd take her like the beast the handlers thought him. The idea disgusted him. He would have this female, but on his terms, not theirs.

Though he could and had performed this function with an audience, on occasion he demanded privacy. Long ago he'd learned to put on a show for the handlers: it gained him some measure of respect and self-determination. He began his routine. With his fists he pounded his chest, then each of the panels in turn, until he'd made a circuit of the room. Then, as if satisfied he'd put his opponents in their place, he returned to stand over the female.

In response the panels turned opaque, no longer reflective. The handlers had agreed.

He crouched over the woman. He knew it would be easier to take her before she woke, but curiosity made him pat her cheek. "Wake."

She blinked up at him. "What the hell?" She scrambled to her feet and away from him. "Who are you?"

Experience had taught him that there was more pleasure in coaxing a reluctant female than in forcing one. A fearful female often objected to his attentions, and his size compared to hers could intimidate, so he continued to crouch.

Her words sounded strange to his ears, but he understood them. The sight of her naked flesh and the scent of the sex stimulant made it difficult for him to concentrate on anything but her seduction. Later he would try to puzzle out why she spoke a different language and why he comprehended it.

"Come to me. I'll not hurt you. Much pleasure we find together." He used the simple language of the herd.

She took another step back and glared at him. "I don't think so."

This was odd. Though at first a female might fear him, none had ever outright denied him—and all left happy. He sniffed the air. The sharp smell of fear overpowered the scent of the sex stimulant.

"You have not been properly prepared." The answer satisfied him. "Do not worry, I will please you." He stood. He grinned as her gaze dropped to his groin. His member responded accordingly, increasing in size. Her eyes widened and she put out a hand.

"Stay where you are. Who are you? What do you want?"

With each word she spoke, her strange language became more familiar. A dull throb started behind his eyes. Later. He'd think about this later. For now, another need took precedence.

"I want what you want. Do not deny me." He stepped toward her.

"You've got to be kidding. I don't want you. Just because you look like Alexander doesn't mean I'm going to have sex with you."

"I know not who this Alexander is, but you will have me." His own natural need along with the sex stimulant the handlers fed him left little patience for this female's game. "Do not fight me. I can be gentle, but I will not be denied."

"That's what you think. I don't care what kind of drugs the Flock gave me or who you look like; I won't be a mindless sex toy for you and put on a show for them."

"The Flock?" He edged closer.

"Your masters. The ones with the rods and power around here."

"They are not my masters." The thought that she believed him to be controlled by the handlers, though it was true, angered him. Still, he gentled his tone. "They cannot see us. The panels are dark." He motioned around. "We are alone."

She glanced at the walls, then turned her wary gaze back to him. "That doesn't change anything. I still don't want you."

"I think you lie. Let me touch you."

Cora's feet refused to move as the man moved closer. She fought to keep her eyes from focusing on his maleness. She didn't remember Alexander's male equipment being so large, so intimidating . . . so enticing. Reluctantly she raised her gaze to his face. The years had added bulk to his body, fine lines to his face and a few strands of gray in his hair, but the features were still Alexander's.

His resemblance to Alexander, combined with the remnants of the stimulating oil on her skin, dissolved her determination to resist. His musky masculine odor filled her nostrils. Her breasts ached to be touched, her nipples hardened in preparation for the feel of his lips. Her sex throbbed with the need to be filled. Alexander or not, who would it hurt if she chose to enjoy herself with this man? It had been so long.

His large, calloused hand slid around the back of her neck, and she shuddered and closed her eyes in surrender. He lowered his head. His lips on her throat sent a bolt of liquid heat through her. She gasped. Feather-light hands stroked down her back. Unable to stop herself, she arched into him. His erection pressed like a hot brand against her belly. He bent and closed his lips over one breast. She quivered in delight as a wave of pleasure broke over her.

"I would go slow, but find I cannot. I must have you now."

Dimly Cora recognized he spoke in Standard, but his next actions drove rational thought from her mind. With a groan he cupped her buttocks in both hands and lifted her. Instinctively she wrapped her arms over his shoulders and clamped her thighs around his hips. Spreading her legs to accommodate his thighs opened her to a touch of air. It felt cool against her dampness.

Hard, hot and throbbing, his erection rested at her entrance. She strained downward, trying to impale herself on him. He held her away.

"Easy. I am large. I would not injure you."

"Do your best, big boy. I'm ready." Rotating her hips, she brushed her moistness over the head of his cock. When he groaned, she laughed in triumph. "I want you hard and fast and—now!"

At her command, his restraint broke. With one quick motion he thrust upward. She gasped in a combination of pleasure and pain as he plunged into her. Filled to overflowing, she struggled to breathe. Nothing she'd learned of sex with Alexander had prepared her for the sensations engendered by having this man inside her.

"Have I hurt you?" he asked.

"N-no. G-give me a m-minute."

Thankfully, he remained motionless to let her body adjust to his invasion. She rested her head on his shoulder. Her breasts pressed against the hard wall of his chest, making her nipples tingle. She could feel the tension thrumming through his body, the rapid thud of his heart and the echo of his pulse deep within her.

After a few minutes the sting of being stretched eased, leaving only a delicious feeling of fullness. Cora lifted her head. The man's gaze met hers. Sweat glistened on his face. She grinned. The strain of remaining still was starting to tell on him. She liked the sense of power it gave her. Then he twitched inside her.

The jolt of pleasure made her back arch. Seeking more of the same, she flexed her hips. Frissons of sensation coursed through her. A heartbeat separated her from satisfaction. Too long—it had been too long since she'd last felt this way, experienced this sense of being complete, of being connected to another person.

She put her hands on his shoulders and asked, "Let me?"

Mouth stretched in a grimace, he nodded. Beneath her palms she felt his body trembling in restraint.

Delighted with the feeling of being in control but unsure how long he could hold out, she threw back her head and arched her back. His size stretched her sex wide, pulling the center of her sensation down and taut so that with every motion it rubbed against him. Tightening her thighs around his hips, she rose upward. Slick with her moisture, he slid easily inside her. The feel of his large shaft's withdrawal left her lightheaded and wanting more. Her body seemed to collapse inward, creating a suction intent upon dragging him back.

Wanting both to prolong this delicious feeling and to reach the end of her journey, she hovered there, only the head of his shaft inside her. Cora's body began to tremble along with his. Giving in to need, she plunged herself down.

A wave of ecstasy shattered her façade of control and stole her breath. Her vision went blank, her body rigid. Shudder after shudder coursed through her until she finally went limp against him. It was done.

Zan stood frozen as the woman's strong inner muscles sought to milk him. The urge to move, to thrust in and out of her mindlessly, beat inside him like a moth against a covered flame. He resisted.

Using the last of his restraint he pulled out and laid her upon the floor. She protested, but once a mate reached her release the aftereffects of the sex stimulant would take their toll: she would sleep for hours. He could finish now, as hard and fast as he chose, and she wouldn't be aware until she woke up later, her sex sore and swollen.

Take her was what he should do. He'd done it before with reticent women, though few under the influence of the sex stimulant remained reticent: forced them to accept pleasure at his hand, then finished the act once they fell into drug-induced oblivion. But something stopped him. What? Servicing, impregnating females was part of his purpose in life, as bearing his offspring was theirs. The drug the guards gave him made sure his need for sexual release overrode his aversion to rape.

Rape? Where had that word come from? What did it mean? The word made his head pound with pain. Only the ache of his still swollen sex hurt more.

He looked down at the sleeping female. Never before had a woman fit him so well. Most accommodated only a fraction of his size. Servicing them merely blunted the edge of his sexual frustration. He gave them his seed, but he never truly found fulfillment. This woman could engulf him all and push him to his very limit. Somehow, he knew if he gave in to his need to take her, he'd never be free of wanting her.

Aside from her larger stature and unusual coloring, though appealing in face and form, he saw nothing about her to attract him so and make him act out of character.

"Alexander," she murmured.

The sound of another male's name on her lips enraged him. A fierce, unfamiliar feeling possessed him. This woman belonged to him; no other would have her. With a roar, he scooped her up and headed to the exit.

The door opened to reveal his handlers. Clutching the woman close, he snarled at them. Chirping in agitation, they stepped back, but kept their stun rods ready. The corridor ahead led to his transport.

Once before when they'd first put him to stud he'd taken a female back to his quarters; he wasn't sure why. Though his handlers had been surprised, they hadn't tried to stop him. She'd been a small, timid creature, eager to please but physically incapable of accommodating him. Still, he'd enjoyed her company. He had performed with the other females his handlers presented him, and he had continued to do well in the arena, and they had let him keep her until her pregnancy began to show. Then, one day when he was fighting they took her away. He never saw her again. Though his attachment to the female hadn't run deep, he missed her. After that he'd never taken another female to his quarters.

This female was different. Let them try and take her from him.

Cora woke with a start. She groaned. Waking up naked in strange places was getting old real quick. She sat up. Where was she now?

From where she sat on a wide pallet on the floor she could see the entire room. Aside from some rough-hewn wooden shelves attached to the stone wall, the room was bare of furnishings. On the opposite wall were two metal doorways. Through an opening she could see a primitive commode and a basin into which water ran continuously from a faucet. On the fourth wall a large window looked out over a concrete moat filled with sparkling blue water. A sheer rock wall rose about six feet over the water. Above that she could see a waist-high metal fence. Because of the angle, she couldn't see beyond that.

"Great. Now I'm in a damned zoo." She got up. Her legs felt wobbly, but it was something else that made her pause. Without thinking she reached down and touched her sensitive flesh. "It really happened."

Remembered pleasure and shame caused her cheeks to heat. She snatched her hand away. Her fingers smelled of her own passion but didn't hold the aroma of male release.

Forcing herself to ignore the questions hammering in her brain about the man who looked so much like Alexander and the things she'd done with him, she set out to investigate her new prison. The metal doors were securely fastened. With a grimace of distaste she used the commode, but unlike the open pits in the women's pen at least it flushed. She washed her face and hands in the basin. The water felt cool and refreshing, and washed away the remaining fuzziness in her mind.

When she straightened, drops landed on her breasts and reminded her of her nakedness. She grabbed up the only piece of cloth in the room, the blanket from the pallet, and fashioned a sarong. Pressing her face against the window, she tried to see more of the outside but her view was limited. Though it seemed to be midafternoon, nothing moved out there.

"Must not be visiting day," she grumbled, and turned her attention to the shelves.

Bits and pieces filled the shelves. A hand-sized shard of what looked like pottery or shell caught her eye. She picked it up. Bright blue in color on the outside, the inside reminded her of mother-of-pearl or opal. She ran her fingers across the smooth side, and then over the pebbled outer bit. One by one she studied each of the other things: a piece of wood worn smooth by water, a rock that sparkled with flecks of color, a scrap of metal polished to a mirror finish, a cup with strange markings on it, a string of colorful glass beads.

About to turn away from the useless junk that was the collection of treasures belonging to this cage's inhabitant, one tiny item shoved nearly out of sight made Cora stop. No. It couldn't be what she thought it was. Trembling in shock and hope, she reached for it.

Behind her, a door slammed open. She pulled her hand back and whirled around. Two Flock, staggering under his weight, carried in and laid on the pallet the man with whom she'd made love. He landed flat on his back. He was naked except for a hard cup covering his genitals, and dirt, sweat and blood streaked his body.

She started toward him. A Flock grabbed and held her back. "Let me go, you overgrown birdbrain. He's hurt."

A third Flock entered the room and kneeled next to the man. From a bag he produced a syringe and injected something into the man's arm. After a short conversation with the other Flock, he rose. Cora's captor released her and they left the room.

Cora rushed to the man's side and searched his body for injuries. Aside from bruising on his rib cage and minor cuts and scrapes on his knuckles, he looked intact. She grabbed the bowl from the shelf and filled it with water from the faucet.

Wetting a corner of the blanket, she wiped the streaks of dirt and blood from his face. His eyes opened. "What happened?" she asked.

She scooted back as he sat up and grinned. "I won."

Unconscious, he'd looked helpless and harmless and so much like Alexander it made her heart ache. Awake, he radiated masculine power that she fought to keep from intimidating her. Thoughts of what it felt like having him inside her made her wary of letting him get too close. Though, where could she run if he decided to pursue her?

"Won what?" Was he aware that while he spoke the herd language, she spoke Standard?

"The fight. I *always* win." His grin reminded her of a little boy who'd just hit a home run.

"If you won, why did they haul you in here unconscious?" She gave in to the urge to ruffle the metaphorical feathers he preened.

"The handlers stunned me. Today they wished only my victory, not the death of my opponent. If I killed him, the handlers would have to send me to service his females."

"That's barbaric! Inhuman! We're intelligent people, not dumb animals to be used and abused for the amusement and profit of another species."

He didn't seem to understand.

"Do not worry, it harms me not." He pulled off the cup over his genitals. His sex sprang free and bounced against his thighs as he strode toward the toilet area. "I will cleanse myself now. I do not fight again for six nights, so aside from my other duties we will be left alone."

"Other duties? What other duties?" She was afraid she knew just what one of those other duties was.

Once inside the cubicle, he pushed down a lever and water gushed over him. The sound drowned out whatever answer he might have given.

Sweat, blood and dirt rinsed away and swirled down the drain in the floor. Eyes closed, he tilted his face into the stream. Moisture pooled in Cora's mouth and between her thighs as she watched the water cascade down his magnificent body. As if he felt her perusal, his cock swelled.

She realized she'd been given some kind of drug earlier that accounted for her uncharacteristic behavior, but what she felt now had nothing to do with drugs and everything to do with hormones. She wanted this man. She wanted to touch him. To have him touch her. She wanted the sense of connection she'd only ever found with one other man— Alex.

If she watched him much longer, she wouldn't be able to stop herself from joining him under the water. And this time, she'd make sure he enjoyed it as much as she had. She yanked her gaze away.

Each passing minute his resemblance to Alexander grew, from his cocky attitude to his apparent habit of collecting useless, shiny objects that caught his fancy. Soon she wouldn't be able to tell fact from fantasy, reality from wishful thinking. This man couldn't be Alexander. Alexander had died six years ago.

But are you sure? Had she accepted Earth League Force's determination of his death too easily? The question hammered at her. *You never saw his body. No one did.* His ship had exploded, light years off course, in an unexplored region of space. No debris or bodies were ever recovered.

Could Alexander have survived? His ship's last transmission had said something about an anomaly that interfered with their navigation. Just before *Freedom* lost power and spiraled into a crash landing on a planet she'd have sworn wasn't there a minute before, there'd been a moment when her navigation went haywire. And she'd been near the region of space where Alexander's ship had disappeared. Could it be possible?

And what of the other humanoids on this planet? Where had they come from? Were they descendants of a lost colony ship? Had whatever grabbed Alexander's ship and hers also grabbed theirs hundreds of years ago?

She buried her face in her hands. Soon she'd believe in fairy tales and happily-ever-afters. She'd rather have the black-and-white logic of an engine anyday.

"Are you hurting?" he asked.

"Yes," she whispered.

Hands gentle, he took her arms and turned her to face him. "Where?"

She wanted to sink into his embrace; instead she put a hand over her heart. "Here."

"I don't understand. You have no injury."

"It's not a physical pain. My heart hurts."

"But why?"

"You remind me of someone I once knew."

"This Alexander?"

"Yes, but he died a long time ago."

"I'm sorry for your pain, but I cannot regret his passing. I will not share you with another."

"Sh-share me! What are you talking about?" She jerked away and scrambled to her feet to tower over him.

But not for long. He stood, and she ended up having to crane her neck to meet his gaze. She didn't remember Alexander being so tall or so broad across the shoulders.

"Don't worry. I feared that while I fought in the pit they would remove you, but the handlers have agreed to my keeping you."

"K-keep me?" she spluttered. "Why, you big hairy ape! I'm not a thing you can keep like a pet or possess like one of your trinkets over there." She waved her hand in the direction of the shelf. "I'm a living, thinking, feeling human being."

"Keep you I do, and possess you I will. Join me on my pallet and we will commence where we left off earlier."

"No way." Though her body screamed for her to give in and enjoy the moment, she refused to be sidetracked by meaningless sex. It didn't feel meaningless. It felt right. They fit together. It felt like more than sex. It felt like . . . coming home.

No. Escape was her first priority—her only priority. She wouldn't let herself become some creature's sex toy. She backed away. Her foot tangled in the blanket and it came loose. When she tried to snatch it back over her breasts, she lost her balance and tumbled forward.

He caught her as she landed on his hard chest. The feel of his warm skin against her nipples and his damp scent in her nostrils weakened her determination. What could it hurt to grab what pleasure she could? Trapped in this cage until a Flock opened the door, she couldn't escape.

"Do you come to me freely? Though it's in my power to bend you to my will, I wish not to force you. I shall give you great pleasure."

The threat in his voice made her shiver in anticipation. She smiled at his confidence in his sexual prowess and knew he didn't overestimate himself. Then she felt a shock as she realized he'd been speaking Standard. As impossible as it seemed, this had to be Alexander. There was no other explanation.

CHAPTER FOUR

Joy and hope exploded inside Cora, but she probed for more information. The man frowned but didn't stop her as she moved out of his arms and rewrapped the blanket around her body.

"What's your name?"

"The herd call me Zan. The overseers call me—" He made a low rumbling whistle. She'd heard the women in her pen make that sound several times.

"Zan? Is that part of Alec-zan-der?" The similarity of the name he called himself and his given name hinted of memories buried in his mind. Could she spark them to life?

"No. I am named for the creature whose attack I survived, the Zanther."

"Do you remember how you came to be here?" At his confused look, she added, "In this compound?"

"I have always been here."

"What about before you were attacked?"

"There is no before." He massaged the space between his eyes. "Enough. Your questions make my head ache."

She risked one more. "Do you know what the Flock are saying?" If he understood the Flock, maybe she could learn to do so too.

"Flock?"

"That's what I call the aliens."

"A-li-ens." He rolled the word around on his tongue. His brows creased then he shook his head. "Some. I know the meaning of their commands. Not"—he grinned at her—"that I obey them." He puffed out his massive chest and thumped it with his fist. "I am Zan, fighter, not a dumb herd beast."

"Can you teach me their language?"

When his strutting didn't impress her, he deflated a bit. "Perhaps."

"Good."

For a moment she wondered if she imagined the resemblance between Zan and Alex, if the desires of her heart played tricks on her mind. She searched his strange yet familiar features. No, there was no doubt of Zan's identity. He was Alex. Despite his lack of memory and the differences in his body, her spirit recognized his.

All the fear, pain and humiliation she'd been through since her ship first lost power became unimportant; to have Alexander back she'd do it twice over again. She'd consider the how and why of his being here later. Until then, she intended to enjoy their reunion. And when she figured out a way to escape this crazy zoo, she was taking Alexander home with her.

He moved closer and her blanket dropped. She put her arms around his neck. "Where were we?"

"Here." With a growl he pulled her down on the pallet.

Moist from his shower, his body felt cool against hers. She shivered, but not from cold. Once she gave herself to this man, no matter if he ever remembered who he really was or what happened, there'd be no turning back. She couldn't leave this world without him, nor could she stay as part of the Flock zoo.

"Are you cold?" Turning her so they lay facing each other, he ran his hand down her back in a comforting stroke. Her body tightened in expectation.

"No."

"Then why do you tremble?"

"Other than earlier, I haven't been with a man for six years," she admitted. Would he remember that he was that man?

"This is strange. You're in your prime. Why would your handler not breed you?" His words blurred from the feel of his hands on her body. He caressed her breasts and fondled her nipples into hard, aching peaks.

She struggled to explain, to make him understand how bizarre his view of life was. "I don't have a handler. I don't belong to the herd. And neither do you. I'm a free person."

"What you say makes no sense, but I'll consider your words later—much later."

He lowered his head to capture one nipple in his mouth. She threw back her head as he suckled. The feel of his hot tongue swirling around that aching peak sent a bolt of lightning straight to her groin. Rational thought melted under scorching heat; with each pull of his mouth on her breast, she let out a moan.

When he splayed his large hand over her belly, she parted her thighs in invitation. Without hesitation he cupped her mound. His fingers strummed over her like a master musician, playing both familiar and unfamiliar notes until the music nearly overwhelmed her. With each stroke he increased his pressure. Moisture dampened his palm. The earthy smell of her arousal filled Cora's nostrils.

He suddenly moved lower and placed his lips where his hand had been, and he slid two fingers inside her. Wave after wave of intense pleasure broke over her. Cora arched her back and cried out her release.

But it wasn't enough. She wanted his cock buried deep inside her. Wanted him to fill the emptiness she'd carried within her for the last six years. No, longer than that. Since her father died, aside from Alex she'd allowed no one to touch her physically or emotionally. Finding him again shattered the dam she'd built around her heart and loosed a flood of need. She didn't want to need Alex, but honesty forced her to admit she did. But she wanted him as mad with need as she.

Damp and warm, his dark hair curled around her fingers as she tugged his head away from her. His lips shiny with her juices, he smiled like a cat that had been in the cream.

She rose to her knees over him. "I need you inside me, *now*."

His smile grew. "No other woman has ever dared to command me."

"Well, get it through your thick skull—I'm not like any other woman you know."

The sight of her breasts dangling in his face and the salty sweet taste of her sex on his tongue made Zan hungry for more of this unusual woman. Though she was a stranger, he felt he knew her from before.

He'd claimed there was no before, but he'd lied. Often he woke in the night, from disjointed dreams of times and places he couldn't fully recall. Some left him shaking and sweating in terror and anguish. Others left him longing for something lost. He now probed the memories of those dreams for her face.

A stab of pain in his head warned him not to pursue this train of thought. Remembrance caused suffering; experience had taught him to live for the moment. His unusual desire for this woman worried him. Soon enough he'd give in to his need to spill his seed inside her and then she'd be taken. Despite his brash claims, he knew the handlers controlled his life. To protect himself from future grief, he couldn't allow her to mean anything to him.

Still, when she reached down and took his erection in her hands he couldn't deny his need to possess her. Against all reason, he knew to keep this woman he would defy the handlers, even if it meant his death.

The feel of her fingers moving over his engorged and throbbing cock drove out further coherent thoughts.

Wanting to prolong their encounter, he forced himself to lie still as she fondled him. She cupped his testicles in her warm, smooth palms. To block his temptation to plunge mindlessly into her again and again until they were both slick with sweat and satiated, he closed his eyes. But with each breath her musky scent filled his lungs and weakened his resolve. He clutched the blanket in his fists to keep from grabbing her.

When he felt her lips, a bolt of remembered pleasure fired though him. He groaned. No female had done this for him before. Not even the boldest of the women he serviced had ever thought to give him pleasure beyond his use of their bodies. So, how could he remember this feeling?

Her tongue stroked up and down his shaft, then swirled delicately across the tip. As she started to raise her head, he couldn't stop himself from clasping it in his hands and holding her to him. He felt her laughter vibrate against him as she took him fully in her mouth. Questions flittered away before he could grasp their meaning. Sweat beaded on his body. Against his will, his hips jerked upward. He gritted his teeth to hold himself rigid, but couldn't stop the sudden exquisite relief as he found release.

He felt her throat work as she swallowed, then swallowed

again. The motion caused him to swell. The pleasure of re-lease battled with his shame at his lack of self-discipline.

She lifted her head and turned to meet his gaze. "Are you ready to get down to business now?" Her bold demand, that challenge posed along with a self-satisfied smile on her glistening lips, infuriated him. He'd allow no mere female to take control.

At his frown her smile wavered, then it died altogether when he rolled her beneath him and positioned himself between her thighs. He rubbed his cock against her slickness and poised it for entrance. One quick thrust and she'd be his.

She squeaked. "Alexander, what's wrong?"

"I'm *not Alexander.* I am Zan. Say my name."

A mutinous expression crossed her face. She shoved at his chest without effect. "Your name is Alexander."

A dull throb started behind his eyes. "No."

With an oath, he lifted himself away from her and stood. His breath came in harsh gasps as he pressed his palms against his temples to block out the thoughts and images flooding his mind. "No! I will not let you steal my identity. I am Zan!"

He'd lost himself once. Broken and battered, his mind a blank, he'd woken from the *before* he'd denied existed. Then, bit by bit, he'd recreated himself body and soul. He wouldn't do so again.

As if he entered the battle pit, fury boiled up inside him. His muscles clenched in preparation. Strike out! Fast! Hard! Defeat his adversary! He raised his arm to land the final blow.

"Alex-Zan?"

Her soft voice quelled the storm raging inside him, and stayed his swing. Horror at what he'd almost done made him groan. His arms dropped limp to his sides. Unable to face the fear in her eyes, he turned away.

A warm hand settled on his shoulder. He winced but couldn't bring himself to pull away.

"It's all right. You didn't hurt me."

"I could have killed you."

"Well, you could have tried. I'm not that easy to kill." Her confident words and soft laugh didn't quite hide the tremor in her voice. "Why do you get so angry when I call you Alexander?" The throb in his head became a pounding. "Because it makes you remember things? Who you really are? Where you came from?"

He shook his head but remained silent.

"I don't know what happened to you, and I'm not a doctor, but traumatic injuries can cause memory loss." She massaged his neck, then ran her fingers up through his hair and over his scalp. Her firm touch eased the ache in his head.

"I don't know how you came to be here, but you're no more one of the herd than I am. We're different than they are, and not just on the outside but *here*"—she moved around in front of him and put her palm against his chest—"inside."

As she touched him, the click of a door opening behind her made Cora spin around. Two Flock entered. With a growl Alexander put himself between her and them. She stumbled back.

One Flock carried a stun rod held out in front of him. The tip glowed blue, indicating it was charged for use. The other carried a tray containing food. Keeping a wary eye on Alexander, he placed the tray down and backed out of the room. The other Flock followed. The door shut with a clang and they were alone again. Or as alone as one could be in a glass-walled cage.

Alexander's muscles relaxed. Their discussion either forgotten or pushed aside, he turned to her. "Are you hungry?"

Her stomach rumbled, but one look at the tray made her gag. "I can't eat raw meat."

He looked surprised, but knelt down and picked out several pieces of fruit and a handful of seedpods, then took

them to the sink and rinsed them off before he held them
out to her.

"Thank you." She took his offering and was about to sit on
the pallet to eat when something pinged against the glass wall.

Her appetite fled. A group of Flock was outside, standing at
the fence and staring in at them. She snatched up the blanket
and turned her back to the Flock. Alexander seemed oblivious to their audience; he crouched and gobbled his meal.

Clutching the fruit, she moved into the toilet cubicle—
the only place in the cage not visible from the outside. Tears
of shame and anger burned her eyes. She refused to let them
fall. She sat on the commode and, though she was no longer
hungry, forced herself to eat. When she finished, she fashioned the blanket into a sarong. Still unwilling to expose
herself to the view of the Flock, she stayed in the cubicle.

"Why do you sit in here? And why do you wear my blanket in such a strange way?" Alexander stood in the opening.
Neither his nudity nor the eyes of the Flock seemed to concern him.

"I'm not used to going naked."

"What purpose does it serve to cover your skin in this
heat?"

"My body is mine. I like to keep it private."

"You are an odd female. But you may wear my blanket if
it makes you comfortable."

"Gee, thanks."

He raised an eyebrow but didn't comment. His face had
matured since she'd last seen him. Lines bracketed his mouth
and fanned out around his eyes. His nose had a bump that
hadn't been there before. A few strands of silver threaded his
hair.

"Where did you get that scar?" She pointed to the jagged
line running from the corner of his right eye up across his
temple to disappear into his hair.

He shrugged. "I don't remember. A fight, I guess." He

put one hand on his hip and stretched the other upward to lean against the wall. Nudity suited him. He looked like an ancient sculpture.

Though he'd always kept fit, now his sun-bronzed skin covered an impressive musculature. Broad of chest and lean of hip, with well-muscled legs, he made Cora's mouth water. She let her admiring gaze travel down his body. Even at rest his cock was imposing. Thoughts of what it felt like when he'd been fully aroused and buried deep inside her heated her blood and started an ache between her thighs. She swallowed hard, looked away and attempted to gather her control.

Again, she wondered how he'd come to be here. Did he even know? And how was she going to get them both free?

"Come, we go outside." He held out his hand.

Though she was loath to expose herself to the view of the Flock, the thought of air not stinking of raw meat made her put her fingers in his.

The second metal door stood open. She followed Alexander outside. Straight ahead was a large courtyard bordered on two sides by high rock walls. Her gaze followed them upward until her fear of heights made her look away.

When she was ten she'd lost her father from a fall while they hiked together in the mountains. It took three days for the rescuers to find her crouched at the top of the cliff staring down at his broken body. Another three weeks before she came out of her catatonic state. She shuddered at the too-vivid memory. Since then she'd had an unreasoned fear of heights, and a determination to take care of herself and those she loved.

Alex had teased her about her career choice. How could a person so fearful of heights be a pilot? She'd answered that in space there is no up or down, no high or low, therefore no heights to fall from. But that didn't solve the problem of takeoffs and landings or low-altitude planet recon. That part took sheer resolve, and whenever possible she used her expertise and instruments to handle her ship.

From the time she'd been a small child and her parents had split up, she'd wanted the freedom to fly, to escape into the sky away from the complexities of human relationships. She'd refused to let fear destroy her dream.

A tall leafless tree stood in the center of the yard. A sparkling pool of water lay to her left and continued in front of the chamber window. The other side of the pool ended in a sheer concrete wall. Rough concrete paved the yard from the doorway to the pool. Waist-high grasses and bushes grew a few yards out from the walls, providing the illusion of a natural setting.

The midafternoon sun beat down on Cora's shoulders. Her toes curled against the sun-warmed stone. Biting down on her lip to banish the queasiness heights caused, she turned her gaze up to the sky and freedom. Above, from the walls to halfway over the pool, a metal grate covered the enclosure. Her stomach lurched as she acknowledged the only way out of this cage. But she'd think about that later.

Above the pool wall a group of Flock, made up of three adults and what looked like about ten youngsters, stood behind the fence. The young Flock varied from the size of a human toddler to almost grown. Downy yellow-white feathers covered the youngest from head to toe. Cute and fluffy, he reminded her of an Earth chick. He danced excitedly alongside the adults. Despite her hatred of the Flock, the baby's high peeping made Cora smile.

The older ones were gangly, their baby down interspersed with adult feathers. Grayish-pink adult skin showed through on their necks, arms and legs.

While Cora hesitated in the shadow of the doorway, Alexander strode forward and dove into the pool. He sank to the bottom, then shot out of the water, sending a spray high in the air. Thrilled by his antics, the Flock shouted and pointed in excitement.

While they watched him, Cora headed toward a cluster of bushes near the far wall that provided an area invisible to the Flock. Before she was halfway there, one of the Flock let out a sharp whistle and their attention turned to her. She ran the last few yards and practically dove behind the bushes. Though she knew they couldn't reach her, the thought of them watching her like an animal made her heart pound in a combination of anger and fear.

Alexander turned in the water and looked toward her. "This is wonderful. Join me."

The urge to jump into the pool and join her body with his despite the audience made her shudder. She wouldn't let her desire for Alexander override her sense of self and turn her into the animal the Flock believed her to be.

"Not likely," she muttered.

When she didn't answer, he pulled himself out. Water glistened like amber diamonds on his skin. He shook his wet hair out of his eyes and moved toward where she crouched.

"Why do you hide?"

"Because I refuse to provide amusement for our captors."

"You are a strange female."

"You've said that before."

"Why do they disturb you so?"

"Doesn't it bother you to be treated like a mindless animal—used for another's entertainment and profit as if you don't have thoughts and feelings?"

His brows drew together in a frown and his mouth tightened. A pulse throbbed at his temple. "You speak of things you don't understand. This is my life. I am satisfied."

She grabbed his arm. "No, it's not. And how can you be? You're a person, not an animal. You have the right to live your life the way you see fit. Listen to what you're saying.

You may not consciously remember who you really are, but inside you know I'm right. You're Alexander Anderly, a xeno-anthropologist with the Consortium of Intelligent Life, whose ship was lost six years ago."

He jerked out of her grip. "I listen no more." He'd reverted to herd speak.

How could she make him understand, make him remember who he was, if he wouldn't listen to her? "Alexander, please."

"I am Zan."

Fists clenched, he stood over her. Strangely, she didn't fear that he would strike. Somehow she knew that enough of the Alexander she'd known remained buried inside him to keep him from venting his anger on her.

At an impasse as to what to say or do next, she stared at him. She hadn't been able to sway the old Alex—the one who claimed to love her—from his goal, so if he didn't remember her, how could she make him accompany her when she escaped? And escape she would.

A splash and a terrified whistle shattered the tense moment between them. Alexander turned toward the pool.

"What's happening?"

Alexander sat down. "A young Flock fell into the water."

Hesitant about exposing herself but curious to get a better view, Cora stepped out from behind the bushes. The Flock's attention focused on the youngster splashing in the water. Spray filled the air. At the rail, Flock leaned forward, gesturing wildly. Their shrill cries made her eardrums ache. Cora didn't need her translator to understand their terror.

"He's drowning. Do something."

Alexander shrugged. "Why? A handler will come for him soon. And when they do, they will stun us."

"By the time they get here it'll be too late. That baby will be dead in minutes."

"Regrettable, but true." With no outward expression on his face, he watched the small creature thrashing in the water.

Cora stared in disbelief at the man she thought she knew. "What happened to make you so callous?" The baby Flock's pitiful cries tugged at her heart. As much as she hated her captors, she couldn't sit by and watch a baby die.

Tearing off the blanket, she ran and jumped into the pool. The water felt refreshing against her heated skin. The baby had sunk below the surface. She dove down. There it was on the bottom. Cora grabbed the limp creature and pushed upward.

Struggling with the baby's waterlogged weight, she hoisted it up onto the concrete and climbed up next to him. Above, the Flock continued to cry out. A small stone hit her shoulder and drew blood. Ignoring the sharp pain, she turned her back to them and concentrated on the too-still baby.

One of the youngest of the Flock, the baby was the same size as the toddler that had been trampled in the pen. Guilt for that casualty made her determined to save this baby.

Downy feathers lay in wet stripes, revealing the baby Flock's grayish-pink skin underneath. A pulse beat in his throat, but he wasn't breathing. Not knowing what else to do, Cora tried mouth-to-mouth resuscitation. With her fingers she covered the creature's nostrils, opened his beaklike mouth and blew.

At first nothing happened. Time seemed to stretch out. The noise around her faded away as she concentrated on breathing life back into the baby Flock. She dimly realized that Alexander moved between her and the other Flock as they continued to throw stones. Perhaps what the Flock might do to him out of fear was why he'd refused to try to rescue the baby. Still, when they sought to drive her away from their baby, he'd put himself between them and her.

Finally, after she'd begun to believe it was hopeless, the baby choked and coughed. His eyes blinked open and he let out a series of wailing peeps. The Flock cries rose in volume.

The baby staggered to his feet and gave a shake. Water showered over Cora. She sank back on her heels and gave a chuckle of relief. Blinking the water out of her eyes, she started to rise.

Before she could, Alexander grabbed her around the waist and pulled her into the pool. Water closed over her head and went up her nose. She came up spluttering. "What did you do that for?"

"Look." He towed her to the far side of the pool against the wall and held her in his arms as he treaded water. Four Flock guards entered the courtyard. Each carried a lit stun rod. "I have no wish to be stunned. It is not a pleasant experience."

She nodded, remembering the sharp pain when the overseer had touched his rod to her breast. "What about the baby Flock? Is he all right?" She turned in Alexander's arms to see.

"Yes, thanks to you. Wet, but alive. Now that we're out of their way, they'll take him back to the others."

Cora watched the guards gently check over the squalling baby, then wrap him in the blanket and carry him out of the courtyard. They closed the door behind them, leaving Alexander and her alone. If any Flock remained above she couldn't see them, and if she couldn't see them, they couldn't see Alexander and her.

"Why did you save the creature?" Alexander asked.

"I'm not sure. If you'd asked me before it happened if I'd do it, I'd probably have said no. I hate them for what they've done to me, to you and the others. But when that baby fell, instinct kicked in. Whatever else it is, it's a living being and an innocent baby. I couldn't sit and watch it die."

The thoughtful expression on his face made her want to ask him again why he had ignored the plight of the baby

Flock, but the feel of his warm slick body rubbing against hers as the cool water lapped around them made it impossible to concentrate. Adrenaline coursed through her veins. Later she knew she'd crash, but right now her body thrummed with energy that needed a physical outlet. "Mmmm."

She pressed her face into the hollow between his shoulder and neck and closed her eyes. Her body felt both languid and stretched to the breaking point all at once. She wrapped her legs around his hips. She forgot his question and his callous disregard for life as the movement of his legs treading water caused his penis to rub against the sensitive flesh between her thighs.

He trailed nibbling kisses down the line of her throat. His hands roved up and down her back, heating her passion to the boiling point. She leaned back in his arms to allow him better access to her aching breasts. Her cry of pleasure when his mouth closed over one swollen peak echoed off the wall and made her remember where she was. The realization didn't last a moment. If the Flock wanted to watch, let them; she no longer gave a damn.

With one arm he held her around her waist; his other hand slid between their bodies and found the center of her pleasure, stroked then pinched it between two fingers. Tension made her body hum. Cora choked back a moan as he slipped two fingers into her.

She moved against his hand. Her inner muscles clenched, but two fingers weren't enough; she wanted—*needed*—more.

"Fuck me," she blurted.

He chuckled at her crude demand.

In flight school, being a woman in a field dominated by men, to fit in she'd learned to curse and swear without embarrassment. Some of that abandon filtered into the rest of her life. When they made love Alex had teased her about her salty vocabulary. Since his death she'd spent most of her time alone, so her language ceased to be an issue.

"If I do, we'll drown," he said.

"I don't care." She reached one hand down between their bodies and wrapped her fingers around his cock. "I need it now!"

Why did rational thought and control desert her with this man? The thought flitted through her mind but soon evaporated.

"Take a deep breath," he said.

Barely had she sucked in air when he plunged into her, and her head sank below the water. Hot and cold, man and water, filled her. Cora clamped her legs around his hips, her arms around his neck, and she held tight as he rocked in and out. Tension coiled inside her. Against the water the movement felt slow and easy, but sensations streaked through her fast as a powerless ship in a planet's gravitational pull.

Her lungs burned, but the demand of her body for release overrode her need for air. She reached a powerful climax; breath escaped from her lungs in a stream of bubbles that tickled her cheeks. Alex pulled out and cold replaced the warmth inside her. A surge of heat washed over her belly. Satisfaction and disappointment stabbed her: she didn't understand why she so wanted him inside her when he came, but she couldn't deny the feeling.

With a strong kick he propelled them upward. Gasping, they broke the surface. Cora coughed and sucked in air. Unable to catch her breath or find equilibrium after her shattering climax, she simply clung to him.

Zan pulled himself and the female out of the pool and onto the concrete. Since she'd rescued the baby Flock the sun had set, leaving the courtyard lit only by the rising moon and the yard lights. A breeze touched his wet skin.

"I'm cold."

Though the air felt balmy to him, the woman shivered and curled into his arms. He stroked the moisture away from her goose-bumped flesh, attempting to warm her with his touch.

"Mmm, that feels nice."

He continued to rub his hands over her until she stopped quivering and her skin felt dry and smooth again. She pulled back slightly and blinked up at him.

"It's dark."

The moonlit night turned her honey-colored skin to alabaster, her golden hair white, and her blue eyes black. He touched his fingertips to her soft cheek. What was it about this female that made him lose control? He'd almost spilled his seed inside her. If he impregnated her, the handlers would take her from him. In response to that threat, he pulled her closer.

Why should it matter if he kept her or not? What about this female drew him like no other ever had? Her unusual yet strangely familiar looks attracted him, but her beauty was not what captured his interest. Other females were physically appealing and aroused his male needs. That she was taller and built to accept his whole length without difficulty shouldn't signify; despite their smaller stature he managed to satisfy himself with other females. Her sharp tongue, independence, defiance and commanding attitude were harder to dismiss. In fact, they should annoy him. Instead they increased his fascination.

The other females, while accommodating his physical needs, did not engage his mind. Her words stirred things in him that, while painful, excited him beyond the physical. For the first time outside the life and death struggle in the fighting pit, he felt alive. He liked talking to her. At the same time, it irritated him that she disrupted the comfortable flow of his life.

Vague, fleeting images reminiscent of his dreams filled his mind. Answers to his questions hovered just out of reach.

"Cora," he whispered.

"You said my name! Do you remember me?" She put her hand over his and pressed her face into his palm.

"Yes—no. I don't know." His head began its familiar pounding as he tried to force buried memories to the surface. "There is something here." He touched his forehead. "But when I try to capture the images, the thoughts, my head begins to ache until I can't think anymore."

"Then don't try to force the memories." She brushed his damp hair off his forehead. "Let them come to you like my name did. Let's enjoy our privacy while we can. Take me to bed—please."

Her husky plea and the feel of her warm lips nibbling on the tender skin between his thumb and finger made him forget his need to remember what he hadn't realized he'd forgotten. She captured his thumb in her mouth and sucked; his cock jumped to attention. Growling in agreement, he gathered her in his arms and strode into his chamber.

As he went, he attempted to regain control. Though he wanted this female with a passion that had been lacking in his encounters for a long time, he also found himself struggling to balance his need to explore the memories struggling to surface in his mind and apprehension of what he might learn. She claimed she knew him from the time before his memories began, from before his life as a pit fighter and herd stud. He shuddered. Until he'd seen her in the breeding chamber he'd been content, if not happy, with his life. He'd known his purpose and his place. Now, everything was different. He knew if he pursued this path his life would be forever altered. If his lost memories returned, could he cope with his life?

He doubted it. Already she'd changed him. Resentment toward the Flock—as she called them—now churned inside him. What right did they have to control his life? To make him fight? To breed? Anger flowed like lava through his veins.

But they weren't there for him to vent it on. She was. He'd best keep his distance from her until he regained control.

While he and Cora were outside, the handlers had been in the chamber. Fresh bedding covered his pallet. The night lamp in the ceiling cast a soft glow. A tray filled with more fruit, bread and meat sat on the floor inside the door.

He laid Cora on the pallet and started to stand. She reached up and stopped him.

"Where are you going?" Her fingers trailed down his chest and splayed over his belly. Blood rushed from his brain to his groin. He groaned.

"Nowhere. But even my handlers allow me a few minutes to recover between females."

She clasped his growing erection in her hand. "I don't think you need any more time. Do you?" She tightened her grip and stroked up then down.

His cock swelled further. "We need to talk," he said.

She smiled. "That should be my line. Yes, we do, but I want to make love with you again, now while we're alone and no one's watching, so let's talk later. Okay?" She stroked him again.

He couldn't deny his desire for her, but because she had caused his awakening he feared he might make her pay the price of his growing anger and confusion. But, no. Years of maintaining his sanity while others directed his life had given him the ability to turn away from rational thought and focus on what he wanted at the moment. At this moment, what he wanted was her. No matter what else happened, she was his. Not on the Flock's terms or hers, but on his.

CHAPTER FIVE

Cora watched the expressions—fury, uncertainty, horror and hatred—chase across Alexander's face. One moment the rage in his eyes made her want to flee in fear. Then in a blink his expression became unreadable. Somehow that frightened her more.

"You are right. Talk can wait. I find I cannot."

Before she figured out what he meant, he captured her wrists in one hand and pulled her arms above her head. She squeaked in surprise. "What are you doing?"

His previous patience and gentleness gone, he shoved his knee between her thighs and spread her legs wide to accommodate his hips. "What do you think I'm doing?"

"Wait. What's wrong with you?"

"That is not what you said a minute ago."

"Yes, but I didn't mean like this. Why are you doing this? I don't want . . ."

"Your wants do not matter." He cut off her objections. "A mere female does not command me. No one will rule me again."

Anger made her deaf to the meaning behind his words. She squirmed in his grip. "Why, you arrogant bastard! What in the hell are you talking about? Get off me!"

His weight pinned her to the pallet as securely as the Flock had strapped her to their examination table. She couldn't budge him. Remembered humiliation stirred her indignation. His cock nudged against her, seeking entrance.

Aware that something she didn't understand had changed inside him, tears blurred her vision. "Please, don't. There's something special between us. Don't destroy it by raping me."

He paused. For a moment she thought he understood what he was about to do, the fragile bond his actions would cut.

"The only thing between us is *this*." He tilted his hips and his cock pushed into her. She snarled in outrage.

She tried to close herself off, but when she tightened her inner muscles she felt Alexander's bulk and heat pulsing against her. Even though she said no, her body cried yes. Somehow what he forced on her left her panting with need and weak with self-loathing. Still, as much as she wanted him inside her, she couldn't let him take her like this, couldn't let him steal her freedom of choice. Her control.

She met his hard gaze with one of her own. "I won't let you rape me."

"And how will you stop me?"

Even as he spoke, she felt him moving away from her. His comprehension snapped the bonds of anger inside her. Relief warred with need. Need won.

"Like this." In one swift motion she surged upward and took charge.

Though his weight limited her motion, she circled her hips and rocked up and down. He released her wrists. Holding his head between her hands, she raised her mouth to his and traced the outline of his lips with her tongue. When his lips parted on a groan, she invaded his mouth with her tongue, running it over his teeth, stroking the inside of his cheeks and circling his tongue. When she flexed her inner muscles and his breath caught, she allowed her lips to curl against his into a smug grin. Emboldened by her success in turning the tables, she thrust her tongue in and out of his mouth in a pantomime of the sex act.

For a second he went still, then Alex's chest rumbled with a low growl. He caught her tongue between his lips and suckled. With each pull of his mouth, liquid heat flowed down through her belly to pool between her legs. He rocked against her. Licks of fire radiated outward from where they were joined.

As if of their own accord, her legs wrapped around his hips and her feet locked together at the small of his back. With one hand he cupped the back of her head and with the other he gripped her buttocks. His hips rose and fell in a pounding rhythm.

No longer able to fool herself that she was in charge, she yielded to the passion blazing lust between them.

Like an approaching storm, her climax built as he moved within her. Small tremors followed sharp streaks of pleasure, each set increasing in intensity until her body felt ready to explode. Then lightning and thunder merged into one and the storm broke, drenching her in exquisite relief.

"Alex!" Her cry shattered the silence.

Aftershocks, as he continued to stroke in and out, rumbled through her. She ran her hands over the sweat-slicked muscles of his back. Her eyelids drifted closed. She wanted to move, to give him the same release, but she didn't have the strength. Limp and trembling with satisfaction, her legs slipped from around his hips.

His breath came in harsh gasps as he buried his face against her throat and increased his pace. Summoning the last of her energy, her hips matched his motion. Her inner muscles contracted around him, sending shivers of enjoyment coursing through her. She felt as his release built inside him.

Then he pulled out. Hot and wet, his semen hit her belly, and inside she again felt cold and empty. As if trying to grab what he'd denied it, her womb contracted. She blinked away her tears, but she couldn't stop herself from crying out, "No."

He lifted his head. "Didn't I please you?"

"You know you did, but why did you pull out?" She blushed as the question escaped. Why did she care how he took his pleasure?

"I would not impregnate you."

"Is that all? Don't worry, I won't get pregnant."

"Are you barren?" The thought seemed to worry him.

"In a manner of speaking. Before I started my mission I had a temporary procedure done. It stops a woman's, ah, you know, her woman's cycle for a time." Why was she finding it difficult to talk about this subject? P/MS—pregnancy/menstruation suppressant—was a common practice for women in the space service. Menstruation and pregnancy while on a tour of duty in space were less than desirable. "The women here do have monthly cycles, don't they?" Or were they different from humans? Did they have seasons instead? Or go into heat?

"Yes. How is this done?" He didn't sound convinced.

"I'm no physician, so I'm not entirely sure. I just know it works and no matter what we do I can't get pregnant for another three months."

"I don't know if this is good or bad. The handlers would leave you with me until you begin to show signs of pregnancy, but if it takes too long for you to conceive, they may decide you aren't worth my time and effort and remove you. I had thought to wait to impregnate you when I judged the handlers began to be impatient. Three cycles may be too long."

Suddenly his weight pressing her against the thin pallet no longer felt warm and comfortable; now it trapped her. Angry with both him and herself, she shoved at his chest. "You were going to impregnate me when it suited your purpose! What then? Let the Flock haul me away to their breeding barn? I don't think so. I'm not some brood mare. Get off, you oaf. You're squashing me."

He rolled to the side. But when she tried to rise, he anchored her to his side with an arm around her waist.

"Trust me, I will find a way to keep you with me."

"You don't get it, do you? I'm not staying in this damned zoo. As soon as possible I'm getting out of here. Let me up." She tugged uselessly at his arm. His ability to control his physical reaction to her, while his mere touch turned her to jelly, angered her.

He leaned over her. "And once you escape, where will you go? The world outside this compound is a hostile place, filled with deadly plants and animals. Even the ground itself is treacherous. I remember little before the Flock brought me here, half dead from injuries and out of my mind with fury and terror, but I do know this world is full of peril."

She ceased her struggles and gazed into his eyes. "You do remember something. What happened?"

A shudder ran through his body. "I don't wish to speak of it. Escape is impossible. Outside you would die, either brutally quick or torturously slow. Here, with me, you will live. It is time to sleep."

"I'm not sleepy," she lied, then added truthfully, "but I need to use the facilities."

Her heart told her to stay in his embrace and never leave, but no matter the danger, self-preservation demanded that she escape. To stay was to lose her humanity and become the animal the Flock believed her to be.

He released her. "Come right back."

She scrambled to her feet and looked down at him. Already his eyes were closed, his breathing slow and even. His big body appeared harmless, like a domestic house cat, but she knew the tiger merely slept, his strength and power ready to pounce at the slightest provocation. What had happened to steal his memories, his identity, and turn him into a caged animal?

With every breath, sensations still radiated out from her center, rippling through her. A breeze cooled the sticky wetness on her belly and brushed the dampness between her legs. She shivered, then turned and headed into the toilet cubicle. Maybe a cold shower would return her to her senses and she could figure out a plan of action.

Zan woke and stretched. Satisfaction and anticipation made him eager to start the new day. Outside the sky lightened from black to gray, but the layer of fog hanging over the pool obscured his view.

For the last several years he'd come to accept his life, even enjoy it at times, but there'd always been a sense of longing for something he couldn't name. Now, he knew what had been missing—Cora.

"Cora." Liking the taste and feel of the syllables, he rolled them around his tongue. But he enjoyed the taste and feel of the woman more.

No other woman pleased him as she did. When they finished having sex, he felt drained yet full. He'd never have enough of her. He'd do whatever it took to keep her with him.

But would she stay? Her talk of escape frightened him. When he'd first become aware of himself, his head and body bruised and battered, he'd run in mindless terror from whatever had happened to him. Eventually terror had given way to numbness. His memories of that time were filled with holes. He recalled wanting to die. But when a beast attacked him, his survival instinct kicked in. He'd fought but hadn't the strength to defeat an animal that out-weighed him three times over and had razor sharp claws and teeth six inches in length. Only the Flock's timely ar-rival had rescued him from being mauled to death. Mem-ories of the horrors that waited outside the compound made him shiver. His failure had nearly resulted in his death. Only the Flock's fast action and medical care had kept him alive.

No, strong as Cora was, she was no match for the beasts that roamed this exotically beautiful world. And if she avoided those, there was little edible food. In places, the ground itself leaked lethal vapors. Surely once she understood the dangers, she'd choose to live with him.

But was he truly alive? Until Cora, his life had consisted of fighting in the pit, servicing the females the handlers brought him and providing entertainment for the Flock who stood outside his cage day after day. He'd thought him-self content with his lot, convinced there was nothing better. Now he found himself wanting, needing something more.

Would forcing Cora to stay with him in his cage provide what he needed? He doubted it. He didn't remember the person she claimed him to be, but her arrival stirred feelings and longings inside him. He doubted her claim of being barren, and once she conceived she'd be taken from him. Though it tested his restraint, he couldn't give in to the need to find his pleasure within her body.

A delicious aroma wafted into the chamber. He sniffed, and his stomach growled in response. Moisture flooded his mouth. What had the handlers brought him to eat now?

He opened his eyes. A swift glance told him Cora wasn't in the chamber or the toilet cubicle. The courtyard door stood open. Had the handlers taken her away while he slept? Heart pounding in fear, he jumped up and rushed outside.

The scene that greeted him made him skid to a halt. Mouth open, he stared at her. Wearing a blanket tied around her neck to hide her body from view, she sat cross-legged on the ground in front of a circle of stones. Her short hair was tousled around her face. Moisture from the dissipating fog beaded on her cheeks. She glanced up and smiled at him. For a moment he forgot the tantalizing aroma.

Then the strange light flickering inside the stone circle caught his attention. She held a stick with a piece of meat on the end over the light. The light licked at the meat. Juices bubbled and popped on its browning surface, then dripped into the dancing light where it made a sizzling noise and released a mouth-watering smell on a smoky cloud.

"What are you doing?" How could he forget something this awesome and powerful? The memory eluded him.

"Barbecuing some meat. Rare is okay, but I just can't eat raw meat." She wrinkled her nose. "Veggies taste better cooked too."

"The light, what is it?" Mesmerized by its radiance, he reached out to touch it.

"Watch out! You'll burn yourself." She grabbed his hand, but not before he felt the heat blistering his skin.

"You really did forget everything, didn't you?"

He sat down next to her and stared at the flickering light. Had he ever seen this phenomenon before? Something stirred in the recesses of his mind, but along with the memory came a searing pain that darkened his vision.

"How did you end up here?"

Her voice brought him back from the blackness threatening to swallow his mind. He blinked. "I remember little about my first days here. I was badly injured and in a lot of pain. The handlers cared for me while I healed. When my body recovered, because of my unusual size and strength they trained me to be a pit fighter." Restless and full of rage, he'd channeled his energy into that training. Despite their early care of him, anger at what they had forced him to become burned inside him. They had sensed that given half a chance he'd savage them, and had handled him with caution. "After I started to win, they brought me women to service."

"Service?"

"Impregnate. Though I knew nothing of who I was or where I came from, I remembered how to do the deed." He grinned.

"I'll bet you did."

He tried to ignore the distaste in her voice. Though it didn't compare to the delight he'd found in Cora's body, thinking about the pleasure those many women had given him broadened his smile.

"What do you remember about before you came here?"

He stared into the flames—yes, that's what they were: flames, *fire*.

Images blasted into his mind.

An explosion. Wailing alarms. Men shrieking. Fire flaring around him. Heat scorching his skin. Acrid smoke burning his nostrils. Lungs screaming for air. Pain. Terror. Bodies flying around the cabin to land twisted and broken, then burning beyond recognition as the ship tumbled at breakneck speed toward the planet's surface. He gritted his teeth and clutched his head to keep from adding his voice to the pandemonium of sight and sound as the vision played out behind his closed eyelids.

"Alex! Alexander! What's wrong?" Cora's voice and hands gripping his shoulders broke the hallucination. That was all it was, all he'd allow it to be—a delusion.

He gave a mighty shake and pushed the images back into the hidden recesses of his mind. Remembering would do him no good. Remembering threatened to steal his sanity.

"Nothing. I am fine."

"You're not fine. You're shaking like a leaf. Sit down. Eat something." She tugged him down to sit beside her and offered him the browned meat.

More to hide the trembling of his hands than from hunger, he took the offering and shoved it into his mouth. The rage and terror of things he saw in his mind vanished as flavors burst on his tongue. With a moan of bliss, he gave himself over to enjoying this unusual meal.

Cora dug out the steaming vegetables she'd wrapped in wet leaves then roasted in the fire and handed them to him. As with everything he did, he gave the food his full attention, savoring every bite. The expression of sensual enjoyment on her face made her want to forget her goal of escape and replace the food with herself. He ran his tongue around his lips to lick away the grease. A bolt of heat shot through her, and her nipples hardened. She tore her gaze away and forced her thoughts into line.

As much as she wanted him to remember, an inner caution told her not to push him too fast. The memories he'd repressed were too painful for him to easily accept. She'd have to allow him to remember at his own rate. The question was, did they have the time? What if the Flock discovered her ship? She hadn't been that far from it when she had fallen into their trap. Would they know what it was? Would they try to destroy it? How would they react if they came to understand that the humans they kept as animals were actually intelligent, thinking beings? Would they even believe it? Or, the thought hit her, did they already know and not care?

It had taken mankind generations to accept and protect the developing intelligence of many of Earth's native inhabitants. Some had become extinct before they could reach their full potential. To this day, many humans thought

Gorillas and Dolphins didn't deserve their status as members of the Consortium of Intelligent Life. Of course, there were nonhuman members of C.O.I.L. who questioned human membership and looked for ways to negate it.

Maybe if she understood the Flock and this world, she could figure out how to escape from both. Locked inside Alex's mind were the tools and knowledge she needed to gain that information: His skill in understanding alien cultures, along with the ability to learn their languages, had earned him a posting as not only the first human aboard a First Contact ship, but also the youngest.

"Tell me what you know about the Flock." She felt a moment of regret as Alex's jaw tightened, banishing his look of contentment.

"What would you like to know?"

If she posed the right questions, would his training and knowledge as a xeno-anthropologist kick in and provide the answers she needed? "You said all the keepers are female—hens." Since the Flock reminded her of big, long-necked, flightless chickens, she might as well use chicken terminology. "What about the male—the rooster, or the commander, as you called him?"

At her questions he relaxed. His look became thoughtful. When he spoke she could almost hear the old Alex. "Calling them the Flock is pretty accurate. Their social structure is built around a group of females ruled by one dominant male. Hens and a rooster, as you said."

"How do they live? Trade?"

"Each compound has its own industry. Some are farms, some manufacture things, some act as distributors for others. This compound specializes in breeding pit fighters. I have been the champion for the last five seasons. Females are shipped here from all over for me to service."

Not sure she wanted to hear more about pit fighting and

the services he provided, or about what he'd been forced to endure, she turned the conversation back to the Flock and its social structure. "How do they reproduce?"

"They lay clutches of eggs. The commander determines which females he will fertilize to produce the strongest young and the most females."

"Why do they want more female offspring than males?"

"Females are a valuable commodity. Young males are tolerated in the compound until they reach sexual maturity. Unless a young male can acquire females, he cannot found his own compound. If his sire is wealthy he purchases or trades for a group of young females from a neighboring flock and helps the youngster set up his own compound.

"And if the sire isn't wealthy?"

"The young male is either driven from his compound to take his chances in the wild or he might challenge his father for control. Usually when a clutch is laid, the commander inspects it and will destroy any male eggs he detects before they can hatch. On the other hand, a wealthy male may allow some male eggs from his favorite females to hatch. The hens favor their male offspring—perhaps because they know that when their rooster is ousted and they're no longer fertile, they can find a place in their son's compound rather than being abandoned. When the rooster sets his sons up with their own compounds, he gains by collecting a portion of that compound's profits.

"Other than that, from what I've observed as the commander ages, either the females get better at hiding their eggs or his ability to detect male eggs from female eggs lessens, and males are hatched. From those few a smart commander will choose and train his successor before he reaches the time when he risks losing a challenge. During that training period a bond forms between them, and when the elder retires he is allowed to remain with the flock. The young one you rescued was the commander's chosen successor."

She wondered if her captors would look on her action favorably or if it would work against her.

"When the males fight, is it to the death?"

"They might as well. The loser is driven out of the compound to die. I have personal experience of the beasts that roam the open land. Without powerful weaponry, one Flock, one man or"—he gave her a long assessing look—"one woman wouldn't stand a chance of survival."

With his words he warned her of the dangers she faced if she attempted to escape. But did it mean he'd stop her from trying? Or just that he wouldn't make the attempt with her? He spoke Standard without pause and he discussed the Flock with the words of a professional xeno-anthropologist. Despite his memory loss, his powers of observation remained intact. Still, she didn't feel confident enough to question him—yet. Somehow she had to stir his memory, to resurrect the man he'd been, at least enough so that he'd no longer tolerate being an animal in a zoo.

"Tell me how you get from compound to compound. Do the Flock have motorized vehicles?"

"Mo-to-rized?" He sounded out the term; then, as if he suddenly remembered the meaning of the word, he shook his head. He seemed to accept each new concept more easily as he remembered. "I haven't seen any. They use armored wagons pulled by strong four-legged beasts to move from place to place. The pace is slow. A trip to the nearest compound takes three days. Within their own groups, the Flock are social animals but prefer to keep their compounds well separated. Males become agitated if they're near other dominant males for too long. The only time they gather is to trade or attend fights. The farthest compound I've visited took two weeks to get to."

"How can they have electric lighting and those stun guns and not yet have figured out how to build some kind of electric or combustion engine?" Cora mused aloud.

"I don't think that technology belongs to the Flock. I believe they borrowed it. From my observations they're resourceful and clever rather than inventive and innovative, but I can't be certain."

Had one of the lost colonies crashed here? Had the survivors and what was left of their technology fallen into Flock hands? In four hundred years had the Flock bred the independence and intelligence out of these humans?

And if they truly were human, what besides relaying their condition to E.L.F. could she do?

Even without his memory and while being treated as a dumb animal, Alex had managed to accumulate a lot of information about his keepers. Were the Flock candidates for First Contact?

"Do you think they have any idea that there's intelligent life other than their own?"

Alex shook his head. "I doubt it."

Cora swallowed her groan of dismay. C.O.I.L. laws concerning first contact were stringent, and the consequences of breaking them severe. Law One stated that before First Contact could be initiated, the species had to be aware of the possibility of the existence of other intelligent life.

Her mind spinning, Cora pushed her fears of C.O.I.L retribution for Alex's and her crimes aside; she'd deal with that problem later.

The excited whistles and whirs of two handlers standing inside the chamber doorway drew her attention. They held their stun rods ready as they pointed at the fire and conversed in rapid tones.

"Our fire seems to disturb them." Cora put out the flames and retreated to the far side of the courtyard where she crouched behind the shelter of a bush to watch. As if they were beneath his notice, Alex ignored the Flock and dove into the pool. His powerful arms cut through the water as he swam back and forth. Cora was torn between her desire to watch the play of water over his bronzed skin and her need to observe her enemies.

They headed toward her. She backed against the stone wall. "Alex!"

He surged out of the water and put himself between her and the Flock. Rivulets of water trickled down his back and over his bare backside. His muscles rippled as he tensed. White against his bronzed skin, a scar slashed around his left shoulder blade. She couldn't see Alex's face, but the two Flock must have; they stopped a few yards away and conversed.

"Come to me," Alex said. She hurried to stand behind him. He pulled her to his side and held her there with one arm, then gave a sharp whistle, several whirs and what sounded like a cackle. Her translator finally kicked in.

"Mine. I keep. No take."

"You can *speak* Flock? Why didn't you tell me?" Apparently the translator had needed to hear the Flock language from a human tongue before it could process the sounds. Now that it had, she'd be able to understand and communicate with them.

His ability shouldn't have surprised her. He'd always had a way with languages that almost made a translator chip unnecessary.

The Flock became excited and began a rapid dialogue. Her translator could only catch a couple of words. "Extraordinary." "Report."

"I can speak only a bit. Our tongues aren't equipped to make many of the Flock sounds. I understand much more. But my speaking their language upsets them. The last time I did so, I spent months in their lab undergoing tests. I have no wish to repeat that experience."

She shuddered at the memory of her short time in the Flock lab. "Then why did you speak now?"

"If I hadn't, they would have taken you away. I had to

stop them. My only other choice would have been to kill them, and if I had, more would come until they had you."

"What happens now?" She watched as the two Flock, still talking, backed out of the courtyard.

"I don't know. Because last time I deliberately flunked all their tests, they convinced themselves I didn't understand the sounds I made."

They sat down together at the far side of the courtyard behind some bushes, away from the door and out of sight of the viewing area.

"What did you say the first time you spoke?"

"I said no to killing an opponent in a battle."

She remembered Alex's gentle nature. The thought of him being forced to kill made her heart ache in sympathy. The Flock had a lot to answer for. "I thought that was the point of the fight—to kill your opponent."

"The handlers decide which fighters live and which will die. Early in my training killing came hard to me. My first opponent was very young and inexperienced, not a trained fighter. He didn't have a hope of defeating me. I could see and smell his fear."

"They wanted you to kill him? Why?"

"The handlers set him against me to allow me an assured victory and build my lust for blood."

Cora had read that in Earth's past some people had enjoyed pitting vicious dogs against each other. To train those animals they would use smaller dogs or other animals as bait. If possible, her opinion of the Flock sank lower. Civilized species shouldn't use other living creatures in this manner.

"You seem to be aware of what was being done to you. Why didn't you just refuse to fight?"

He gave a humorless laugh. "The handlers are well versed in training reluctant fighters. In the end it's less painful to give in and do what they want than to say no.

And it took me a long time to understand what was going on, and even longer to learn how to get my own way. Now, I choose the opponents I kill. If my choice differs from the handlers, they must stun me or he dies."

She wanted to ask how he chose, but was afraid to know the answer. What had happened to the Alex she'd known? Was he still alive, buried deep inside the creature the Flock had created from his injured shell? Or had the man she loved died?

"Why don't we just tell them the truth?" But she knew that wasn't an option, not if they wanted to return home. The Consortium didn't look kindly on those who broke their laws, intentionally or otherwise.

"And what is the truth?"

"That we're intelligent beings with minds of our own, not animals to be kept in their zoo and used for their entertainment."

"Until you came this thought hadn't occurred to me. I was content with my life here. I had food, shelter, females and no concerns beyond winning my next fight. What more could I want?"

"And how do you feel now?"

"I don't know. You are different from any female I've known." He lowered her to the ground and covered her body with his own. "I will not give you up. You are mine."

As he was hers.

She tugged his face to hers. "Kiss me."

"Kiss?"

"Don't tell me you've forgotten that too. Here, like this." She lifted her lips to his and brushed a gentle kiss there.

"Ah, I remember from before." He plunged his tongue between her lips as she had done to him earlier. Slick and hot, he explored the recesses of her mouth. Taking control, she pulled her mouth free of his.

"You don't like?"

71

"Yes, but that's only one kind of kissing." He didn't object as she shifted until he lay flat on the ground and she leaned over him. "Let me show you another."

She closed her lips and pressed them over his in a chaste kiss. The gentle touch of his lips on hers sent a shockwave of emotion through her. How had she lived without him for so long?

She'd believed she'd dealt with his loss in a manner fitting a space pilot; rationally, without emotion. Those who explored unknown space knew the risks and accepted them. Now, the true answer stunned her. She hadn't. Since news of his death had reached her, she'd merely existed. Her heart had continued pumping blood through her veins, but it had ceased to beat with true life. Her mind had propelled her through the days, but had stopped dreaming. Without Alex she'd become an automaton, going through life in an emotional vacuum. Now, she woke to renewed life. Whatever came next, she couldn't regret the circumstances that had returned him to her.

She pulled away. "Oh, Alex. I've missed you so."

"Talk later. I like this kissing."

Rolling her beneath him, he pressed his mouth against hers. She drank in the savage sweetness of his possessiveness. He showered kisses around her lips and along her jaw, then his mouth swooped back to capture hers. Blood pounded in her brain, leapt from her heart and made her tremble with longing.

"Make love to me," she begged. It seemed impossible, but she couldn't get enough of him. She caressed the strong tendons of his neck and explored the muscled ridges of his shoulders and back. Her fingers trailed across the ragged scar.

"Patience, little wild one," he whispered as he began.

Later, she lay in his arms, body sated, her emotions in turmoil. At the last moment he'd pulled out and spilled his hot seed over her belly. Disappointment that even in the throes of passion he retained his control while she lost hers left her feeling alone and confused.

CHAPTER SIX

Zan watched the female—no, Cora was no mere female—as she slept curled against his side. Her head and upper body rested on his chest. One arm draped possessively across his waist, she'd nestled her thigh into his groin. A tangle of golden blond hair hid her face. He pushed aside a strand and stroked the soft curve of her cheek. As she shifted, his cock stirred to life, then went lax again.

Time after time through the morning hours they'd taken pleasure from one another until she'd fallen asleep in his arms. Despite her insistence that she wouldn't conceive, each time he made sure to spill his seed outside her body. Much to her increasing displeasure in this, he refused to waver.

Though well used to servicing many females in a short span of time, he'd never come away from those sessions feeling so drained—and also full. What he did with the females the handlers brought bore no resemblance to the act between Cora and him. But aside from her ability to accommodate his entire length, how did it differ?

The physical sensations, though more intense, were similar. It was what he felt *inside* that disturbed him. With this female—with Cora—it wasn't just his body that engaged in the act. Being with her involved his heart and mind as well. The thought frightened him.

Sooner or later, the handlers would try to take her from him. He tightened his hold on her. She twisted away as if even in her sleep she refused to be held captive.

The memories she stirred inside him made his head pound, but he could no longer deny them. She was the key that had unlocked the door in his mind; now he needed to pull that door open and explore the truth of who he was.

Disrupting his thoughts, she reached up and touched his face with her fingertips. "Do you remember when we first met?" she murmured.

"In the breeding chamber?"

She sat up and pulled the blanket around her body, and air chilled his flesh where she'd lain against him. But it was his heart that grew cold.

"No, the first time we met at the academy. I was a starry-eyed freshman while you were a senior and big man on campus."

Memories, pictures of his past flickered through his mind in rapid succession. "Hardly a big man. I don't think women ever even noticed me."

"Oh, they noticed you all right. They just didn't know the right way to approach you. They thought because you were handsome and well built that you lacked a brain. Their bold frontal attacks on your body sent you running for cover. I knew better. I appealed to your mind, but"—she trailed her hand down his cheek to his chest and pinched his nipple—"I was really after your body too."

Their first encounter played out in his mind. He snatched at the memory, but it faded away like early morning fog beneath the sun's rays, until only drops of dew remained. He massaged the ache at the back of his neck.

"What do you remember?"

"I remember you." With each word he spoke the picture grew clearer in his mind, his voice firmer. "Your hair glowing like spun gold in the sunshine, smiling at me, asking for my help with your classwork. Astro-navigation. I was so stunned by your attention, I forgot that it was my worst subject and agreed to tutor you. Only later I learned you were top of your class and you ended up tutoring me." The words, some familiar, some strange, poured out of him. He shook his head.

"And within days we were lovers."

"Yes." He remembered how she'd taken charge and seduced him. He saw her stretched out naked on a field of white. A soft flickering light sent warm shadows dancing over her smooth pale skin. She reached up her arms, and he lowered himself down and close to her. He closed his eyes to savor the memory.

"We had big plans," she continued. "Together we were going to explore uncharted space. I'd map the stars and planets while you made first contact with their alien inhabitants."

Plans—her plans—he'd accepted them without question until . . . Another memory surfaced: He and Cora stood together on a broad field of concrete. Tears streamed down her face. Acrid smoke and pungent odors burned his nose. Engines roared, deafening him to her words. She held him tight, kissed him hard, then took a step back as he turned and walked away. Ahead rose a strange silver and white craft—a spaceship.

Stay with her! Don't go! he screamed at his ghostly image. "What happened?" Was that calm voice his?

"During my last year at the academy you received your first posting. I never saw you again until now. When the authorities declared your ship lost and all hands dead, I felt as if I'd died too." Her voice wobbled. "I think a part of me did die. My body continued. I finished school and began my career as a pilot, but inside I stopped feeling or caring whether I lived or died. I took every difficult, dangerous assignment that came along. I took foolish risks. I don't know if it was skill or luck, but I managed to survive and not get anyone else killed. Still, no one wanted to be posted on a ship with me. Finally I purchased my own ship and contracted with Command to scout the far edge of mapped space."

Of the bits and pieces of memory that continued to tumble and twist in his mind, Cora remained the only clear image. An incessant pounding blurred his vision. He rubbed his eyes.

"Is your head hurting?"

His nod sent a shaft a pain shooting through him. He groaned.

"Rest now." She pulled him to the ground with her and tucked his head against her shoulder. "Don't worry about remembering."

"I remember you," he whispered as they fell asleep.

As the days passed, to avoid having their every action observed, and much to their viewers' disappointment, Cora and Alex chose to sleep through visiting hours. During the night when they were alone, they swam, ate, talked and made love. Despite his refusal to believe she couldn't become pregnant, the sex left Cora breathless and always eager for more. If they weren't prisoners in the Flock zoo, Cora would have thought it heaven, but the thought of escape never left her mind.

Several times a week the handlers came for Alex. The few hours he was gone she tried not to consider where he went or what he did. She wanted to ask, but wasn't sure she could bear to hear the answer. It gave her some comfort that when he returned, though he was sweaty, he didn't smell of sex.

Over the course of several weeks, Alex's memory returned bit by bit. He didn't remember everything, and most of what he did recall left him with more questions than answers. In some ways he was the man she'd known, in others he was a stranger. His ability to accept his life as a Flock captive baffled her. Nothing she said or that he remembered convinced him that they stood a chance of escaping captivity. What had caused him to retreat so far into his mind?

As the sun started to set and the last of the day's visitors trailed away, Cora tried to stretch. Alex's arm held her against his side. He slumbered on. She eased out of his embrace and rose. Though the air was mild, leaving his warmth made her shiver. He murmured a complaint at her absence.

She draped the blanket over him. In the last few days she'd grown more comfortable being naked. When they were alone she no longer felt the need to cover herself. If there was a chance of the Flock seeing her, she wore the blanket.

Her stomach growled. She went out into the courtyard to cook something to eat. Since her first fire, the handlers now stocked the enclosure with kindling and firewood. She smiled. It had helped drive home their request when Alex had pelted the handlers and viewers with raw meat.

She wondered what the Flock made of the changes in Alex's behavior, and what they might do about it. Chances were something would happen soon. Nearly two months had passed since her arrival. She just hoped nothing happened too soon; she wanted more time with Alex before she decided what came next.

Her escape plans remained sketchy. She'd stashed away food and water, but from what Alex told her about the dangers of this world, without a weapon they didn't stand a chance outside the Flock compound. She sat back on her heels and stared into the fire. Could she manage to steal one of the Flock stun rods? Not without Alex's help.

First she had to figure a way out of this cage. She'd thoroughly investigated every inch of the chamber and the courtyard. She'd even dived to the bottom of the pool and searched the submerged walls. Other than the main door, which the Flock kept securely locked, there was only one way out. She raised her gaze up the rock wall to the metal grating overhead. What lay beyond this cage, she didn't know, but she intended to find out—tonight.

Warm hands came to rest on her shoulders. "Something smells delicious. I'm hungry."

"I haven't started cooking yet. You'll have to wait." She looked back over her shoulder at Alex.

He nuzzled her neck. "I wasn't referring to food."

As much as she wanted him, the time had come to talk about escape. She couldn't let him distract her. She batted his hands away. "Food first. Sex later."

Alex grinned and sat cross-legged on the ground. He was hungry, but the sight of her, her golden hair tangled around her flushed face, her body bare, roused a different kind of hunger inside him.

Would he ever have enough of this woman?

While she cooked, the sun set; now the fire lit the courtyard. Through the flames he could make out the shape of several Flock standing in the viewing area, but behind the fire Cora and he were invisible. He didn't mention their presence, not wanting to destroy this moment of contentment.

Cora's hopes and plans of escape were nothing but a dream. Every minute and every day his memory of his past increased. He didn't understand all he recalled, but he accepted that his life here was a lie. So, if they couldn't remain here and they couldn't escape, where did that leave them?

In the morning the handlers would come for him to fight. How would she react when they took him away? And would she be here when he returned? Her arrival had changed more than just his thinking. Since the incident with the baby Flock, the handlers had left Cora and him alone. He hadn't been summoned to fight or to stud; his only duties had been working with the young boys.

Before a fight the handlers usually didn't send him to the breeding chamber, but they always took him to train. Aside from his sessions with the young ones, he'd had no training for over a month. If he fought tomorrow he would be unprepared. And being unprepared left him open for defeat. His muscles tightened. He would not, could not lose. Without him, Cora would be defenseless.

Honesty then forced him to admit he provided her no shield from the Flock. Against their stun rods and drugs, how could he protect her?

"Here." She handed him some roasted meat. The smell teased his nose and made his stomach rumble in response. While he'd been thinking, she'd prepared their food. Though the element of novelty was gone, he still savored the way cooking enhanced the meat's flavor.

"Mmmm. How could I have forgotten this? Fire? My past? You?"

"I don't know, but it doesn't matter. You're remembering things again."

Appetite gone, he put down the food. "Small bits of my life. Like shattered pottery, I want to put them together in my mind to make a whole, but I can't. In my mind I see faces, but can't remember names or who they were to me. Even my memory of you is a tiny fragment of what you tell me we shared. I can't remember how I ended up here. Everything before the Flock found me is a jumble of sights, sounds, tastes, smells and sensations. When I try to make sense of them my head pounds. I don't know who I was. And since you came into my life I no longer know who I am."

"Be patient." She put her hand on his arm. "These things take time."

"We might not have time."

Unable to bear her sympathy, he stood. She raised her face to look at him, which brought it level with his groin. The feel of her warm breath brushing across him made him swell.

"I'm scheduled to fight tomorrow. The handlers will come for me in the morning."

She laid her cheek against his thigh. "How do you know?"

"During my training session with the young ones I heard them talking. I've never gone this long without a fight. They must be determined for you to conceive."

"Oh, Alex. What are we going to do?"

"I don't know."

"Why haven't you ever turned your swords against the Flock?"

"I tried once."

"What happened?"

"The handlers are extremely careful to stay out of my reach when I have swords in my possession. One day when they came within reach, I believed they'd grown careless and turned to strike them down. The next thing I knew I was back in my cage. As close as I can figure out, the swords are equipped with stunners activated by something the Flock wear. If the sword comes close enough to strike a Flock, the holder is shocked into unconsciousness. They stay out of reach not to protect themselves, but to spare me being rendered senseless more than necessary."

"Maybe if I could get my hands on a sword I could deactivate the mechanism."

"Unlikely; they only give me my swords just before I enter the arena."

"We'll think of something."

"My life as a Flock captive has taught me to enjoy each moment. And if this is our last night together, I intend to savor it. Make love with me?"

"Yes."

81

★ ★ ★

Cora half-smiled as he tangled his hands in her silken hair and tugged her head to his sex; she shared his lust. Following his lead, she cupped his testicles in her palms. Blood rushed to his cock as she took it into the hot depths of her mouth.

His thick erection throbbed against the inside of her cheek as she licked and sucked. Kneeling at his feet, she worshipped his body. She felt the tremors of his restraint vibrating through him. Working her mouth over and around him as she would her hips if they'd been joined there, she sought to shatter his control, to make him as wild for her as she was for him. With a groan he clasped her head and thrust his hips forward.

Satisfaction made her lips curl into a smile. Moisture dampened her thighs, which she pressed together to still the growing ache. Heat from the fire that warmed her backside couldn't compare to the inferno raging inside her.

Alex gave a strangled cry and pulled away. Wet with her saliva, his erection trailed across her cheek. When she reached for him, he took her hands in his and lifted her to her feet.

"Not that way." He brushed the hair from her face with gentle fingers. "I want to feel your body convulse around me—I want *you* to come."

She found herself moved to say, "I'm always with you. Even when I thought you were dead, my heart was with you." She cupped his smooth cheek in her palm, noticing that after all this time his beard suppressant still worked.

He splayed his hands under her buttocks and lifted her, and she locked her legs around his hips. The hard length of him pressed against her belly. He raised her until he probed her warm, wet, willing entrance. Her body trembling with need, she buried her face against his throat.

"Now, please." No matter what they did, she couldn't get enough. She needed this—so badly.

In one smooth motion, he filled her. "Alex!" Tiny ripples of pleasure rushed over her as her inner muscles tightened around his pulsing flesh. He began to rock against her. Slow and steady, his movements tantalized, made her crazy with wanting, brought her to the brink of gratification but didn't push her over the edge into the mindless bliss she craved.

She tried to urge him to go faster, harder. She squirmed. Dug her nails into his back. Nipped at his neck. But he held her still, ignored her wordless pleas and continued to torment her, making her accept his pace. With each stroke the pressure inside her grew until she moaned in frustration. Muscles tense and hard, he kept up his maddening rhythm. Breathless with need, she clung to him.

"Please, Alex."

He gave a growl filled with male dominance and pride. Pushing her back against the stone wall he slammed into her. She caught his face between her hands and kissed him hard. Their tongues dueled as each fought to control the other. Rough rock scraped Cora's back as she met Alex thrust for thrust, squeezing him and demanding he give her what she wanted—total surrender. Then, she couldn't wait. A fierce wave of sensation crashed over her as she reached the crest and plunged into the swirling depths of her climax. Head thrown back, her body stiffened as wave after wave of ecstasy flooded her. Once again, he pulled out as his own release claimed him.

Despite the aftershocks of her climax, she felt empty, defeated. Nothing she did broke his control. He'd never be hers. Her legs dropped from around his waist. Limp, she would have sunk to the ground if not for his arm that held her against him.

The salty musky smell of sex permeated the air, and suddenly her wanton behavior embarrassed her. Over the last few weeks they'd come together so many times. In the dark, in the light, standing, sitting, in the water, against the wall. So many times she'd come apart in his arms, while he maintained control. She needed him to be as wild with wanting as she.

She tried to move away, but sticky with their combined fluids, his now flaccid flesh stuck to her thigh. He tightened his hold. She looked up at him. Light from the fire cast menacing shadows over his beloved features. She blinked and the fearful image faded. No matter what he'd been through, he was still her Alex.

But one thing was clear: they'd wasted enough time. She couldn't let the Flock take him from her again. Somehow they had to escape—tonight.

"What mad scheme are you planning?"

His tone reminded her of all the times he'd asked that question while they were at the academy. Now, as then, she knew he would try to talk her out of doing anything dangerous. He'd always been the cautious one, looking before he leaped and weighing the odds of success before he tried anything. His careful study of the facts would have served him well as a First Contact diplomat. She on the other hand preferred to gamble. Pilots had to be willing to take calculated risks. And now as then, she'd prevail. She had to. Their lives depended on it. In this she couldn't give him a choice. Couldn't let him retain control.

She led him into the chamber and sat with him on the pallet. "We need to get out of here, to escape. You can't be here for them to take you tomorrow."

"I've told you, escape is impossible."

"Us here together is impossible, but it happened. We—I can't . . . I *won't* stay here. I'd rather die trying to escape than remain an animal in a cage, but . . ." Her voice broke. "I can't leave you behind."

"If we can get out of this cage, where would you go?"

His cautious question stirred her hope. "To my ship, to *Freedom*."

Five years of hard work, along with the remainder of the inheritance from her parents, had bought her *Freedom*, along with her commission in the Earth League Force—or ELF, as members like to call it—recon squad. More than a means for her to make her living, *Freedom* was a part of who she was. For her, losing *Freedom* and the position that went with it would be the same as stripping the wings from a bird.

"Do you know where in the Flock compound we are?"

He hesitated before answering. "Yes."

"Good. Once we're out of here I can find my bearings. When my ship crashed I noted a pair of mountains with dusky pink peaks that look like a woman's breasts. I could see that same range from the field where the Flock took the women and me to graze."

Alex nodded. "I know the range you speak of. But they are many miles away, across dangerous territory. We'll need a weapon to attempt crossing. A stun rod would be best."

She breathed a sigh of relief: he would leave with her. "Any idea how we can get one?"

"Each handler is issued a stun rod at the beginning of her shift. They're kept in the commander's office. If we can get there and get one, I know how to operate them. A stun rod has six settings. Settings one through three are for discipline . . ."

Cora hid a smile as he slipped into lecture mode. If he hadn't opted for space service, he'd have made an excellent teacher.

"The first setting delivers a mild jolt, like a zap of static electricity. Setting two packs a bigger charge. Both are painful, but leave no lasting damage. Setting three is a different matter. It disrupts the body's entire electrical system. When you're hit by it, it feels like every nerve in your body is on fire. The guards don't often use this setting because it can cause serious injury. Afterwards your muscles ache, your skin feels like it's on fire and your head pounds for days."

Cora wasn't sure which setting she'd been stunned with, but she shuddered in memory. "What about the other three settings?"

"Setting four causes paralysis. It shuts down all your body's voluntary muscle control. You're awake and aware, able to feel everything, but unable to move. An unpleasant experience. It lasts a few hours. Setting five renders you unconscious, but when you revive it's as if you've been asleep. This is the Flock's, and my," he added with a grimace, "preferred setting for when they need to perform any procedures on me,"

"And setting six?"

His face looked grim. "It stops your heart."

She laughed, trying to keep things light. "You've really been paying attention."

"Despite what you might think, I've never enjoyed being an animal in a cage." But then he cupped her face in his hand and looked into her eyes. "Escape is impossible. I won't let you risk your life."

Tears burned her eyes. What could she say to convince him? And what would she do if she couldn't?

Before she could argue further, overhead lights came on. She blinked against the sudden glare as six Flock poured into the courtyard. Alex covered her retreat as she made a dash for the pool. At its edge she paused to check on Alex. Four Flock surrounded him.

"Alex, look out!"

The Flock behind him shoved a stun rod against the back of his neck. He went rigid, then collapsed. Paralyzed or unconscious? She couldn't tell.

They started to lift him.

"No!" She couldn't let them take him.

Not considering the cost, she ran forward. A Flock, the

same one she'd attacked, intercepted Cora and used a stun rod to herd her into a corner. The Flock trilled something that sounded like a laugh; then, before she could dodge out of the way, jabbed the stun rod against her shoulder. White-hot agony shot through Cora. She screamed and fell writhing to the ground. Again it pressed the stun rod against her until she curled into a ball, sobbing in rage, pain and fear, and unable to see what had happened to Alex.

"Stop!" She barely heard or understood the sharp command from another Flock. Eyes glinting in satisfaction, her nemesis touched her one last time with the stun rod and Cora couldn't move. Paralyzed, she stared in horror until the guard bent over and closed her frozen eyelids.

Because they could not obtain what they wanted from Zan while he was unconscious or paralyzed, the Flock strapped him to a table in their lab before they revived him. He woke to the feel of their hands on his limp penis.

Usually he fought this process with every fiber of his being, physically struggled against the constraints and mentally battled the sexual stimulants they injected into him. On several occasions he'd even thwarted their efforts to get his seed. His satisfaction at frustrating them just about made up for the pain when they used other, less pleasant, ways of obtaining it. Though he found the procedure degrading and humiliating, this time he wanted it over with as quickly as possible, so he remained passive and accepting of what was to come. The sooner it was done, the sooner he could get back to Cora.

To his dismay, his handlers proceeded with their normal caution. He felt the sting of the stimulant injection and waited impatiently for it to take effect. He could sense his handlers' confusion when he didn't thrash or roar or pull against the constraints. He didn't try to fight the surge of blood to his cock as they stroked and fondled him to erection.

Nor did he ignore the ripe scent of the young teaser female they placed at his side. She bent over his groin and let her full breasts brush against him. Engorged and ready, his cock jerked out of the Flock's hands and stood at attention. At the Flock's direction the female closed her small warm fingers around him and began to pump. Sweat beaded his body.

Closing his eyes, he filled his mind with images of Cora—her body wrapped around his as she rode him to fulfillment; lying beside him, their bodies limp and sated from physical ecstasy; sitting with her before the fire, talking; relearning his past; playing tag in the water until he caught her, and teasing laughter turning again to passion. The bond they shared went far beyond the physical.

Inside him, the pressure built, an eruption waiting to happen. Struggling to reach his release, he strained against his bonds. Flock hands replaced the female's, cupped his balls, lifted and squeezed, all the while maintaining the forceful stroking of his cock.

His hips jerked upward and like hot lava his seed spewed out. Shame and anger at being used threatened to swamp him. He summoned his resolve to find and free Cora.

CHAPTER SEVEN

Trapped sightless and motionless in her own body, Cora struggled not to succumb to terror. *Concentrate on what you can feel, hear, smell and taste. Don't yield to panic.* Hands lifted her. A few minutes later she was placed on a padded surface. The room smelled of disinfectant, was probably an infirmary.

She tried to comprehend the Flock conversation as they probed and prodded her helpless flesh. Their chirps and trills remained undecipherable. Maybe the electrical charge from the stun rod had further disrupted her translator chip.

Her sarong was stripped off, leaving her naked. Hands spread her legs and lifted her knees until her feet rested flat on the table. Though she tried to resist, her body refused to answer her mind's commands. Cool air touched her inner thighs. The scent of her arousal and Alex's passion teased her nostrils. She tried to focus on what they had between them and ignore the feel of cold Flock hands invading her person.

Through the degradation, she attempted to maintain rational thought and not descend into madness. She tried to sort the sounds she heard—the clink of glass, the scrape of metal against metal, and the swoosh of liquid—to discern what might happen next.

Fingers combed through her pubic hair and pulled open her labia; then something wet and cold that stung and smelled of antiseptic was dragged over her genitals. A Flock inserted two fingers in her, and at the same time pushed down on her belly. She shuddered and screamed inside, thoughts of Alex unable to take precedence over her rage at being violated, but her body didn't move and no sound escaped her throat.

The Flock trilled and Cora's translator chip caught the word. "No."

Nothing could prepare her for the thick object that was jammed deep inside her, for the bite of pain as it pushed hard against her cervix—then the searing heat as liquid flooded her womb. Suddenly she knew what was happening, but her mind balked at accepting the knowledge. She tasted salt as tears trickled from her eyes down her cheeks to the corners of her mouth.

Like any brood mare that didn't conceive when covered by the stud, she was being artificially inseminated.

Hours later, her body aching, her head pounding, her dignity shredded, the Flock returned Cora to the cage and laid her on the pallet. Alex was already there, locked outside. After the Flock left the room they released the door lock and allowed him inside. When he approached she turned her back to him. Still, she didn't object when he lay down beside her and pulled her against his chest. Silent sobs wracked her. Hot tears slid down her cheeks.

"Shhh," he whispered as he held her close. "It's all right. I was afraid they wouldn't bring you back. You're safe with me now."

"No, I'm not safe. We're not safe." She twisted until they were face-to-face. "You can't keep us safe. You couldn't stop what they did to me." The awareness of what had been done to her was reflected in his eyes; his torment was clear. "I won't stay here another day. I won't be made into an animal. No matter the risk, I'm getting out of here."

His eyes closed for a moment before he met her gaze. "I'll help you escape."

"Now?"

He nodded.

"Why now?" She saw his guilt, but anger made her ask, "Why not before?" If he'd agreed earlier, she wouldn't have had to endure the humiliation.

"Because it's what you need to do."

His answer didn't satisfy her, but it would have to do; she didn't have the energy to probe further, to make him admit he also needed to be free.

Ignoring her aching muscles, she got up and started to wrap the blanket around herself, then stopped. "My sarong will be a bit skimpy, but you need covering, too." Tearing the blanket in half, she fashioned a pair of loose short pants for him and a thigh-length sarong for herself. The humor of the way they looked eased a bit of the humiliated rage burning in her breast. "Aren't we the height of fashion?"

Alex plucked at the fabric wrapped around his lean hips. "It feels odd."

"You'll get used to it." She pulled out the small cache of supplies she'd managed to accumulate. "Let's get going."

"Wait." He went over to the wooden shelving, picked up an object and held it out to her. "I don't remember what it means, but I was wearing it when I came here. Is it yours?"

How had she forgotten what she'd seen on that shelf her first day? She took the gold ring she'd given him as her pledge of love from his outstretched hand and tried to slide it onto his ring finger, but his fingers had thickened. Instead, she put it on his pinkie and curled his fingers into a fist under hers. "No, it's yours. I gave it to you."

He fingered the ring. "It interested the Flock."

"I'm sure it did. Are we ready now? Any other trinkets you want to bring along?" She used sharp words to hide how much the memory of his departure still hurt. That he was alive and with her again should be enough, but she admitted it wasn't. He desired her, but she wanted more. She needed his love, his commitment and his belief in their future.

He cast a glance around the dim chamber, then shook his head. "No. There is nothing else *here* that I want."

His intonation puzzled her, but she didn't have the time to figure it out.

She led the way out of the chamber. Nothing but embers remained of the fire. They stopped at the edge of the pool in the shadow of the rock wall. There a smooth concrete replaced the rock and ended halfway below the metal grating. The grating extended ten feet over the water and continued past the concrete wall. They'd have to climb, then make their way under and over the grating to reach . . . to reach what? She didn't have a clue what they'd find at the top. If they even got that far.

She looked up. A chill rippled down her spine. The wall rose twenty feet straight up.

But her anger burned hotter than her fear. She turned to Alex. "How are you at climbing?"

"Go. I'll follow."

As if he sensed her fear, he took the bag of supplies from her and slung it over his shoulder. Then he put his hands on her hips and lifted her up.

Pressing tight against the rough rock, she scrambled to find handholds. Halfway up she glanced down and froze. In the darkness it seemed an endless plunge to the ground. A wave of dizziness made her sway. Her hands clenched and her breath stalled.

"I'm right behind you. Only a few more feet to go."

The feel of Alex's warm hand on her bare calf eased the panic building inside her. Cora took a deep, shuddering breath and reached up for the next handhold.

Bit by bit she crept up the steep wall until her fingers touched the cold metal grate at the top. Then she realized: "I can't do this. I'll fall." How had she thought she could cling upside down twenty feet above the ground?

Alex climbed up beside her. "I'm right here. Trust me. I won't let you fall."

The feel of his warm, solid hand against her back and the sound of his firm voice helped steady her nerves. She took a deep breath and nodded. They couldn't stop now.

Fear slicked her palms with sweat. Her heart pounding against her chest, she reached out and grabbed the grating. Inch by inch she peeled away from the rock wall and pulled her body along the underside of the metal grid until only her feet touched the wall. To keep from scrambling back to its relative safety, she bit her lip. Salty and metallic, blood filled her mouth.

Alex didn't say anything, but she could feel his presence behind her. Heat from his body eased the chill of fear that coated her body in icy sweat.

She lifted one leg, then the other, and hooked her feet into the metal grid until she hung suspended above the courtyard. As she swayed, she could feel the ground trying to pull her loose, to make her fall. Dizziness swamped her. This was nothing like the weightlessness of space. Squeezing her eyes shut, she clutched the fragile wire.

The grid sagged beneath Alex's weight as he moved out next to her. "Are you all right?"

She looked at him. The darkness hid his expression but the light in his eyes revealed his excitement. "Y-yes," she lied.

"Then let's go. The sooner begun, the sooner finished."

He waited until she began the slow, difficult process of crawling across the underside of the metal grid. Each step required her to move a hand forward, unhook one leg from the grid and reposition it in the next opening, then repeat the process with her other hand and leg. Her muscles trembled at the unaccustomed strain. Though round and smooth, the thin wire bit painfully into her flesh. With his greater weight the wire would dig deeper into Alex. If it cut through his skin, could he maintain his grip on a wire slick with blood?

Though she knew he could move faster, he stayed by her side. Concern for him overrode her fear. "Go on ahead. I'm fine." He continued to keep pace with her. Only his greater strength and longer arms had him reach the edge of the grid first. A few feet ahead a bar of metal about an inch thick ran the length of the grid. Relief that this ordeal was almost over made her smile.

"Stay here," Alex said. "I'll swing to the top, then help you over." He hooked one arm through the grid, let his legs slip free to dangle in the air, then reached out with his free hand to grab the metal bar.

Because of the light from the stars above she hadn't noticed the faint blue glow emanating from the bar. "Alex, wait!"

Too late. His fingers curled around the bar. A shrieking alarm rent the air. His body went rigid, cutting short his cry. Before she could grab his arm he fell. With a small splash he disappeared into the inky water of the pool. Ripples marked the spot. He didn't resurface.

"Alex!"

She stared down. The pool seemed to recede into the distance.

Before she could think about what she was going to do, Cora let go of the grid and plunged toward the water. Cool and dark, it closed over her. The impact left her disoriented.

Where was he? Unable to see in the shadowy water, she reached out with her hands, searching. Lungs straining, she dove deeper.

Warm and solid, his arm brushed past her fingertips. She grabbed hold and propelled herself upward. When her head broke the surface she gasped for air. Alex bobbed up beside her, but he didn't move or make a sound.

She towed him to the edge of the pool, and using strength she didn't know she possessed, heaved him out of the water. Panting, she pulled herself up beside his limp form. He wasn't breathing. Had the shock from the bar stopped his heart or had he drowned? She felt his neck for a pulse. Though faint, his heart still beat. She bent to resuscitate him.

The sudden glare of the overhead lights made her head snap up. Blinded by the brightness, she blinked. Stun rods ready, four Flock burst into the courtyard. As the Flock approached, Cora pulled Alex against her.

"Wait! Let me help him!"

They ignored her curses and pried him out of her arms. Hands curled into claws, she flung herself at them. A Flock grabbed her from behind and pinned her arms. Screaming and crying, she reared back, kicked out with her legs and tried to break free. Rage and fear lent her strength. She clawed and bit at the Flock's arm until the bitter taste of its blood filled her mouth.

Despite her efforts, she couldn't escape. No match for the Flock, she watched helplessly as they carried Alex away She ended up lying on the ground, bound hand and foot, naked and at the mercy of her captors—again. The fact that they hadn't stunned her meant nothing. Hot tears streamed down her cold cheeks. Was Alex dead? Did the Flock know how to resuscitate him?

Two Flock stood above her, talking. She fought to control her dread, to listen to them. By listening maybe she'd learn what had happened to Alex. Could her translator decipher what they were saying? Forcing herself to lie still, she concentrated on their whistles and chirps. She comprehended about one word in ten. The effort of trying to fill in the blanks in their conversation started her head pounding again.

". . . Unars display . . . behavior . . . bitch bit . . ."

Cora had a fleeting moment of satisfaction as the Flock rubbed the bite mark on its arm.

". . . treated," the other Flock said. "Unar bites . . . hazardous . . . female arrived . . . male . . . dangerous . . . difficult . . . handle . . . commander . . . informed."

". . . Unar . . . escape." The Flock looked up at the grid, then back at Cora and shook its head.

". . . devotion . . . male . . . female . . . female . . . observation . . . checked . . . commander . . . hides . . . injured."

". . . pregnant . . . loses . . . kit."

"Help . . ."

The disjointed conversation made her head ache, but it didn't seem like they were going to hurt her—at the moment—so when the Flock picked her up, she didn't resist.

Zan opened his eyes and blinked until his vision cleared. When he tried to rise he found that he was bound to a table. Several Flock stood over him, deep in a conversation. He recognized the commander, the head physician and her assistant. Though the assistant had always been gentle when she dealt with him, he could smell the physician's fear.

Instinct screamed at him to fight for freedom, but Cora had changed him. He forced himself to remain calm and listen. His head pounded as he struggled to understand the Flock's exchange, but with each chirp and whistle his comprehension grew—as did his dismay.

"Physically he'll be fine," the physician said. "The stun didn't damage him and the female pulled him from the water before he drowned. We'll have to watch him for a few days to make sure he doesn't develop a lung infection from inhaling water, but other than that he's in good shape."

"Is it safe to return him to his compound?" the commander asked.

"Not until you fix the problem with the grating," the physician said.

"You think he'll try to escape again?" The commander looked down at Zan.

"I don't know." The physician shook her head. "Since the female arrived, his behavior has become erratic. Look at him. Every other time we've had him on the exam table, we've had to keep him drugged or he'd kill himself trying to get free. Now he's lying there watching us. It's almost as if he understands what we're saying. Makes my feathers twitch."

The second female spoke up. "This male has always been unusual. His larger size and coloring differentiate him from the other males. Wasn't he captured in the wild? And I heard that he can speak, that he's intelligent."

"False feathers! The ability to imitate a few sounds makes him clever, not intelligent. I taught my pet sanlog to whistle and I'd hardly consider it intelligent."

Inside Zan had always known the Flock viewed him as an animal, but he found hearing it disturbing. Cora was right. He was a thinking being, not a dumb creature to be used.

"And 'captured' isn't the way I'd put it." The physician gave a humorless chuckle. "A scouting party saved him from a Zanther attack. It cost this compound thousands of credits to keep him alive."

"Credits that he's more than earned back in fighting and stud fees." The commander gave her a warning look.

"I advised against treating him then and my advice now is to put him, his offspring and the female down. They're abnormal. I believe it's a mistake to breed this bloodline. Wild unars are unpredictable and dangerous."

With a piercing whistle, the commander turned on the female. "Your opinion on this subject is clear, but their fate is my decision, not yours. Follow my orders or I'll be forced to replace you as head Unar physician." His headfeathers stood straight up as he strode out of the room.

Her own feathers flat to her head, the female cringed. "Yes, Commander." She turned to the second female and snapped, "See to the Unar's transfer to an isolation chamber."

"What about the female? Should I put them together?" the other Flock asked.

"No."

After the physician left the room, the assistant leaned over Zan. In her hand she held a syringe. He tried to pull free of the restraints.

She brushed the damp hair off his face. "Easy. Don't worry. You'll be fine. I'm just going to put you to sleep to transfer you."

He felt the needle sting his arm. "Thank you," he chirped.

His vision blurred on the sight of her astonishment.

Strapped naked and spread-eagle on a table again, Cora couldn't control the tremors that ran through her as she suffered another invasive exam. Against her will, tears leaked out from beneath her tightly closed eyelids. Her humiliation didn't matter; Alex was dead, and she was the one who had convinced him to try to escape. Her body ached and she shivered with cold as her skin dried, but the chill came from her heart. Nothing the Flock did to her could hurt as much as losing Alex again. Her need to control her life had killed him.

A hand stroked her cheek. She turned her head and tried to bite it.

The translator chip turned the Flock's chirp into a trill of laughter. She opened her eyes to glare.

"No need for that." The Flock turned to another Flock and said, "We're done here, Ansal. She doesn't appear damaged. The commander wants her placed in an isolation chamber for observation."

Cora listened without interest to the conversation as the translator turned the Flock's chirps, clicks and whistles into words. Ironically, now that she no longer cared what they said, their words came through without difficulty. In other circumstances the situation might have struck her as funny.

"I can't imagine why she hasn't caught yet. The male's potent and she's fertile," Ansal said.

"Who knows?" The first Flock shrugged. "Unar are a fragile species. In the wild they're nearing extinction."

"With a lot of help from our hunters and traps," Ansal muttered under her breath.

Cora didn't think the first Flock had heard her, because she continued without pause, "If it weren't for our breeding programs, they'd already be extinct."

"Perhaps that would be for the best." Ansal stroked her hand over Cora's hair. "They really don't have much purpose, do they? I did my studies in native species and none of the experts can explain how or why they exist."

As Cora suspected, the Flock saw humans as a lower life form, without intelligence, to be used and misused for profit and entertainment. Could she convince them otherwise? How many C.O.I.L. laws would she be breaking if she did? And if Alex was dead, did she even care to try?

But if he were still alive? Hope flickered inside her.

"Bite your tongue," the first Flock chided. "Unar breeding is this compound's prime function."

"You mean pit fighting, don't you? That's what it's all about. Making credits by pitting male Unars against each other or wild animals. It's a disgusting sport."

"Don't let the commander hear that or you'll be out of here faster than you can say fickle feathers. Pit fighting may be bloody, but it's popular with the men, and breeding winners supports this compound."

"I know, but I don't have to like it."

"If you don't like it, why did you choose to come to this compound?"

"I didn't. My sire traded me as a stud fee. Like this female here"—she touched Cora's head—"I had no choice. He wanted a champion pit fighter more than he cared for his daughter. While we do all the work, males have all the power."

"My sympathies. Whatever your personal feelings about this compound's livelihood, you owe the commander your loyalty. When you have chicks of your own you'll understand better how the world works."

"Perhaps," Ansal muttered. "What happened with the male? Did he die?"

The first Flock shrugged. "I don't know. Looked dead to me. It's a shame, but maybe for the best. Prepare the female for transfer." As she left the room, she said, "Be careful who you speak to so candidly. Others might not be as open-minded as me."

Alex, dead. Nothing else mattered. Grief and guilt swallowed Cora. Physically and emotionally numb, she lay limp as Ansal moved around the room.

Ansal swabbed Cora's upper arm with something cold. She felt a sharp prick.

"That didn't hurt, did it?" Ansal patted her arm gently. "Sleep now, that's a good girl."

Cora tried to speak, but consciousness slipped away before she could make her lips and tongue work.

Zan paced the small chamber. His feet stirred the layer of sawdust covering the cold concrete floor. Anger made him want to pound his fists against the walls. Instead, he paced.

Where was Cora? Had the Flock hurt her? Unlike the

cool confidence he felt when he entered the pit, this rage was different, more personal. In the pit he separated his mind from his emotions and fought with restrained fury. The thought of Cora injured tore away any notion of control. If they'd harmed her in any way, he vowed to rip out their hearts.

Before Cora, he'd been content with his life. Now he found the thought of life without her intolerable. He'd do whatever it took to find her and help her escape.

He stopped and stared at the observation window. Did they watch him? What should he do?

When he'd spoken their language, the consequences had been physically and psychologically painful. They'd put him through test after test, but even when he responded they didn't believe the results. Finally he'd stopped trying to communicate with them. They refused to hear him; to do so would be to admit that they'd enslaved an intelligent species, and in this compound the Flock's sense of self was too fragile to accept that burden of guilt. Also, that knowledge would destroy the basis of their compound's livelihood.

Zan wondered how he understood the Flock so well. He searched his memory. Like a ship broken on jagged rocks, pieces of knowledge floated to the surface of his mind, the flotsam and jetsam of his shipwrecked past. He sensed he had buried inside him the training and skill to deal with the Flock, but did he have the strength to unearth it?

Naked, Cora huddled in a corner of her cell. In the three days since they'd brought her into the ten-by-ten room, she hadn't moved from her spot except to relieve herself in the far corner. When she did, she kept her back to the observers, refusing to let them see her fear and pain.

Though the air was warm and dry, she couldn't stop shivering. Her mood swung from hopeful to defeated. Tears left a crust of salt on her cheeks. She knew she should eat, keep up her strength to escape, but the sight of food made her nauseated.

The door opened. Instinct forced her to turn and face whatever threatened. Crouched in the corner, she hissed at the Flock who entered. Some part of her mind realized she acted like the animal they thought her, but she couldn't stop her reaction.

The Flock held a stun gun in one hand and a piece of cloth in the other. "Easy, little Unar."

Some of the tension seeped out of Cora as she recognized Ansal.

"That's right, relax. I've brought you something. It's all right. Take it. I know you like to wear clothing. You're a most unusual Unar." As if speaking to a dangerous, wild animal, Ansal used low soothing tones. She held out the cloth as she approached.

A chuckle lodged in Cora's throat. She was a dangerous, wild animal. She shifted her gaze between Ansal and the offering—a simple tunic—then back to Ansal. She snatched the tunic and drew it over her head.

Putting on the covering changed something inside her. Grief still held her heart, but she no longer wanted to curl up and die. If she died, then Alex had died for no reason. She owed it to him to escape, to return to Earth, to report what she'd found here. First contact with the Flock would be Alex's memorial.

Fists clenched, mouth tight, she stood and faced the Flock.

"That's good. I'll take you outside." Ansal's wavering tone and shaking hands betrayed her nervousness. She clutched the stun rod and motioned Cora to the open door. "Be good now, please. I'm going against orders letting you out."

Cora paused at the door and spoke in Flock, "Why?"

Surprise and fear widened Ansal's eyes. She took a step back, then answered, "I'm not sure. But any creature who cares so much for another, who wants freedom so bad it risks death, can't be a mere animal. I can't bring back the male and I can't set you free, but I can let you out of this cage."

Cora nodded and moved out into an empty corridor. The sharp smells of disinfectant and humanity stung her nose. Ansal steered her toward another door at the far end.

Moving cautiously past Cora, Ansal opened the door. Fresh air swirled around them. Cora took a deep breath and stepped out into the open. Sunshine warmed her face as she looked up at the clear blue sky.

She kept pace with Ansal through an unfamiliar area of the compound. Though the Flock treated humans like animals, Cora couldn't deny they were a sentient, intelligent species; their compound, their buildings, their language, their technology screamed the fact at her. But were they ready for First Contact? Somehow she doubted it. If they weren't and if she managed to escape, what would be her fate once she returned home and made her report? With Alex dead, she couldn't find it in herself to care.

She squeezed her eyes shut and tried to summon her rage against the Flock. Ansal's gentle tap on her shoulder dissolved it. Her shoulders sagged. Without anger she felt directionless. Eyes open, she moved as if in a dream.

A few minutes later they reached an open field. Watched by three guards, a dozen young human females in groups of two and three wandered around the field grazing on seedpods and the occasional grub.

Ansal spoke briefly with one of the guards, then turned and left.

The Flock guard, the one who hated her, glared at Cora as she entered the field. Though she had no appetite, she picked a pod, dug out the seed and popped it into her mouth. The bland taste stirred her hunger. Forcing aside thoughts of the past and the future, for the present she concentrated her attention on sating her body's needs.

Her stomach full, she headed toward a tree where several

women lounged in the shade. Three days of tears, no food and little sleep had left her feeling woozy. Later she'd decide what to do next.

The women stirred briefly but didn't object as Cora settled next to them. Their musky aroma mingled with the rich earthy smell of the moss-covered ground. Cora curled against the trunk of the tree and sought the oblivion of sleep, but memories of Alex past and present flooded her mind. Fresh tears moistened her cheeks.

Once before she'd lost him and survived; she didn't think she could again. This time, the pain went deeper. This time he'd died because of her.

Despite her grief, exhaustion crept over her and her body went lax. A high shrill scream jolted her awake.

CHAPTER EIGHT

Something jostled Cora. She blinked. The women who moments earlier had dozed in the shade at her side now scrambled to their feet in panic. Sitting up, she watched in confusion as they fled across the field toward the compound. Several guards herded them to safety inside the gates.

She turned toward the sound of the screams, and her mouth fell open in shock. A creature out of a nightmare, twice the size of a grizzly bear and covered in thick gray scales, had three women cornered against the side of a cliff. One woman, her leg twisted in an awkward position, tried to crawl away. Screaming in fear, the other two cowered together.

Under the creature lay a guard. Alive, but unable to move, the guard's pleading gaze locked on hers. Another guard—Cora noted it was the one who hated her—attempted to jab the creature with her stun rod, but couldn't get close enough. The two women helped their injured companion to her feet and hurried toward the compound. At the sight of its prey escaping, the creature roared and swung a massive paw. Cora's enemy pushed the women aside and took the blow. It hit her and sent her flying backward. She landed with a thud. The women ran.

The creature clamped its massive jaws around the first guard, who gave one last strangled shriek of agony and then fell mercifully silent. In the sudden quiet, the sound of cracking bones made Cora gag. Grunting, the creature tore into the guard's body with teeth and claws.

The second guard groaned, but didn't rise. Cora headed toward her. What was she thinking? Why risk her life for a Flock guard who'd taken delight in torturing her? She should behave like the women had, run away. Why should she care? But her feet kept moving forward.

As she approached, the creature lifted its head and looked directly at her. Its deep-set eyes held a primitive intelligence. Cora froze and waited for it to attack. Instead, with a dismissive snort it turned back to its meal.

The living Flock guard tried unsuccessfully to stand. Cora scanned the ground for a weapon. A few yards away lay the first guard's stun rod. The end glowed blue, but it hadn't helped any. And if Cora tried to get it, she'd put herself within reach of the creature. But what choice did she have? There wasn't anything else around.

Keeping a wary eye on the creature, Cora crept forward. Occupied with the dead guard's rapidly disappearing body, the feeding creature paid her no mind. Obviously it didn't consider her a threat. Probably it figured she was another course, maybe dessert.

She snatched up the stun rod and scurried out of reach. Unsure of what to do next, she went over to check on her enemy. The guard trilled and motioned for her to run.

At the sound, the creature paused in its feeding and looked up. Blood and feathers decorated its face. Cora yanked the guard to her feet.

"Run!"

The guard hesitated. When Cora gave her a shove, she took off. With an enraged roar, the creature rose on its hind legs and swung a paw, but the guard ducked and kept going. The creature fell to all fours and started to lumber after her. Cora jabbed her rod against the creature's side. It yelped and stopped.

As the creature turned, Cora scrambled away. Growling deep in its throat, the thing stalked her. Blood-soaked feathers fell away from its muzzle. Cora clambered up the face of the cliff. Unable to climb higher, she stopped at a small ledge a few feet above the creature's reach. For a few minutes the creature paced below her, then tried to climb up behind her. In a shower of loose rock and gravel it tumbled backwards. Rising on its hind legs, it leaned into the cliff and swiped at her with its paws. Cora scooted aside and hit the creature's snout with the stun rod. It roared in pain and fell back on all fours.

Shaking its head against the sting of the stun rod, the beast settled back on its haunches, tugged the remainder of the dead guard to itself and continued feeding. The metallic smell of blood and the stench of the creature stung Cora's nose. She tore her gaze from the grisly scene and looked back toward the compound. The guard she'd rescued was gone. Nothing moved. The outer gates were securely closed. No help there. Behind her the cliff rose smoothly for fifteen feet. Even if she could force herself to climb that high, there was no way to do so.

As it was only a foot deep and three feet wide, she couldn't sit on the ledge, so she crouched and waited. Maybe after the creature finished eating it would leave. Cora doubted it. The look the creature had given her after she hit it with the stun rod was full of intent. Though it might not be terribly intelligent, it understood enough to want retribution.

It took only minutes for the creature to devour the body. All that remained were some feathers, bones, and a bloody splotch. Cora shuddered. Sunlight glinted off the creature's gray-green scales as it stretched. It raised its head and belched. The rank smell of undigested meat wafted upward.

Cora gagged and waved her hand. "Whew! You should do something about that breath. Of course, with that ugly mug, good breath really won't help much."

Bracing its front paws on the side of the cliff, the creature stood on its rear legs and stared at her.

"So, what now? You can't get up here and I'm not coming down. How long are you going to wait around?" Talking to the beast kept her panic at bay.

She moved aside as the creature leapt and curled its four-inch-long claws onto the edge of the ledge. What now?

With a grunt, the creature pulled back its paw. A large chunk of rock crumbled off the edge of the ledge.

"Damn!" Cora shoved the stun rod at the creature's paw but missed.

Again and again, the creature tore at the ledge. When able, Cora hit its paws and muzzle with the stun rod, but the sting no longer seemed to phase the creature's determination to get to her. Occupied with keeping out of the beast's reach, she couldn't figure out how to change the setting on the stun rod, and even if she could she feared it wouldn't make a difference.

Soon there was next to nothing left of the ledge. If the creature swiped at her now she'd have no place to jump. Cora prepared to leap off the ledge and over the creature. She'd have to take her chances on outrunning it.

The creature braced itself against the cliff, and its massive paw started toward her. A sudden shout made it pause. It turned its head toward the sound. Cora looked as well. The compound gates were open. A dozen guards stood there, but it was the man running toward her that grabbed Cora's attention.

"Alex!"

The creature whipped its head back toward her and swung its paw. Cora leaped out into the air over the creature's head. Landing in a roll, she found her feet and ran. With a roar the creature dropped to all fours and followed. She felt the vibration of the ground as it pounded after her; its hot putrid breath touched her shoulders. But large and powerful as the creature was, she was more agile. Its short legs and a belly bulging with its undigested meal made it slow and cumbersome. Ignoring the pain of her bare feet hitting the hard ground, by dodging and weaving she stayed out of its reach.

Cora kept her eyes on the man running toward her: Alex, alive and well! For a moment she forgot everything but her joy, then her pursuer roared and reality flooded back.

She was leading the deadly beast straight to Alex. The swords he held in each hand seemed a puny defense against the creature's size, teeth and claws. Aside from a covering over his genitals he was naked. None of the Flock guards followed him; they would let him face the creature alone. Her steps faltered.

"Cora, don't stop! Come to me! Run!"

"No." She darted to her left, then left again, doubling back toward the creature. The creature attempted to turn. Dust filled the air as its paws churned up the ground. Its size and awkwardness gave Cora a head start, but she began to tire while the creature's stamina held fast.

Still, whatever happened to her didn't matter as long as Alex was safe.

Zan watched in horror as Cora turned back toward the beast. What was she thinking? Once a cayadil chose its prey, it never gave up. And this cayadil had set its sights on Cora.

Quick and agile, she darted back and forth in front of the beast, never giving it an opportunity to attack. But when she tired, the cayadil would strike. He had to reach Cora first. Over the years Zan had fought cayadils and won, but none so large as this.

As the cayadil moved away from the gate, disappointed shouts came from the Flock guards gathered there. He knew that when the guards had come to get him, they'd hoped he'd fight the cayadil within view. He'd accompanied them reluctantly. Since Cora, his need to fight seemed to have diminished. Before, he'd found a release for his rage in his battles against wild creatures and other men, but now he only wanted to focus his energy in another direction—setting Cora free.

Fear for her lent him speed. He closed in on the cayadil just as Cora stumbled. She landed on her hands and knees. The stun rod flew out of her hand. She curled into a defensive ball and the cayadil's momentum carried it over her. One paw grazed her head, knocking her sideways. She lay motionless. Blood trickled from her scalp. A few yards away, the creature skidded to a stop and turned.

Zan launched himself between Cora and the cayadil. The creature snorted.

With a stomach full of meat, the chase had to have exhausted it. Though known for great strength and tenaciousness in stalking their prey, cayadils disliked long periods of activity. They preferred to hide in the muddy shallows along the riverbanks and surprise their prey rather than having to chase it down. Coldblooded creatures, their heavily armored bodies didn't tolerate being out of the water in the hot sun for too long. Already this cayadil's scales were dry. Its breath came hard and heavy.

Still, Zan knew better than to underestimate it. He planted his legs and tightened his grip on his swords.

The Flock were unlikely to intervene. They enjoyed

watching his battles, but they never willingly put themselves in harm's way. Their long fragile necks and short arms made them awkward and less than competent in a fight.

The creature paced in agitation. Its need to curl in the mud and digest its meal fought with its desire to kill the being that had hurt it. The smell of blood tantalized, but the presence of another being confused. At the top of the food chain, cayadils were challenged by few creatures, and fewer still did so and survived.

The sun beat down. Cold sweat slid down Zan's body. The need to go to Cora, to make sure she was all right, made him tense. But he couldn't let his concentration waver. One second of inattention and the cayadil would attack.

The creature gave a hacking cough and belched. It sat back on its haunches. Distended from feeding, its belly brushed the ground. The scales protecting its tender underside gaped apart. A blow there wouldn't kill it, but given a bit of luck, a sword thrust between those scales might discourage the creature. A cayadil had two hearts and could live for days even when mortally wounded. Only a precise plunge through the back of the animal's neck could sever the connection between its small but well-armored brain and large body, and drop it in its tracks.

He moved to stand over Cora. She moaned. The cayadil's head lifted in renewed interest. Zan forced himself not to glance away. Equal amounts of joy and fear flooded him.

He heard her stir. The cayadil rose and sniffed the air.

"Lie still," he whispered.

"Wh-what happened?" From the corner of his gaze, he saw her stagger to her feet. She gave a small gasp as her memory returned. Cold fingers curled around his forearm.

"Stay behind me," he said.

She took a step away. The cayadil's gaze followed.

"What are you doing?" He wanted to snatch her back, but any sudden action might trigger the cayadil's hunting instinct.

She moved slowly into his line of vision and bent down. When she came up she gripped the still-glowing stun rod, but now she was between him and the cayadil.

"Get back here."

She grinned at him and moved to his side. "This might help."

Blood matted hair to the side of her head. A bruise darkened on her forehead, and scratches marred the smooth skin of her bare arms and legs. Still, she smiled at him. She fiddled with the controls on the stun rod. "How do you change the setting? Level two didn't even phase the beast. Aha!" She slid the switch to level six. "Got it. This setting should get its attention."

"Its attention is the last thing we want. With its belly full, be still and it might give up."

She stood at his side. "And if it doesn't?"

"Then we'll find out how big a charge that stun rod carries." He couldn't hold back a grin. Though he wished her to safety, having Cora at his side felt right. The warmth from her body eased the chill he'd felt when he saw her fall.

The cayadil gave a hoarse grunt and lowered its head.

"Prepare. It's charging. Go right."

He gripped his swords. The cayadil barreled toward them. At the last moment Zan dove beneath the beast, slashed upward with his swords. Scales parted. Two lines of tough skin separated. Blood sprayed over him. The beast rose up on its hind legs, roaring in pain. Coils of intestine spilled out and dragged in the dirt. The cayadil staggered as its hind claws caught and tore the slimy membranes.

Lumpy liquid rained down. The rancid odor burned Zan's nostrils. He rolled out of the way of slashing claws and snapping jaws, and jumped to his feet. He searched for Cora. As he'd directed, she'd flung herself to the right. Mad with pain, the cayadil now zeroed in on her.

Holding the stun gun in front of her, she scrambled

backward. The cayadil dropped back to all fours. Leaving a trail of blood and gore in its wake, sides heaving, it stalked forward. Pinkish foam dripped from its panting mouth. In seconds it would be on her. The stun gun might finish it off, but not before it sank teeth or claws into Cora. She had one chance.

Cora clutched the stun rod as the cayadil started its lunge. She didn't think the stun rod would stop the creature. Even if it did, the weight of the beast would crush her. Then Alex leaped on the cayadil's back and clamped his thighs around its shoulders. The creature lurched upward, nearly falling over backward. Slime, blood and bits of half-digested meat splattered Cora.

Roaring in pain and fury, the cayadil sought to dislodge its attacker by twisting and turning. Alex's body jerked to and fro. Sunlight glinted off the blade as one of his swords flew into the air. Cora ducked aside, then darted forward and jabbed her stun rod repeatedly into the beast's trailing intestine. It didn't seem to notice.

She looked back at Alex. Ignoring the swipes of the cayadil's claws as it reached for him, he gripped the hilt of his remaining sword in both hands and raised his arms above his head. When the creature bent its head in an attempt to bite his leg, he slammed the blade downward. The sword sank hilt deep between the scales at the base of the cayadil's neck. Along with a spray of blood, the point and an inch of blade erupted from the creature's throat. With one last gurgle, the connection between the cayadil's brain and body ended.

Alex leaped free as the beast crumpled to the ground and lay twitching.

"Alex!" Cora ran around the fallen cayadil to where he sprawled facedown. "Are you hurt?" Though she wanted to gather him to her, she ran her hands over his blood- and dirt-covered body, searching for injuries.

He gave a ragged cough and sat up. "Had the wind knocked out of me. Are you injured?" With gentle fingers he pushed aside her matted hair and touched the discoloration on her forehead.

"Aside from a few scratches and bruises I'm fine." Her voice broke, and tears blurred her vision. "Oh, Alex, I thought I'd lost you."

"I'm tough to kill." He pulled her into his arms.

Unmindful of the gore that coated them, she leaned into him. He covered her mouth in an aggressive kiss. She answered in kind until the acrid smell and taste of blood, bile and mud on their lips penetrated her consciousness.

He didn't object as she eased her mouth from his and rested her head against his chest. The rapid beat of his heart in her ear eased the chill that had settled in her heart. She knew they should move, but, afraid this might all be a dream, she didn't want to let go of him. Though danger surrounded them, she felt safe in Alex's arms.

Reluctantly she raised her head. "We'd better get out of here. The carcass might draw other predators, and the Flock are going to come looking for us soon."

"No other predators will approach a cayadil. Even a dead one is dangerous. The Flock will steer clear for a while. See?" Alex tossed a rock at the cayadil. The body heaved and its leg jerked. Massive claws flailed the air.

"Is it alive?" She shuddered, then relaxed as Alex's arms tightened around her.

"No. That's just a reflex action. I'm surprised it came so far from the swampy area it calls home." He pointed to the left, at a waving sea of grass and reeds where the cliff sloped down to the river. "They dislike being out in the open. And they need the buoyancy of the water to help support their heavy bodies. Though normally solitary beasts with large territories, this is the brooding season so there might be young around. Since young cayadils are always ravenous, leaving this area is a good idea. Perhaps now would be the time to find your ship." He pulled her to her feet and stood.

She looked around. The Flock compound was out of view. How far had they come? Things had happened so fast she couldn't judge. The cayadil explained why the Flock had refused to allow her and the other women near the river. "Any chance we can wash the muck off first? It reeks and my skin is starting to itch and burn."

"Yes, we should bathe. Though the smell of its blood will discourage other predators from approaching us, cayadil bile is caustic. Proves helpful in digesting the bones of its prey. If we don't wash it off, eventually it will eat through our skin. Among other things, the Flock use it to clean rust from the wheels of their wagons."

"Lovely thought," Cora muttered.

He picked up the sword that he'd dropped and headed toward the river but away from the swampy area. "Follow me."

Relieved he didn't attempt to retrieve the sword stuck in the cayadil, Cora turned off the stun rod and tucked it into the rope belt around her waist. The thought of approaching the beast again made her shiver.

As they got closer to the riverbank, the roar of rushing water grew. Sunlight flashed off the ripples on the expanse of water. A tree branch moved at a fast clip in the rapid current. At the river's edge the water swirled slowly in a clear shallow pool surrounded by an area of tangled brush. Large trees shaded the pool from the glare of the sun. Aside from the sound of water, the hum of insects and the titter of some bird, the small glade was a serene refuge from the blazing sun and dry field.

At the edge of the pool, Alex held up a hand. "Wait here."

Before she could ask why, he disappeared into the brush. One moment he was there, the next he was gone.

Alone, suddenly the quiet shelter no longer seemed

peaceful. The breeze stirred ominous shadows. Unfamiliar sounds made the hair on Cora's arms stand at attention. She slipped the stun rod from her belt and flicked it on. "Alex, damn it, where are you?" At the sound of her voice the birds and insects fell silent. She peered into the gloom of the trees.

He didn't answer. Nothing moved. After a few moments the insects started their song again. A bird chirped. The sound reminded her of the Flock.

Cora scratched at the crusty scum covering her arms and looked with longing at the crystal pond. "This is ridiculous." Turning off the stun rod, she laid it at the edge of the water within easy reach and stepped into the pool.

Soft silt pressed between her toes. Cool liquid eased the burn on her skin. With a sigh of relief, she ducked beneath the surface and slipped out of her tunic. She used a handful of silt to scrub her skin clean of cayadil blood, and rinsed out the tunic.

After a few minutes, common sense returned and she reluctantly left the pool. She draped the damp tunic over a low branch. Being unclothed no longer left her feeling vulnerable; it felt almost normal. She sat cross-legged on the mossy ground and let a warm breeze dry her skin.

Minutes dragged by, and her temper heated as she waited for Alex to return. When he appeared she didn't know whether to leap into his arms and cover him with relieved kisses or smack him upside the head for making her worry. Unable to decide, she didn't move. Desire coiled inside her as she watched him stride toward her.

Apparently he'd stopped to bathe. His dark hair lay in wet clumps over his broad shoulders. Naked except for the leather straps crossing his chest and the cup over his genitals, his skin glistened with moisture. Bronze skin moved smoothly over muscle. He looked at her, his gaze sliding from her face to her breasts to lower. Her nipples pebbled. Water trickled through the curls at her groin and joined the growing wetness of her desire. She let her gaze travel from his head down his chest, over the angry red marks where the cayadil's claws had raked his flesh, to the hard cup hiding his genitals. With a sigh of disappointment she looked up to meet his eyes.

He smiled. In one hand he gripped his sword, in the other he held up a cluster of reddish-yellow fruit. "Are you hungry?"

"Famished." *But not for food,* she added silently. Yet now was not the time to think about sex. Suddenly shy, she stood and snatched up her tunic. "Maybe we should eat as we move. I wouldn't want to run into any more cayadils or Flock."

He stopped in front of her and lay down his sword and the fruit; he was clearly filled with some intention. "There's no need to rush. The sun will set soon. Cayadils do not prowl in the dark, and the Flock do not leave their compound after the sun is gone." He plucked the tunic from her fingers and tossed it aside.

"What about other predators?" Her breath caught as he trailed a fingertip across the top of her breasts.

"There's only one predator who'll taste your flesh this night." He nipped her neck.

"Ouch!"

The cry had barely left her lips before the slick stroke of his tongue soothed the sting. She didn't object as he took her with him to the ground. Hungry with need, she dragged his head up and met his mouth with her own. In a wordless battle for control their tongues tangled.

Cora's body shook with fear and desire: fear over having almost lost him for a third time, desire for reassurance that he was real and not a fevered dream.

Warm and solid, his body covered and surrounded her. His weight pressed her into the ground. The clean fresh

117

smell of him filled her nostrils. Hot, hard and heavy, his cock throbbed against her belly. The feel of his skin beneath her palms sent a bolt of sensation to her groin. She spread her thighs and cool air touched her, arousing the need to be filled by him. Without him she felt incomplete, empty, half alive.

When she tried to wrap her legs around his hips, he lifted himself away.

"No!" She clutched his shoulders in panic.

"*Shh*. I'm not leaving, but I've no wish to grind the ground into your tender skin." She held tight as he carried her to a patch of moss.

"I don't care. I want you in me now!" She locked her ankles at the small of his back and bucked upward, ignoring the mindlessness of her desire.

His chuckle rumbled through her. "Ever demanding, my little she-beast."

He teased her with the tip of his erection. She wiggled, trying to force him to enter her, but with his greater size and strength he controlled the dance until tremors of need coursed through her. Cora's hands curled into claws, nails digging unconsciously into his muscled shoulders. Still, he continued. A heated rod, his cock slid around the edge of her desire, tracing a path of fire that left her breathless and quivering, hovering on the brink of release.

When he lowered his head to her breast and drew one aching nipple into the hot cavern of his mouth, her body convulsed in a climax. Wave after wave of pleasure poured over her. But it wasn't enough. Her womb contracted with a need for more.

"Please, don't torture me." She strained her hips upward to capture him.

"Not yet."

★ ★ ★

Zan tormented himself with his restraint. Full to bursting, he felt his cock throb painfully against her warm and wet flesh. He resisted the urge to plunge mindlessly into her.

Outside the Flock compound, they faced many dangers. Even if they evaded the Flock, who would certainly look to recapture them, predators and a hostile landscape blocked their way to *Freedom*. And if they made it to her ship, honor, duty and love demanded he send her off alone.

If this was to be their final time together, he wanted it— *needed* it—to last.

Ignoring her cries to finish, he trailed his mouth down her chest. The rich aroma of her desire drew him south. Her heels rubbed across his back. He paused at the indentation in her flat belly and plunged his tongue into her navel. A ripple moved through her. The tang of salt and body-heated pond water burst on his tongue. His scalp stung as she twisted her nails there.

Lower, he went. He breathed deeply, inhaling her rich scent pungent with passion. He touched her thigh, and with a sigh of surrender she released his head and let her legs settle on the ground. He pushed them apart until she lay spread open.

He knelt between her thighs, draped her legs over his shoulders and lifted her to his mouth. Like tiny jewels, her juices glistened on the crisp short hair between her legs. He pressed his face against her and inhaled the heady scent of her desire.

With his fingers, he parted the hair guarding her woman's secrets and stroked his tongue up her swollen slit. Thick and salty, her taste filled his mouth and stirred him to a fever pitch. A quiver raced through her and she strained upward. He burned with the need to be inside her, to feel her heat surround him, to enter the inferno together with her and let the flames incinerate and restore them. Instead he continued to lick, his tongue rasping across her engorged, moist flesh, dipping in and out of her, then up to, around, but never quite touching the small nub at the top, until she gasped and moaned and writhed in his grip.

Again and again he teased her, almost but never making contact.

"Alex! Please!" Her head whipped back and forth while her feet beat against his back. Unconsciously she clenched and unclenched her hands, ripping up clumps of moss that filled the air with its rich, moist scent.

Finally he took pity on her—and himself—and swirled his tongue over her nub. Before she could react to that assault, he pulled it into his mouth and sucked.

Eyes closed, head thrown back, spine arched, she went rigid in his clasp. He held her as tremors rocked through her; then when she went limp, he eased her to the ground. He looked at her face. Mouth parted, eyes closed, aside from the rapid rise and fall of her chest, and the delicate shudders coursing over her body, she looked asleep. Her eyes opened and her gaze snared his in a mute appeal.

Damn. As much as he wanted, needed to make this last, he couldn't wait. He had to be inside her. When he lowered her legs from his shoulders, she arched her back and he slid into her. Her inner muscles gripped him. Resting her hips on his thighs, he took his thumbs and stroked the outer edges of her inner lips where they stretched around him. At his touch, she trembled and locked her ankles at the small of his back.

In time with the slow stroke of his thumbs, he moved in and out of her until her body began to shake and her breath came in small gasps. With every beat of her heart her inner muscles pulsed.

His cock throbbed with his need to explode, but he held back. He caught the nub of her pleasure between his thumb and forefinger and squeezed. Crying out, she pulled herself up against his chest.

Again and again, he slammed his hips forward. She clung to him. Fire surged through him to equal her answering blaze. Together they rode the flames. Higher and higher they climbed. They burned from the inside out, yet were left unconsumed. Another her climax took her. As her inner muscles contracted, Zan fought the need to remain inside her as he reached his own peak, to bind her to him in the most primitive way. He was successful. Refusing to increase the risk of her conceiving, he pulled out and spilled his seed uselessly onto the cold ground.

Side by side, bodies damp with sweat, they lay limp and breathless.

Cora woke to sunlight on her face. Enjoying the warmth, the sound of twittering birds and the pleasant ache that came from passion spent, she laid still until the tantalizing smell of roasting meat made her stomach growl. She looked around the small glade at the edge of the river until she found Alex.

His refusal to lose control preyed on her mind but she pushed it away. Part of her understood his continued restraint. Her pregnancy suppressant had likely expired, and who knew the effect of the drugs the Flock had given her. But now that they were leaving this planet, the possibility of her becoming pregnant was less dangerous. Damn, thanks to the Flock, she might already be pregnant. The thought both pleased and frightened her, but either way there was no reason for Alex to deny himself or her what they both wanted. Next time she wouldn't give him any option.

She grinned at the sight of him bent over a small smokeless fire. Comfortable in his nakedness, he balanced on the balls of his feet as he turned a small animal on a spit above the fire and dug out from the coals some items wrapped in leaves. Muscles rippling beneath his skin as he performed his self-appointed task, his back gleamed in the morning sun. She rubbed the sleep from her eyes and eased up on her elbow to watch. He'd secured his long hair at the back of his head. At the sight of the angry red scratches that joined the tracing of white scars marring the smooth perfection of his skin, she sucked in her breath. The deeper marks had come from the cayadil, but the fainter ones were from her.

He turned to her. "Are you hungry?" His gruff tone and grim look barely registered in her mind.

"Mmmm." She licked her lips and let her gaze roam over the broad expanse of naked flesh.

"Insatiable female," he muttered. "Eat." He shoved a plate made of bark and loaded with steaming meat and vegetables into her hands. Between his legs his cock twitched, giving lie to his tone of exasperation.

Torn between two hungers, Cora settled for the food in her hands; in minutes nothing remained of their meal but a few well-gnawed bones. While she lounged naked and licked the last of the grease from her fingers, Alex doused the fire and gathered their meager possessions.

"We need to leave." He tossed her tunic across her hips. "Dress."

"Let me take a look at your sword first."

"What?"

"Let me see if I can disable the stunner, so if the Flock do show up, you can use the thing against them."

He handed it to her. After a few minutes she shook her head and handed it back. "Without tools there's no way for me to get into the housing. I'll try again when we get to my ship."

She pulled her tunic on over her head. When she looked at him again, he'd strapped his sword to his chest and donned his protective cup. By the pained expression on his face, she knew it was a tight fit. She grinned in satisfaction.

He turned away with a grunt and her grin faded. Despite his obvious arousal, something wasn't right. When she reached out to touch his arm, he jerked back.

"We've no time to dally." He walked away.

Hurt by his rejection, she snapped, "Who said I was asking?" She wanted to question him, to find out what was wrong, but not now. The sun stood high in the sky. They'd slept longer than was wise. Once they were aboard *Freedom* and well away from this place, they'd have time to sort things out.

The thought of the long weeks alone together on her small craft made her forget her wounded feelings. Once aboard, she'd have the time and opportunity to destroy his control and have what she needed from him—total surrender. Her body hummed in anticipation.

"Since I know the way to my ship, maybe I should lead."

Back stiff, he paused and waited while she caught up to and moved in front of him. She glanced back, but he wouldn't meet her gaze. Unease slid down her spine. Something was wrong. She just couldn't figure out what.

CHAPTER NINE

Zan followed close behind Cora. Though he realized she needed to lead—not only because she knew the way, but also to assert her independence—he didn't want her out of reach. This jungle held many dangers. Occasionally she had to stop and wait while he went ahead to clear a path through the dense foliage. As he passed her on the narrow trail, their bodies brushed, and her warm, musky scent filled his nostrils. He swelled uncomfortably inside his protective cup.

He knew his silence disturbed her, but he hadn't the heart or the courage to tell her his thoughts. The question remained: what would he do next?

Because he'd taken his sword and the stun gun, the Flock would know at least one of them had survived the cayadil attack. It wasn't arrogance that made him certain the Flock would attempt to recapture him; a good portion of the compound income came from his services—fighting and breeding—so no matter the risk, they couldn't afford to lose him. The fact that they'd let him face the cayadil told him they also valued Cora. Oh yes, they would come.

If they made it to her ship, the Zan part of him wanted nothing more than to climb aboard and leave this planet behind without another thought. But the part of him that was Alexander Anderly, xeno-anthropologist, knew it wasn't that easy; there was more to fear. He didn't remember everything about C.O.I.L. laws, but he recalled enough to realize that he'd broken more than one of them. Would the fact that he'd committed them unknowingly excuse his lapses? Because of Earth's probationary status with C.O.I.L., Earth's government dealt harshly with the slightest transgressions. Even if he escaped that, another bigger—or perhaps he should think of them as several small problems—existed. The image of those small problems brought a smile to his heart.

Until Cora had awakened him to his humanity, he hadn't realized how much he enjoyed working with the young boys in the compound. Teaching them satisfied a need he hadn't known he had, filled him with joy. Their trust and, yes, the love he saw in their eyes when they looked at him, filled him with an answering devotion. That would be hard to leave.

As well, the reality of what he'd done wiped away his inner joy. The fact that he'd taught them to fight, that he'd prepared them for lives of blood and violence and ultimate death, weighed on his soul. He longed to find a way to teach them what Cora had retaught him—to be human, to be free. He owed them, and the other humans imprisoned by the Flock, that much and more.

If he told Cora his plans, he knew she'd insist on helping him. He couldn't saddle her with his responsibilities. She deserved her freedom, not the burden of his guilt. Silence was his only option.

They walked through the morning, stopping once to drink from the stream they followed. Aside from a "yes" or "no" to the questions Cora asked, he didn't speak. He felt her agitation and growing anger, but could think of nothing to say to ease it.

They pressed on through the afternoon heat. A sudden rain shower offered a moment's respite. He watched as Cora paused and turned her face upward to catch droplets in her mouth. In seconds she was doused, rain plastering her hair against her head in a sleek golden cap, and the thin tunic to her lithe body. Moisture that had nothing to do with the deluge flooded his mouth. He couldn't contain his groan of longing. He adjusted his protective genital cup in a futile attempt to ease the pressure.

As quickly as it began, the rain ended and the sun's rays turned the air thick with moisture. They trudged onward.

As the day progressed and the shadows lengthened, the jungle gave way to an open grassy area. They'd emerged at the base of the mountains.

"Yes!"

At Cora's cry and sudden stop, Zan nearly crashed into her back. Lost in thought, he'd allowed himself to become distracted from his surroundings. In one move he pulled his sword and put her behind him.

"No, Alex." She gripped his arm. "Nothing's wrong. We're almost there. My ship is just over that foothill near that stand of trees." She pointed to a haze of green peeking over the rise.

He relaxed. "You're sure?"

Her annoyance at his distant attitude clearly forgotten for the moment, she straightened, fisted her hands on her hips and grinned. The action pulled the fabric of her tunic tight across her breasts. "I'll have you know I was top of my class in astro-navigation."

He cocked an eyebrow at her. "Astro-navigation?"

"Yeah, well, stars or rocks, navigating is navigating and I'm damned good at it."

"Yes, I remember."

Her arms dropped to her sides. She searched his face with her gaze. "Do you?"

He knew what she wanted. He could only say, "I don't remember everything, but my memories of you are the clearest."

Her gaze softened. She reached out and stroked his cheek. He knew he should pull away. Instead, he closed his eyes and savored her touch. His arms ached to pull her close and never let her go. Reluctantly he opened his eyes and stepped back. Soon enough he'd lose her.

He said, "The light's fading. We'll have to camp for the night. It's not safe to travel in the dark, but we should reach your ship by midmorning." Then he turned and walked away.

Her hand still tingling from touching his skin, Cora watched as Alex sheathed his sword and strode off. She followed. With each step her feeling grew that something was wrong. No longer the sweet, quiet lover from her past, nor the Flock's bold, confident prize stud, this Alex confused her.

They made camp at the base of a foothill next to a small stream. She built a fire while Alex went in search of their dinner. Before the sun sank behind the mountain, he returned carrying two limp rodents and a handful of tubers. Neither of them spoke as they prepared the meal. He skinned and gutted the animals, then fashioned a roasting spit while she washed and buried the tubers beneath the fire's embers.

The smell of roasting meat stirred Cora's appetite, but it was the sight of Alex lounging next to the fire that made her mouth water. Firelight bathed his flesh in golden hues, and she felt her lust return. She needed to recapture the accord between them. But when she scooted closer and slid her hand up his thigh, he shifted away.

Her appetite gone, she moved back. They ate in silence.

Somehow their easy conversation had died. Lost in thoughts she couldn't decipher, he stared back in the direction they'd come.

The fire burned low. Cora shivered in the night air. Without speaking he reached out and pulled her down between his body and the fire. With a sigh she accepted his embrace. A grin tugged at her lips when she felt his cock swell against her backside. He might not be saying anything, but his body spoke loud and clear.

"Are there any humans outside of the Flock compounds?" It wasn't the question she wanted to ask, but it was one long overdue.

He looked at her, but took a moment to answer. "Yes. It has happened occasionally, that the Flock capture wild ones and bring them to the compound."

"What happened to them?"

He hesitated before answering. "The females were brought to me."

"Did they say anything about their lives outside the compound, their communities?"

He lowered his gaze. "We had no conversations."

She understood what he avoided saying. The women had been stunned or drugged before being brought to him for impregnation. "What about the men?"

"From what I saw and heard, the males were uncontrollable. When not drugged they attacked the guards. After that, the Flock decided it was easier to breed Unars than to tame them. Only the very young children and girls were kept. The men, older women and boys over the age of puberty were . . . destroyed." He looked straight into her eyes. "During my early training some of them were brought to me in the fight arena. And like the beast the Flock believe I am, I slaughtered them."

Before she could stop herself, she recoiled in horror.

Then the guilt in his eyes for what he'd done, for what the Flock had forced him to do, brought her to tears.

When she'd thought him dead, something inside her had died as well. She'd turned cold toward the people who wanted to grieve with her, pushing them away, retreating into herself. She'd turned all her energy into her career, not allowing another person to penetrate the shell she had erected around herself. Until she saw him alive, she believed her emotions were dead.

But he'd suffered much worse. He'd lost himself, the knowledge of who and what he was. The Flock had taken the gentle man of peace and diplomacy he'd been and created a killing machine for their entertainment.

He brushed a finger across her cheek. "Don't cry for my crimes."

She turned in his arms to face him. "You're innocent of any fault. The sin belongs to the Flock. They made you what you were. You didn't know any better."

He looked unconvinced. "Perhaps. But what inside of me allowed me to become their creature? To do what they commanded? To kill. To r-rape." He stuttered over the word as if he'd just realized exactly what he'd done.

"You always told me survival is man's first instinct. You did what you had to do to survive."

"What purpose did my survival serve if I gave up my heart and soul?" His voice broke on his whisper.

"You stayed alive for me to find. Did you take pleasure in killing those men? Torture and toy with them?"

"No! I killed them quickly, cleanly, and as painlessly as I could."

She put his hand over his chest. "Your heart and soul are intact."

"But—"

"No buts. Don't think about it anymore. It's done. What

matters is what you do from this point on." She looked for something to change the subject. "Since I came, have you been with other women from the compound?" The question slipped out before she could stop it.

"I—"

Aghast at what she'd asked, she put her fingers against his lips. "You don't have to answer that. I have no right to ask. You did what you had to do. I don't blame you."

He gripped her wrist and kissed her palm. "I want to answer."

But she wasn't sure she wanted to know.

"At first I was left alone with you, probably to ensure that you became pregnant quickly." She felt his smile against her palm.

As much as she didn't want to know, she had to ask, "What about lately, when they took you out of our cage?"

"After the first few weeks they started putting me with other females."

Unwanted jealously washed over her. She stiffened.

His low chuckle vibrated through her. "Don't worry. Even with the sex stimulants they fed me, I wouldn't perform."

Relief spread through her. She snuggled up against him, but feminine curiosity and the need for reassurance made her ask, "Why not?"

"Because I want only you." He thrust his hips forward and his cock pushed between her thighs.

Distantly she recognized that he was using her physical desire for him to distract her from further questions, but she didn't care. She lifted her leg over his hip and gasped as his hard heat penetrated her. "Yes!"

He thrust deeper, and the angle caused her to wince in remembered pain.

"Are you all right?"

"I'm fine." She wouldn't allow the atrocities she'd endured to come between Alex and her.

As if he understood her sudden need for control, he gripped her hips and twisted until he lay flat on the ground, putting her in charge. She arched upward to straddle him; the action thrust him deeper. She welcomed the pressure of him against her cervix and pushed aside the memory of what had been done to her. He moved one hand to her mound and parted her damp curls, and the breath caught in her throat as he caressed her. The promise of release crawled through her veins, but refused to deliver. Fear, pain, rage and sorrow surfaced, products of the last few days, stoking her passion to the boiling point but allowing her no further. Inside her, pressure built.

"Harder," she demanded.

He complied, stroking and tugging harder. Tendrils of pleasure twisted in her belly and radiated outward. Still, it wasn't enough.

She lifted up, then slammed down and ground her pelvis against his. "*Fuck* me!" she demanded.

He met her stroke for stroke, his hips rising to meet hers in this primitive, savage mating. The scent of sex filled her nostrils and inflamed her senses. The sound of wet, slapping flesh echoed in the quiet. Again and again they crashed against each other, reaching for what they wanted, giving desperately what the other needed.

Sharp and fierce, her climax was explosive. With a strangled cry she released control and fell limp against his chest. But he didn't stop. He rolled her over, buried his face against her neck and continued to pound into her. Crushed beneath his weight, unable to catch her breath or regain her senses, she rode the aftershocks of her climax.

After a moment he attempted to withdraw, but she wrapped her arms around his shoulders and locked her ankles at the small of his back. With each thrust her womb contracted. Pleasure spiraled through her, left her panting. It took every bit of energy she had to hold on to to him, to move with him. If he didn't end soon, she'd crumple. But instead of lessening, her desire grew. Now her nails dug into his shoulders. Her heels drummed against his back, urging him on. Renewed energy flowed through her, drove her on toward her goal.

She reached it: with one last powerful thrust, Alex pushed her over the edge a second time and leapt after her.

"Cora!"

Heat filled her as he lost control. Breathless with satisfaction, she smiled against his throat.

Cora was curled against Zan, asleep. Her head rested on his chest, her breasts pressed into his side; her thigh was draped over his, her knee nudging his now limp penis. Her soft curves molded his hard angles. Tendrils of hair stuck to her damp cheek. Moonlight filtered through the trees, turning her skin pearly white.

Though exhausted, his body aching, sleep eluded Zan. He stroked a fingertip down the line of her throat. He sucked her scent deep into his lungs.

Despite her words, the things he'd done still haunted him. He had to atone. He couldn't leave those innocent children behind as victims of his crimes. But what he had to do, he needed to do alone. He couldn't ask or let Cora give up the freedom she craved to assuage his guilt. And now that his control had shattered and he'd spilled his seed inside her, it was doubly imperative he set her free; he'd breed no more children for the Flock to abuse, and he wasn't sure when he'd be able to leave here. If ever.

Come morning, he'd have to tell her of his plans to return to the compound and attempt to free the people there. He had set himself an impossible task, but win or lose, to restore his soul he needed to try.

"What plans?" Her murmur sent a shudder through him. Had he spoken aloud?

"Nothing. Morning is hours away. Go back to sleep."

"I have a better idea." Her warm fingers closed around his cock.

Beneath her touch, thoughts of what was to come dissolved. Since he'd first wakened in the Flock compound, his body torn and wracked with pain, his mind devoid of memory, he'd learned to put aside thoughts of the past and the future, to live in the moment. "Again?" he asked. "Is there no satisfying you *ever*?"

She chuckled, and her warm breath filled his ear. "We have six years to make up for."

He groaned in protest as her hand left his erection. Cool night air dissipated the warmth of her touch. She straddled his hips and positioned herself over him.

He knew he should refuse her. Push her away. Maintain his distance. Making love with her only made what he planned more difficult for both of them. But as she lowered herself and her wet heat enveloped his shaft, he couldn't deny her. One last time she'd be his and he'd be hers. One last time.

Waking the next morning, Cora shivered in the chill air. She turned to share Alex's body heat, but he no longer lay beside her. Unreasoned panic seized her. Logic said if something had happened to him in the night, she would have awakened. But eyes wide open, heart pounding, she bolted upright.

His back to her, Alex sat a few yards away. She paused to let her heart rate return to normal before she stood. Over the top of the horizon the first rays of the sun turned the dusty gray sky to shades of pink and blue, and started to warm the air. No longer uncomfortable with her nakedness, she padded to his side and plopped down next to him.

"We will locate my ship this morning. In a few hours we'll be off this godforsaken rock and on our way home." A breeze made her shiver again, so she leaned against him for warmth.

He jumped to his feet and stalked a few feet away from her.

Rubbing her arms to dispel her goose bumps, she stood too. "What's wrong?' Unease slid through her. She'd thought— hoped—that his complete surrender to the passion between them had boded well for their future.

"I won't be leaving with you. After we reach your ship, I'm going back."

"W-what! You can't. You'll end up back in a Flock cage." Fear, anger and confusion boiled over inside her. She grabbed his arm and swung him around to face her. Had her need for control driven him away again? "Why in the seven galaxies would you want to go back?"

"My reasons are my own. They don't concern you." He stared past her, his gaze shuttered.

"That's space crap and you know it." Once before he'd left her without truly explaining why. Not this time. She smacked her palm against his chest. The noise startled them both. He took a step toward her. She stood her ground. "Tell me what's going on in that mind of yours or I swear I'll—"

"You'll what? Hit me again?" His smile didn't reach his eyes. "Since you arrived you've been telling me I should be free to live my life as I see fit, to make my own decisions. Do you now rescind your words? Would you again make me a slave to your commands?"

Again? Had he felt trapped by her love? Could she have driven him away? When? How? Fear made her unsure of what to do next. "Of course not. But I don't understand why you want to stay here."

He didn't answer her question; instead he said, "We need to go. The Flock will soon follow our trail. Here. Eat." He handed her a piece of fruit and strode away.

To keep from screaming, she bit the fruit. Tart juice puckered her mouth. Struggling to absorb Alex's decision to remain behind, and trying to figure out how to change his mind without really understanding his reason, she hurried to follow. The area looked strangely familiar in the light. Memories resurfaced. "Wait! Look out for the pit!"

Too late. She heard a thud, then a curse. Around the curve of the trail she crouched down and peered into the pit. More than ten feet down Alex lay on his back in the moist dirt and leaves. He glared up at her.

"Are you hurt?"

"No." He sounded more angry than hurt. "Only my pride. Why didn't you warn me earlier?"

She remembered well her chagrin at falling into the Flock's simple trap. Relieved that he was uninjured, she smothered a chuckle. "You took off too fast. Hold on. I'll see if I can find something to help you climb out."

"There's no time. Leave me. Go to your ship."

She ignored his command. It took some time, but in the underbrush she found a large dead branch with lots of short outshoots for handholds. By the time she dragged the branch back to the edge of the pit, the sun was fully up and sweat trickled between her breasts. Alex stood at the bottom. Dirt streaked his arms, chest and legs. Apparently, like her, he'd attempted to climb out. And, like her, he'd discovered the sides of the pit crumbled away rather than holding his weight.

"I told you to go. By now the Flock have discovered our trail and are close behind us. Go now."

"If you think I'd leave you here, you don't know me very well." It hurt and angered her that he believed she'd leave him behind. "For some mysterious reason you want to stay on this blasted space rock, but I'm sure you don't want to fall into the Flock's hands again. Or do you?"

"No," he muttered.

"Then stop arguing and use this to climb out." She tipped the branch into the pit. It came to rest so that the top rested insecurely two feet below the pit's rim. Lying down on the ground, she leaned over to steady it. Alex started his climb, but the branch creaked and slid lower against the side of the pit. His sword slipped free of its sheath against his back. He caught it with one hand. The shifting of his weight forced the branch deeper still into the soft dirt.

Cora knelt, dug her toes into the ground and gripped the branch. Rough bark scraped her palms with each foot upward he climbed. Her muscles burned. She'd forgotten how quickly an amusing annoyance became a deadly obstacle on this planet. "Hurry!"

She cried out in pain as the branch finally pulled through her hands and slipped down and out from under him. At the last moment he lunged upward and grabbed the edge of the pit with one hand; in the other he kept his sword. Legs flailing for purchase, his body swung precariously. Now the short outshoots on the branch posed a risk. If he fell, they could impale him.

Cora reached for his free arm. "Let the sword go. Take my hand." Beneath her she felt the ground starting to crumble. Soon it would collapse, throwing them both into the pit.

"Move away or we'll both fall," he commanded.

"I'm not leaving you."

"Stubborn woman." He dropped the sword and clamped his fingers around her wrist.

She grabbed his other hand and held on just before the ground gave way. For a moment his full weight wrenched her arms. Agony scorched her. Then he found a foothold and pushed himself upward. Ignoring the pain, inch by inch she pulled back from the edge of the pit. Her tunic bunched up under her arms. Rocks and sticks scraped her bare torso.

Between her pulling and his pushing, his chest soon cleared

the crumbling edge of the pit. He heaved himself onto solid ground and flopped onto his back.

Cora knelt, breath rasping in her throat. When she tried to move her arms back to her sides, her vision blurred and she moaned in pain.

Alex rose and leaned over her. "Foolish, stubborn woman. You could have been killed. The sooner you're off this planet the better."

She blinked away tears and looked into his angry beloved face. "I couldn't agree more." Grimacing against the pain in her arms, she reached up and brushed a clump of dirt from his cheek. He shook his head. Leaves and twigs rained down on her.

"Are you hurt?"

She sat up and tested her arms. The burning had subsided, but she knew within hours they would ache with a vengeance. "No permanent damage. I'm just a few inches taller. You?"

He grinned. "This was nothing compared to a training session." His grin faded as he helped her straighten her tunic. He brushed away the dirt and twigs from her chest and belly, his fingers gentle on the scratches there. "These are because of me." He bent his head and feathered a kiss over each small mark.

Cora's nipples hardened. Heat rushed into her cheeks. She closed her eyes to hide the truth from him, but her body told the tale.

Without warning his mouth came down against hers in a punishing kiss. His tongue speared between her lips and took brutal possession. She didn't care. Spurred by the thought that she'd almost lost him, she met his violence with her own. Pain forgotten, nails digging into his shoulders, she dragged him to her. They were alive. Together. Who knew what came next? They had only this moment in time.

Brief and intense, their coupling lasted mere minutes. Cora cried out as Alex's powerful thrusts pushed her over the edge. A second later he spilled his seed and collapsed against her.

The glow faded quickly. They'd rutted in the dirt like the animals the Flock thought them, but despite a twinge of shame she couldn't regret it. She stroked her hand through his tangled hair. In the distance an animal shrieked in fear or anger. Alex lifted his head.

"We need to go." He pulled her with him as he stood. Nothing about him gave a hint of what they'd just done.

Cora winced at the pain in her arms and shoulders, but it was the ache in her heart the hurt the worst. After everything they'd been through, he didn't retain the love they'd shared. Would it return before it was too late?

Though they gave wide berth to the edge of the pit, Cora saw Alex glance with regret at the sword lying at the bottom. At least they still had the stun rod.

CHAPTER TEN

Over Cora's objections, Zan continued to lead the way. He needed to think and the sight of her half naked in front of him was distracting. After an hour of hard travel she fell silent.

He swore to himself to keep her safe until he put her aboard her ship and watched her leave this planet. Or, was he lying to himself? It was she who'd saved him—more than once. Regardless, he needed to get her away. He'd come to a decision. But something told him getting her to abandon him wasn't going to be easy.

The Flock were surely close behind. Hours or minutes? He was unsure. Had they overcome their fear of traveling after dark?

Though he had told Cora he understood the Flock, in truth his knowledge of their thought process was that of a farmer from the perspective of a farm animal. Now that his memory—his humanity—had returned, he realized how much he'd misinterpreted about their behavior. It would take him time and observation to get things right. They had neither.

Raising humans as fighters for profit had to be a time-consuming, expensive and risky proposition. From what he'd seen and heard, this Flock compound had no other enterprises; their entire income came from breeding fighting humans. Common sense and his study of social structures told Zan this was probably a narrow niche in Flock society. It wouldn't do to underestimate his value to them or their tenacity in regaining him.

He also found himself thinking that, though he abhorred the Flock's treatment of him and the other humans, was what they'd done worse than what humans did to the intelligent nonhuman species of Earth? Against his will the Flock fascinated him—their culture, how they'd managed to carve out a civilization and a life on this dangerous planet. And the more he thought, the sharper his memories became.

In existence for thousands of years and made up of tens of thousands of planets, the Consortium of Intelligent Life survived by constantly growing, by pulling more and more planets and species under its ever expanding wing. The rules imposed by C.O.I.L. were both simple and complex. Cora, like most people, had no idea what it meant to be a member planet; most saw only the benefits and ignored the restraints. Because he'd studied as a xeno-anthropologist and had chosen to sign on as an FCA—First Contact Agent— Zan had spent many hours learning the intricacies of C.O.I.L. law. His head ached as he dredged up the knowledge buried in his mind.

As a newcomer to C.O.I.L., Earth membership, a mere fifty years old, was still probationary. While older member planets sometimes flaunted the laws with a degree of impunity, infractions by new members were harshly dealt with. The Earth government couldn't afford to let any violations, no matter how minor, go unpunished. Doing so risked Earth's expulsion from C.O.I.L. Expulsion meant not only the loss of the many benefits of C.O.I.L. membership—medicines, technology, goods and services—but it opened Earth as a target of aggression from other planets wishing to increase their resources.

Even though his memory still had gaps, Zan remembered enough to know the Flock's intelligence, ingenuity and resourcefulness, not to mention their planet's wealth of natural resources, made them a prime candidate for First Contact, which was governed by C.O.I.L.'s strongest laws—laws put into place to prevent member planets from deliberately alienating possible new members so they could claim the planet as rogue and plunder it. Though he knew the governing of C.O.I.L. and the implementation of its laws was not perfect—no form of government, no matter what species it was run by, could be—he still believed in its basic principles.

Part of him longed to be a part of First Contact with the Flock, while another more primitive part of him wanted nothing more than to destroy them. What he planned satisfied neither desire and broke C.O.I.L. law.

It also destroyed any chance of his being with Cora. So far he might be forgiven for his actions with the Flock, but if he carried out his plan, Earth and C.O.I.L. must never know Alexander Anderly had survived the crash of his ship. He had to remain dead.

Thus, he needed to get Cora off-planet and to safety or she would be as guilty as he of breaking C.O.I.L. law. He wouldn't risk her or Earth by including them in his actions.

"Alex . . . please . . . stop." Cora couldn't keep pace with him. She bent over and rested her hands against her thighs. Every muscle in her body screamed in protest. Her shoulders and arms ached. The scratches and bruises on her chest and belly throbbed in unison with her thudding heart.

In a moment he was at her side. "What's wrong?"

She shook her head. "Nothing. I just need to catch my breath. Guess I'm more out of shape than I thought. I used to be able to outrun you."

Her reference to when they used to run together didn't ease the frown on his face. Since he'd fallen into the pit his demeanor had changed. No, it went further back than that. Ever since they'd fought the cayadil and escaped the Flock he'd been pulling away, becoming more Zan and less Alex. The only time she felt connected with him now was when they made love.

"This path we're traveling is too well used for it to be wise to pause here."

"It is a Flock route?"

"I don't think so. The Flock prefer to travel in large groups and wheeled conveyances. This trail is narrow. There are no wheel ruts, and the foliage alongside isn't damaged. Perhaps it's an animal trail."

"Cayadils?" A nervous shudder went through her. She peered into the heavy foliage of the surrounding woods and clutched the stun rod.

"No. Cayadils don't come this far from water." When she started to relax he added, "But this planet has other predators that roam the woods and mountains."

"What kind? No, never mind. I don't really want to know. You're right. Let's go. I'll be fine."

"How far is your ship?"

Cora looked around the wooded path running through the foothills, then toward the mountains rising above them. "Hard to tell for sure. I was a bit dazed when I came this way. *Freedom*'s sitting on a plateau near the base of that peak. About half a mile."

Brows drawn together, Alex peered back the way they'd come. "Sit here." He directed her behind a rock that bordered the trail.

"Are you sure it's safe? What about other predators? I'd rather not be lunch."

"I haven't seen any sign of them along the trail. Besides, you're too small and dirty to appeal to all but the hungriest animal."

For a second she thought his mouth twitched; then his grim look returned. Still, he couldn't hide the ravenous look in his eyes. What little remained of her strength drained from Cora's limbs. Her pulse, which had decreased, began to race again, and for the first time she felt self-conscious about her ragged appearance.

"Thanks. You look especially delicious right now too." As soon as the mocking words left her lips she realized she spoke the truth. Despite the dirt and blood smeared over him, the twigs stuck in his hair, and the pain she knew he must feel from his injuries, he radiated strength and confidence. His stamina amazed her, left her feeling inadequate. She wanted nothing more than to rush into his arms, to surrender her hard-won control. When she started toward him he stepped back. Pain that had nothing to do with her sore muscles or bruises shot through her. She wrapped her arms around her middle.

He lifted his hand. "Cora, there's something I need . . ." His fingers curled into a fist and his arm dropped to his side. "Stay out of sight. I'll be right back."

"Where are you going?" What had he been about to say? That he'd changed his mind? That he'd go with her?

"To find some food. I'm starving."

She heard the lie in his voice. Would he leave her now? Without saying good-bye? Where would he go? Back to the Flock? Unlikely. She tried to brush aside her fears and doubts. Though he'd changed and she didn't understand his decision to stay on this planet, nothing she knew of Alexander—or Zan—could lead her to that conclusion. He wouldn't abandon her to find the way to her ship alone, unprotected. "So am I. Take this." She handed him the stun rod.

"You need it for protection."

"And you need it to catch our lunch." She pushed it into his hand. Whatever he planned to do, at least he'd have some defense.

Before she could voice more objections, he took off at a trot the way they'd come. With a groan, she eased herself down. She knew she should keep alert, but she tilted her head back against the rock and closed her eyes. The last few days had taken more out of her than she'd thought. Now Alex's strange behavior knocked the last support from under her. If he didn't come back she'd just sit here until her bones turned to dust.

She laughed. What nonsense. She knew he'd never leave her alone, and if he didn't come back she'd soon be on her feet looking for him. She'd give him thirty minutes.

Coward! You should have told her the truth, the reason you can't leave with her. He'd started to, but the look in her eyes had stopped him. She'd thought he was going to abandon her. Her doubt hit him like a stun rod. She should know him better.

But honesty forced him to admit her fears were justified. She did know him—too well. He'd left her once before and he was going to leave her again. He had to. But not unprotected on the side of some trail. When they reached her ship he'd tell her.

And then what—she'd calmly climb aboard and fly away without him? He couldn't stop his grin. Unlikely. More likely, determined to save him, even from himself, she'd club him over the head and drag him aboard.

His grin faded. Could he make her understand why he needed to return to the Flock compound? Maybe if he told her the absolute truth. If he did, could he convince her to let him do so alone? Again, unlikely. She'd insist on helping him.

No, in this case being honest would serve no good purpose. As much as it would rip out his heart, he had to make her believe he didn't want to be with her, that he preferred his life here to the life she offered. The way he'd done before. Only, this time he'd have to convince her he didn't love her. Did he have the strength?

Yes. He'd do what needed to be done. Cora's future, her life depended on it.

The sudden cessation of insect and animal sounds alerted him that someone or something disturbed the forest. He slipped off the trail into the surrounding woods and continued to move forward.

Through the dense foliage he saw them: the Flock, at least twenty of them. All were well armed. A ways behind them, pulled by four large dracas, came an armored transport vehicle. It surprised him to see the Flock commander. Leaders rarely left their compounds. By doing so he not only put his life in jeopardy, he also risked that another male would learn of his absence and try and usurp his power. The loss of their champion fighter was clearly critical to the compound.

How had they tracked them so quickly?

In the forest's filtered light, he saw the leader lift a stun rod. The end flickered green rather than its normal steady blue glow. Zan looked at the stun rod he carried. Its tip also flickered green. During their mad dash neither he nor Cora had noticed this. Perhaps the stun rods contained a homing device. His first instinct was to toss the stun rod away, but he thought better of it.

The Flock moved at a surprisingly rapid pace. And aside from the creak of the transport's wheels and the silence of the forest creatures, they gave no warning of their approach. At this rate they'd reach Cora in less than fifteen minutes. He had to draw them away. Moving through the woods, he doubled back behind them. Once out of their sight he broke out of the woods onto the trail and ran.

Cora jolted from her doze. By the position of the sun in the sky, at least thirty minutes had passed. Alarms went off inside her. In spite of her doubts she knew Alex should have returned by now. She shot to her feet. A surge of adrenaline helped her ignore her stiff, sore muscles. She moved onto the trail. Something was wrong. Alex was in trouble.

Without making a conscious decision, she ran in the direction he'd gone. Ten minutes later her adrenaline rush faded. Breathing heavily, she stopped. This was madness. What was she doing? He could be lying a few feet away and she'd never see him for the dense underbrush and deep forest.

She opened her mouth to call his name, but sounds not normal to the forest—the creak of wood against metal, the pad of footsteps, and the rustle of clothing—stopped her. Against her better judgment, she moved off the trail into the underbrush. Branches snagged her tunic and scratched her skin. Her toes curled. Who knew what kind of creatures lurked in the bushes and crawled in the damp, rotting vegetation under her feet? Not for the first time she cursed her lack of clothing and footwear.

Cautiously she picked her way alongside the trail. She froze as she caught sight of a large contingent of Flock. She recognized the leader deep in conversation with a guard. Too far away to catch more than a whistle or a trill, she couldn't make out their words, but she could guess the subject—Alex and her. They seemed to be arguing. The other Flock stood or sat along the trail, listening with varying degrees of interest and waiting for orders.

The guard held two stun rods. The tips of both flickered green. The second stun rod had a strip of cloth tied around it—the same cloth she'd used to tie the stun rod to her waist. Her heart skipped a beat. Had they caught Alex? She scanned the group but saw no sign of him.

An animal snorted. The sound drew her attention to a large armored vehicle at the far end of the group. Was Alex locked inside? What could she do if he was?

Careful to stay out of sight, she moved along the trail parallel to the group. From the position of the vehicle, it appeared the Flock were traveling away from her. No guards stood near the front of the vehicle. She crept closer and breathed a sigh of relief. The transport stood open and empty. Alex wasn't here.

How could he have disappeared so completely? Had he left of his own accord? From the time he'd killed the cayadil, he'd been pulling away from her, putting up barriers between them. Doubt niggled at her. Anger replaced fear.

An arm circled her waist and yanked her backwards off her feet. Before she could scream a hand clamped over her mouth. Her back hit a hard chest. Afraid to kick or thrash and make noise that would alert the Flock, she bit down on a hand—a human hand—and the salty, copper taste of human blood flooded her mouth.

Alex! For a second she went limp and let him carry her away. By the time she realized the man holding her wasn't Alex, it was too late.

After leading the Flock miles back the way they'd come, Zan had dropped the stun rod at the edge of a steep ravine. He'd also trampled the brush and broke some branches there, as if he and Cora had fallen. Then he'd circled back around behind the Flock. Would they take the bait?

Hidden alongside the trail, he watched as the column halted near the ravine. A guard found the stun rod and took it to the leader.

Though he'd always understood much of the Flock's language, only since Cora's arrival had he bothered to listen.

The leader kneeled and studied the trampled weeds at the edge of the ravine. After a few moments, he stood and said, "The search is ended. They have fallen to their deaths. We return now."

"But, Sire." Though the guard was probably a consort rather than the leader's offspring, she called him by his customary title. "This makes no sense. Why did they come back this way? It could be a trick."

"Unars are not that clever. Perhaps something scared them and they thought to return to the compound. Who knows? We've wasted enough time and resources."

"We must find him," the guard insisted. "Without our champion our compound will soon have no resources."

The leader's head feathers fanned upward. "Do you question my authority?"

"N-no, Sire." The guard bowed her head in compliance.

"Don't worry." Mollified by the guard's submissive pose, the leader patted her back. "For a while things may be tight, but he was old, his fighting days nearly done."

Zan growled deep in his throat. He itched to show the leader how wrong he was, to take revenge for the degradation he and Cora had suffered at Flock hands.

"What of his stud fee?" the guard asked.

The leader clacked his beak rapidly, an action that passed as a smile for the Flock. "If not for our new technology that would be a grave blow to our income, but now that his seed is limited it will command an even higher price. Perhaps his loss will prove a boon, eh?"

Not if he could prevent it. Zan remembered with distaste the many times he'd been milked. Whenever he refused or was unable to perform with a female, the Flock had taken his semen in other, less pleasant ways. He added another objective to his list—destroy the Flock's means of creating more humans to abuse.

"Besides, we have a new champion to train," the commander continued. "Now, lead us home."

Finished with their hunt, they no longer bothered to be silent. The guards chattered as they headed home.

Until she'd asked to stop and rest, Cora's inner strength and determination often made Zan forget how fragile she was. Necessity had forced him to leave her alone and unprotected. Now he needed to get back to her. Weaponless, he proceeded with caution. So far fortune had favored them. They'd not run into any predators, deadly reptiles, poisonous plants or insects.

Even at a run, the trip back seemed longer. Lungs straining and muscles burning, he rounded the last curve on the trail. The boulder came into view. He slowed to walk and fought to bring his breathing under control.

"Cora?" He spoke softly so as not to startle her.

She no longer sat on the far side of the boulder. She'd left. He sank to his knees.

No, not the Cora he knew. She'd never desert him. Not willingly.

He looked back the way he'd come. Had she followed him? Even if he'd been looking, the leaf-strewn trail would show little evidence of her passage.

Had the Flock found her? He examined the ground for tracks. He saw no indication they'd come this far. Nor did he see any sign that she'd been attacked by wild animals and dragged away.

Where should he search?

Had she grown tired of waiting for him and gone ahead to find her ship? Though it was doubtful she'd taken this action, the thought sustained his hope. Purpose restored, he headed toward the plateau she'd indicated.

Half an hour later, hope crushed, he stood on the empty plateau.

He could see where she'd crashed. Already the planet's lush vegetation tried to reclaim the burned and gashed ground. A green blanket of new growth covered the scorched foliage, but nothing could hide the raw furrow the ship had gouged into the ground when it skidded to a stop near the edge of the plateau. Another few feet and the ship would have plunged headlong down the side of the mountain and he would have never known.

Though his heart wanted to, he couldn't deny what his eyes told him. The ship was gone. She was gone. She'd left.

Reason told him this was for the best. All along he'd planned to send her away from danger.

But while her betrayal shouldn't hurt, it did. He shouldn't feel anger, but he did. He shouldn't want her back, but he did. His years with the Flock had changed him in ways he didn't comprehend. Sending her away was different than having her leave him.

Before Cora came, he'd been content with his life. Food. Sex. Fighting. What more did a man need?

Her arrival had unleashed difficult, uncomfortable emotions inside him, turned him into a stranger she called Alex. For her he'd been willing to give up the life he'd created as Zan, to kill him off, to be the Alex she claimed to love. As his memories returned he knew she spoke the truth of his past, but the warrior he was now refused to die easily.

Now he found that everything he'd thought between them was a lie. All her words were a lie. She wasn't who or what he believed her to be. She'd used him to escape the Flock and then left him. For that he'd never forgive her. *You left her and she forgave you,* a small voice inside reminded him.

He shook away the remnants of his tender feelings, Alexander Anderly would cry for love lost. Zan would not. At that moment Alex died a second time and Zan was reborn.

Zan refused to mourn the woman's departure. Still, she'd given him one precious gift—freedom.

CHAPTER ELEVEN

Throat sore and muscles aching, Cora woke slowly. The sensation of softness beneath her and the feel of smooth material against her skin made her reluctant to open her eyes. This had to be a dream. A feather mattress and soft sheets weren't part of the Flock's idea of caring for its stock.

"So you're finally awake."

The sound of a strange voice jolted her eyes open. She found herself looking at one of the most beautiful boys she'd ever seen.

Any woman would envy and long to run her fingers through his hair; the color of polished chestnut, it flowed thick and straight over his head and halfway down his back. Smooth caramel-colored skin covered sculpted cheekbones, making his age difficult to determine. He could be anywhere from his mid to late teens. The lack of any hint of beard made her believe the former.

As he gave her a small smile, even white teeth peeked between his lips. Her mouth watered as his tongue ran over his lips to dislodge a strand of hair that clung there. He had a mouth made for kissing, a nicely shaped upper lip slightly thinner than its fuller lower partner. If not for his strong square jaw, his face would be femininely pretty.

Her gaze moved to his torso. She caught her breath. His loose-fitting shirt with its deep V did little to hide broad shoulders, well-muscled arms and a powerful build. Dark brows arched over azure blue eyes. He studied her with an almost childish curiosity as she gazed at him in awestruck wonder.

She pulled herself together and demanded, "Who the hell are you? What am I doing here?"

He stared at her in confusion. "I'm sorry, I don't understand your words. I'll bring someone who speaks the language of the slaves." His voice sounded almost feminine, definitely young. He rose.

She realized he was speaking an old Earth language, one that had been abandoned centuries ago when Standard was adopted as a way to help unite the factions of the planet before they destroyed each other. She'd taken the obligatory course in ancient languages, but only remembered a little; her translator chip was filling in the rest. But as had been the case since she crashed, accessing it caused her head to pound. The chip was definitely damaged in some way. Thank the stars it still functioned.

"Wait." She touched his arm then jerked back. The feel of his skin under her hand sent a jolt of heat to her groin. She forgot the ache in her head. She felt her sex respond; her skin itched and her breasts felt swollen and tender, the nipples sensitized. What was wrong with her? Sure the boy was gorgeous, but he was just a boy and she'd seen other handsome men before without having this kind of physical reaction. Despite his betrayal, she loved Alex.

She wrapped her arms around her waist, glared at the boy and said in his language, "Who the hell are you? Where am I? And what have you done to me?"

GET UP TO 4 FREE BOOKS!

You can have the best romance delivered to your door for less than what you'd pay in a bookstore or online. Sign up for one of our book clubs today, and we'll send you **FREE* BOOKS** just for trying it out...**with no obligation to buy, ever!**

HISTORICAL ROMANCE BOOK CLUB

Travel from the Scottish Highlands to the American West, the decadent ballrooms of Regency England to Viking ships. Your shipments will include authors such as CONNIE MASON, CASSIE EDWARDS, LYNSAY SANDS, LEIGH GREENWOOD, and many, many more.

LOVE SPELL BOOK CLUB

Bring a little magic into your life with the romances of Love Spell—fun contemporaries, paranormals, time-travels, futuristics, and more. Your shipments will include authors such as KATIE MACALISTER, SUSAN GRANT, NINA BANGS, SANDRA HILL, and more.

As a book club member you also receive the following special benefits:

- **30% OFF** all orders through our website & telecenter!
  (Plus, you still get 1 book FREE for every 5 books you buy!)
- **Exclusive access** to special discounts!
- **Convenient** home delivery **and 10 days to return any books you don't want to keep.**

There is no minimum number of books to buy, and you may cancel membership at any time. See back to sign up!

*Please include $2.00 for shipping and handling.

YES! ☐

Sign me up for the **Historical Romance Book Club** and send my TWO FREE BOOKS! If I choose to stay in the club, I will pay only $8.50* each month, a savings of $5.48!

YES! ☐

Sign me up for the **Love Spell Book Club** and send my TWO FREE BOOKS! If I choose to stay in the club, I will pay only $8.50* each month, a savings of $5.48!

NAME: _____

ADDRESS: _____

_____

TELEPHONE: _____

E-MAIL: _____

☐ **I WANT TO PAY BY CREDIT CARD.**

☐ VISA   ☐ MasterCard   ☐ DISCOVER

ACCOUNT #: _____

EXPIRATION DATE: _____

SIGNATURE: _____

Send this card along with $2.00 shipping & handling for each club you wish to join, to:

**Romance Book Clubs
1 Mechanic Street
Norwalk, CT 06850-3431**

Or fax (must include credit card information!) to: 610.995.9274. You can also sign up online at www.dorchesterpub.com.

*Plus $2.00 for shipping. Offer open to residents of the U.S. and Canada only. Canadian residents please call 1.800.481.9191 for pricing information.

If under 18, a parent or guardian must sign. Terms, prices and conditions subject to change. Subscription subject to acceptance. Dorchester Publishing reserves the right to reject any order or cancel any subscription.

JOIN NOW!

He took a step back. "You speak our language?"

"Obviously, but that doesn't answer my questions."

"We didn't expect anger. Fear and confusion are more common. You are unusual in many ways beyond the obvious." As he spoke, he continued to back away.

She could see the apprehension in his eyes. Her arousal faded as quickly as it had come. Handsome he might be, but daring he wasn't. Despite his impressive physicality, he was a child.

"I must leave. Don't be afraid. Someone will answer your questions soon." He headed toward the door.

For the first time since she woke, Cora looked around the room. With no windows and only one solid door, it appeared to have been chiseled out of rock. The flickering light of an oil lantern cast a yellowish glow over everything. The furniture—a bed, a chest of drawers and a straight-backed chair—though plain, was of good construction and quality. She'd already noted the sheets covering the mattress. A few drab woven rugs softened the hard floor, but no pictures decorated the room's rough gray walls or knickknacks adorned the top of the chest. Alex's cage in the Flock compound had more personality than this clean, comfortable but barren room.

Before the young man could leave, the door opened and another man entered. Against the light that flooded in, Cora could make out little more than a massive silhouette, but a sense of power and command surrounded him.

"Father! She is unusual and speaks our language," the younger man said.

"You may leave now, Atier," the newcomer said. "We'll speak later."

"Yes, father," the boy answered in a subdued manner.

The door clicked shut, leaving Cora alone with a man she feared would affect her even more than his son. Goose bumps prickled her arms. Naked again, she huddled behind the blanket. Someday she'd like to wear clothing when she had to confront a strange man.

Though her hair and skin were clean and the blanket around her felt soft and smelled better, she found herself wishing for her old sarong. The man stood motionless. She could feel him studying her.

If she had thought Atier the height of male beauty, his father shattered all her ideals. Tall, broad-shouldered and powerfully built, with the face of a fallen angel, his eyes and the lines etched into his features showed experience and hard-won wisdom. Only the gauntness of his cheeks kept him from total perfection. An older, more mature version of Atier, he made her wish her heart didn't belong to another.

He stepped toward her. She shook off her fanciful musings—her heart belonged to no one but her—and faced him.

"You have nothing to fear here." Like hot chocolate syrup over frozen cream, the sound of his voice caused Cora's heart to thump in anticipation.

"Who said I was afraid?" She wrapped the blanket around herself and stood.

He came closer. A few inches shorter than Alex, he still towered over her. She tipped her head back to maintain eye contact with him.

"My son is correct. A most unusual female." He ran his gaze over her body in a way that brought heat to her cheeks. His eyes seemed to see right through the thin cloth. She hadn't felt this naked since she'd woken up in the Flock compound for the first time.

"I wish you'd stop talking about me like I'm not here. I'm human. You're human. And you're obviously not part of any Flock herd." She motioned at the shirt, trousers and boots he wore with casual ease. "So let's get down to it. Who in the intergalactic blazes are you people? Why am I here? And could you get me some clothes?"

His laughter made her jump. She glared at him until he stopped.

"I don't understand more than half of what you say, and answers—for both of us—will come later, but clothes I can provide." He opened the door, called out some orders, and then turned back to her. "My people are called the Erath."

She tried to peer past him out of the room, but his bulk blocked her view.

"Are you hungry?"

She hadn't thought about it, but her stomach growled in response to his question. "Yes."

He added another request to someone she couldn't see.

She thought about making a dash for freedom, then decided against it. Even if he hadn't been blocking her path, she had no idea what she'd find outside. Barefoot and naked, how far could she get?

With Alex she'd almost made it to *Freedom*.

He'd warned that he wasn't going with her, but his betrayal cut deep. At least the first time he'd left her he'd had the decency to say good-bye. He'd been the first person since her father died who she'd let into her heart. She'd learned at a young age that loving someone left you vulnerable, so even though madly in love with him, she'd kept a tight rein on her emotions, never letting herself lose control. Then he'd left her, choosing his career over her love.

After she'd thought him dead, she'd closed herself off from people, determined never again to count on another person for anything. That decision had served her well. For six years she'd found a way to survive and even thrive. When she'd found him again, how easily she'd thrown away that hard-won autonomy and put her heart in his keeping a second time. She blinked the threatening tears from her eyes. She wouldn't make such a mistake again.

The man sat on a chair. Feeling at a disadvantage with his head now level with her chest, she sank down on the edge of the bed. The move provided less than the desired result. Now they were inches apart. She could feel the heat from his body. Unwilling to meet his questioning gaze, she looked down.

Judging by the bulge in his pants, he wasn't unmoved by her either. She bit the inside of her cheek to keep from smiling. This was no laughing matter. She'd been abducted—again—to what purpose she had yet to determine. Well, at least this time she could talk to her captors.

Or could she? Based on thin evidence—their human appearance and old Earth language—she guessed them to be descendants of one of the Lost Colony ships. Those ships had been sent out several hundred years before Earth joined C.O.I.L., so technically, communicating with these people didn't violate any First Contact laws, did it? She hoped not.

Of course, if she wanted any part of her old life back, silence was her only option. When she returned to Earth alone she would bend the truth a bit about where she'd been and what had happened. Recon ships were often out of contact for months. Her long absence shouldn't raise any red flags. Despite her anger with Alex, she wouldn't go back to Earth and report everything that had happened. C.O.I.L need never know about Alex, this planet, the Flock or the humans on it. That was the best move. By keeping her mouth shut there'd be no consequences to her, to Earth's C.O.I.L. membership or to Alex, whatever life he chose to live here.

She'd get her ship back and find a new job. During her captivity her current enlistment contract with Earth League Force would have expired. As an independent pilot, she could reenlist with the Earth/C.O.I.L. authorities for planet recon or hire herself out to private industry. A good recon pilot with her own ship was always in high demand. She was free to do what she wanted and go where she wanted, in control of her life again. Strangely, the freedom felt empty and meaningless.

"My name is Ro'am of Clan Radolf. How should I address you?" The man interrupted her thoughts.

" 'So long' would be good," she muttered.

"Solong. A pretty name."

She couldn't prevent her chuckle. "No, my name's Cora."

"I'm pleased to welcome you to my home and my village, Cora Solong."

She grinned, but didn't correct him. He answered her smile with one of his own, and her body went into meltdown. Surprised, she sucked in her breath. His clean masculine scent filled her nostrils. Heat flowed through her veins. Dizziness washed over her. She swayed.

"Do you feel unwell?"

"No. Yes. I don't know. What's wrong with me?"

He leaned toward her. The thin blanket felt oppressive against her skin. She wanted to rip it aside along with the clothes he wore and press her burning flesh against his. Desire grew. Her breasts ached. Her consciousness and self-control seemed to be burning away. Not even the Flock sex stimulant had made her feel this way.

Sex stimulant! She'd been drugged! A wave of desire threatened to overwhelm her. "No!" She refused to become the animal the Flock thought her. "Get away from me!"

She slapped away his outstretched hand, scrambled to the far side of the bed and huddled against the wall. He jerked back. She didn't have the strength to flee, and knew if he touched her she'd attack him like a bitch in heat.

Rather than decreasing it, rage fed her lust. Tears of shame and frustration coursed down her flaming cheeks as she fought to keep from taking what her body screamed for.

He reached out to her again. She cringed. "What did you drug me with?"

His arm dropped to his side. "A mild tranquilizer."

"Liar."

His cheeks reddened. "The other is merely an unfortunate side effect some women experience. It will pass soon." He moved to the door, turned and added, "Rest now. We'll speak later."

She heard a bolt clank into place as the door closed behind him.

Wrapping her arms around her middle, she rocked on the bed. Despite her effort to restrain them, tears beaded on her lashes. Why had she felt such overwhelming desire? And worse, honesty forced her to admit that even without the effect of the drug in her system, she wanted Alex. That would never stop.

Mind and body she missed him. She missed his smile, his laugh, the feel of his body against hers, his warmth. She wanted his arms around her, his mouth on her breasts and his cock buried so deep inside her it would take him a year to pull out. She pressed her knees together to ease the ache in her sex. Moisture dampened her thighs. A low moan escaped her. A ball of misery, she clutched the blanket around herself and curled up on the bed.

Zan didn't understand his reluctance to leave the crash site. Cora was gone; lingering here would not bring her back. Nor did he wish it to. The lie tasted sour. Despite her betrayal, he wanted her back. He missed her.

He was wasting time.

What else did he have but time?

He had no weapon, no food, and, he admitted grudgingly, until Cora had arrived he'd had no purpose. Everything he'd needed or wanted—aside from freedom—the Flock had provided. They'd decided how he lived his life. Now, good or bad, he was free to make his own choices, his own decisions.

At the sound of a piercing cry, he looked up. He hadn't lied to Cora about the dangers this planet held. A pair of Alavan hawks soared in the wind, their sharp eyes searching for prey. High against the blue sky they looked like tiny specks, but he knew they possessed wingspans wider than a man stood tall, razorlike talons and bad attitudes.

No, it didn't pay to linger unarmed in this territory. Without his sword, he felt naked and exposed in a way his lack of clothing had never made him feel.

As he turned to leave the plateau, something sharp stung the back of his neck. He reached around to slap the annoying insect and felt the feathered shaft of a dart. The world began a slow spin. He tried to turn, to face his assailant. His limbs refused to obey. His legs folded under him. Unable to stop himself, he crumpled face forward. Pain flared as his head hit the ground. A rock gouged his temple. Warm liquid burned his eye and blurred his vision.

He blinked. Whatever he'd been shot with rendered him incapable of movement but left him conscious. Had the Flock found him? Like a stupid Flock chick, he'd wandered about as if this world weren't filled with peril. Fuming with rage at his own negligence, he waited and listened.

A rock clattered as someone approached, coming closer, but out of his field of view. He counted two sets of footsteps.

A voice spoke. At first the speech sounded garbled, neither Flock nor Standard nor Herdspeak. He strained to distinguish what was said. With his translator chip, in seconds the sounds became words.

"Bind him. The tranquilizer will wear off quickly."

Pain bit into Zan as his arms were yanked behind his back and tied together, then his ankles were secured.

A second man spoke: "We should have used a larger dose."

"No, Boro, we wanted to capture not kill him."

Hands grabbed Zan's shoulder and rolled him onto his

back. He took stock of his two captors. Disgust rolled through him that he'd allowed these two to take him unawares. One was ancient, his shoulders stooped, his body withered and frail. Lines creased the leathery skin on his face. Gray obliterated any sense of what color his hair might have been. The other, though tall and muscular, was little more than a lad. Whiskers had yet to sprout on his chin.

The younger one, Boro, frowned down at him. "Drac it all, Telan! A pissing Verian slave beast." He prodded Zan's side with the toe of his boot.

Telan shook his head. "Hardly. Take a closer look."

Boro crouched down, put his face almost in Zan's and chuckled. "He seems angry."

Hatred coursed like acid through Zan's veins. He gathered every ounce of his strength and willpower.

"I wouldn't get that close," Telan warned.

"Why? He's trussed up like a suckling pig for the fire, what can he—"

Zan whipped his head forward, catching the man off guard. Their foreheads hit with a resounding crack. Boro grunted in pain and fell backward. His brief surge of strength depleted, Zan slumped to the ground.

Telan threw back his head and laughed. "I tried to warn you. He's not as helpless as he appears."

Boro sat up rubbing the growing bump above his left eye. Awareness dawned in his eyes. "A Verian *warrior.*"

"Possibly. He has the size and strength, not to mention the scars for one."

Dizzy from his futile attempt to fight back, Zan stared. The man studied him in return.

"What's he doing out here by himself?" Boro moved to what he probably considered was a safe distance away.

"That is the question, isn't it," Telan said. "Get the cart. We'll take him back to the village for questioning."

Boro looked unsure. "If he's not the one we've been searching for, should we leave the site unguarded?"

What or who were they looking for? And why? *Think.* His body might be paralyzed, but his brain functioned. The answer hit Zan. Cora. Somehow they knew about the ship. They'd been watching for her.

But if they'd been watching the crash site, how had she left without them seeing her? And what about the ship? Where was it?

"If the pilot returns he'll follow the trail of his ship and we'll capture him," Telan assured the lad.

Joy exploded inside him. She hadn't deserted him. His elation was short-lived. If she hadn't left in her ship, where was she? Had the Flock caught her? He'd seen no evidence. Nor had he seen any indication that a wild animal had attacked her.

Feeling tingled in his hands and traveled rapidly up his arms. He wiggled his fingers. In minutes his body would again be his own to command, and these two would regret whatever they'd done to Cora.

The door opened and a woman came into the room carrying a tray. Cora blinked in surprise. The woman wore an enveloping robe of drab brown fabric over her body, as well as a veil made of a lighter weight material across the lower portion of her face. All that was visible to reveal her tender age was her eyes.

"Who are you?" Cora uncurled herself from the bed. "Why are you keeping me locked in this room?"

The woman didn't answer. She kept her head bent and, after depositing the tray of food as well as an armload of clothing inside the door, she hurried out.

There were people on the other side; Cora could hear their muffled voices but couldn't make out their words. For a few minutes she pounded on the door and demanded to be released.

When no one responded, she sorted through the articles of clothing and dressed. It felt decidedly odd to be wearing clothing again. With every movement, the simple white blouse and multicolored calf-length skirt, though made of a soft material, grated against her skin. She ignored the heavy robe, the veil and constrictive undergarments. She tried on the leather boots, but quickly removed them. After going barefoot for so long, the boots pinched her toes.

Tantalizing aromas drew her back to the tray of food. She didn't recognize the fare, but the smell convinced her to try it. If Ro'am and his people wanted to harm her, they'd had the opportunity; poisoning her food wasn't necessary.

In addition to an array of colorful fruits, a selection of cheeses and crusty bread, there was a steaming bowl of stew. After the first bite she forgot her concerns and dug in. Soon nothing but crumbs remained.

A sip of the provided beverage made her sigh in delight. Hot, black . . . *coffee*. She savored the treat. Somehow the MAT unit on *Freedom* never got it right, so she carried real coffee beans along with an ancient pot for brewing it that Alex had found for her in one of the dusty antique stores he loved to peruse.

Suddenly, the coffee tasted bitter on her tongue. How could the man she'd come to know change so totally? Granted, Alex had been through a grave ordeal and much of his past was a cipher to him, but with each passing day she'd watched as the old Alex reemerged. No, not reemerged so much as merged with Zan. Much of this man remained the person she'd come to know in the Flock compound. In some ways, this new man comprised the best parts of both previous. Intelligent. Strong. Caring. Protective.

But nothing of what she knew of either Alex or Zan made what he'd done by leaving her make any more sense.

Could she be wrong? Could the Flock have recaptured him? Had she judged him guilty without evidence?

She had to get out of here. Though her captors were human and didn't seem inclined to harm her, so far they hadn't given her any information. Every instinct inside her screamed that they had a hidden agenda, and one she wasn't going to care for.

The door handle turned. On impulse Cora jumped off the bed. Aside from the heavy side chair there was nothing in the room she could use as a weapon. The wooden tray!

She snatched it up. Plates and bowls tumbled away, spilling their contents across the bed. She moved out of sight alongside the door. With both hands she lifted the heavy tray over her head.

The door swung inward. Cora squinted at the glare of light. By the shape of his silhouette she recognized Ro'am. For a split second she hesitated, then she swung the tray at his head.

He ducked. The tray slammed against the doorjamb and dropped out of her hands. The impact numbed her arms and sent her reeling back. A strong arm wrapped around her waist and lifted her off her feet. She threw back her head. With a thud it connected with Ro'am's.

"Ouch!" He tightened his hold until she could barely draw a breath. Her bare heels kicked against his shins. Pain shot up her legs, making her regret not keeping on those boots.

"Enough!" he roared in her ear.

Feet dangling, she went limp in his arms. The pressure on her lungs eased. Her feet touched the stone floor. If not for his arm clamped around her waist, she would have sagged to the floor in a heap. He turned her to face him.

"Are you injured?"

She looked up at him in surprise. Concern etched his features.

"Me?" she managed to croak. "You're the one whose head almost got bashed."

One corner of his mouth twitched upward, then he frowned and spoke over her head. "Go back about your business."

She glanced behind her. Outside the door a group of people clustered, watching with expressions varying from amusement to anger. She shuddered at the look of hatred directed at her from one man.

At Ro'am's command they dispersed. Cora's senses returned in a rush. She was plastered against him from breast to thigh. Though she didn't hate the feel of his muscled chest pressing her breasts flat or feel disgust at the hard length of him jabbing her belly, she felt no answering arousal. It confirmed her belief that she'd been drugged earlier. Anger flared.

"Put me down!" She pried at his arms with her fingers.

He released her, and she staggered. He reached out as if to steady her, but she took a hasty step away from him. For a moment she thought a look of hurt flashed across his face.

Heat rushed to her cheeks when she saw the knife strapped to his waist. During their struggles it had slipped around to his front. Apparently she hadn't had the effect on him she thought.

"Do you always attack your host?" He cocked an eyebrow at her. "As a guest you leave much to be desired."

"Guest?" She snorted. "Let's talk about your attributes as a host. Guests aren't normally drugged and then locked in their rooms."

He had the grace to look away. "The door was locked for your protection."

"Protection from what? Who *are* you people? Why did you bring me here? Where's here?"

He didn't answer; instead he said, "Come, there's something I want to show you." Damn, the man matched her talent for sidestepping questions. He started out the door.

"Wait." She tugged on her boots and wobbled after him.

CHAPTER TWELVE

Once outside the door to her room, Cora realized that if she'd escaped she wouldn't have gotten far. A dozen men filled the outer chamber. Every one of them stared at her, their expressions varying from curiosity to sexual awareness to hostility. Their looks made her wish she hadn't ignored undergarments or the robe and veil. She felt more naked dressed than she'd felt running around naked in the Flock compound. At least the Flock hadn't looked at her with lust in their eyes. Unsure which attitude disturbed her more, the hatred or the lust, she avoided their gazes and followed close behind Ro'am.

They passed through a common room. Though also hewn from rock, this chamber was ten times as large and twice as high, capable of holding dozens of people. Lanterns lining the walls filled the chamber with light. Tables were scattered all about. A massive hearth filled one wall, but it contained only a small fire. A woman sat in a rocking chair nearby. In spite of the voluminous robes and sheer veils the women here wore to hide their faces, Cora could tell this woman was very young, barely out of childhood. In her lap she cradled a swaddled bundle. Her gaze met Cora's. Innocent curiosity, free of fear or hatred, shone in her eyes. Then she turned her head and smiled at Ro'am. Every fiber of her being radiated love and contentment. He paused. Behind him, Cora couldn't see his response, but something told her he returned the girl's feelings.

Something pink poked out of the bundle and waved in the air, and the woman turned her attention to the infant in her arms. Deep inside, Cora envied the girl her ability to find calm and serenity in this hostile place.

"Who's that?" she asked Ro'am.

"My wife, Analyn, and daughter Breal."

The affection in his voice created a longing inside Cora couldn't afford. In defense she lashed out. "She's much too young to be a wife, much less a mother. How old is she?"

"Old enough to bear a child." His voice was hard. "Our numbers are few and dwindle each year. Women must bear children early or we'll soon be none." He stalked away, leaving her alone in the midst of the others.

She caught up to him at the far end of the chamber, almost outside, and touched his arm. He turned to her. The bright glare of sunshine prevented her from seeing his features.

"Why?" she risked asking.

He took a deep breath before answering. "This world is hard on women. For some reason our healers can't determine, their fertility is limited and their life spans unnaturally short."

She remembered the youth of the women in the Flock compound. Aside from the woman in the bathing chamber, she hadn't seen any females over the age of thirty.

"The Verians are also a grave danger. They raid our mountains often, kill our men and boys and steal our women and girls."

Cora sensed that Ro'am had personal experience in this matter. "Where is Atier's mother?"

"She was captured by Verians."

She heard the old pain in his voice. "What happens to them?"

"You probably know more about that than I do." He gave her a questioning look. When she didn't respond he sighed. "I pray they killed her."

"Why would you wish her dead?" Nothing she knew about the Flock indicated they killed women—at least not young healthy ones. *Freedom*'s computer had a large medical data bank. Something there could help these people. And her MAT unit could synthesize whatever medication was required. What help could she offer these people without breaking C.O.I.L. law?

"Few who are captured by the Flock return. Those who do are never the same." He leveled his gaze at her. "Who are you, Cora Solong? You speak our language but know little of our ways. We found you half-naked in the forest, hiding from the Verian, but you don't have the manner of a Verian slave. Where are you from? Who *are* you?"

Unsure of how, what or if she should answer, Cora looked away from his searching eyes. These people were likely descendants of one of the many lost colony ships Earth had sent out hundreds of years ago. But her knowledge of C.O.I.L First Contact law didn't cover this scenario. Would she be breaking any law if she made contact with them? Alex would know. She shoved away her longing for the man. He'd made his choice. Now she had to make hers.

She turned and, as her eyes adjusted to the brightness, she gasped. They stood on a plateau halfway up a mountainside. Bigger than the one she'd crashed on, this plateau lay deeper into the mountain range. As far as she could see, mountain peaks rose and fell around her. Snow blanketed the highest points. High above a distant cliff, specks soared and dipped against a cloudless blue sky, their keening cries a faint sound in the silence.

Cora shivered in the crisp air. Nothing looked familiar. If she managed to escape from these people, could she navigate her way back to her ship using the night sky? How far had they taken her?

Deep green forests covered the area below. Almost out of view in the forested valleys she could barely make out hidden enclaves of humanity—a patch of lighter green revealed a crop field, a puff of smoke a secret abode, a flash of color the clothing of people going about their lives.

Ro'am swept his arm from one side of the view to the other. "This is our world. We hide like rodents in these mountains, scraping a living from the steep, rocky soil, afraid to congregate or to venture out onto the fertile plains for fear of the Verians. So again I ask, who are you?"

"Is this what you wanted me to see?" Unsure what her answer should be, she evaded his question.

"No." His arm dropped to his side.

The disappointment in his response made her long to tell Ro'am the truth. But to what purpose? Caution kept her from giving him the information he asked for, or voicing the questions filling her mind.

If they were descendants of a lost colony ship, did they know? How much did they know about the Flock—or Verians, as they called them? What did they know about her? What did they want from her? Though they'd treated her with a certain amount of consideration, they had abducted and drugged her, and she was, as far as she knew, their prisoner.

But the biggest question of all was what C.O.I.L law required of her in this situation. She kept her lips tightly sealed. She couldn't prevent her wish that Alex were with her to solve this dilemma; his skills as a First Contact agent would come in handy.

"Come," Ro'am said, "we have a ways to go."

She followed him. Having successfully turned his attention away from who she was, she found herself curious about what he wanted to show her.

They moved across the broad plateau toward a trail leading down the mountainside. "Are we walking?"

"For a small way. Then we'll ride dracas."

Cora remembered the large, shaggy animals the Flock used to pull the transport, like an Earth ox only sturdier and stronger. "Good. I don't think my toes can handle a long trek in these boots."

"How long were you with the Verians?"

"About two months. It took a few weeks for my feet to toughen up, but now wearing shoes feels strange." How easily he'd tricked her into giving him information, she mentally chided herself.

Sunlight filtered through the thick canopy of trees hiding the trail down the mountainside. She and Ro'am walked side by side without speaking. A thick blanket of leaves littered the trail. Her feet stirred up the scent of moist dirt and vegetation. Insects filled the air with a steady buzz of sound that sounded loud in the silence.

The lower they went, the warmer the air became. Beads of sweat dotted her forehead and trickled between her breasts. She felt trapped in a seemingly endless green tunnel. No breeze ruffled the dense foliage surrounding them.

Then a roar broke the air. A woman screamed. Something crashed.

"Stay here," Ro'am said, running off down the path.

"You wish," Cora muttered. She followed close on his heels.

They broke into a clearing where chaos reigned. In a glance, Cora took in the scene.

Made up of a dozen thatch-roofed buildings, a tiny village sat in the clearing. In the open area in the center, half a dozen men circled one man. Body tensed yet loose-limbed, in a half-crouch he moved with them, never giving them an opening. Apparently they wanted him alive. Though they had weapons, knives and swords at their waists, none were used.

Blood streaked the man's nearly naked body. Bruises darkened the skin not covered in dirt. And even though the snarled mat of hair around his head obscured his face, Cora recognized him. *Alex*. She started forward. Ro'am snagged her arm and dragged her back. She twisted against his grip but he held firm.

At first Alex managed to hold the other men at bay. If one ventured too close, he was easily fended off. Then three men tackled him at once. They all crashed to the ground in a tangle of arms and legs.

Fists flying, they rolled across the ground. Grunts and curses filled the air. The second three men stayed out of reach. Men and women, along with a few children, watched from a distance.

With deceptively casual ease, Alex plucked away one man and sent him flying into the second trio. The men went down in a heap. He lifted a second man above his head and threw him to the ground. Something snapped. The man screamed. Clutching a twisted arm, he crawled away.

The third man clung to Alex's back. With a twist of his body, Alex got the man in a choke hold. He plucked the knife from the sheath at the man's waist and brought it toward the man's exposed throat. . . .

The man whose throat he was about to slit was Atier. He might be an enemy, but he was barely more than a child. He didn't deserve to die.

"Alex, don't!" Cora screamed in Standard.

For a split second, Alex's attention wavered. He turned

his face to the sound of her voice. That was all it took. A man sprang up behind him and a club smashed down on his head. He collapsed. Eyes closed, his skin devoid of color, he lay motionless.

Rage held back the tears burning Cora's eyes. She glared at Ro'am. "You've killed him. Let me go."

He tightened his hold, ignored her accusation and asked Atier, "Are you hurt?"

"Only my pride, Father. Thank you, Charic." Atier rubbed his bruised throat, then looked down at Alex.

"How did he get loose?" Ro'am asked.

"We didn't expect him to wake so soon." Atier picked up a length of rope lying in the dirt and examined it. "He chewed through the rope binding him. As we reached the village he smashed his way out of the cart. Who is he?"

Ro'am glanced at Cora. She averted her face.

"I'm not sure," Ro'am said.

"Is he dead?"

At Atier's question, Cora's heart skipped. She strained against Ro'am's grip. He let her go, kneeled next to Alex, and placed his fingers against his neck.

"His heart is as strong as his head is hard. He'll ache when he wakes, but he's not dead."

Shooting Ro'am a hate-filled look, she sank to her knees next to Alex. She stroked the hair from his scraped and bloodied cheek.

His eyelids fluttered open. "Cora? Am I dreaming?" he whispered in Standard.

"I'm here. Rest."

Seeing him crumpled at her feet destroyed her facade of not caring that he'd left her. No matter what he did, she loved him.

"You left," he said.

Her heart skipped a beat. He thought she'd abandoned

him, as she believed he'd left her. Tears wet her cheeks. Why did he doubt her? What had she done to make him think she'd leave without him?

Everything. With every word she spoke she'd told him she'd escape the Flock and get off this planet. She'd ignored his concerns and doubts and almost got him killed. In spite of that he'd come to her rescue, and when the opportunity presented itself, had helped her run for freedom.

With or without his consent, by whatever means she could, she was going to get him home. If that meant hitting him over the head again and dragging him away, so be it. Even if he hated her for it, she couldn't leave him here.

"For the best. Nothing here for you." He slipped into unconsciousness.

He was wrong. Everything she wanted in life was here.

Ro'am rose. "Boro, Atier, take him to the holding cell, and this time make sure he's contained," he said. "The rest of you clear up this mess and go about your business."

"Leave him alone." Cora put herself in front of Alex as the men tried to obey Ro'am's orders.

Ro'am grabbed her from behind and pulled her away. She twisted and kicked. This time she felt satisfaction as her boots connected with his shins, and she heard his grunt of pain. But she was no match for his strength. Helpless, she watched them carry Alex away.

"Let me go with him. He needs medical attention."

"Are you a healer?"

"No." She wasn't quick enough to lie.

"Then our healer will see to him."

When she ceased struggling and sagged in Ro'am's hold, he let her go. She turned to face him. "Then what'll happen to him?"

"Who is this man to you?"

"That's none of your business."

"If you wish me to answer your questions, then you must first answer mine."

She bit her lip to keep from swearing at him. "No one. He's just a man."

Ro'am snorted. "He said your name."

"It means 'angel'," she lied. "Maybe he thought he was dying."

"If you don't know him, why did you jump to his defense?"

"Why the hell not? It was six against one. I didn't like the odds."

"You spoke to him in another language, and it wasn't the language of Verian slaves."

She ignored his unasked question. "I answered you. Now it's my turn to ask a question."

"Your answer leaves much to be desired, but it will do for now. Ask."

"What will to happen to him?"

Ro'am folded his arms across his chest and regarded her evenly. "That depends."

"On what?" she demanded.

"We'll speak of his fate later."

"And if I want to talk about it now?"

"I've already answered your question."

"As you said, your answer leaves a lot to be desired," she shot back.

"If you don't wish to hear the answer, don't ask the question."

She gave him a sweet smile and muttered a nasty expletive concerning his parentage, but she did so in Standard. Common sense warned that she'd pushed the man as far as she could for the time being. No sense in aggravating him more than necessary.

"Someday you'll have to enlighten me as to what you just said. But this is not the time or place for conversation." He

173

nodded his head at the people watching them with degrees of interest and hostility as they cleared the broken cart from the square.

Cora lowered her voice. "I'm not sure what yet, but you want something from me. I promise you that if anything happens to that man you'll never get it." She couldn't refrain from pushing a tad harder.

She was surprised when he let out a muffled curse, grabbed her arm and propelled her toward a corral holding several dracas at the far side of the clearing. Once there, he whirled her around until she was forced to grip his forearms to keep from falling.

"Be warned, woman. Willing or not, I will have what I want from you. The fate of my people depends on it."

Speechless, she stared at him. The force of his passion for his people held her motionless more than the strength of his grip on her arms.

He made a sound of disgust, whether with her or himself she couldn't tell, and let her go. She shivered and rubbed her arms; not from cold, the air was still and warm, but from delayed reaction.

"Ro'am, I . . ." She started to reach out to touch his arm, then thought better of it. "I'm sorry." She wasn't sure why or what she apologized for.

He paused from saddling the dracas, then turned back to her. "No, it's I who need to apologize. You've been drugged, abducted and threatened. You have every right to be angry and confused about your position here. There's no reason for you to trust or confide in me, but I ask it of you anyway."

At that moment she wasn't sure she wanted to know the truth. "Let me see that the man is all right and I'll answer your questions," she offered.

He ran his hand around the back of his neck. "Soon. There's something you need to see first."

He helped her mount a draca. A short while later she again found herself wishing she hadn't forgone undergarments. Though the animal's rocking gait wasn't uncomfortable, with her legs splayed wide to accommodate the animal's broad back, each movement chafed her thighs and crotch against the saddle. After attempting to no avail to tuck her skirt under her, she gritted her teeth and endured the torment.

For an hour they traveled single-file down a steep, narrow trail again covered by a thick canopy of greenery. She distracted herself from thinking about Alex by focusing her attention on what Ro'am thought so important he'd drag her down a mountainside to see. Soon pain drove all other thoughts out of her head. The insides of her thighs, as well as a more sensitive portion of her anatomy, were raw from rubbing against the saddle.

Just before she begged Ro'am to stop, he halted his mount. She looked up to see they'd reached a small valley. A few hundred yards ahead, across a patch of rocky ground, rose a stone wall. She craned her neck to see where the top pierced the sky.

Large birds circled the peak. Their shrieking cries sent a shiver of dread down Cora's spine. Even at this distance their shadows rippled across the ground like ominous black clouds. She didn't have any desire to see them up close.

As if sensing her apprehension, Ro'am turned in his saddle and said, "Stay close to the cliff and the Alavans probably won't bother us. Dracas are generally too large a prey for them."

"Your assurance is underwhelming."

He grinned, then urged his mount out of the cover of the trail. She took one last glance upward at the menacing birds, then followed.

Separated by deep cracks, thick slabs of gray and black striated rock angled toward the sky. Dark shadows hid what lay beyond the gaping spaces between them. As they grew closer she discovered that the openings were bigger than she'd first thought; several were wide enough to fly her ship through with room to spare. A sense of foreboding crept over her.

In front of the entrance to one opening, Ro'am halted and dismounted. He came to her side. She didn't object when he reached up to lift her down, if she had tried to dismount by herself, she doubted her legs would hold her weight. Once her feet touched the ground, she teetered for a moment before she found her balance. When her legs came together she bit her lip to keep from crying out in pain. No matter what happened she vowed not to climb back up on that beast.

At their approach, three men stepped out of the darkness of the opening. Slightly unkempt, their clothing ragged and much patched, and well-armed with knives and swords, they regarded her with suspicion but said nothing as Ro'am urged her forward into the black maw.

After about a hundred yards the tunnel widened into a massive cavern. The damp air smelled of mineral-laden water and tasted metallic. She peered into the expanse, but couldn't make out the far walls. Though the ceiling was high above and disappeared into the dimness, she felt as if it pressed down on her, smothering her with its weight.

"You wanted me to see a cave?"

Cave. Cave. Cave, her voice echoed eerily back at her in the vast space.

"No. Just a bit farther."

She wanted to object but didn't when he took her arm and led her deeper into the cave. Walking on a moisture-slicked rock floor she could hardly see left her disoriented. The ache in her neither regions had her trembling. Or was it the sense of apprehension she felt about what he would show her?

Ahead, shimmering in the gloom loomed a silvery shadow. Her heart thudded against her chest. Her breathing escalated. Suddenly she knew what lay in front of her.

Freedom.

Her ship.

The thought blossomed in her mind as the outline took shape in front of her eyes.

She turned to Ro'am in confusion. How? When? "Why did you bring me here?" she asked, when what she really wanted to know was why they had *Freedom* here.

He hesitated for a moment then said, "To discover what you know about this . . . thing." His pause made her think he knew more about *Freedom* than he wanted to reveal.

"Why would you think I'd know anything about a strange piece of metal?" Calling *Freedom* just a piece of metal was like calling Alex just a man. *Freedom* was more than metal and circuits.

"Like you, this thing doesn't fit in my world."

"What do you mean I don't fit here?" She used his words to distract his attention from *Freedom*.

He studied her for a few seconds. His perusal made her want to cross her arms over her chest. Instead, she met his look with her own.

He looked away first and chuckled. "You're not like the other women here or the women who come from the Verians. You're bold, brash and demanding. Few women have your strength of mind and will."

She coughed to hide her snort of disgust. Like most men, Ro'am was blind to the true nature of women. "What does that have to do with anything?"

"Our legends tell us of a time before my people lived in these mountains. Until recently, most discounted them as myth."

"What happened to change that perception?"

"This object fell from the sky and revived the legend of

how my people arrived here in a great metal ship from the heavens. Since the object's arrival, our scholars have scoured the ancient texts for more information."

"What did you learn?" She wished she could discuss this turn of events with Alex. His knowledge of history and C.O.I.L. would be helpful.

"There are little more than the briefest of passages left, but we believe this object to be another ship from beyond the sky. Some believe *you* arrived here in this ship."

"What do you think?"

"I reserve judgment."

She slipped free of Ro'am's hand and moved forward until her fingertips touched *Freedom*'s hull. Like a lover long separated from her mate, she ran her hands over the smooth metal. "She's beautiful, isn't she?"

Made of a tough alloy—one of the newest benefits of being a C.O.I.L member—the fiery trip through the planet's atmosphere and the hard impact on its surface had left only a few scratches and dents on the ship's outer skin. No other type of ship would have survived the crash. Inside was where the damage had occurred. Slamming against hard rock had caused equipment and passenger alike to bounce and break.

Dark and sleek, her ship was a top-of-the-line RCB— recon bird. She touched the blistered scar where reentry had burned away the logo of the hawk in flight she'd had painted on the side of the ship along with its name. *Freedom*. The burnt paint flaked away under her hand, leaving behind shiny metal.

"You know what this object is?"

Ro'am's question jarred her from her thoughts. She pressed her cheek to the satiny hull. What to tell him?

From the outside, *Freedom* appeared as nothing more than a smooth cylindrical lump of metal about fifteen yards long and five yards wide. With her hatches closed they became nearly invisible and almost impenetrable. The amount of force necessary to blast her open would vaporize her passengers and her contents long before that happened. Though it appeared to rest on the ground, an anti-grav field held it just above the surface and allowed it to remain stable.

"How did you get it here?" She answered his question with one of her own.

He let out a breath. "It looks heavy, but it moves easily. We hooked up dracas to pull it."

In her daze she'd forgotten to lock *Freedom* down. Thank the stars she'd sealed her before she'd wandered off. Without her voice command no one could enter or fly her, but they obviously could cart her away. "I'm sorry, sweetheart," she whispered in Standard. She shuddered to think what would have happened to herself and Alex if they'd reached the plateau with the Flock close on their trail and found *Freedom* gone.

"How far away did you find her?"

Ro'am paused and raised an eyebrow, but when she remained silent he answered, "A few miles down the other side of the mountain."

He laid his palm against *Freedom*'s side. Cora smiled as a puzzled look crossed his face. Despite the chill damp atmosphere of the cave, *Freedom* felt warm and dry. She seemed to hum beneath Cora's cheek, a soft purr of sound as if she were alive and pleased to welcome her mistress back.

He snatched his hand away. "What is this thing? Is it alive?"

"In a way, I suppose she is," Cora murmured.

"Her? She?" Ro'am's look of boyish confusion disappeared and the hardened leader returned. "It's time for you to speak to the Ruling Council. Come."

Reluctantly, Cora pushed away from *Freedom*. Could she speak the command and enter *Freedom* before Ro'am or his men could stop her? Ro'am stood less than arm's length from her and a dozen men guarded the ship. And if she did, what about Alex?

Perhaps she could use *Freedom*'s small laser canon to break Alex out of whatever prison he was in, but first she had to know where he was, and then she had to be willing to kill some of these people to do so.

She sighed and followed. She'd figure it all out later; right now she had to decide how much to tell Ro'am.

CHAPTER THIRTEEN

Zan's bare feet slapped against the stone floor as he paced his cell. It was carved from rock, its rough walls and floors slick with moisture, and a solid wooden door barred the ten-by-ten room's one opening. There were no windows. A single gas lamp mounted on the wall provided a smoky, flickering light. Shivering in the chilled air, he stopped at the door and strained to hear. The rasp of his breath provided the only sound.

He sank onto the cot, the room's only furnishing. His bladder cried to be emptied, but his captors hadn't seen fit to provide a place for him to relieve himself. He refused to urinate on the floor.

Nor had they given food or water. He winced when he licked the dried blood from his split lip. The Flock treated their humans better than these people treated their own. But then, to the Flock he had value. These humans saw him as a dangerous enemy to be contained and possibly destroyed, not an expensive investment.

Just how dangerous he'd soon show them. He stomped down his surge of rage; brute strength and anger would not serve him here as it had with the Flock. Here his mind would be his greatest asset.

He berated himself for his impulsive escape attempt. It had earned him nothing but additional cuts, bruises and an aching head. He should have waited for a better moment and been prepared for a sneak attack. Cora's voice had distracted him for that split second.

Had he really heard her? Seen her? Touched her? Or had it been a delusion brought on by the blow to his head or the tranquilizer? His heart wanted to believe, but he couldn't be sure. To know for certain, first he had to escape.

He lay back to rest and plan. Eventually his captors would come for him. When they did they'd get more than they expected.

"Until I see for myself that your other captive is safe and well, I'm not telling you anything." Cora crossed her arms over her chest and stared back at the five men watching her from seats across the table.

When they'd first entered, Ro'am introduced them. Charic of Clan Eachan. Telan of Clan Gavan. Baylan of Clan Kinnell. Samal of Clan Ceara. And himself of Clan Radolf. Something about the names seemed familiar. Were they some of the family names from a lost colony ship? She couldn't be certain. History hadn't been one of her better subjects.

Even if these were descendents of a lost colony ship and they capitulated to her terms, she wasn't sure exactly what she'd tell them. In the twenty-four hours since she'd seen Alex she'd formulated a dozen possibilities, none of them ideal. Until she spoke to Alex she couldn't settle on any of them.

She needed his expertise in First Contact law to devise a plan that would be acceptable to the Consortium. Though

E.L.F. did what it could to protect its pilots when they inadvertently violated a first contact law, C.O.I.L had the ultimate authority concerning any and all FC situations.

"I say we execute her," Charic, the youngest man in the group, said.

A sling held his arm against his chest, and she recognized him as the man who'd hit Alex over the head—the one Alex had tossed aside as if he were an annoying insect. That obviously had stung his pride, and she was the recipient of his ire.

Refusing to let them intimidate her, she lifted her chin.

"For what crime, Charic?" Ro'am leaned casually back on his seat.

Charic blustered a moment, then blurted, "For being a Verian spy."

The other men tried to hide their chuckles. Cora caught Charic's hostile glare, and she gave him a sweet smile. His face reddened and his mouth grew mutinous.

"Charic, you know very well the Verian do not send humans to spy on us." When an elderly man spoke, the others fell silent in respect.

"She carries their brand," Charic insisted.

Cora rubbed her wrist and fought the urge to hide its humiliating mark in her lap. She met Charic's accusing look without flinching.

"That does not make her a spy, merely an unfortunate victim. If she escaped from the Verians' compound, then she is a refugee and we must treat her with kindness and understanding so she can assimilate into life here."

"Well said, Telan," Ro'am remarked.

"She's no more a Verian slave than I am," Charic muttered.

"I'm glad we agree." Ro'am turned his gaze on Cora. "The question is, where is she from?"

A fourth man said, "Whether a spy or a Verian slave, she's female. Are we so depraved that you'd have us destroy our people's hope?"

She met their questioning looks with nothing more than a raised eyebrow.

"And what of the male? He too is branded. Is he also a 'mere unfortunate'? Shall we cosset him as well?" Charic asked.

"Enough," Ro'am snapped. "We forget our guest understands our language. Excuse us for a moment," he said to her.

As if she had a choice in the matter.

The men conversed in hushed tones that she couldn't make out. Charic gestured wildly with one arm, his voice the loudest. Several words came through: future, children, force, torture. She shivered in apprehension. If they tortured her, was she strong enough to hold out? Would Ro'am allow it? Finally their conversation ended.

"Then it's decided?" Ro'am asked the other men.

Three gave brisk nods. Charic's head barely moved. He shot her an angry look.

Cora steadied herself with a deep breath and looked at Ro'am. She refused to ask what they'd decided. "Wait here," he told her. His face revealed nothing of the decision they'd made.

After the men filed out of the room, she jumped to her feet and rushed to the closed door. Locked. She took Ro'am's seat at the table and waited. Buried deep inside the twists and turns of the cave system that honeycombed the mountain, even if she found a way out of this room she doubted she could find her way back to *Freedom*.

Being alone had never bothered her before. Recon pilots had to be able to spend long stretches of time by themselves. During a mission, months passed when she neither saw nor spoke to anyone. Why did she feel the isolation now?

The answer came: Alex. She groaned.

Finding him again, being with him had changed her. When she'd thought him dead, she'd closed down that part of herself that connected to other people. If she didn't care, didn't love, she couldn't lose. It was a lie. By refusing to open to people she lost part of herself.

Discomfited by her thoughts, when Ro'am had come to escort her to the meeting with the Ruling Council she'd gone eagerly. Action kept her from dwelling on her mistakes, past, present and future.

Now she could only wait. And think.

The door to the cell creaked open. Zan sprang to his feet, slipped to the side of the door and waited.

"Friend. No attack. We speak?" a masculine voice said.

Zan had to grin as the man mangled the Herd language. Communicating in Herd was going to be a tedious process. Though it used simple words and structure, the Herd language was far more complex, made up of not only the verbal, but also the nonverbal. Hearing the words alone would lead a person to believe a Herd human to be simpleminded; this was far from true. Ro'am knew the words but not the subtleties.

Still, Zan had no difficulty understanding the man's meaning. Some of the tension eased out of him. That they wanted to talk was a good sign. If they'd desired him dead they'd had the opportunity. He stepped in front of the door.

A man entered. "I Ro'am. Leader." He pointed to himself, then to Zan. "You?"

Zan remained silent. Who was he? Zan, Flock champion? Or Alexander Anderly, xeno-anthropologist?

He made the decision he'd avoided since the first moment he'd seen Cora in the breeding hall. "Alexander Anderly."

The man looked at him, taking in the dirt and blood caking his naked body, and frowned. He spoke in Old Earth to the armed men standing just behind him. "Bring food, water and fresh clothing." When the men hesitated, he snapped, "Immediately!"

Ro'am stepped into the room and shut the door behind him, leaving himself and Alex alone.

"Sit." Ro'am gestured to the cot.

Alex sat and waited.

"You. Where from?" Ro'am asked.

Alex pretended not to understand Ro'am's slow, careful Herdspeak. Until he knew for sure if Cora was here, he couldn't decide how to answer. Did Ro'am suspect his identity? If so, the man had courage.

Though a few inches shorter than Alex, Ro'am was well-muscled and armed with a knife and a sword. Still, Alex doubted the man could match him in a fight. Years of training, fighting and killing had honed him into a lethal weapon.

The Flock rarely contaminated their herd with wild humans, but they did occasionally try to exterminate them. As he'd told Cora at the start of his training, Alex had been called to the arena to fight and kill obviously untrained opponents—wild humans. At the time he'd thought little of it, killing the men with ease for the amusement of the Flock. Later, as his skill grew, he'd disdained fighting or killing unworthy opponents, merely rendering them unconscious, much to the disappointment of his handlers. Now shame at his actions burned inside him.

Alex tamped down his guilt. If these people discovered who he was, whom he'd killed, his life was over—perhaps deservedly so. But before he surrendered to their judgment, he had to know if Cora was here and see to her safety.

"Woman? I see?" he asked.

By dredging up long-buried skills, he kept his expression blank and maintained an outward calm while inside he battled with himself. The Zan part of him demanded he grab Ro'am by the throat and force the information. The look in Ro'am's eyes told Alex the man felt the same way. Alex enjoyed an inner smile as he realized Ro'am could read nothing of his feelings on his face.

Ro'am studied him for a moment, then nodded. "First eat. Bathe?" He gestured to clarify his meaning.

"Good," Alex said and fell silent.

Ro'am left the room, and a few minutes later several men brought in a tray of food, a tub and steaming water and some clean clothing. They eyed him nervously and quickly left. Once they departed, Alex wasted no time in eating and bathing.

He'd lost his opportunity to make a good first impression with these people, so he needed to surprise them even more now. Success, perhaps even his life, depended on it. Using his fingers he combed his now clean but tangled hair and secured it with a strip of cloth at the nape of his neck. He probed the bruises and cuts on his face. They didn't feel too bad, but without a mirror he had no way of knowing for sure how he appeared.

Undaunted, he dressed with care, adjusting the loose-sleeved shirt so it highlighted his size and strength while not making him appear too intimidating. The material of the tight trousers chafed his groin. Grimacing at the discomfort, he repositioned himself as best he could. He stamped his feet into the boots provided and frowned at the constriction of his toes. Becoming a civilized human again would take time and work.

Less than forty-five minutes later, the door opened again. Ro'am entered and stopped. He looked at Alex, shock obvious on his face. He quickly recovered his composure and motioned Alex to exit.

This time, Alex didn't hide his grin. He strode out of the room. Six armed men waited for him. They flanked him as Ro'am took the lead and the parade began.

They moved through a series of tunnels and caverns of various sizes. In each cavern they passed, people stopped their activities and watched. Without turning his head or acknowledging their interest, Alex surveyed them and took stock of their community and culture. He assessed the number of men, women and children. The state of their technology. The type and quality of the clothing they wore. The kind and quantity of food they ate and how they prepared it. The chores they performed, along with the tools they used.

Part of being a First Contact Agent was the ability to quickly and accurately evaluate a society. Though brief, his appraisal told him much about these people. Without further data he couldn't be one hundred percent sure of his analysis, but based on what he saw, he concluded this culture was on the verge of collapse.

Cora nibbled on a ragged fingernail and, despite the soreness of her thighs and groin, paced the floor. Over an hour had passed since Ro'am and the others had left. Her throat felt tight and raw. She rubbed her hands up and down her arms to generate some warmth.

The door swung open. Ro'am entered. Right behind him came Alex.

Dressed in a loose white shirt that emphasized his broad shoulders, muscled arms and sculptured chest, and tight-fitting trousers that did little to hide his masculine endowments, he appeared both civilized and untamed. He'd secured his wet hair at the back of his neck. Though bruises and scrapes marred his face, he seemed intact. She clenched her fists to keep from throwing herself into his arms.

"Alex?" she whispered.

He glanced at her without obvious recognition, then turned his attention back to Ro'am. Her breath caught in her throat. Had the blow to his head affected his memory again?

"Sit," Ro'am directed Alex in Herdspeak.

Cora shot Alex a sharp look, but he didn't respond. He took a chair.

Ro'am also seated himself. As he did, the other four

members of the Ruling Council entered the room and situated themselves on the far side of the table across from Alex. Cora remained standing. These people weren't taking any chances; six heavily armed guards lined the walls.

"Will you sit as well?" Ro'am asked Cora in Old Earth.

She squirmed mentally as all eyes but Alex's turned to her. Hatred for both her and Alex blazed in Charic's gaze. Telan regarded them evenly, a small smile playing around the corners of his mouth and eyes. Ro'am looked weary. The other two men looked puzzled but neutral.

She plopped herself down next to Alex and peered at him from the corner of her eye. Questions flitted through her mind. *Are you hurt? What happened? Why won't you look at me? What should we do? Why did you leave me?* She both admired his calm control and found it exasperating.

As if he'd heard her, hidden from the others' sight by the table between them, he captured her hand in his grip. Warmth flowed up her arm, swirled around in her chest and settled in her belly. His touch promised answers and much more.

Ro'am introduced the members of the council to Alex. As he did, Cora whispered to Alex in Standard. "Telan, the eldest. He's the wise counselor of the group. He'll hear and weigh all evidence before rendering a verdict tempered with compassion. Charic, the youngest." A chill, owed only in part to the room's coldness, ran down her spine. "What kind of society would place this angry hothead in a position of power? Baylan. Middle-aged. Comfortable with himself and his life. He'll be slow to judge, but once he makes up his mind difficult to sway. Samal. Handsome." Alex tightened his grip on her fingers. "I can't read him."

"Good assessment," Alex whispered back. His words created a glow inside her. He nodded to her unspoken question about the clan names.

"You've already had the pleasure of meeting Cora So-

189

long," Ro'am continued. Cora grinned. Someday she'd have to correct him about her name.

"And this is Alexander Anderly."

Ro'am called him Alexander? She tried to catch Alex's attention. He stared straight ahead.

She tried to process. Did introducing himself as Alexander Anderly mean he'd accepted his past and who he was? Or was it just a means of self-preservation? As a Flock champion, Zan had done things that would condemn him in these people's eyes.

"We talk. Together." As if unaware of Cora's tension, Ro'am gestured between himself and the other council members as he spoke to Alex in garbled Herdspeak. "Agree?"

When Alex nodded, Ro'am said to the council, "As I speak the language of the Verian slaves, I will translate for the captive male. Ask your questions."

"How do we know that what you say is true?" Charic asked, staring at Ro'am.

Cora cringed at the look Ro'am gave the youth.

"Do you challenge my honor as head of the council?" Ro'am's low, even tone sounded more ominous than if he'd roared.

"N-no, of course n-not." Charic sank back in his seat. "I-I just meant that the prisoner might lie."

"That is a possibility, but we won't know until we question him."

Charic cast a dismissive glance at Alex. "You can clean him up and dress him in clothes, but that doesn't make him human. When has a male Verian slave ever answered our questions?"

"The fact that he dressed himself and is sitting before us calmly says much about who he is," Telan said. "A Verian fighter would die before allowing himself to be captured. Nor would he refrain from attacking his captors whenever possible."

Charic made a rude noise.

"What about the female?" Baylan asked.

"She speaks our language, so you may question her directly." Ro'am smiled. "But I doubt she'll give you a direct answer."

"I think we've given these prisoners too much time and too much leeway in explaining themselves." Samal spoke for the first time. "We've danced around them, accepting their non-answers to our vague questions. It's time we demand straight answers to hard questions."

"I agree," Baylan said. "Ro'am, the woman's been with us for over a day now and what have you learned about her? Next to nothing. We've wasted enough time coddling them." He turned his gaze on Cora. "Who are you? Where are you from? How did you get here? What do you know about the Verians? How do you know our language?" One after another he shot questions at her. "And what is that thing we saw fall from the sky?"

Alex squeezed Cora's fingers, then released them and rose to his feet. "Allow me to respond," he said in perfect Old Earth.

All eyes turned to him. Too shocked to respond, they fell silent and he took control of the gathering. The force of his personality dominated the room.

Ro'am stood. The two men fought a silent battle. Then, without a word spoken, they both sat.

"What is it you wish to know about us? Ask your questions. We will answer."

"Who are you?"

"Where are you from?"

Charic, Baylan and Samal blurted a slew of questions. Ro'am and Telan remained quiet. Cora could see the anger in the set of Ro'am's mouth. He didn't appreciate being made to look a fool.

Alex held up his hand and smiled. "One at a time, gentlemen. As Ro'am told you, I am Alexander Anderly and this is my partner Cora Daniels." He corrected her name. "We've been on this planet two moon cycles."

Used to the world of mechanics, where there was only working or not working, right or wrong, black or white, she admired the way he shaded the truth to suit his story. Apparently he'd remembered his training.

"How did you get here?" Samal asked.

"The object you found is m–our ship," she added.

"Why are you here?" Baylan asked.

"Before I answer, can you tell me something?" Alex asked.

"What is it you want to know?" Telan leaned forward.

"What do you know of the origins of your people on this planet?"

Ro'am studied Alex for a moment. "Why is this your concern?"

"How much we share with you about ourselves depends on this information."

Face red, Charic jumped to his feet. "Verian slime! You don't make demands! You're our prisoners! You'll tell us what we want to know or we'll—"

Ro'am cut him off. "Charic, sit down."

The man sank back into his seat, but his anger didn't abate.

"He's right." Ro'am looked at Alex. "Why should we let you dictate to us? There are ways to make you reveal everything, you know. Just because we've exercised restraint in our treatment of you so far, that doesn't mean we'll continue to do so."

Cora shuddered at the barely veiled threat in Ro'am's voice and eyes. She couldn't contain herself. "You call this restraint? You almost beat him to death." She touched Alex's face. For a second he tilted his head so her palm cupped his cheek, then he straightened away from her.

"Torturing me won't gain you what you want," he said.

"Who said anything about torturing *you?*"

Charic's words sent cold dread through Cora. The other members of the council's horrified looks at his threat didn't comfort her. She feared that if they became desperate enough they'd use whatever means they had to force Alex to tell them what they wanted to know.

She inched closer to him. Out of the council's sight he took her hand again and gave it a warning squeeze. His movement stirred a breeze that made her shiver in the room's chilly air. She welcomed the warmth of his hand and watched him from the corner of her eye. This was an Alex she hadn't seen before. Not the shy, unassuming Alex of old, nor the bold, brash Zan, this Alex was cool and confident against overwhelming odds. Between the two of them they could probably defeat the council members in a straight fight, but even Alex's strength and fighting skills couldn't prevail against six well-armed guards. What did he have planned?

"There's no need for threats," Alex assured them. "I'll tell you what you want to know. But first let me tell you what I know of you."

"Bah! What can you know of us?" Charic spat.

Alex let go of Cora's hand and leaned forward. Keeping his voice earnest he began: "Because of constant harassment by the Verians you're forced to hide in these mountains, which both protect and crush you. Crops don't thrive in the rocky soil and neither do your people. Your presence has scared away most of the game animals and forced you to range farther and farther afield to hunt. When you do, you leave yourself vulnerable to attack by large predators and the Verians. Poor nutrition renders you less capable of providing for yourselves. Your birth rate is dropping and your young, weak and elderly are perishing in alarming numbers. In short, your society is in a rapid decline." He finished his speech and sat back.

The council erupted in shouting. Cora couldn't make out more than one or two words of their rapid speech, but their anger was clear. She took advantage of the chaos to speak with Alex.

His calm attitude confused her. Though she wanted to ask him where he'd gone and why, those questions could wait. First they had to get out of this mess, so instead she asked, "What are you doing?"

"Shock and awe." He looked pleased with himself.

"What?"

"Part of First Contact with a new species is their first impression of you. Well, I blew that, so I had to improvise. First I shocked them with my radically changed appearance, then I awed them with language and insight into their society."

"Not too confident, are you?" She laughed. His attitude reflected all three sides of him, the old Alex, Zan, and the new Alex, his boyish excitement at figuring out a plan, his confidence that it would work, and his calm execution of that plan. From the little she'd seen of these people, she had to agree with his method.

"I trained long and hard to be an FCA. I know what I'm doing. Follow my lead. Trust me."

She bit back her objections. As much as it pained her to relinquish control, he was right. She knew nothing of diplomacy, and she knew just enough about First Contact protocol to screw things up. This was his field of expertise. Give her the clean logic of an engine to repair any day. People—human or alien—were too unpredictable.

"Silence!"

Ro'am's roar made Cora jump. The council ceased their shouting.

Once the room became quiet, Ro'am turned his attention to Alex. "Your comments on our society are irrelevant. And you have no need to know our history. The issue is you and the woman. Who are you? Where are you from? And why are you here?"

"My insights are far from irrelevant," Alex replied. "And your people's history is pertinent to my ability to reveal my identity to you." Even as the men began to murmur again, in anger at his refusal to answer their leader's direct questions, Alex kept his voice and expression calm. Despite the room's humid air, he couldn't afford to let them see him sweat. He rapidly formulated a plan that with Cora's help might work.

"This is getting us nowhere. I say kill them," Charic growled.

Samal and Baylan murmured their agreement. Telan remained silent.

"Charic is right," Alex said. "No, not that we should be killed. But that this back and forth is futile. One of us must take a step toward trusting the other." He directed his comments to Ro'am. Though the council was divided, this man wielded considerable power. Where he led his people would follow.

Ro'am leaned back in his chair and smiled. "As our guest, I insist you go first."

Confident now that his plan had a fighting chance, Alex returned the smile. "Cora and I are from Earth—"

"You lie!" Charic shouted. "Earth is a story we tell our children at bedtime."

"Charic!" Ro'am commanded. "We'll hear him out."

"Our ancient texts tell us Earth is more than a myth," Telan said.

Charic sank back into his seat. "Ancient nonsense," he muttered.

Cora gripped Alex's hand. Heat radiated off her in waves. He knew how hard it was for her to sit silently and let him take charge of this situation. It went against everything inside her. Her trust eased his qualms.

Charic's outburst told him that these people were aware of where they'd come from, but what they knew for sure and what was mere legend he'd yet to determine.

"I don't lie." As an FCA he could twist his words into creative truths, but he'd never outright lie—a tricky balancing act. "We crashed here and were captured by the Verians. We just managed to escape." He watched Ro'am and Telan's faces as he spun his tale. The two men accepted what he said without questioning the time line.

Samal shook his head in disbelief. "That thing is no ship. I saw it fall from the sky and crash into the mountain."

"No one could have survived that crash," Baylan added.

"Then how do you explain the fact that the ship is undamaged?" Cora asked.

All eyes turned to her.

"What can a woman know of these things?"

Charic's dismissal of her question reaffirmed Alex's appraisal of their culture as a patriarchal one. Women, though sheltered and cosseted for their childbearing ability, had little power or say in the governing of their lives or their society. A fact that would not sit well with Cora. Alex almost looked forward to seeing the sparks fly.

"Why didn't you tell us this to begin with? Why such secrecy?" Telan directed his questions to Alex and ignored Cora's outburst.

"To answer your questions, you have to understand the changes that have occurred on Earth in the last four hundred years."

"Yes, tell us your fairy tale," Charic spoke up.

"Open your mind," Telan chided.

Alex nodded. "Earth is now a member of a group called the Consortium of Intelligent Life."

"What is this Consortium?" Ro'am asked, skepticism obvious in his voice.

"An organization of thousands of planets."

"Must we listen to this wild tale?" Charic whined.

"Yes," Ro'am answered, despite his obvious doubts.

"Though Earth is an independent world with its own laws and government, in matters concerning other planets and races of people, the Consortium has jurisdiction," Alex continued. "The ruling council of the Consortium makes and enforces the laws regarding first contact with new planets. The consequence to a member planet who violates those laws is severe. As a probationary member, Earth could be expelled. Expulsion means doom. Without the protection of C.O.I.L., Earth would fill prey to other planets greedy for her resources."

"Why should we concern ourselves with a planet that may or may not even exist?" Ro'am asked.

"Because before Cora or I can fully answer your questions, we have to determine if you are the descendants of the colony ships Earth sent out four hundred years ago. If so, then as citizens of Earth you fall under the protection of Earth League Force and the Consortium and their fate is yours as well."

"The council must discuss this before we come to a decision," Ro'am said.

"There's nothing to discuss. Kill them now, before they destroy us!"

Ro'am ignored Charic's outburst. "We'll meet again in the morning. Guards, take our guests to a holding chamber. Rest well, Alexander Anderly and Cora Solong Daniels. Tomorrow we'll decide your . . . *fate.*"

Alex tamped down his anger at the man's mocking echo of his own words, but he couldn't control the possessive part of him that bristled at the smile Ro'am directed at

Cora. When the guards motioned for Cora and him to move, he put his arm around her waist. She leaned into him. The feel of her body pressed against him shattered his calm façade. Whatever else happened, he wouldn't let them be separated again.

CHAPTER FOURTEEN

Questions flashed in Cora's eyes as they were escorted to a room. Before the door clicked shut and they were alone, Alex whirled her around and brought his mouth down over hers. As her lips parted in protest, he plunged his tongue between them and savored the hot, sweet taste of her.

She attempted to pull away. "We need to talk."

"Yes, but later." He yanked her flush against him. "Much later," he whispered as he trailed his lips down her throat.

For a few seconds she fought his hold, then her body molded to his.

"Oh, Alex, I thought I'd lost you again." Her voice cracked on the last word.

"Never. I'm here and I'm not going anywhere without you." She was his woman. He'd never let her go.

When he thought she'd left him he'd buried his pain under fury at her betrayal, vowing to make her regret the action. Now he discovered his anger went deeper.

In school when they'd first met, she'd been the aggressor, the one who directed their relationship. Amazed that she, the brightest star on campus, had even noticed such a shy, awkward guy, he'd allowed her to control the course of their affair. It was she who encouraged him to study and apply for a position as an FCA. Insecure in their love and afraid that if he challenged her she'd move on to another man, without a murmur of protest he'd abandoned his original career choice, social anthropology.

But once he began his training, he'd discovered how much he loved the work. Success fed his confidence and self-assurance. When he'd graduated ahead of her and was offered a position as the youngest-ever FCA, he'd jumped at the opportunity.

Though he should have, given her need to control every aspect of her life, he hadn't expected her reaction to his news. The hardest thing he'd ever done was refusing to comply with her demand that he not accept the position, that he remain Earthbound until they could be posted together. He knew if he caved in he'd lose not only her respect, but also his own. In order to keep her, he'd taken the risk of losing her.

His gamble had paid off; she'd grudgingly given him her blessing.

But his victory was short-lived. That self-determination had cost him his identity and nearly his life.

While he'd thought himself a beast, he'd held himself in check, but now that he'd accepted himself, he let the control he'd maintained with Cora crumple and the civilized man gave way to the primitive male. He claimed his mate.

She slipped her hand inside his shirt and ran her fingertips across his chest. Memory dissolved in a flood of sensation. He couldn't think of what was to come. Nothing mattered but the here and now. The feel of her against him. The smell of her in his nostrils. The taste of her skin on his tongue. The look of passion in her eyes. The sound of her breathless whimpers of longing.

He plundered her mouth. She answered his hard kisses by licking and nipping at his flesh with sharp, insistent little teeth. Eager to feel her flesh against his, he pulled down her blouse, trapping her arms at her sides and exposing her chest to his eyes. A rosy pink colored her golden skin. Lush and warm, her breasts spilled into his waiting palms. He bent his head and sucked one ripe bud into his mouth. The taste of her exploded like nectar on his tongue.

She arched back, thrusting her breast deeper into his mouth. Her moan of pleasure sent a rush of blood to his groin. His cock strained against the restraint of his trousers. With one hand he freed himself. He used the other to lift her skirt.

Her soft cry made him pause and lift his head to search her face. "Are you hurt?"

"Yes. No. It doesn't matter. Don't stop." Cloth tore as she reached out to pull his hand back to its task.

Ember-hot, feather-soft and butter-slick, her body welcomed the invasion of his fingers. He stroked the swollen flesh until her passion drenched his hands. Her breath ragged, she buried her face against his chest. Together they stripped off their clothing and made their way to the chamber's narrow cot.

He braced himself on his arms and hovered over her. The ends of his hair brushed against her breasts. She stroked her hands over his broad chest, her fingers gently exploring his many injuries.

She choked back a sob. "So many cuts and bruises. Do they hurt?"

"They mean nothing." The feel of her moistness against his cock rendered him oblivious to pain.

The flickering yellow light of the room's lantern turned her tanned skin to warm gold as she lifted her head and pressed a kiss to each wound. Her velvet lips moved over him. A different kind of agony made him groan. His arms quivered.

"What's wrong? Where does it hurt?"

"I ache here." He gripped his erection.

With a smile, she pushed him onto his back and straddled him. The cot creaked. Crisp moist hair brushed his knuckles. Mere inches from paradise, his cock jerked in his hand. A bead of liquid glistened on the tip.

She looked down. Her small pink tongue left a glossy trail across her lips. To keep from disgracing himself, he tightened his grip. She adjusted herself and lapped away the bead of moisture. Eyes closed, Alex savored the anticipation. When her mouth enveloped him, his control slipped. He rolled her beneath him and stared into her eyes.

"Don't tease, woman."

"Who's teasing?" She smiled up at him. "Kiss me. Fuck me."

Unable to delay a moment longer, he plunged his tongue between her parted lips and buried his cock deep inside her.

Cora gasped at the difference in Alex. For the first time since he'd left her so long ago, his need truly matched her own. It was raw, unquenchable, unstoppable. This was what she felt for him, what she'd always felt.

Catching her breath, she wrapped her legs around his waist and ignored the scrape of his hips against the sensitive skin of her inner thighs. The burn of his cock stretching her raw flesh sent her careening toward the edge; they'd done this so much—and yet not enough. Pain blurred into bliss as he sank deep, filling her.

Fingers tangled in her hair, he tugged her head back to expose her throat. The sting of suction from his lips on that tender skin burst into pleasure as he branded her. Sweat slicked their bodies. To hold herself steady as he rocked into her, sliding himself in and out, she clutched his arms. The tempo increased along with the force. Each stroke took her higher. Anticipation and excitement built. Harder and harder he pounded into her until she couldn't contain the exhilaration flowing through her veins. Crying out in rapture, she arched her back to meet his final thrust. Warmth flooded her as he came.

Beneath them, the cot cracked and collapsed to the floor. Entwined in each other's arms and caught in the glow of their release, some time passed before Cora noticed the poke of the broken slates pressing into her back through the thin mattress. Her sore inner thighs and raw intimate flesh brought tears to her eyes, and though she never wanted to let him go she had to breathe, to get relief from the growing distress in her groin. She pressed her palms against his chest.

He rolled onto his back. She started to rise. As much as she wanted to ease the fiery pain, she didn't object when he anchored her to his side with an arm around her waist.

The cold of the stone floor seeped through the thin mattress as they lay on the cot barely wide enough to accommodate one of them. Shivering, she pressed closer to his heat. He turned on his side and pulled her alongside him. Heat from his breath warmed her cheek.

Nestled against her belly, his flaccid cock twitched. Her belly tightened in response.

"Already?" she asked, unable to keep the laughter out of her voice.

In answer he slid his hand between her thighs. Her chuckle became a strangled cry of pain. He stopped instantly. "What's wrong? Did I hurt you?"

She pressed her thighs together. "No, it's nothing."

Sitting up, he spread her thighs and frowned. "You're scraped raw. Did I do this?" His fingers hovered over the reddened skin on her inner thighs, then moved higher. When his fingers separated the swollen folds of her sex she couldn't stop her flinch or her whimper.

"By the stars, woman, why didn't you say something? I would have stopped."

She blinked away her tears. "You needed me."

He jerked his hand away and ran it over the back of his neck. "Despite evidence to the contrary, I'm not an animal. My needs can wait." Concern and self-condemnation etched his features.

"Mine couldn't." Despite the return of his control, she smiled at the knowledge that she could push him beyond it. "Don't berate yourself. We both needed it. Now it's time we talked."

"First let's make you more comfortable."

Eyes half shut, she watched him searching the room, which began to revolve around her as she tried to fight off the exhaustion washing over her.

He went over to a chest of drawers. On top sat a basin and pitcher of water, along with several towels. He poured water into the pitcher and wet a towel. Then he sat next to her. As he gently parted her thighs she tensed in anticipation of more pain. But when he placed the cool towel over her flaming flesh, a sigh of relief slid through her lips and her eyes closed.

"Better?"

She cracked one eyelid. "Yes, thank you."

"How did this happen? Did these people do this to you?" His tone hardened. Pressed against her crotch, his fingers clenched. She flinched at the added pressure. His touch gentled even as his expression darkened.

"Did Ro'am's people rape you? I'll see that they pay." The fierce Zan-like look on his face made her shiver.

If Ro'am and the others found out about Alex's life in the Flock compound, there was no telling how they'd react. She couldn't take that chance. Even if she had been raped she wouldn't tell him. Thank the stars she hadn't.

"No, nothing like that. I'm sore from riding a dracas without any undergarments."

"What? Why?" Some of the fire died out of his eyes.

"It doesn't really matter. Though their hospitality"—she glanced around the bare room—"leaves a lot to be desired, these people haven't hurt me." Watching his face, she wasn't sure if he believed her. She changed the subject. "What do you think you were doing back there with the council? Granted, I'm not the expert on First Contact law—"

"No, *I* am." He gave her a cocky grin.

"Yeah, but, you told these people a lot more than what's allowable."

"As descendants of a lost colony ship these people are already citizens of Earth; speaking with them violates no laws. And because they made First Contact with the Flock long before Earth's admission to C.O.I.L., there's no First Contact breach there either."

"Are you sure your memory is totally clear? Your assessment of the situation is probably right, but you don't have the authority to make it. By speaking with these people without prior approval from the Consortium, ELF or at least your superior officer, you're most likely breaking several laws."

He looked annoyed. "My memories are intact, as is my judgment. As the only surviving member of my team, I'm the superior officer. I have the right and duty to make this decision and carry it out."

"I hope ELF agrees with you." She chewed her bottom lip.

"Earth League Force doesn't argue with success."

"Yes, but first you have to succeed."

"Trust me. I have a plan to help both these people and ourselves."

"Tell me." The Erathians, the Flock and this entire planet couldn't be her major concern.

She had one goal: go home and have Alex with her.

Alex breathed a sigh of relief. Cora hadn't been raped. He believed her. She was a lousy liar. When the Flock had forcibly inseminated her, she'd reacted emotionally and physically to that invasion of her person.

He'd been with enough women to recognize an abused one, too. Some came to him in the breeding barn having been misused by other males. Though they'd been unwilling at first to accept his attentions, he'd never had to force himself on them. Patiently he'd eased their fears and seduced their bodies, then he'd pleasured them until they welcomed him. And even at the cost of his own satisfaction, he'd never injured them in any way.

Liar. By submitting to the Flock's control of him, he'd damaged those nameless women. No matter his gentleness, he'd treated them like animals and in the process made himself one. Only by finding a way to free them, to restore their humanity, could he regain his own.

As he and Cora spoke, he revealed nothing of his inner thoughts or guilt. It amazed him how easily he slipped back and forth between the two halves of himself. On the surface the Alex part of him appeared easy-going, trustworthy, without deceit, when in truth he manipulated those around him. Zan on the other hand presented a fierce front, wild and dangerous, treacherous, but in actuality was more honest: he didn't bend reality to suit his agenda.

The Zan part of him demanded he tell Cora the truth rather than manipulate her. He shut Zan away. Alex needed to deal with this situation.

"Tell me your plan," she repeated.

He could see the wheels turning in her head. Single-minded, once she set herself a goal she didn't waver. And her goal was to get off this planet and back home.

Service. Dedication. Loyalty. Earth League Force's motto was more than just words to her. She'd die before she broke the vow she'd made when she joined at the tender age of sixteen. With her parents dead, and no siblings or extended family, it had become her family, her home, her reason for existence—until she met him.

Her love for him gave him power over her. A power she both craved and fought with every breath she took.

It grieved him to know he was about to take advantage of her feelings, but other lives depended on his success. He knew he could influence her, but was her love for him strong enough to overcome her loyalty to Earth League Force? Once before he'd used that loyalty to convince her to let him go, had left her alone with nothing but Earth League Force to sustain her. Now he'd ask her to forgo that loyalty for him.

Service. Dedication. Loyalty. He'd also made that pledge. But to him it went beyond Earth League Force or even C.O.I.L. As an FCA his duty lay with the preservation of humanity. These people and those he'd left behind in the Flock compound needed his aid. No matter what his heart demanded, he couldn't leave them to their fate.

But without Cora's knowledge and skills, his new plan wouldn't get off the ground—literally. He knew if she agreed to what he asked she'd demand something in return. Whatever she asked, he'd give.

At his long pause, she slid a warm hand across his thigh.

"I need your ship," he blurted, his carefully worded speech forgotten. "Stop that. I can't think when you're touching me." He grabbed her hand away from where it played. How she tempted him to again abandon the control he'd worked so hard to obtain, the control of his mind and body that had allowed him to survive.

"*You're* touching *me*." She wiggled her fingers suggestively inside his. His cock jumped in response. Somehow the towel slipped out of his hand and his fingers stroked her. He started to snatch his hand away, but she closed her thighs, clamping it in place.

"I'll hurt you." Who manipulated whom, he wondered briefly before desire swamped rational thought.

"No. Feels good." But suddenly she jerked her hand away and bolted upright on the cot.

"You need *Freedom*? What for?" Eyes narrowed, she shifted until his fingers slid out of her, and she pulled the blanket around her bare body. "I think you'd better tell me this plan of yours before we get distracted again."

Cool air swirled around his groin, but it was the frosty look in her eyes that made him shrivel. Cora could spot a lie from fifty feet. Even before his memories returned she'd known who he was and forced him to act accordingly. Desperate as he was, he'd found he couldn't maneuver her into helping him. She deserved better. She deserved the hard truth. And if she refused to assist him he'd find another way.

He stood. Crouched on the cot as she was, her head was level with his groin. The warmth of her breath stirred his pubic hair. In spite of everything, he still wanted her and it showed.

"First, put on some pants." A faint blush colored her cheeks as she averted her gaze.

Hiding his grin at her sudden shyness, he pulled on his trousers. "Better?" His erection pressed uncomfortably against the trouser placket.

"No, but it'll have to do," she snapped. "Now talk."

"There are many ways to institute First Contact." He paced as he started. "Some involve infiltrating the native population for years before revealing ourselves a bit a time. Because of the physical differences between humans and the Flock—or Verians, as our hosts call them—this is not a viable option."

Cora nodded, but she didn't comment.

Encouraged by her willingness to listen, he continued. "Another way is the direct approach, walking up to their leaders and introducing ourselves. This works best with species who are on or near our level technologically, who have some knowledge of the galaxies and believe in the existence of other intelligent life.

"The Verians, while on the verge of technological advancement, are still far behind the most primitive of C.O.I.L. planets. Also, they believe humans to be a lesser species. When I spoke their language in the compound they assumed I was an aberration and acted similar to the way humans responded to the great apes when they made their first attempts to interact with us. Even if we approach the Flock directly, they probably wouldn't accept the evidence of their own eyes and ears. Too many deviations from what they expect from humans, and they'll react with fear and most likely violence."

"Why? Wouldn't they feel guilt and shame for having enslaved another intelligent species? And want to make amends?"

"It's possible but not likely. Verians have a strong sense of self. And though we may not like what they do to us, among their own kind they have a code of honor, of right and wrong. If we challenge those codes they're more likely to turn their anger on their victims than they are on themselves."

"That doesn't make any sense."

"It's human nature."

"But they're not human."

"Not physically. Their society may be structured differently than ours, but at their core they are just as . . . human as we are."

She snorted. "We'll have to agree to disagree on that, but go on. If we can't infiltrate them or approach them directly, what option does that leave us with?"

Her use of the word *us* gave him hope.

"Shock and awe."

She leaned forward. Cheeks flushed and eyes bright, she

watched him. The blanket slipped lower, revealing the tips of her breasts. Distracted by the sight of those rosy peaks, he lost his train of thought.

"Is it cold in here?" Despite the warmth of the room, she shivered and drew the blanket back up around her shoulders. "What does 'shock and awe' mean this time, and how does my ship come into it?"

He looked away and continued. "First we have to shock the Verians out of their preconceived notions of what a human is, and then we have to awe them with our power and strength. That's where your ship comes in. The sight of it landing in the center of their main city will shock them, and a blast or two from your laser cannon will awe them into listening to us." That was the bare bones of his plan; the rest he'd share later. Much later, after she'd agreed and when it was too late for her to back out.

Surprised at her lack of response, he turned to look at her. She lay on the cot, motionless. The flush in her cheeks was now two spots of bright red. Her eyes looked glazed and unfocused.

"Cora?" He knelt next to her. Heat scorched his palm when he smoothed the tangled hair from her forehead.

"I'm so hot." She tried to rip away the blanket. "What's wrong with me?" she rasped.

"Rest now. We'll talk more later." He brushed his fingertips over her eyelids.

"Hold still." She tried to grab his wrist but missed. Her arm flopped to her side. "I'm cold."

As she reached for the blanket, a shudder wracked her body. With a cry she bolted up, then crumpled. Alex caught her. Wherever their skin touched heat seared him, but she shivered uncontrollably in his arms as fever raged through her.

He gathered her close, as if his physical strength could

fight off the unseen enemy attacking her from within. But he knew it couldn't.

Alex paced the corridor outside the room where the healer examined Cora. He barely noticed the cold, damp stone beneath his bare feet, the fact that he wore no shirt, his trousers gaping open at his hips or the four armed guards warily watching his every step.

Seeing Cora lying there helpless had shattered his brief surge of confidence, elation, and calm. If she died, nothing else mattered. Sheer terror at the thought of losing her made him want to strike out. He wanted, needed the release of smashing his fists into someone, something. But he couldn't fight this unseen enemy. Only constant motion held his rage in check. So he paced.

Arms crossed over his chest, Ro'am waited with him for the healer's verdict.

"This woman is important to you?"

Alex stopped and faced Ro'am. "She's my heart."

A look of reluctant understanding, as if he didn't want to identify with Alex in any way, flickered across Ro'am's face. "Don't worry. Elder Maran is our most skilled healer. And the woman is strong in both body and spirit."

"Easy for you to say. It's not the woman you love lying there raging with fever."

A shadow crossed Ro'am's face. He stepped away from the wall. "I've sat and watched helplessly as more than one of my loved ones has died. This world is harsh and unforgiving to the weak and unwary."

Before Alex could respond, the chamber door opened and the healer came out. As a mark of his profession he wore a thigh-length white tunic with a scarlet sash around his round middle, and white trousers. A man of middle years, a sprinkle of gray in his hair and lines on his face, he projected an air of surety. He looked at Ro'am and said, "The woman will be fine."

Relief drained the starch out of Alex's spine. He sagged against the wall.

Maran continued, "She has Laric fever. Nasty, but if treated early not fatal. Can't imagine where she picked it up. Close contact with a cayadil or its kill is required to contract Laric fever. They carry the infection in their intestines."

"We fought a cayadil."

"You fought a cayadil and survived?" Ro'am asked.

"Was she bitten or scratched?" Maran asked.

Alex ignored Ro'am's question in favor of the healer's. "No, but when we killed it, its guts spilled out."

"Perhaps if she inhaled the fumes that would have done it." Maran scratched his head. "I've given her a potion to counteract the poison in her system. Her fever has already dropped. Let her rest a day or two and she'll be back to normal." He looked at Alex. "Were you bitten or scratched by the beast, or did you inhale the fumes?"

"Scratched." He tilted his shoulder so the healer could examine him.

"Amazing." Maran probed the wound. "This should be infected, and you should be sick. You must possess a natural immunity."

"Or the Verians inoculated him against the fever." Suspicion laced Ro'am's voice.

"When I was captured I was given many shots. The Verian like to keep their stock healthy." Alex's explanation didn't seem to ease Ro'am's mistrust, but he didn't ask why Cora hadn't also been inoculated.

"Perhaps. Either way I must study this. Bring him to my laboratory," Maran told Ro'am.

"No. I've been a lab rat long enough. I have to see Cora."

"Yes, yes, of course." In the face of Alex's scowl Maran backed away. "I understand. I can examine you later. She's been asking for you. But don't stay long. She's weak and needs to sleep. Don't be concerned if she rambles or seems incoherent. I've also given her a mild sedative."

Alex hurried into the room. He barely noticed as Ro'am entered behind him, or that the guards remained outside.

Ingrained training as an anthropologist and as a warrior had him scanning the room, but without real curiosity or concern. While he had waited for the healer to see to Cora he'd been only half aware as the room was refitted. Though still bare of decorations, a stove now sat in the corner and gave off a fragrant, smokeless heat. Fur rugs softened the stone floor. The broken cot had been replaced with a larger bed frame covered with a thick mattress and soft bedding.

Only the woman lying still in the middle of the bed captured his attention. When he sat on the edge of the mattress she opened her eyes and looked up at him with a small smile.

"Sorry I zonked out on you like that. Guess you're more man than I can handle."

Even though she spoke Standard and Ro'am couldn't understand, unexpected heat flooded Alex's cheeks.

"You looked flushed." Cora cupped his face in her palm. "Are you ill too?"

Her skin still felt warm, but much cooler than before. "No. I'm fine." He captured her hand in his and tried to tuck it beneath the bedding. "Sleep now."

She resisted, clutching his hand with surprising strength. "Don't leave me. I couldn't bear it again."

Her whispered plea tore at his heart. Never before had he seen her so vulnerable. Since the day they met she'd been strong and sure. No matter what obstacles or adversaries she faced, she didn't protest fate or complain about the inequities of life.

As a student she'd been at the top of her class, destined for great things. Her intelligence, drive and dedication made her stand out amid the elite. Without doubt or hesitation she went after what she wanted. She allowed nothing and no one to stand in her way. Memories of her calculated pursuit of him brought a grin to his lips.

Even as a captive in the Flock compound she had always had a plan, insisted on leading the way, resisted being broken. Nothing the Flock did to her changed her inside as it had him.

Her eyes drifted closed and her grip eased. Again Alex tried to tuck her arm under the bedding. At the last moment her eyes flew open and locked on his. She pressed his hand against her breast. "Promise me you won't leave me again."

"I promise." He could no more leave her than he could rip out his own heart. But when she learned of his plans to stay on this planet, she'd leave him.

CHAPTER FIFTEEN

"One way or another I'm getting out of this bed and this room—today," Cora told Maran. "I'm bored out of my mind stuck in here." She didn't mention that it wasn't until this morning that she was even in her mind. The last three days—no, the last five days—were a blur.

"You've been very ill. It would be best if you rest a bit more. At least through today," Maran advised. "Your recovery has been miraculous, but you don't want to risk a relapse."

"I'd risk damnation if it meant I'd get out of this blasted room," she muttered.

"What did you say, my dear?"

Maran was a good doctor and man, but he was a fussy old woman. "Nothing."

"If you insist, you may rise for an hour this afternoon."

"Only an hour?"

"Believe me, my dear, after an hour you'll be glad to return to your bed." Maran chuckled.

"I don't think so."

"Would you like to make a wager?" His eyes twinkled.

"No." She knew he was right, but it didn't make accepting the forced inactivity any easier. Even in the Flock compound she hadn't been this bored. There at least she'd had Alex to keep her company. At the thought of his company her body tingled. Since she'd taken ill she'd seen little of Alex, and when he had come to see her, she'd either been sleeping, too out of it to notice, or he'd been distracted.

Flashes of memory of their conversation from before she took sick disturbed her, but she couldn't nail them down. As she thought back over the last few days, she realized that Alex had come and gone from her room with ease. Ro'am had also visited several times. Occasionally they came together. Though the air around the two men crackled with tension, she sensed a growing trust between them. They also exuded an excitement that made her nervous. What in the stars were they planning? She wished she knew. Then again, maybe it was better she didn't, because she had a feeling she wasn't going to like it.

"I'll send in your meal. Afterwards you may bathe and rise. I'm sure your friend Alex will be pleased to escort you on your outing. Or perhaps you'd prefer Ro'am?" He winked at her and bustled out of the room.

An hour later, when Alex came in, Cora was ready and waiting. She was also exhausted. He gave her an assessing look.

"Are you sure you feel well enough for an outing?"

A look in the mirror had warned her what he saw. Dark circles under her eyes made her look pale and gaunt. Even after shampooing, her hair hung in lank, lifeless clumps. Altogether she looked a hag. Female vanity had almost had her refusing Alex entry to her room, but the need to escape its confines prevailed.

She returned his look. "You look fit." *Enough to eat,* she added silently. Dressed in a crisp white shirt and dark trousers, with snug calf-high boots, he cut a dashing figure. He'd tied his long hair at the nape of his neck. The swelling and bruises on his face had subsided and faded to faint discolorations. She envied him his good health. Eating, bathing and dressing had left her ready for a nap. Instead, she hurried to the door before he changed his mind.

She snagged his arm. "Get me out of here."

The long walk through the maze of caves from her room to the outside nearly undid her resolve. She found herself leaning on Alex more than she liked. When she tried to pull away, he secured her arm in his.

"Are you sure you're up to this?"

The concern in his voice both warmed and irritated her. She needed to be strong, to stand on her own two feet. Depending on anyone else made one weak. And in the end one was alone again. Realization came to her. That was what she'd wanted from Alex, for him to be dependent on her. As much as she hated to admit, it hurt that he'd survived and even thrived without her.

"I'm fine." Immediately she regretted her harsh tone; still, she forced herself to stand straighter and not lean against him so much. "I'm sorry I snapped at you. It's not your fault. I just hate being sick."

"Forgiven."

"You seem to know your way around." She looked around with interest. "No more guards either."

"Ro'am and I have reached an agreement."

His cryptic answer made Cora wonder again what the two men were up to. She wished she could remember more of what had happened before she fell ill. Part of her wanted to just come out and ask. Another selfish part didn't want to disturb the accord between them.

Halfway through one of the larger caverns, a little girl of about three dashed away from a group of women.

"Lana, come back," a woman called.

The little girl ignored the command and rushed up to

Cora and Alex. Something about the child's bold gaze and fearless attitude struck a chord in Cora. Dark hair, which someone had obviously sought to tame with a colorful ribbon, straggled down her back and hung over her eyes. Dirt smudged her baby-fat cheeks. Chubby bare toes peeked from beneath the drab smock she wore. In her hands she clutched a bedraggled bouquet of weeds. She studied them with wide brown eyes, then shoved the bouquet at Cora. "For you."

When Lana lifted her arm, Cora caught sight of a familiar brand burned into the flesh of the little girl's wrist. Fresh anger surged through her.

She accepted the gift of weeds, the stems warm and damp from the toddler's grip. Tears burned the back of Cora's eyes. The child's acceptance and lack of fear touched her.

The woman who'd called out hurried forward to stand behind the little girl. She looked from Cora to Alex, then down at the girl. Her eyes widened and her fingers tightened protectively on the girl's shoulders. "Forgive her. She's newly come to us and has yet to learn caution with strangers. I'm Nala and this is Lana. We welcome you."

"Come to you from where?" Cora asked. "Isn't she yours?"

"She will be as soon as the council rules." Above Nala's veil, Cora could see love for the girl in the woman's eyes. Nala added, "The raiders brought her in several days ago."

"The raiders? Who are they? What do they do?" But Cora feared she had a good idea of the answers.

The woman's gaze shifted away. "I've said too much. You need to ask the council. Come along, Lana." She took the little girl's arm and led her back to the others, the group of women watching Cora and Alex with curiosity.

From behind the woman's skirt, Lana smiled and waved. Cora looked up at Alex and was surprised to see a look of pain and guilt on his face. "Do you know her?"

"Who, the woman? No."

"The little girl, Lana."

"No, but she reminds me of someone."

She reminded Cora of someone as well. Alex. "She's yours, isn't she?"

Alex shook his head, but refused to meet her eyes. "I don't know. Possibly."

A hard rock of unreasoned anger and jealousy formed in Cora's chest. All along her mind had known that Alex fathered children on the women in the Flock compound, but until this moment she hadn't let the knowledge invade her heart. Warm, breathing, flesh and blood evidence now shattered the lie she told herself.

Reason told her he'd had no more control of what happened to him than she had. Still, she wanted to fling herself at Alex, to vent the pain and rage churning inside her. She held herself rigid.

When they were first together, she'd thought of children as something for the future. Galaxies waited to be discovered and explored; children would come later, much later. Only, they hadn't had a future. Now Cora found that she wanted Alex's children to be her children. She envied and detested every woman who'd carried his seed. And she wanted Alex to give her what he'd given those other women.

Memories of what he'd told her before she fell ill came rushing back. "You don't plan on leaving with me, do you? Your loyalty is here, with the children you fathered, isn't it? You don't trust ELF, C.O.I.L or even me to rescue them. Instead you tried to trick me into using my ship."

"Cora, I—"

"Let me go. I need some fresh air." She pulled her arm from his and strode off.

Alex followed slowly. What could he say? Cora was right. Though logic told him his actions in the Flock compound were not fully his fault, he couldn't stave off his guilt. No matter the reason, in the last five years he'd fathered dozens, perhaps hundreds of children. All along he knew Cora had blocked that knowledge from herself. He should have told her, made her understand. But understand what—that he was a mindless stud animal?

No. She needed to know that since she'd arrived back in his life, he'd realized what he'd done. That he had to make amends. Those nameless children were his. They were human. They deserved their freedom and happiness more than he deserved his. And whatever it cost him, he'd see to their liberty and their care.

Ahead, the tunnel widened to an opening. He blinked against the glare of the light streaming in. Cora continued outside. Shoulders stiff, she stomped down the trail without care or caution. Though this was a well-used path down the mountainside, dangers lurked in the surrounding forest. He hurried after her.

She paused several minutes later at a clearing that looked out over the mountainside. Knee-high grass waved gently in the breeze. Standing well back from the edge of the cliff, she stared at the view. He came up behind her. Her body quivered slightly as her gaze fell to the valley below. She stepped back and came up against his chest. When he put his arms around her she didn't object.

"This world is beautiful," she said.

Specks of color—red, yellow and orange sprinkled throughout the lumpy green blanket of forest covering the mountainside—hinted at the coming change of season. Once the trees were bare and snow fell, the mountains would offer little protection from prying eyes. From this vantage point a person traveling the trails would be visible for miles. Harsh weather and cold would force the residents to hole up in their caves for weeks on end.

Above, white-tipped peaks pierced the fat white clouds drifting through the blue sky. Near a rocky cliff face, a pair of nesting Alavan soared on the wind, eyes sharp for unwary prey. Their shrill cries broke the silence.

"We need to talk about this."

When he spoke, Cora jerked away and crossed her arms over her chest. "About what? Your lies? Your children?"

"I've never lied to you."

"Lies of omission are still lies." She refused to look at him. "You should have told me about them."

"And what should I have told you? You knew what my life in the Flock compound was. The results had to have been obvious."

"Yeah, well, I guess I'm guilty of lying too—to myself."

Her response stirred an answering anger in him. He spun her to face him. "I didn't ask for any of this."

For a moment, body rigid, she resisted. Eyes sparking, she glared at him. "Yes, you did. You went gallivanting off into the unknown without me." Her voice broke on a sob. "You left."

His grip eased as she sagged against him. Her tears dampened his shirt. "Don't cry. I never could bear it when you cried. Your tears almost kept me from leaving."

"I didn't cry. I never cry," she argued with a hiccup.

"Then what are these?" He brushed his fingertips across her cheeks. "Raindrops?"

She rubbed her hand across her face, leaned back in his embrace and looked him in the eye. "If I had cried, would you have stayed?"

The question haunted him. "I fear I would have," he answered honestly, "but it would have been wrong. I left because I had to become my own person, not just an extension of you." The look of pain in her eyes almost made him stop. "You were the strong one. You always knew exactly what you wanted and how to get it. I loved you, but if I stayed I would have lost my identity."

Instead, he'd lost himself. Become less than human. Only

with her arrival back in his life had he reclaimed his humanity, his soul.

He waited for her reaction. It didn't come. Instead, her face was blank as she pulled out of his arms. "So, what happens next?"

"Even if they weren't my flesh and blood, how can I leave them to live that life? And what about these people? As a race, they're dying. The Flock are hounding them into extinction."

"We can take *Freedom* home and report what's happening here to ELF and C.O.I.L. We don't have the authority or the resources to handle this situation. A team will be sent back to solve the problem."

"How long will it take us to get to Earth? Do you even know where we are?"

"Well, no, not exactly. Just before I crashed, *Freedom*'s nav system went haywire. But once I get aboard I'll know and I can send a message to Earth. We could get their answer before we leave."

"I doubt it'll be that easy. Neither Earth League Force nor the Consortium are known to act quickly on any matter. It could take months, perhaps years for them to discuss the problem and even longer to decide to act on it. These people don't have that kind of time. From what Ro'am tells me, the Flock have been increasing their forays into the mountains. They're determined to wipe out the free human population."

"I won't stay here. I can't. As soon as I can I'm getting off this blasted rock."

"I won't ask you to stay. But help me to help my children." He watched her face as she struggled with her decision. "I can't do this without you."

"You mean, without *Freedom*." She paced to the edge of the plateau and stood with her back to him.

To keep from grabbing her shoulders and shaking her, Alex clenched his fists. Force would get him nowhere. Zan would demand her compliance, but he was no longer Zan; he was Alex. He couldn't compel her. She had to choose this path for herself.

"Yes, your ship plays a vital role in my plan, but it's you I need at my side."

He waited while she stared out at the mountains.

Eyes narrowed she asked, "And if I agree to go along with your plan, what do I get in return?"

"Whatever you want."

She cocked her head to one side, looked him up and down, then stepped closer until they were inches apart. "Anything?" She breathed the word against his lips.

The sudden shift in her demeanor worried him, but the sweet taste of her breath quashed his misgivings. "What is it you want?" he found the strength to ask.

Her arms slid up around his neck as she pressed herself against him, shoulder to knee. Soft and warm, her curves fit his angles. His body sprang to attention.

"You. All of you. Nothing held back."

Alex hesitated for a moment, then answered by wrapping his arms around her. She rose on her toes and met him kiss for kiss. As always when they came together the world around them disappeared. Nothing else mattered, not freedom, not control. She forgot about the Flock, the secretive Erathians, and the children that weren't hers. Everything else, even *Freedom*, could wait. She wanted him.

The fact that they stood out in the open didn't matter. She tugged at his shirt. Buttons popped and were lost in the grass. In a fever they stripped away their clothing. When she tried to pull him down to the ground he pressed the grass flat and used their garments to fashion a pallet before he lay down and pulled her on top of him.

Around Cora and Alex the grass formed a green bower that rustled softly in the breeze. The rich green scent of the broken stalks perfumed the air. Insects whirred a rhythmic song.

Warmth from his body eased the chill inside her. She wouldn't let him go. Not this time. Without him she was only half alive. Whatever it took, she'd keep him with her.

Afterwards, as they lay tangled together, Cora struggled with the pain and anger inside her. She'd forced him to give her what she thought she wanted, so why did her victory feel hollow?

Alex lay back and tucked Cora against his side. He felt her body go lax as she fell asleep. Body sated, he wanted to give in to that lure as well, but his mind churned. He cursed himself as a selfish bastard. Maran had warned him she was still weak and needed to rest. Instead, he'd given in to her demand. He'd rutted like an animal and risked impregnating her.

She stirred restlessly. From where it lay on his hip, her hand shifted and curled around his cock, which jumped to attention. She murmured something indiscernible, then settled back to sleep, his growing sex clutched in her fist.

He chuckled, but the sound held little humor. Where she was concerned he had no restraint, no pride, no shame. With an ease that frightened him, she made him lose his reason and his focus. Wherever she led he followed blindly. He lost control. If he didn't take care, she'd have him aboard *Freedom* and halfway back to Earth before he realized what had happened.

He couldn't allow that. Though he loved Cora beyond life, he had an obligation to the children he'd fathered and the women who birthed them that he couldn't forgo.

The shrill sound of a bird's cry roused Cora from sleep. Another unknown animal screamed. The sound sent a shudder through her. She stretched, blinked away the grit in her eyes and sat up. Her body ached in a pleasant after-sex way, but her heart felt heavy. She'd stolen from Alex the thing she valued above all—the freedom to choose. Lengthening shadows showed the afternoon was nearly done.

Silhouetted against the sky, Alex stood at the edge of the plateau. He'd put on his trousers and boots, but his shirt still lay beneath her. She tugged on her rumpled clothing; then, shaking the broken grass stalks from his shirt, she went to stand next to him.

A rock dislodged by her feet tumbled down the side of the cliff. Her stomach lurched as she watched its descent down the boulder-strewn slope. Images, sounds flashed in her mind: Her father, his body cartwheeling backwards, falling. The sick wet sound as he hit the rocks. His final aborted scream. Then silence. Honesty forced her to admit that that moment of helplessness had defined her as a person, made her attempt to control every aspect of her life.

She shoved Alex's shirt at him and took a hasty step back. "Here. We should be getting back."

He shrugged his arms into the shirt, but without buttons it hung open over his chest. "Have you made up your mind? Will you help me?"

"Do I have a choice? If I say no, are Ro'am and his people going to allow me to take *Freedom* and leave?"

When Alex didn't say anything, she had her answer. "I didn't think so. Yes, I'll help. What is it you need me to do?" Once inside *Freedom* she'd have more options. Until then she'd go along.

"Give me access to fly the ship."

"You're not qualified to fly her."

"I have a pilot's rating."

"That's over six years old. *Freedom* is a new class of recon ship. Her systems are far different from anything you trained on. It would take you weeks to learn her systems. Besides, where she goes, I go. I can pilot her."

"That may not be possible."

"Why not?"

"The Erathians assumed I'm the pilot."

"Why didn't you tell them the truth?"

"Ro'am's society is highly patriarchal. Though they cherish their women, they don't consider them equal to men in any way. I doubt they'd believe that you're a pilot."

"So just what do they think I'm doing aboard ship?" she demanded.

Alex's cheeks reddened, leaving it obvious who and what they thought she was.

"Why, those dirty-minded space garbage. They think I'm your whore, brought along for your amusement."

"Of course not. They believe you're my wife. In their culture, unmarried men and women don't travel together."

"If they think you're the pilot, why haven't they made you open her?"

He looked sheepish. "I led them to believe that after we crashed and just before we were captured by the Flock, we'd had a fight and you'd locked me out."

"And they bought that story? No wonder they took such good care of me. If I die their hopes die with me. Nice to know I have value even though I'm just a woman."

"You have value to me."

"Well, once I'm flying the damn ship they'll see how much I'm worth, won't they?"

"There. I *told* you they left the caves unaccompanied." Charic's strident voice carried across the clearing. "Seize them."

Cora turned to see Ro'am, Charic and the rest of the Ruling Council coming toward them. The five men were heavily armed, as were the guards who followed.

"Hold." Ro'am strode up to Alex. "I gave you the freedom of the caves. Is this how you honor my trust?"

Alex faced Ro'am without flinching. "I don't recall being forbidden to leave the caves."

The anger in Ro'am's voice and face made Cora want to

back away. Instead she met his hostile stare with one of her own, and smiled inwardly when he looked away first.

"Cora wished some fresh air." Alex slipped his arm around her waist and pulled her against his side. She wanted to reject his strength, but her legs felt rubbery.

"Right, blame me," she whispered in Standard.

"Then you're foolish instead of deceitful," Ro'am said. "The mountains are rife with peril, yet you wander them without a single weapon. You risk not only your life and that of your woman's, but my people's future."

"I need no weapons to protect myself or my woman from danger." Alex's fingers tightened on her waist. He glared at Ro'am and challenged, "Shall I prove it?"

Ro'am's fingers moved to the hilt of his sword and he took a step forward. Alex's body stiffened. He shifted so he stood in front of her.

Like heat lightning, tension sparked between the two men. As if sensing the coming storm, Charic and the other council members, as well as the guards, hung back. Cora could feel Alex struggling to keep himself in check.

"All right, that's enough." She stepped between the two men. "Quit squabbling like children. No harm's been done. We're here and we're fine. Let's return to the caves. There's a lot that needs to be discussed about your plans." She looked from one man to the other. At her words, both relaxed just enough for her to start breathing again.

Charic spoke: "This is the man you want us to trust with our future, Ro'am? He lets a woman fight his battles. I say we go with my plan to save our people instead of his. Kill him." Charic's gaze moved to Cora. Lust and something darker stared out at her. "And let his woman bear us many fine children."

The way the space slug looked at her left little doubt in her mind who he thought should father those many fine children. She shuddered in revulsion.

Without a sound of warning, Alex's control snapped. In a blur of motion he surged forward, snatched Charic's knife from its sheath and grabbed the man in a chokehold. Gasping for breath against Alex's grip, Charic's face turned red. The knife pressed against his exposed throat. His eyes bulged.

But it was Alex's eyes that held Cora's attention. Fierce and wild, Zan looked out at her. It made her question: Which was the real man—Alex or Zan? Who would remain at the end of this? Or were they each a half of the whole?

"Seize him!" one of the others shouted to the guards. They started forward. A bead of crimson appeared on Charic's neck. He gave a strangled cry.

"No! Wait!" Ro'am ordered, then said to Alex, "You've proved your point. Now let him go."

"Let him go, Alex." Cora held his gaze with hers. "Please."

For a moment he hesitated; his grip tightened. Charic whimpered. Then the fire went out of Alex's eyes and he let his arm drop. Charic staggered, clutched his throat and fell coughing to his knees. Alex stood motionless while the guards, weapons drawn, surrounded him.

They didn't stop Cora as she rushed to his side, prised the knife from his hand and tucked it in her waistband. If their lives hadn't hung in the balance, the frozen tableau might have made her smile. What would Ro'am do now? Had Alex's actions turned the man against them, undermined his authority? She glanced over at him. He stood in deep conversation with the other members of the council, except of course for Charic, who still crouched on the ground trying to catch his breath.

She couldn't help her grin of satisfaction. Turn her into a baby machine, would he? In some ways the Erath were no better than the Flock, treating the women, half their population, like livestock, ignoring what they could contribute. No wonder their society was in trouble. Alex was right. They needed help.

The question was, did she want to give it? Part of her screamed no. Their fate wasn't her problem. She just wanted to go home. Let the Consortium sort it all out. Another part argued that as a fellow human she owed them her assistance.

In the Flock compound, unsure of the status of the humans around her, she'd been able to ignore their plight. Now that she knew the truth about these people and where they'd come from, the situation was no longer black and white. And shades of gray were Alex's color palette, not hers.

A wave of physical and mental exhaustion washed over her. Legs trembling, she swayed. Alex's arm came around her waist. Reluctantly grateful for his support, she leaned into him and met his gaze. Gone was his wild look; instead, regret filled them.

She grinned at him and whispered in Standard, "Not a very diplomatic move."

He gave her a rueful smile. "It seems you can take the warrior out of the compound, but you can't take the warrior out of the man."

"So what happens now?" She looked at the guards. Weapons in hand, they eyed Alex nervously. Blades flashed in the waning sunlight. One sudden move and a mistake might be made.

"We wait and see." He directed his gaze toward where Ro'am and the others still stood in some kind of debate.

Cora strained her ears but couldn't make out their words. "What do you suppose they're arguing about?" The subtle tightening of Alex's fingers at her waist warned her that he knew more than he revealed. "I think you'd better explain."

"There are three different factions. One thinks they can attack and defeat the Verians. Given the difference in populations and strength, it's a totally improbable outcome. Another seeks to maintain the status quo, to continue to raid the Verian caravans to steal women, children and goods, and remain hidden in the mountains. This scenario is doomed to failure as well. Ro'am tells me in the last several years the Verians have increased their efforts to wipe out free humans. Even with the influx of new women and children from the raids, the human population is still dropping."

"Why didn't you tell me all this sooner? Did you think I'm too stupid to understand?"

"Would it have made any difference?"

Honesty forced her to say, "No, probably not." She didn't repeat her belief that this was a problem for the Consortium to sort out. Right or wrong, she'd already agreed to assist. "I assume your plan is where the third faction comes in."

"Yes. Ro'am believes his people's best hope of survival is to make contact and forge a treaty with the Verians. I agree. To do that he needs us, and your ship."

"All right, tell me your plan to make the Flock sit up and take notice."

"Even with the information I've gotten from the Erath about the Verians, my observation of the few compounds I've seen doesn't give me a broad enough base of knowledge to finalize my plan. I need more detailed information about the Verians, their society and government. The layout of their main city would be helpful too. Does *Freedom* have long-range scanners?"

She grinned. "Do the Flock have feathers?" Then she proceeded to list the ship's capabilities.

When they'd finished going over how they'd get the information he needed, Alex said, "Good. Once I have the data, I can formulate an exact plan."

"Does Ro'am know just how tentative this plan of yours is?" Cora glanced over at the men who were still arguing, though the arm waving had ceased. "Are you even sure they're still on board with it?"

He followed her gaze and gave a rueful grin. "No and

no. But I was top of my class in negotiation, and I'll con–vince them to go along."

"How can you be so sure?"

"Rule number one in First Contact: Doubt is the first step in defeat."

"And if you can't?"

His grin widened. "Rule number two: Always have a backup plan."

"What's yours?"

"We'll do it your way."

CHAPTER SIXTEEN

Ro'am broke away from the group and came toward Alex and Cora. "There have been enough delays. You'll show us your ship now."

Alex felt Cora's body tremble. Just before her legs gave out, he swung her up into his arms.

"Has she relapsed?" Samal hurried forward, along with the other council members. Their expressions of concern seemed genuine. Alex tightened his hold on Cora. With a small sigh she curled against him, apparently unconcerned about the council and confident in his ability to handle the situation. Her faith swelled his heart.

"We've been precipitous," Telan offered. "The hour grows late and the woman needs to rest. The ship will wait until morning."

A frown drew Ro'am's brows together as he studied Cora, but he nodded in agreement. "At first light then. Take them to their quarters. This time post a guard. And double the guard on the ship." He turned and strode away.

Alex hoped his actions hadn't destroyed what little trust he'd developed with Ro'am, but only time would tell.

The council followed.

Rubbing his throat, Charic paused in front of them. He said nothing, but his angry look promised retribution. When Alex glared at him, the man, like the rodent he was, scurried away.

"Watch out for him, he's dangerous," Cora whispered. Her warm breath brushed across Alex's bare chest. Along with a primitive need to claim and protect his woman, heat surged to his groin.

"He's an insect. If he annoys me again, I'll squash him."

"Even insects can sting." She chuckled and looked at the guards. "Time to go. The natives are getting restless."

"I'll squash them as well."

"What would it gain us?" She cupped his jaw and turned his head. "Look at them. They're just boys. Most of them don't even have whiskers yet."

She was right. Either Ro'am still trusted him or was a fool; despite their number and weapons, these beardless boys posed no threat. He believed Ro'am was no fool.

Cora curled her hand behind his neck and pulled his face to hers. "Take me to bed," she breathed into his ear. Without another word he headed back toward the caverns. The feel of Cora's breath teasing his bare flesh hurried his steps. Confused by his sudden compliance, the guards rushed to keep pace.

Weariness washed over Cora. In order to buy them more time to talk and plan, she'd faked her collapse, but now she realized the weakness wasn't feigned. Content for now to let Alex take charge, she pressed her cheek against his hard warm chest and closed her eyes.

Despite the pain she felt at his deception, the rapid thump

of his heart in her ear as his blood raced through his veins sent an answering rush through her. It was amazing: nothing he did stopped her from wanting him. She trailed the tip of her tongue across the flat disk of his nipple. It sprang to life. His fingers pressed into her thigh and the side of her breast. His pace increased.

After the door to their chamber closed with a solid thud, he strode to the bed. As he laid her down she clutched his shoulders. "Stay with me."

He kissed her fingertips. "You need to sleep."

This might be their last time together. If his plan failed they could soon be dead—or worse, captives of the Flock again. She shuddered and vowed to destroy *Freedom*, herself and Alex along with it before she allowed that to happen. And if his plan succeeded and she held him to his vow of granting her anything she asked in return, he'd end up hating her. She didn't think she would dare that.

She clutched his hand. "Don't leave me."

He didn't answer, but lay down and tucked her to his side. As much as she wanted him, her eyelids drooped. She was too weary to think.

She knew forcing him to leave this blighted planet was the right thing to do. So why did it feel so wrong?

A fist thudded against the door. Cora jerked awake. Despite her best efforts she'd fallen asleep. Regret for time wasted flickered through her.

"Get dressed. The council comes soon," a gruff voice ordered.

Cora tried to get up, but Alex's arm tightened around her waist. The noise from outside hadn't roused him. Sprawled on his stomach across the bed, he slept on.

"Wake up," she whispered in his ear.

With a growl, he pulled her against him, his intent obvious. As much as she wanted to remain where she was, Cora squirmed out of his hold. She snatched the sheet around her and stood next to the bed. Alex smiled and reached out for her.

Swatting his hand away, she scrambled for her clothing. "Get up. Ro'am and the others will be here in minutes. I don't know about you, but I don't want to be naked when they walk in."

Instantly he became alert. The sleepy, sexy shine in his eyes disappeared, replaced by a look of hard resolve that was neither Alex nor Zan, but rather a merging of the two.

They finished dressing as the door swung inward. Together Alex and Cora turned to face the council.

Ro'am stepped through the doorway and paused. His gaze went from them to the twisted sheets on the bed. His lips twitched. Refusing to meet the knowing look in his eyes, Cora ducked her head and ran her fingers through her tangled hair.

Ro'am escorted them to the great cavern where *Freedom* lay. Cora wasn't sure if Ro'am was aware of it, but his young wife followed at a discreet distance. Cora hid her grin. Apparently, Erath women weren't as cowed as their men would like to believe.

Once at the ship, barely able to contain her excitement, Cora forgot Analyn's intrepid action. Fingers itching to touch *Freedom*'s sleek silver side, Cora almost danced in place. Only Charic's hostile stare and the presence of the council kept her from shouting in glee. Instead, with a calm she didn't feel, she waited at Alex's side.

Ro'am stepped in front of them. "Show us."

She looked to Alex for approval; this was his show. He nodded.

"Open sesame." To activate the hatch on her ship it took both the simple command she'd found in an ancient book of tales and programmed into *Freedom*, and her voice. In a millisecond the ship analyzed her voice pattern and responded. The hatch slid open soundlessly and the gangway descended.

Except for Ro'am, the group gasped and took a step back. A murmur of noise went through the crowd of men, women and children gathered in the cavern. A few women, bolder than the rest, clustered to one side of the gangway and peered into the open hatch.

Without waiting for permission, Cora walked up the gangway and into the ship. Inside the hatch she turned and looked at the group. Frozen in fear and awe, no one would have time to stop her if she closed the hatch behind her. Her gaze went to Alex. He stood with his arms crossed over his chest, watching her, giving her this last opportunity of escape.

Knowing her path was set, she heaved a sigh of resignation. "Well, come on, let's get this party rolling."

Several hours later, after the council had received a tour of *Freedom* and she'd dispatched the LARCs—low-altitude recon probes—she busied herself making repairs to the ship's systems while Alex sat at the ship's command console and watched the feeds from the probes. He scribbled in furious bursts on a data pad. In between, he chewed on the end of his writing stylus. Cora grinned. His habit of chewing on whatever was handy while he worked hadn't been lost along with his memory. In school his fondness for old-style pens had often left him with ink stains on his fingers and occasionally his lips.

While Ro'am and the other council members gathered in the ship's small lounge area several feet away, she forced herself to watch the video feeds from the LARCs. As the tiny probes zipped unnoticed through the Flock city, she bit her lip to hold back her nausea. It was bad enough having to see hundreds of Flock going about their daily lives—shopping, eating, working and, generally, aside from their birdlike bodies, resembling human beings in more ways than made her comfortable—she had to view it all from a perspective of fifteen feet above the ground. She pressed her fingertips into the counter behind her to distract her from her growing vertigo and panic.

"Verian society is more complex than I first supposed." Alex leaned back in the command chair and swiveled around to face the council.

Grateful for the reprieve, Cora turned with him.

"Though theirs is a male-dominated culture, its population is predominately female—a hundred to one ratio in favor of females. Definitely not a natural occurrence."

This was the Alex she remembered, the academic who found the inner workings of human and alien cultures so absorbing. As he lectured the council—whom aside from Charic listened intently—on Flock society, the scholar subdued the warrior.

"From what I can tell, each city is made up of hundreds of individual compounds or cells. Each cell consists of a dominant male and his females. It also appears that the Flock control the planet. I didn't see any evidence of another intelligent species. We'll approach the capital city to make contact."

He tapped the stylus against his chin. "There's a strict class system in place. Each cell is a specialized guild. One guild makes cloth, another provides transportation services, and still another bakes bread and so on until all functions of society are covered. This is an efficient method of running a society, but also a risky one. If one cell is damaged beyond its ability to recover, the city as a whole suffers, at least until a new cell can be created to fill the gap. And if the damaged cell is critical to running the city, the city may never recover. Adaptability is often the key to a species' survival. Extreme specialization limits adaptability."

"How can you tell all this from just a few hours of observation?" Samal asked.

"Because I understand the Verian language, and I'm a

trained xeno-anthropologist as well as a First Contact Agent. Plus, I also spent several months as a captive in a Verian compound. These things give me the expertise to evaluate and form a valid opinion." Without sounding like a braggart, he stated simple facts. "Any other questions?"

Cora grinned at the slightly dazed look on Samal's face.

"A male's status in Verian society is determined by the number of females he can support, and that number is interdependent on his compound's productivity in their chosen specialization. A delicate balancing act."

"Sort of which came first, the chicken or the egg," Cora quipped. The blank expressions on their faces indicated that neither Alex nor the council got the joke. She shrugged and fell silent.

Alex continued his lecture. "Because the females vastly outnumber the males, it's the females who carry out most of the day-to-day activities that maintain Verian society. They provide all the labor. Even the governing is handled by the females."

"How is that possible?" Baylan asked. "Women don't have the bodies for physical labor or the mental capacity for business and trade."

Cora coughed to hide her snort of disgust at these people's archaic attitudes.

"Women—females, whether they be Verian or human—are capable of as much if not more than men," Alex responded, then continued with his lecture. "Each cell selects females to sit on the governing council. The number per cell is determined by the size of the cell, as well as its productivity. Once on the council they formulate and pass laws, handle disputes between cells and make judgments. Though inside their individual cells they are completely under the control of the dominant male and have little power to rule their own lives, while on the ruling council they determine the direction and fate of the entire society. Fascinating."

Ro'am walked over to Alex. "Yes, but is it helpful?"

"Extremely. I'll have to adjust my plan to merge this new data." He plucked the stylus from between his teeth and wrote some more. "The makeup of our contact team must be precise. One male and at least a half a dozen females should be right," he muttered. Cora doubted anyone besides her heard him.

Ro'am leaned toward the screen. "There don't appear to be many humans in the city. Why not? The compound nearby is filled with them." He turned and stared at Alex, and Cora bit her lip as she waited for Alex's answer. Did Ro'am suspect his identity?

Alex looked directly at Ro'am and said in an even tone, "To the Verians, humans are livestock. This local compound has specialized in the breeding of humans for a specific purpose. I'm sure you're aware of the function they serve."

Ro'am searched his face, then straightened. "Yes, we are."

"What I've discovered from my observations is that this function is not generally approved of by Verian society. In fact, there's a strong movement in place to ban it entirely."

This information surprised Cora, and caused a flurry of discussion among the council.

"Does that mean the Verians realize that humans aren't animals?" Ro'am asked.

"No. Just the opposite. To them humans are animals, difficult and expensive to own, dangerous to handle and not of much practical use. The movement to ban human fighting is based more on the Verians' sense of compassion to lesser creatures, rather than any true understanding of our nature."

"Verians have shown us little in the way of kindness. I doubt they have the capacity." Ro'am's eyes darkened with restrained emotion. "Not only have they enslaved humans for generations, they destroy our meager crops and leave us to starve. They attack our encampments, steal our women and children and slaughter our men either immediately or . . ." He paused and fixed Alex with another hard stare. "In their fighting arenas."

Cora braced herself for Alex's reaction. Ro'am knew more about Alex than he'd let on. Usually he managed to hide his anger better, but occasionally, like now, it slipped out of his control. Aside from a flicker of emotion in his eyes, Alex didn't react.

"Why don't they see us as intelligent beings?" Telan's question broke the tension between the two men. "We wear clothing, grow crops, and use tools much as they do."

"They don't see these things as evidence of intellect," Alex answered. "To them communication is the only indicator of intelligence. Until the language barrier is broken, I'm afraid there's no possibility of peaceful coexistence between our species."

"Then why didn't the Flock accept us as thinking beings when we spoke to them?" Cora couldn't resist asking.

"As I said to you before: because to do so put their way of life at risk. This nearby compound makes its living by breeding fighting humans. Without humans they have no livelihood. Also, no species wants to believe what they do is cruel or heartless. For this compound to accept humans as an equal, intelligent species would shatter their sense of who they are. That's why our approach must be made to the Verian main city. The Verians there don't have their livelihood invested in us, so they'll be more likely to believe what they hear and see."

"Bah! As if we want to coexist with them," Charic said. "I say we should wipe them off the face of the planet."

"Charic, your opinion has been noted," Ro'am said. "But the council has ruled on this. We don't have the strength or numbers to defeat the Verians. Our only hope of survival is to forge a treaty with them. How do we learn to communicate with the Verians?" he asked Alex.

"For the moment you can't. Cora and I both have translator chips imbedded in our brains that allow us to understand and speak the Verian language. Once Earth League Force is made aware of the situation here, they'll send in a team and supplies. Then you'll be outfitted with translator chips."

"How long will that be?" Ro'am asked.

Alex looked to Cora to answer.

Once aboard, and after she'd dispatched the LARCs, she'd gone to work on the nav system. It hadn't taken her long to get it up and running, but neither Alex nor Ro'am was going to like the answer.

"Anywhere between twelve months and five years."

"What?" Alex and Ro'am said in unison.

"In *Freedom* it'll take about five months to reach the nearest Consortium base. I figure it'll be a minimum of two months before they can reach a decision and send out a team, then another five months for them to get back." She didn't mention that she doubted a ruling of this sort would be made in anything like two months. Things like this often took years.

"The ship doesn't leave," Ro'am stated flatly.

Cora stated the alternative: "A long-range message will get to Earth League Force headquarters in about four and a half years. Then it'll take them at least six months to get here."

"Then your plan and our hopes are doomed." Ro'am's shoulders sagged.

"Not so," Alex assured him. "Cora and I can communicate with the Verians. We can forge the treaty for you."

She glanced at him sharply. He didn't think she planned on staying around any longer than she had to, did he? Five more years on this rock was not an option.

"There's an alternative. *Freedom*'s MAT—matter absorption transformation unit—can produce translator chips," she blurted before she could change her mind. The less the

Erathians knew about *Freedom* and what she could do, the better chance she had of taking her out from under their noses. Even without complete knowledge of the things *Freedom* could provide, they'd realized her value. But she wanted to get off this planet and take Alex with her.

"Then do so," Ro'am said.

"Just one small problem. Neither Alex nor I have the skill or the knowledge to implant the things."

"Does *Freedom* have a medical database?" Alex asked.

"Of course. Her computer is top of the line and completely up to date." She couldn't help bragging.

"Perhaps with some assistance, healer Maran can learn to perform the task."

"I'll send for him." Ro'am gave orders to a guard, who hurried off. "Now tell us your plan."

Alex laid out his plan for contacting the Verians. He, along with Cora and five Erathian women, would take *Freedom* and enter the city. Before landing he'd fire *Freedom*'s laser cannon into the air as a show of force and power. Once in the city they would demand a meeting with the Ruling Council and attempt to start negotiations for a treaty.

Charic jumped up. "No!" The other council members started to argue.

Ro'am held up his hand. The group fell into an uneasy silence and waited. "Charic is right in this. We can't allow women to go along. It's too dangerous," Ro'am said. "I and other men will accompany you."

"It won't work," Alex said. "The Verians will expect a dominant male to be accompanied by an entourage of his females. A male without any females commands no respect. They won't understand a group of men. In their culture males rarely gather together. And when they do, the usual result is fighting."

"Sort of like human males," Cora said.

"We'll dress as women," Ro'am said.

Cora laughed out loud. All eyes turned to her, and she sputtered, "Even in the tentlike dresses and ridiculous veils you make your women wear, I doubt any of you could fool a Flock."

"Perhaps not, but the decision is final. We'll not risk any women, not even you, in this endeavor. Guards!" he called.

"Ro'am." Alex stood. "Be reasonable. Going into the Verian city with a group of men is tantamount to suicide. In their council it's the females who do the negotiating; Verian males are not allowed to participate. At least allow Cora to come along."

"There's nothing unreasonable about safeguarding women, yours included. Thank you for your suggestions, but this will be done the way we decide or not at all." Ro'am turned away as the guards crowded into the ship. "Take him to his chamber and lock her in the single women's quarters," he ordered, then said to Alex, "Think on your options overnight. We'll meet again in the morning."

All Cora's rage and frustration came to a boiling point. She snatched up the laser pistol she'd slipped out of its compartment earlier and pointed it at the two guards as they came toward her. "Stay back or I'll fire!" Though they seemed unsure of what she held, they hesitated and looked to Ro'am for instructions.

"Don't look at him. I'm the one with the weapon. Alex, get them off my ship and we'll get the hell out of here."

When he didn't respond, she turned to see Ro'am standing with his knife pressed against Alex's throat. "Drop the weapon, Cora," the man said. "I don't wish to hurt either of you, but I will if I have to."

Alex stood perfectly still. The look of despair in his eyes defeated Cora. She knew Zan could overpower Ro'am and fight his way free, but in the resulting chaos she and others might be injured or killed. Alex wouldn't take that risk.

For a second she wished for Zan back; he wouldn't hesitate. Then she laid her pistol on the console.

"Take her away," Ro'am told the guards. "I'll see to the man myself."

She submitted meekly as the guards escorted her away from Alex and *Freedom*.

Alex remained motionless as the guards and the rest of the council filed out of the ship, leaving him alone with Ro'am. The blade nicked his skin before Ro'am pulled it away and sheathed it.

"Sit," Ro'am said.

"I prefer to stand."

Ro'am shrugged. "As you will." He crossed his arms over his chest, leaned back against the console and studied Alex. "Do you think me a fool?"

Alex raised an eyebrow but didn't answer.

"The others have their suspicions about your tale, but I don't. I know who and what you are." The desire for vengeance burned in his eyes.

"If you know the truth, why do you hesitate to kill me?" Alex wanted to ask forgiveness, but Ro'am didn't appear interested in apologies. Nor would an apology suffice. Only by helping these people survive could he find peace within himself.

Ro'am sighed. "Who and what you were doesn't matter. Only what you can do for my people concerns me now." His ability to put aside his own needs spoke volumes about his character and devotion to his people, and Alex was impressed.

"Nothing I do or say can change the past. If you let me, I can make peace between your people and the Verians, but not if you insist on doing it your way."

The fire died in Ro'am's eyes. he took a deep breath and said, "Tomorrow you'll take this ship and a contingent of men and put your plan into action. If you refuse, you'll be judged a danger to our community and executed."

"And Cora?"

"She'll be given in marriage to the first eligible man who applies for her hand." Ro'am paused and eyed Alex in speculation. "I believe Charic is next in line for a spouse."

Alex's fists clenched in fury at the thought of Cora in Charic's hands. "She'll chew him up and spit him out," he growled.

"Perhaps." Ro'am grinned, again the diplomat. "But, although we dislike using it, we have the means and the will to keep a woman amenable. Our survival as a people depends on it."

"And when your way fails and I don't return, what happens to her then?"

"I will see that she is given in marriage to a man more suited to her spirit and temperament."

"If such a man exists." Alex tamped down his need to shake sense into Ro'am. "What of this ship? It has much to offer in the way of knowledge and technology, but without its pilot you won't learn it easily."

"Our scholars will study and glean what they can. As for the rest, we can't miss what we've never had." Ro'am straightened. "What is your choice?"

He had no true choice. If he refused, Ro'am would have him executed. He could kill Ro'am and attempt an escape, but despite his strength and superior skills the odds were against him. His death and Ro'am's would leave Cora undefended and the Erathians worse off than before their arrival. And his children would have no champion. He had one slim chance.

"I'll attempt first contact with the Verians under two conditions."

"You're in no position to demand conditions."

"Mine are simple and easily granted. One, I go alone. Neither you nor any other men accompany me."

Ro'am stroked his chin and studied Alex. "Agreed. And your second request?"

"If I don't return, you'll allow Cora to chose her own mate."

"This condition is harder, but I'll see it done. Do I have your word?"

"You'd trust my word? Why?"

"Do I have another option? My men can't fly this ship or speak to the Verians, so they couldn't risk doing you any harm. In the end they'd be at your mercy. Why risk their lives?"

"I could just fly off." Alex watched expressions flicker across Ro'am's normally impassive face: doubt and fear, then finally determination.

"Only a coward abandons the woman he loves. And whatever else you might be, you're no coward." He held out his hand. "Your word?"

Alex clasped the man's hand and nodded. They left the ship together.

Back in his chamber, guilt ate at Alex. Ro'am was wrong. History had proved him a coward. Once before, fear had sent him running from Cora, when he'd feared he could never create an identity while she was around. Now, a different sort of fear was making him do so again.

He'd made a pledge he couldn't honor. Even if he wished to attempt First Contact alone, his examination of *Freedom*'s console told him that Cora was correct; without further instruction he couldn't fly the ship—at least, not without crashing it again. Come morning Cora would lose both her ship and her freedom. His inevitable death counted for little.

CHAPTER SEVENTEEN

Oblivious to the warm fire burning in the hearth, the tantalizing aroma of roasting meat and fresh-baked bread, Cora paced the comfortable single women's quarters in short angry strides.

"Stupid. Stubborn. Wrong-headed. *Men*." Her words kept time with her steps. With each pass, as if she were some exotic wild beast thrust into their presence, the girls flinched away in prudent caution.

A hand touched her shoulder. Startled out of her tirade, Cora swung her arm at the offender. At the last moment she reached out and kept the girl from falling.

"Analyn. I'm sorry. You caught me off guard. Are you all right? Did I hurt you?"

"I'm fine. You did me no harm," Analyn assured her.

"What are you doing here? I thought this was the single women's quarters."

"It is. We came to speak with you." She pointed to another woman. Cora recognized Nala, the woman who'd been with the little girl, Lana. "Sit with us, please." Analyn patted the seat beside her. "I and my sisters wish to know what's happening."

Nodding in agreement, their fear of Cora forgotten, the girls crowded near. Cora looked at the dozen or so girls ranging in age from early teens to the oldest of twenty. Here in the single women's quarters they had shed their robes and veils, revealing the real, vibrant young women beneath. "You're all sisters?"

Analyn laughed. "Only in the sisterhood of all women."

Women? Hah! They were girls, mere babies. Kept in a gilded cage by their fathers and brothers as they waited to be sold to the highest bidder as brood mares. In their treatment of women, the Erathians were little better than the Flock.

Analyn leaned toward Cora. "Is it true you and the warrior came from the sky in that silver transport? That on your world women are equal to men?"

"Yes, tell us," another girl prompted. "The men tell us little or nothing. We only know what we glean through gossip and eavesdropping."

"They think us too simpleminded and weak to understand," a third added.

"They make decisions that affect our lives without consulting us." Tears wetted Nala's cheeks. "The council ruled against my husband's petition for Lana and gave her to another clan. They claimed our clan already has its quota of female children from the raids, but the truth is that the other man offered more in trade. It's not fair."

Cora smelled a rebellion brewing. Apparently Erathian women were not as meek and biddable as their men believed. She grinned as a plan grew in her mind. Alex wasn't the only one who could make treaties and forge alliances.

"Ladies, ladies." She held up her hand. "One at a time. I'll answer all your questions."

She quickly explained the situation to the women, who caught on quickly. Then she used everything she'd ever learned from Alex about handling people to sway the women to side with her against their men. Awestruck, they listened as she spun them tales of Earth and the freedom women had there.

It didn't take much convincing. In a short while she had them agreeing to help her, and she laid out her hastily conceived plan.

"Are you sure you understand how dangerous what we're going to do is?" she asked Analyn one last time. Despite her young age, the girl was the obvious leader of the others, maybe because of her position as wife to the head of the council, but more likely due to her strong personality. Doubts about her plan churned in Cora's gut. Did she have the right to ask them to take this risk? She gave one last warning. "A lot can go wrong. If we're caught, your men will be angry. You'll face punishment from them. You could lose what little freedom you have now."

"It isn't true freedom if someone gives it to you. Freedom must be taken," Analyn said.

Cora wondered how the girl had gained such wisdom at so early an age. "And if my plan succeeds the stakes are even higher—death or a life as a Flock breeder."

The girl smiled grimly. "I may be young, but I'm not stupid. Though Ro'am's a good man and I love him now, I didn't come to him by my choice. My father arranged the match. As did or will the fathers or brothers of all of us here. We wish more from life for our daughters." Determination rang in her young voice.

"Okay then." Cora glanced at the women, for despite their tender years she revised her previous opinion. These were women, not girls. "Everyone know what they need to do?"

She watched in satisfaction as the women nodded in agreement. She pulled the hood of her robe up to cover her pale hair, and for the first time since arriving among these people secured a veil across her face. "Let's go."

The plan went off without a hitch. Cora and eight helpers slipped out of the women's quarters undetected. First they went to the ship. One young girl served as a decoy. She offered the guards mugs of warmed ale, to ward off the chill of standing guard in the cavern through the night, but it was her flirtatious demeanor that lured them from their post at the end of the gangway. While they were distracted, Analyn and four other women slipped aboard *Freedom* and hid where Cora had directed in the cargo hold.

At the same time, Cora and two other women made their way toward Alex's chamber. This time the proferred ale was laced with a sedative. When the two guards slumped unconscious against the wall, Cora helped the women drag them out of sight and change into their clothing. She'd chosen two of the larger women for this role, but even over their own clothing the guards' shirts and trousers still sagged on them. Their disguises would only fool from a distance. Looking at each other, they giggled.

"Ladies, behave," she chided, choking back her own laughter. "Stars help us if anyone comes along. You two are less likely to pass as male than they could pass as female."

"Don't worry. We'll be fine. See your man." Nala smiled and urged her on.

On impulse Cora reached out and hugged the woman. "Thank you." She opened the door and slipped inside.

Arms behind his head, Alex lay on the bed staring sightlessly at the rock ceiling. Sleep wouldn't come. He didn't even look up when the door clicked open and shut. What could Ro'am want now, he wondered without true interest. The intruder stood silent, his soft, rapid breathing not sounding like Ro'am's. Innate curiosity won out over forced apathy, and Alex turned to see who'd come to pay him a visit.

A woman hovered just inside the door. Her traditional

Erathian garb, enveloping robe and veil, hid her identity, but he recognized her all the same. He bolted to his feet.

"Cora."

With a cry she rushed into his arms and buried her face against his chest.

"How did you get here? Why—"

Without pausing to remove her veil, she stopped his words with her mouth. They kissed through the fine lace until he couldn't resist the urge to taste her. His lips never left hers as he tugged the veil free. The damp cloth fell to the floor. He plunged his tongue deep into her mouth. All the while their hands worked feverishly to free themselves from their clothing.

Good sense told him to stop, to question her, to find out how she'd gotten here and why, but fate had given them one last chance to be together, and he wouldn't throw it away.

Bedding twisted around her waist, damp thighs bare and chilled, Cora forced herself to move out of Alex's embrace. As she attempted to pull on her clothing, she looked down at him sprawled on his back on the narrow bed. His shirt still hung off his shoulders, but he was bare from the waist down. Damp with sweat, his dark hair clung to his forehead. She licked her suddenly dry lips. Unabashed, he grinned up at her.

"Get dressed. We haven't much time." She tossed him his trousers.

She used the moments while he shrugged into his clothing to silently berate herself and gather her composure. Where he was concerned she had no sense of restraint; she lost all control. They'd wasted precious time, but no matter how she tried she couldn't regret it. She could no more resist him than a starving man could resist a feast. Like that man needed food to survive, Cora needed Alex to sustain her. When the rustling stopped she turned back to face him.

"How did you get here?" he asked.

"With a little help from some new friends."

"Why, besides the obvious"—he looked at the bed—"are you here?"

She ignored his satisfied grin and the warmth flooding her face. "To keep you from getting yourself killed. Listen, here are the commands to reprogram *Freedom* to accept you as a pilot." She rattled off the sequence of commands.

"That's fine, but I don't think I can fly her."

"That's why I'm here. To give you a crash course."

He groaned and sank onto the bed. "I don't think crash is the word you want to use."

"While I was working on *Freedom*'s systems I made a few modifications. With a bit of coaching you'll be able to fly her much as you would an older-style ship."

"It's been over six years since I've flown anything. I'm not sure those memories are intact." Taking her hands in his, he tugged her between his knees and met her gaze. She could see the battle raging inside him.

Finally he heaved a sigh, released her hands and said, "Take *Freedom* and leave. Go back to Earth."

"What about you? The Erathians?" She hesitated—saying it made them real—then added, "Y-your children?"

"I'll do what I can to help the Erathians survive until you can bring back help."

"What about your plan?"

"As it stands now, it's doomed to failure."

"Then we'll leave now, together." She tugged him to his feet.

"I can't."

"Why not?"

"I gave Ro'am my word."

Men and their honor. "Why on earth would you do that?" She threw up her hands. She didn't have time to argue with him. "Never mind. It doesn't matter. What matters is, if you go aboard *Freedom* and can't fly her, the Erathians will kill you."

"My fate doesn't matter. Take *Freedom* and leave now."

"Whatever you say," she lied. "But just in case for some reason I can't, listen closely. We only have time to go through this once."

In the next half hour, she gave him a crash course on how to fly *Freedom*. Afterward it took every ounce of willpower she possessed to leave the stubborn man behind; she nearly succumbed to the urge to feed him some of that sedative and drag him bodily aboard *Freedom*. Common sense told her that plan wouldn't work. Once he was unconscious she doubted she and the two other women could drag him all the way to the ship, distract the guards yet again and get him aboard without being discovered.

When he reached for her, she sidestepped. If she let him touch her again, she knew she'd never be able to leave.

Outside the room she and the pseudo guards redressed the real guards and dragged them back into their positions. When they woke and found Alex still locked inside the room she didn't think they'd reveal their dereliction of duty. Satisfied she'd done as much as she could, she sent the women back to their quarters and moved forward with the rest of her plan.

Alex sat through the remainder of the night in anticipation of hearing an alarm raised when Cora took off in *Freedom*. The alarm never came. She hadn't made it.

The only thing left for him to do was honor his word to Ro'am, and when the Verians captured him, make sure *Freedom* didn't fall into their hands and give them the means to destroy the Erathians. He straightened his clothing, bound his hair at the nape of his neck and waited.

Ro'am arrived. "Are you ready?"

"Yes."

Ro'am, along with two strangely subdued guards, escorted him out of the room. When the corridor split Alex paused. One way led to where *Freedom* was held; the other led to the living quarters and Cora. "Before I leave, may I see Cora?" he asked.

"I anticipated your request, but the women have informed me that she refuses to see you."

"Or you're preventing her from doing so," Alex challenged.

Ro'am ran his palm around the back of his neck. "No. I wouldn't deny her the opportunity to wish you farewell and good luck."

"Then why won't she see me?"

"I don't know. The women are acting strange. None have left their quarters. Instead they remain cloistered with your woman. Even Analyn has joined them." He shook his head and straightened. "The action of a few women is unimportant. Come. The council waits at your ship."

Every instinct in Alex's body screamed that something was wrong, but he couldn't determine what it might be or what he could do about it, so he followed Ro'am.

As Ro'am had said, the council waited at the foot of *Freedom*'s gangway. Though they'd been inside the day before, now they eyed the ship with mistrust. Alex grinned. Their fear might have something to do with the fact that Cora had blithely told them that once the hatch closed only the pilot could open it. They obviously didn't want to get trapped inside and forced to ride along into the Verian city.

A crowd of people milled around the cavern, but women were noticeably absent. Without waiting for permission or further direction, Alex started up the gangway. To his surprise, Ro'am followed close behind. Standing in the opening the man held out his hand. "I wish you luck and divine guidance in your endeavor."

Before Alex could respond a voice cried out, "Close! Abracadabra!"

Just before the hatch clanged shut and crushed the man, Alex grabbed Ro'am's outstretched arm and yanked him inside the ship. Together they tumbled to the floor.

Stunned by Ro'am's weight, Alex blinked at the sight of feet surrounding his head and torso. He shoved at Ro'am and the man shifted off of him. They scrambled to their feet. A group of women, eyes wide, mouths open in O's of surprise, stared at them.

Ro'am recovered his dignity first. "What's the meaning of this?" he demanded, then sputtered as he recognized his wife. "Analyn? What's going on? Why are you women here?"

"Because one of them has more brains than all you men put together." Hands on her hips, Cora glared at them. "I told them about the suicide mission you were forcing on Alex and the probable results. They decided to take matters into their own hands."

"Analyn, come to me. And you"—Ro'am pointed at Cora—"open this door at once."

"No," the two women said in unison.

"W-what?" Mouth gaping, Ro'am stared at Analyn and struggled to regain his self-control. "Alex, control your woman."

Cora glared. Alex laughed. "This is your battle. Keep me out of it."

Ro'am turned his attention back to Analyn. "You dare to defy your lawful husband? I've never raised a hand to you, but you push the bounds of propriety."

"Hit me, husband and I'll make you wish you'd never been born." Like a little cat, she spat back at him.

The other women moved out of the line of fire. Ro'am wasn't as wise. He took a softer tone and attempted a different tactic. "You'd risk your life and leave your daughter without a mother."

"I'm doing this so that she can have a life. So *I* can have a life."

The fight seemed to drain out of Ro'am. He looked at his wife as if seeing her for the first time. "What of your life with me? Does it count for nothing?"

Analyn touched Ro'am's arm. "I love you and our daughter, but I want a say in our future."

"I wish only to protect you. You"—he looked at her and the other women who watched the exchange silently—"are our future. Without you we'll cease to exist. We must see to your safety and well-being."

"Even at the cost of our freedom, our very souls?" She moved closer and took his hands inside her smaller ones. "Fear has driven you and the other men to imprison us in cotton-lined cages. We have no liberty, no choices. Our lives are controlled first by our fathers and brothers, and then by our husbands and sons. In many ways our lives are no better than that of the Verian slaves. We wish for more."

As Alex listened, understanding dawned. How like Ro'am and Analyn's were Cora's and his differences. Both wished to protect the other, while neither willingly relinquished control. Instead of embracing the other's strengths, they spent their energy fighting their own weaknesses.

Now, in her unique way, Cora had taken control of the situation and made it her own. He'd asked for six women and she'd provided them.

"As much as I hate to interrupt your argument, Ro'am, you'll need to speak to your people before they hurt themselves trying to get into *Freedom*," Cora said. Alex became aware of the muffled sound of objects striking *Freedom's* hull. The words of the shouts didn't penetrate.

"Let me out and I'll do so."

Cora chuckled. "Nice try, but no chance." She walked over to the console and pressed the com-board. "Talk. They'll hear you." She had shed the Erathian robe and veil, along with the skirt and blouse they'd provided her, and now wore a flightsuit and space boots. The sleek silver material hugged her curves from neck to ankle in a way that made Alex's mouth water.

"I'm your prisoner," Ro'am said. "What would you have me say?"

"Not a prisoner. More an uninvited guest. Tell them what you like." Cora shrugged her shoulders and leaned against the console.

The tightening of her jaw told Alex that Ro'am wasn't part of her plan, but once the man understood he had no choice, his presence would come in handy.

He could see Ro'am fighting an inner battle. The man's basic instinct insisted he use superior strength to solve this dilemma. But using force against women went against every code he lived by. His hand hovered over the hilt of his sword, then fell away in unspoken defeat.

Alex took pity on the man. "Tell them you're coming with me to make sure things go as planned."

"You'd have me lie?"

"It won't be a lie if you make the decision to join us," Cora snapped. "Otherwise, just tell them they'll find you at the plateau where they originally found my ship. I'll drop you off there on our way."

Ro'am pulled Analyn to his side. "It seems I have little choice. I'll not leave my wife unprotected."

"Good, then tell them and we'll get this show on the road." Cora waved a hand at the console.

After Ro'am calmed the Erathians outside, Cora seated herself at the console. Ro'am and the women found seating in the lounge portion of the ship just behind the bridge. Alex took the copilot's seat. Using instrumentation, Cora glided *Freedom* through the cave and into the sky.

"Fly low. And open the viewscreen," Alex said.

"Why? Sub-orbital will get us there in a third of the time."

"I need to see how this world is laid out."

"You can tell that from the instruments."

"I don't have the talent to convert numbers and graphics into a mental picture of the land below. Besides, your passengers need time to adjust to flying. They're turning a delightful shade of green. I doubt they're ready for weightlessness." *Freedom*'s gravity generator didn't work in sub-orbit; it took the vacuum of space for it to kick in.

One of the women let out a distressed moan and dashed for the ship's head. Cora gave a reluctant nod and activated the viewscreen. Once their eyes and inner ears adjusted, the others seemed to enjoy the view.

Below them, the planet flew by. Cora resolutely kept her eyes on the console as she maneuvered *Freedom* through the craggy mountains to the planet's broad plains.

At first Alex divided his time between reviewing the LARC videos, adjusting his first contact plan and watching the viewscreen, but soon the outside view captured his entire attention.

Though filled with danger, this world claimed its share of untamed beauty. From this height the forests turned to lush rolling green blankets, the rivers to twisting ribbons of shimmering silver, and the lakes to swatches of crystalline blue. A huge herd of shaggy beasts grazing in an endless field of wild grass turned the area from a dusty green-gold to mottled brown and black. On a rocky outcropping overlooking the plain, he caught sight of a pride of Zanthers sunning themselves. Flocks of brightly colored birds swooped against a cloudless blue sky.

Watching this untamed world, he could understand why some people were drawn to the challenge of new colonization.

The occasional Verian compound they flew past drew gasps of fear from the women. Alex watched the compounds slip by, gleaning as much information as he could from those brief glimpses.

After a few hours the women lost interest in the view,

and tired from their long night, dozed off. Eyes closed, their argument forgotten for the moment, Analyn leaned trustingly against Ro'am.

"I'm going to talk with him," Alex told Cora.

Eyes glued to the instrument console, she didn't look up. "Good idea. See if you can get him to be reasonable. He's agreed to go along, but somehow I don't think he's going to be happy about Analyn trotting around in a Verian city."

"I'll try, but his protective instinct toward women runs deep." Alex himself understood the need to keep the woman he loved safe, even when she didn't need or want him to.

"Let's just hope he uses his brain to make decisions rather than his . . . gut."

Alex shook his head. "Where women are concerned, men rarely think with their brains."

Cora's soft chuckle sent a shaft of longing to the center of his thoughts. Sunlight caught in the tousled gold of her hair and glinted off the metallic silver of her flight suit. Her strong, slender fingers moved tirelessly over the console as she made adjustments in speed, altitude and direction. She nibbled absently on her lower lip. Alex wanted, *needed* to get her alone one last time before they attempted contact with the Verians. Once they entered the city they might never have another chance.

Like stinging insects, doubts about his plan and what it might cost Cora, the others and him, swarmed into his mind. Each stabbed at his self-assurance. But he had no choice; he'd given his word to make this attempt. Was Ro'am right? Was he wrong to put Cora and these women at risk? Maybe, but without them he was destined to fail.

Oblivious to his attack of self-doubt, Cora continued, "Well, he needs to be convinced to let Analyn participate. Without her I don't think the other women are up to the task."

"Won't they follow you?"

"Maybe, but the confidence isn't there. I'm a stranger to them. They trust Analyn. She's the strong one, their leader. With me in charge, at a critical moment they might falter."

Stunned by Cora's willingness to give up control, Alex leaned back in his seat. The choice wasn't and had never been his to make. Like her, he couldn't control everything. But he'd take charge of what he could and make it work. Determination banished doubt.

Cora didn't seem to notice his silence.

"When you're done with him, send him over here. I want to brief him on *Freedom's* systems."

"Is that wise?"

"Probably not. But if anything happens to you and me, someone should know how to lock *Freedom* up so the Flock don't get their hands on her."

"Good point. Maybe he's capable of learning some basic flying as well."

She grinned at him. "Better not push our luck."

The sun dipped below the horizon as *Freedom* settled without a noticeable jolt in an isolated area several miles outside the Verian city limits. Night and a swale of land hid the ship from all but the most curious eyes.

In the lounge area Alex sat in deep discussion with Ro'am. Though they didn't appear to be at each other's throats, neither were they in complete accord. Content to leave the problem to Alex, Cora studied the women curled together on the benches like tired children. She'd recruited them. They were her responsibility.

She stretched. Her stomach let out a loud rumble. Alex looked over and smiled. Unashamed of her bodily needs, she grinned back.

Another, stronger need rolled over her. The sudden urge to dump Ro'am and the women out the hatch and have

Freedom to herself and Alex left her weak with longing. She'd never realized just how big and empty her bunk on *Freedom* was. The look in his eyes said he felt the same. Heat coiled in her belly, her nipples rasped against the soft material of her flight suit and she felt the tingle of desire.

With effort, she pulled her gaze away from his and re-ordered her priorities. If all went well, soon enough she'd have Alex and *Freedom* to herself. If not . . . A shudder went through her.

She stiffened her spine. Doubts and fears had no place in her life. For now she had more important issues to deal with. First off: food.

"Ladies." She clapped her hands together. "Time to rise and shine. There's work to be done."

The next few hours passed in a blur of activity. Cora organized and directed the women in assembling a simple meal using the MAT unit. In the morning she'd have to see to replenishing the raw material the unit required to function. Her scanners indicated that several feet below ground lay a wealth of minerals. Along with a tank of water and some vegetation, the unit would be primed to provide anything they programmed in.

Once the women got over the ease of food preparation—one simply typed in one's order and the MAT unit spit it out—they all settled down at the table Cora lifted from its storage place in the floor to a dinner of succulent roast beef, steaming fresh vegetables, crisp salad, warm crusty bread and wine. She doubted any of them truly understood that what they ate was merely rearranged atoms. As a mechanic and engineer she knew the machinery and science behind the MAT unit; she could take it apart and put it back together with her eyes closed, but even to her it seemed like magic— a magic that she'd sorely missed in both the Flock compound and the Erathian caves.

The women chatted, adapting easily to their change in

circumstances, seemingly unconcerned about the dangerous task they'd undertaken. Ro'am on the other hand sat silent.

Seated across the table from her, Alex raised his glass. The warmth of his smile told her he remembered his favorite foods and thanked her for them. Heat that had nothing to do with the wine she'd drunk swirled inside her.

Finally, as the reality of where they were and what they were about to attempt sank in, the women's conversation wound down. Exhaustion and growing fear left them pale. To Cora they appeared nothing more than little girls playing at being adults.

Ro'am put his arm around Analyn. She rested her head on his shoulder. The other women fell quiet and tension built. The chin of the youngest girl—probably no more than fifteen—started to quiver. Another brushed her fingers over her eyes. Something needed to be done or this mission would end before it began, but Cora was at a loss.

Ro'am stared as Alex began to clear the table. The women reacted immediately. This was something they understood: Men didn't do household chores. They pushed Alex back into his seat and took over the task. With Cora's direction—another nice benefit of having a MAT unit—all the leftovers, plates included, got fed back into the unit to be recycled. In minutes they had cleaned away the mess; then they arranged the lounge to provide sleeping areas for everyone. Cora helped by obtaining bedding, sleeping attire and personal hygiene products. Ro'am and Alex retreated to the bridge chairs and watched in male fascination as the women reordered the ship into a homey space.

Soon all the women except for Cora and Analyn were bedded down. Cora dimmed the lighting and retreated to the bridge with Analyn, Ro'am and Alex. Like a contented kitten, Analyn curled into Ro'am's lap. Though Cora longed to do the same with Alex, instead she leaned back against the console. Disappointment flashed in Alex's eyes.

Late into the night they discussed and hashed out the details of Alex's First Contact plan. Ro'am surprised Cora by listening carefully to Analyn's suggestions as well as hers, and by not restating his objections. In the end, on issues in question they deferred to Alex's judgment. Long before they finished Analyn fell asleep.

Ro'am fell silent as Cora and Alex continued to talk softly.

"He's asleep," Alex finally said. He nodded his head at Ro'am, who leaned back in the comfortable copilot's chair. His head lolled slightly to one side, his chin resting atop Analyn's head.

"I can use some of that myself." Cora tried to stretch the kinks out of her back from where it pressed against the console.

"Go to bed." He turned to the instruments.

"Not alone." Fortune had handed them a time and place to be together; she wasn't about to waste it on sleep. She took his hand in hers and tugged him out of his seat. "Come on."

They made their way around the sleeping women. At the door to the sleeping compartment, Alex looked down at her. "I thought you were tired."

The teasing light in his eyes challenged her to give back as good as she got. She walked her fingers up his chest and peered at him from under half-closed eyelids. "Well, I guess if you're not up to it . . ."

With a growl, he yanked her hand down to his groin. His erection strained against his trousers and filled her palm. "I'm *up* to it. I merely thought to let you rest."

She stroked him through the fabric, delighted when she felt his pulse quicken and he groaned. "We can rest a long time when we're dead."

"Which if I'm wrong might be sooner than later."

"Then let's not waste a moment of the time we have left."

Once inside the sleeping compartment, they came together as equals, neither seeking to dominate or control the other. First he undressed her, slipping the jumpsuit off her shoulders. The slick material slid down her body until she stood naked before him. His admiring gaze heated her blood. Moisture gathered in her mouth and between her nether lips. Her breasts swelled and her nipples hardened in excitement.

Running her hand over his skin as it was revealed, she helped him out of his clothing. His small tremors of desire empowered her, as did the sight of his cock jutting out from its dark nest of hair.

On the bunk they lay facing each other. Using fingertips, palms, lips and tongues, as if it were their first time, they explored each other's bodies. With her tongue she tasted the small hollow behind his ear and probed with her fingertips the bumps and scars hidden beneath his hair. He stroked his palms down the outer sides of her upper arms, then nibbled the skin between her thumb and forefinger.

Slowly on this voyage of discovery, passion built. His hands cupped and caressed her swollen breasts; his lips and tongue teased and suckled her aching nipples. Her lips found his, and her tongue slipped inside his mouth to explore and taste the moist recesses while her hands slipped lower and investigated his hardness.

Desire surged ahead. Together they flew. Neither one controlled or directed the flight. Faster and faster they went, a fiery meteor streaking through the night sky until they could go no more. To the ground they fell in a blaze of glory to burst on impact.

Limp and sated, Cora curled against Alex. This was how it should be between them. She longed to hold on to the peace she felt at this moment. But the difficulties facing them and their love loomed large in her mind. Would they ever be together for good? Her last thought before sleep claimed her was, she couldn't see how.

* * *

Alex held Cora and tried to hold on to his sense of contentment. No matter what happened tomorrow, he wanted to remember this moment of perfect accord between them. It wasn't enough. He wanted more. He wanted her love and commitment. He wanted her by his side through all their tomorrows. But he knew it wasn't going to happen. If he forced her to stay, whether physically or emotionally, an essential part of her would wither and die. He had to set her free.

With the rising sun would come the worst challenges he'd ever faced, but for now he tried to push those concerns to the back of his mind and enjoy what little time he and Cora had left.

The next morning, during breakfast, spirits ran high with excitement and fear. After Alex and Ro'am checked out their surroundings and found them safe, they collected the materials Cora had requested for the MAT unit; then Alex took the women outside to give them instructions on how to comport themselves during the upcoming encounter. He left Cora in charge of programming the MAT to supply the clothing, weapons and gifts he'd specified they'd need.

Later the sun would warm them, but for now the women shivered in the crisp morning air. Though the land was still green, the chill in the air heralded the coming of winter.

Ro'am, arms crossed over his chest, eyes hard and expressionless, watched as Alex led the women through several warm-up exercises. Though Ro'am had stopped voicing his objections to Alex's plan, he didn't appear convinced. Alex kept a wary eye on the man.

"Analyn, you must face the Verians head on. Slumping or crouching will be seen as threatening gesture." The large feathered headdresses and robes he'd designed would go a long way toward helping her maintain the proper stance. Concerned by the girl's unexpected timidity, Alex put his fingers beneath her chin. As Cora said, this girl was this group's leader. If she faltered, so would they.

Behind him he heard Ro'am cough. A spot between his shoulder blades began to burn from the man's stare.

"I'm frightened," Analyn whispered. Fear made her appear little more than a child. "What if they want to eat me?"

Alex couldn't stop his chuckle. "Verians are vegetarians," he assured her. "They don't eat meat." Especially not human meat.

"Oh, that's good." Some of the tension drained out of her body. A sigh of relief ran through the women.

Doubts about his plan threatened to swamp him. If he failed, these people would pay the price for his mistake.

"Perhaps the council is right. I should go alone," he said. "I don't have the right to ask you to take this risk."

"No." Analyn threw her head back. "This is our world. Our lives. It's our place to do this. We're grateful for your knowledge and assistance, aren't we, Ro'am?" She pinned her husband with a hard look that belied her tender years.

Ro'am grunted. Alex watched as the man disappeared inside the ship, and wondered what other scare stories the Erathian men had fed their women to keep them in line.

Again and again he drilled them, covering every scenario he could imagine happening and a few he couldn't. By the time the sun stood overhead he saw improvement in the women, but knew they had a ways to go before he'd feel confident in their ability to face the Verians without flinching. Though young in both years and experience, purpose shone in their eyes.

The sun beat down on their heads. Sweat trickled down Alex's back. The women's energy lagged.

"We'll break for mid-meal now," he told them.

Released from training, they changed from dignified

women determined to do their duty to boisterous children, laughing as they dashed inside the ship. The sight reminded him of the young boys he'd trained in the Verian compound. For a moment the sight of the youngest girl, eyes sparkling in excitement, dark hair flying in the breeze as she ran, blurred, and in his mind he saw another child: a boy of four. His child. His son. Of all the children he'd sired from the moment he'd arrived for training, for some unknown reason this one had touched Alex's heart. Even before Cora arrived the boy had stirred feelings inside Alex, begun the changes that Cora completed.

He shook off the images. In the afternoon he'd show the women some simple self-protection moves. He hoped they wouldn't be necessary, but if things went badly with the Verians and First Contact failed, he planned to get the women out of there and back home. Then he'd find another way to free his son and the other captives.

Resolute, he entered a chaotic sea of feathers. Cora had been busy. Like a flock of colorful, exotic birds, large feathered headdresses sat in a row on the console. Full-length cloth robes covered in feathers hung along the ship's hull. Being surrounded by the vivid colors of each headdress and robe, crimson red, royal blue, emerald green, purple, yellow and orange, created the effect of being inside a rainbow. Though he'd designed the costumes to astound and impress, the sight awed him as well. Cora had outdone his wildest expectations.

Over the heads of the women he sent her a smile of gratitude. Her answering grin and easy confidence eased his apprehension. Strong and self-assured, she faced each challenge head-on without doubts. Once she set herself a goal she never wavered.

After a lifetime of wearing drab clothing designed to blend into their surroundings, the beautiful garments delighted the women. Chattering, they milled around, picking and choosing which they would wear.

In the midst of the colorful display, two robes and head-dresses stood out. Both consisted of pure white feathers. A shimmer of silver trimmed the smaller one; gold the larger. As the two humans who could speak to the Verians, Alex and Cora would do the negotiating. The other women were for show.

So they could become comfortable with the size and weight, he had everyone don the robes and headdresses. Once garbed, weapons at their sides, the transformation left him dazed. The frightened little girls disappeared. In their place stood five warrior women. They stood tall and proud, their faces reflecting their youthful assurance that they would prevail. The sight gave him hope that his plan might succeed.

But in the end its success or failure lay on his shoulders.

CHAPTER EIGHTEEN

Cora couldn't see him, but she could feel Ro'am's eyes boring a hole in her back as she worked on making the last of her repairs and adjustments to *Freedom*. Finally finished, she turned to face the man. As always, his incredible good looks threatened to disarm her. She hardened herself to his appeal and glared at him. Leaning back against the console she crossed her arms over her chest in an unconsciously defensive gesture. "What?"

"There are only seven robes," he said without preamble. "Why?"

Oops, he'd noticed. She was surprised he hadn't mentioned it sooner. "You don't need one."

"Why not?"

"Well, ah, because you'll be staying aboard *Freedom*," she blurted.

"And if I refuse and insist on joining the contact group?"

"Then you'll probably get us all killed or captured."

"You expect me to sit in safety while women under my protection put themselves at risk?"

"I thought you understood that having you with us creates an even bigger danger. The Flo—Verians won't comprehend or accept the presence of two males." It amazed her to hear herself lecturing him on Flock society in an attempt to make him realize what was at stake. Being around Alex had rubbed off.

"You're willing to risk your freedom, your life, that your man's plan will succeed?"

"Yes." Her answer rocked her. "Yes," she repeated with more force. "I am. Alex is an expert in his field. His training in xeno-anthropology and First Contact is intensive. If he says it'll work, I believe him." As she spoke, she realized she did.

All her doubts and fears about relinquishing to Alex control of her life, destiny and freedom evaporated. Even if his plan failed she'd have no regrets. Her faith went beyond the ultimate success or failure of his plan; it went far beyond reason, to her very heart.

Without him, freedom was an empty word. For six long lonely years she'd had it and it meant nothing. Her greatest freedom lay in her love for him, in trusting him with her life and her soul.

"You trust him despite what he is?"

Cora sucked in her breath. "W-what do you m-mean?"

Ro'am fixed her with a hard stare. "The others may have suspected, but you and I know who and what Alex is. A killer."

Trying to regain her shattered composure, she looked away. Explanations flittered through her mind, each one discarded before it could reach her lips. She had no answers. He took her chin in a firm but gentle grip, forcing her to meet his gaze.

"From the moment I saw him I knew he was a Verian fighter."

"How did you know?"

He dropped his hand. "You mean, aside from his fero-cious fighting skills?" He grinned for a moment then his expression grew thoughtful. "When I lost Zera, Atier's mother, in a Verian raid, I went a bit crazy. Thinking I could rescue her, I made my way to the Verian compound."

"What happened? Did you find her?"

"She wasn't there. I still don't know what happened to her. But while I observed from hiding I saw him—Alex. He was in an arena, fighting another man. Watching him re-turned me to reason. I realized that by myself I couldn't save Zera or the other humans from the Verians."

"If you knew who Alex is, why didn't you tell the others?"

"They would have killed him without pause."

"Is that what you want?"

"I thought I did. I almost ordered his destruction when he fell."

"What stopped you?"

"You rushed to his side and I couldn't risk you being in-jured."

"What difference did that make?"

"You're a woman," he said, as if that alone explained his actions. "An unusual woman, different from any Verian slave I've ever encountered. Plus, the question of the ship and its missing pilot were uppermost in my mind. Also, his reaction to you intrigued me."

"How do you feel about Alex now?"

"My feelings are of little consequence. Alex is far more than just a Verian fighter. Someday I'd like to know the full story about your arrival here, but for now it doesn't matter. What matters is the future of my people and my wife. Can you guarantee her safety?"

"No," Cora admitted. "But I can promise that we'll guard her with our own lives."

"Will you stop me if I forbid her to go?"

"No, but I doubt you can stop her. Ro'am, Analyn is not

271

a child or a fool. She's an intelligent woman capable of making her own decisions. And she believes she can do this."

"I want only to keep her safe."

"By keeping your women helpless you lose half your strength. As a man and as a people you need to let women be who and what they are."

"If we do, then what is our purpose?"

His question surprised her, but her answer that came in a breathless rush stunned her even more. "Don't you know how important you are to Analyn? How vital a man is to the woman who loves him? A woman wants more from a man than protection. She needs him to sustain her in ways that have nothing to do with safety, food or shelter—she needs him to listen to her thoughts and ideas, to support her while she chases her dreams and helps him achieve his." As Alex did with her.

A man needed the same from the woman he loved. Ever since she'd found Alex in the Flock compound, she'd been demanding he see and do things her way. Even after he'd rediscovered himself, she'd tried to force him onto her path. When that didn't work and she'd agreed to his plan, she'd done so with an ulterior motive. She couldn't stay here, but if she forced Alex to leave against his will, she'd be no better than the Flock or the Erathian men. But did she have the strength to give him the freedom to choose—to let him go?

Ro'am listened, then sighed. "What you say is true, but I don't have to like it." He looked at her straight on. "I was mistaken. Alex is not the man I saw in the Verian compound. I won't interfere with his plan."

Relief flooded her. She'd decide what to do about her and Alex later—if there was a later. "So, you won't try to stop us?"

"No, but I have a feeling that if this works Verian society isn't going to be the only one shaken up. Erathian women are never going to be the same." His lips quirked in a rueful smile. "And neither are the men."

Shaken by her own inner revelation, Cora gave a strangled laugh. "Change is never easy, but it's essential for the survival and growth of any society." *Or person*, she added silently. "Since you're staying aboard, let me show you how to operate *Freedom*'s systems."

She spent the next few hours teaching Ro'am everything she thought he might need to know to keep *Freedom* safe and out of Flock hands. Though Erathian technology was simple and *Freedom*'s operation was not, he caught on fast. With time and training she believed he might even make a good mechanic or pilot.

In a leap of faith she gave Ro'am the command codes, and in case First Contact with the Flock failed, she set *Freedom*'s autopilot to take it back to the Erathian caves. After that it would be up to Ro'am and the other Erathians to use *Freedom* to serve and protect as best they could. Whether or not Ro'am would have the strength of purpose to leave them behind, she couldn't be sure.

The next morning, Alex, Cora and the five women donned their feathered costumes. They sat in tense silence as Cora piloted *Freedom* straight into the heart of the Verian city.

If she didn't look close at its inhuman inhabitants, the city appeared much like any city on a pre-space-flight world. Bricks paved the narrow streets between the walled compounds that housed the separate Flock groups. Shops surrounded the marketplace set up in the main square. At one end stood a white stone building: the council hall.

As planned, she hovered the ship a few feet above an open area in the busy central marketplace. Alex had learned from his study of Verian society that today was not only market day, it was also the day the council held session. Once they had the Flock's attention, using the laser cannon she launched a display of pyrotechnics—loud and colorful, but harmless—in the sky.

The Flock scattered. Some ran away; others huddled together in doorways lining the square, too scared to flee. A few stared in openmouthed wonder at the metal object invading their city airspace.

The council hall doors flew open and a group of Flock emerged. They gripped weapons and stood ready to defend themselves and their people.

Alex used the ship's loudspeaker to speak to the crowd. His elegant words of peace and friendship filled the square. He asked to meet with the council to discuss a treaty between his people and theirs. Cora translated for Ro'am and the women. When Alex finished his speech they smiled in approval.

One by one, the Flock came forward until they filled the square. Swayed by his words but wary, the council members sheathed their weapons and clustered together in quiet conversation. Cora steered a LARC in close so she and Alex could eavesdrop.

"What are they saying?" Analyn asked.

"More importantly, what are they going to do?" Ro'am added.

Before Cora or Alex could answer, one of the council members addressed the ship.

"'The Palia welcome the visitors from the sky,'" Alex translated. "It seems the Verians have considered the possibility of other intelligent species from the stars," he gave as an aside, and continued to translate. "'We invite you to meet with our council to forge a treaty beneficial to both our species.'" He looked at the women. "Ladies, you're up."

Cora set *Freedom* down and lowered the gangway. In a flurry of nervous energy, the women stood and smoothed their ruffled feathers.

At the last minute before Cora opened the hatch, Ro'am gripped Analyn's arms, pulled her to him and slanted his mouth over hers in a kiss of love and fear. "Be safe," he said, then stepped back.

Cora longed to do the same to Alex, but he stared straight ahead. She moved to his side and opened the hatch.

In seconds her eyes adjusted to the sudden flood of daylight. At the top of the gangway they stood eye to eye with the Flock council twenty feet away. Fear and rage paralyzed her as she remembered her pain and humiliation at Flock hands. What had made her believe she could face them again, present the human case in a calm, rational manner? At the same time she wanted to turn and run, she wanted to strike them down. Her nails dug into her palms as she clenched her fists.

As if he sensed her conflicted emotions, under the cover of their robes Alex folded her hand inside his own and stroked until she relaxed.

"Be strong." He spoke to her through the com-link set up between them all. He could hear whatever she heard and speak to her through the small earpiece she wore, as could Ro'am and the women.

His soft words and the warmth of his fingers over hers chased the chill from her soul and helped Cora regain her composure. These were not the same Flock who'd captured and abused her. She forced herself to believe that like humans, each Flock was an individual, and to judge them on their own merits. If she faltered now, Alex's plan would fail.

Alex exited first, with her a mere step behind. Their hands slid apart and the chill of doubt returned.

Analyn and the others followed. Once they were clear of the hatch Cora shut and sealed it. In case the Flock reacted badly and took them captive, she'd changed the commands so that now only Ro'am could open it.

The Flock waited as she and Alex mounted the steps. As

they'd practiced, the other women stopped and waited at the bottom of the gangway. Just before the top step Alex also stopped, gave a low bow and waited.

In Flock society the men might dominate their women in their homes, but the women ruled outside. Though Alex had made the first overture of peace to the Flock, Cora would have to negotiate the terms—alone. To prevent the possibility of fighting, males were not allowed in the council hall.

The Flock council watched and waited as she continued forward until they stood face to face. She held her head high and back straight. Sweat trickled down her spine and prickled under her arms as the bird people studied her in obvious confusion.

Alex held his breath. This was the moment of truth. This close, Cora's elaborate feathered headdress and robe couldn't hide her obvious human appearance. He couldn't predict with certainty how the Verians would react to the knowledge that humans were sentient beings; he could only calculate the possibilities based on what he knew of their culture. Rational analysis told him one thing would happen, but his heart feared another. Had his conceit in his ability sent her back into the captivity she so feared?

Finally, the Verian counselor allowed her crest feathers to flatten against her head. "Take the male to the petitioner's chamber and see to the comfort of his entourage," she directed several guards, and then said to Cora, "Come, we will speak of how your people and mine can form a profitable alliance."

Cora and the Verian council members disappeared into the building. Alex let out his breath. They weren't home free yet, but they'd jumped the first hurdle.

Guards surrounded him and the women. "Relinquish your weapons and come with us."

The Zan part of him wanted to strike out at his captors, but the Alex part of him weighed the odds of attacking and overpowering them. He knew he could prevail against these few guards in a fight, but to what purpose? Even if he escaped, Cora would still be a captive. And he couldn't defeat the entire Verian population.

He repeated the command to the women, then reluctantly handed over his sword and knives. The women did the same. Before the guards led them away, he softly reminded the women not to speak while in the presence of any Verians.

The petitioner's chamber consisted of a small bare room with one hard bench, no windows, and a single door. Though the plan might be his, if it succeeded, the success would belong to Cora. The conversation he'd overheard earlier between Cora and Ro'am ran through his mind. Her words had opened his eyes. By agreeing to his plan she gave up more than control; she gave up a bit of who she was to support him.

No matter the outcome he vowed he'd find a way to give her what she wanted most—her freedom.

Once the door closed his optimism faded. His com-link was dead. He tapped the earpiece without result. He couldn't hear Cora or contact Ro'am and the women. The building's thick stone walls blocked transmission.

He paced the small space. And worried. Had he properly prepared Cora for this meeting? He'd thought he'd have the com-link between them, to help her navigate the tricky waters of First Contact and treaty negotiation. Instead he'd led her into a trap she couldn't escape and left her to fend for herself. As a First Contact Agent he was schooled in patience, but this sitting and doing nothing left the Zan part of him frustrated and angry. Through the long night he dozed the hard bench.

Cora was on her own. Their fate rested in her hands.

* * *

After nearly twenty straight hours of negotiations with the Flock, Cora's head pounded, grit scratched her eyelids and her back ached from the strain of wearing the heavy head-dress. Her only satisfaction was that the Flock council looked as tired as she felt.

When she'd first realized the com-link no longer functioned, Cora had almost panicked. But it soon became apparent that Alex had prepared her well.

Early in the negotiations she'd arranged for the women to be allowed to return to the ship, but found the council unwilling to release Alex. They considered him their greatest bargaining chip. In their society, females, though their numbers indicated a male's wealth and power, were expendable. A group could survive the loss of most of its females, but without its dominant male it faced destruction. A compound with no dominant male would soon be attacked and raided. A wise male always had a strong female at his side, and one if not several young male offspring designated as his heirs. Of course, with young, virile male heirs, the dominant male had to be careful of an uprising.

Cora couldn't claim to agree with the structure of their society, but she had no qualms about using their lack of insight into human nature to her advantage. With Ro'am, the women and *Freedom* safe, she negotiated from a position of strength. All she had to worry about was herself and Alex.

With unaccustomed ease she slipped into the role of ambassador. As she communicated with the council members and learned their individual personalities, if she could have closed her eyes, she could nearly forget the creatures she spoke with weren't human, forget they were the same species that had imprisoned, abused, humiliated and degraded her. Though she hid her reactions from them, the sight of their feathered ovoid bodies, long necks and expressionless faces still made her shudder in disgust and shiver in remembered dread.

Hil-Rath, first minister of the Ruling Council, a Flock whom Cora had determined after a short period of time was of middle years, even temperament and keen intelligence, a true leader, looked up from the treaty she patiently read. Unfortunately translator chips didn't give their users the ability to read the language, only to speak and understand it.

"Is clause 321 acceptable?" Hil-Rath asked.

Cora sighed and nodded; only 689 more clauses to go.

Once she'd negotiated peace between the Flock—or Palia as they called themselves—and humans, the freedom of all human captives and the right of humans to claim unowned land, Cora had thought her work was done. She was wrong. Sticklers for detail, the Palia insisted on spelling out a way to handle every possible situation that might arise between their two species. One by one they plowed through seemingly endless clauses. By the time they finished, Cora could only pray she hadn't agreed to anything that might prove awkward or dangerous in the future or worse, violated C.O.I.L protocol.

As she penned her signature on the massive document, the council members, pleased by the promise of gifts and trade agreements they'd negotiated, cackled in excitement. Alex's plan had succeeded beyond their wildest dreams. But Cora couldn't rejoice. Soon she'd be leaving this world and him. Though the treaty was a success, the people here, both human and Flock, needed him far more than she did. There was work to be done. Work she knew he needed to do to purge the shame he felt deep in his soul. She couldn't force him to leave. If she did, guilt would eat him until he was no longer the man she loved.

Could she stay too? Make her life on this planet where the ruling species was the Flock? She shivered in remembered dread. No, even if the memories of captivity, abuse, humiliation and degradation weren't fresh in her mind, tying herself to a life on the ground would destroy her. She needed to fly.

If she loved him, she had to set him free.

An hour later, the door of the room to which she'd been shown opened and Alex strode in. The sight of him, head high, shoulders back, sent a bolt of longing through her. He'd abandoned the heavy headpiece, but the gold feathers he'd woven into his dark hair fluttered against his cheeks. He searched her face for an indication of the outcome of her meeting with the council, a question in his eyes: Are we still welcome guests or once again captive animals?

When the door closed with a solid clunk behind him, Cora stood and waited as he approached.

She wanted to launch herself at him, to rain kisses over his face, to feel his arms close around her, burrow her hands under his clothing and stroke them over his chest and around to his back. She wanted his lips on hers and his cock buried deep inside her. Only his heat could chase away her chill.

Instead, when he came within arm's reach she looked away. "Your shock-and-awe trick worked. Though it'll probably take the Flo-Palia populace time to accept humans as equals, the council agreed to most of our demands. The fighting compound will be closed immediately, the humans there freed and given into the Erathians' care. A grant of land is being drawn up for the Erathians."

"It sounds like everything went as planned. You did great." He put his hands on her upper arms. "So what's wrong?"

"Nothing." The warmth of his palms against her cold flesh nearly defeated her. She shook him off and wrapped her arms around herself in a defensive gesture. "From our negotiations, it was obvious that the Palia council recognize that their society is on the brink of a cultural and technological revolution. They're greedy for the technology we can offer them. The possibility of joining the Consortium excites them. They should make a nice addition to the C.O.I.L. family. And they didn't refuse the promise of trade."

If he touched her again, her resolve would crumble and she'd beg him to leave with her. If she did, she knew he'd agree. And that would destroy him. So when he reached for her she sidled away. She had to tell him now, before her courage failed.

"I'll stay until things between the Palia and the Erathians are underway, then I'm taking *Freedom* and heading home. Once there I'll make my report. A settlement team should arrive back here in a year or so."

"It'll take some time to get things in order. We'll need *Freedom*'s resources to provide translator chips for the Erathians."

She could see Alex analyzing the situation, determining what needed to be done and how long it would take. She could also see inside him the conflict between his need for her and his need to stay with these people—his people. If she forced the issue he'd honor his promise to her, but in making him do so she'd kill the very thing inside him she loved.

"I'll give it a month, no more. That should be enough time." Could she hold out that long?

He shook his head. "I can't possibly do everything that needs to be done in that short a period. I need more time."

"You'll have all the time you need. You're not coming with me."

"What?"

"I'm going alone. I release you from your promise."

"You mean to go without me?"

"Yes. I won't ask you to leave. You're needed here."

"Then stay here. With me."

To counteract the heat of his gaze, she infused ice into her words. "No, I can't. You belong here. I don't. It's simple. I'm leaving and you're staying."

Stunned by her announcement, Alex stared at Cora. This was wrong. Not even when he'd first found her in the breeding chamber had she seemed to so cold, so distant. All along he'd known she'd eventually leave, that he'd have to free her. But now that the time had come, something inside him snapped. She was his. Without her he'd lose himself again. His life would have no meaning. He wouldn't, couldn't let her go.

Fear and rage, long repressed, shattered his restraint, let loose the creature that dwelled deep inside him. The Flock had done everything they could to unearth the beast, but though he'd fought and killed for them and lain with women at their command, in the end he'd retained control.

By clinging to a memory of Cora buried deep inside his mind, he'd held on to his basic humanity, refusing to become the animal they thought him. Now, faced with losing her, memory and conscious thought gave way to his instinct to claim his mate, to bind her to him in the most primal way. Where amnesia, captivity and conditioning failed to open the door between his animalistic self and his thinking self, love succeeded.

He yanked her hard against his chest. She gasped in surprise. Her gaze flew to his. Before she could protest he captured her mouth in a punishing kiss.

She fought his hold. Without effect she beat her fists against his back as he plundered her mouth. The metallic taste of blood filled his mouth. Hers or his? He couldn't tell. Instinct drove him to claim her, to mark her as his. Forcing her backwards onto the bed he ripped aside her clothing. As she tried to squirm away he shed his as well, then leaned forward and cupped her breasts in his palms. Driving need made his grip rough.

"Alex, what are you doing? That hurts. Let me go!"

She kicked out at him. Her foot connected with his hip,

inches from his erection. With a growl he grabbed her wrists in one hand and pried her thighs apart with his knee. Despite her frantic struggles, his weight pinned her to the bed. The tip of his throbbing cock pressed against her entrance, and as usual her body reacted to his. Part of him wanted to slam himself home into her warm, wet depths, but on the brink of doing so he paused. A glimmer of awareness told him physical joining was only part of what he needed. He raised his eyes to meet hers.

Cora looked up into Alex's eyes. Zan stared back. Pain and confusion turned those eyes black. By leaving him she'd finally cracked his control. The result wasn't what she'd expected or wanted.

Her breath came in strangled gasps. With her arms held securely above her head, her thighs pried wide by his, she was powerless to stop him from forcing her. But did she even want to?

Yes and no. She didn't want to be forced, but neither did she want to stop him. She wanted him, needed him inside her. Her body ached for him. The feel of his thighs pressing firmly against hers, his fingers clasped tight around her wrists holding her helpless, the tip of his cock probing the swollen, ready entrance to her body all conspired to rob her of reason.

Her heart longed for him. Since the first moment she'd seen him she'd wanted this man. Whether he was the sweet and shy Alexander of old or the sexy and commanding Zan from the compound, she loved him. Lost in the here and now, she could forget the coming heartbreak that love meant.

His body poised above hers, he questioned her with his eyes, demanding compliance at the same time he begged permission. With one breath he took control and with the next he relinquished it.

But as with freedom, control can't be given; it must be

taken. So, as she'd done once before, she took charge. She thrust her hips up. His cock plunged deep, stealing her breath and banishing rational thought. Physical sensation took over.

When he released her wrists, she curled her arms around his sweat-slicked shoulders. His chest pressed against her aching breasts. His lips closed over hers and his tongue mimicked the action of his hips as he rocked in and out of her. In perfect rhythm their bodies met and parted. He pulled back until her body held just the tip of him, then slammed down as she rose up. Wild and frantic with need she met each powerful thrust. A spring of tension coiled in her belly, winding tighter and tighter with every stroke.

Beneath her fingers his muscles bunched and hardened as he struggled to hold back his release, to continue his pounding pace. They moved together in perfect unity, the way it was meant to be. Equal partners. Neither dominating nor controlling the other. She wanted it to last forever, but needed to finish, to reach the peak where nothing else existed but pure ecstasy. Need won.

She let go. Inside her the spring snapped. Wave after wave of sensation surged through her. As she screamed out his name he thrust into her one last time and went rigid. A flood of liquid heat filled her. Still convulsing, he took her with him as he rolled to his side. Each throb of his cock sent quivers of delight through her.

Sated by passion, their bodies still linked, for a while they lay together. Finally his cock shrank and slipped out of her. When his breathing turned slow and even, she slid out of his arms and wrapped the bedsheet around her body. He didn't try to stop her. Once away from the warmth of his body, she shivered in the cool air.

Outside, night had fallen. The fire in the hearth had burned low and cast only a little light. Cora collected her clothing from the floor and kept her eyes averted from Alex, afraid if she looked at him she wouldn't have the courage to do what needed to be done. Now that she'd discovered the true meaning of love, she had to leave him; she had to set him free.

CHAPTER NINETEEN

"Where are you going?" he called out.

Cora whirled around. Caught under her feet by her action, the bedsheet sarong she'd fashioned pulled from her body, leaving her exposed. Alex rose on his elbow and drank in the sight of her standing nude, her skin glowing like pale cream in the dim light. A golden halo of tousled hair framed her face. Her eyes widened and she took a step back.

Memory of what he'd done slammed into him. He groaned and started to rise.

"Stay there!" She snatched up the sheet and twisted it around herself, clearly planning to flee the room.

What had he done? "Cora, I'm sor—"

"Don't say it! I'm not. There's nothing to apologize for. We both wanted it. But it doesn't change anything."

"I'll come with you. I just need a bit more time to set things up."

"No. I have to go, but you need to be here. You want to be here. If I make you leave this world, these people, your children, a big part of you will wither and die. The choice isn't yours." For a moment her voice broke; then before he could press his advantage it strengthened. She looked him straight in the eye. "It's mine."

As much as he wanted to argue with her, to convince her he could leave with her and still live with himself, he knew she was right. But if he let her go would he be any better off? Without her his soul would shrivel and his heart would break.

"Then choose to stay with me," the Zan part of him demanded. "Without you my heart and soul will be empty."

She turned away from him. "I can't."

He got up and walked to her side. When he reached for her, she cringed away. Pain and guilt stabbed his heart. "Don't be afraid. I won't hurt or force you again."

She gave a short mirthless laugh and turned her tear-streaked face to his. "A little rough sex I can meet and match. You didn't force me to do anything I didn't want to do. The sex was consensual. But I am afraid of you."

Her words deepened his shame. He dropped his hand to his side. "Why?"

She stared at him, disbelief in her eyes. "Don't you know the power you have over me? I spent the last six years living in hell thinking you were dead. All I really wanted was to curl up in a ball and die, but I couldn't escape that way, so I ran away into the emptiness of space. Everything I did— becoming a recon pilot like we'd planned, searching the galaxies for alien species—I did to honor your memory, to find a way to be closer to you in mind if not in body. Finding you was like waking from a never-ending nightmare." She paused and searched his face. "If I asked you to, would you leave with me, now, this minute?"

"Yes," he found himself answering without hesitation. Though it would break something inside him, she would be his first choice. Always. "Do you ask?"

"No. I thought I'd do anything and everything to keep you with me, but I discovered I love you too much to make you choose between who you are and me. To take away your freedom to decide your destiny."

"How does this make you fear me?"

"Don't you see? You have the same power over me. If you ask, I'll stay, and then we're both doomed."

"I did ask."

She gave him a small smile. "No, you demanded."

She was right. He hadn't asked her to stay; he'd commanded her. Independent to her core, she could refuse an order, but if he requested it she'd give him whatever he wanted. His mouth opened to speak the words. The look of distress in her eyes froze them on his lips. He couldn't do it. Couldn't rob her of her freedom. Defeat slumped his shoulders. To hide the plea in his eyes, he turned away.

Over the next few weeks Cora had no time to think about or regret her decision. In gratitude for the peace she'd helped forge between them and the Palia, the Erathian council accepted her decision to leave. Even Charic, subdued by all he'd seen, no longer argued.

To speed the time along she kept busy using the MAT unit to fabricate translator chips as well as the first of the trade goods promised to the Palia. Ro'am's people helped keep her supplied with the multitude of raw materials it took.

As she, Ro'am and representatives from each of the Erathian clans used *Freedom* to scout the planet for land suitable for them to settle on, she had little opportunity to see Alex. Though she told herself it was for the best, she missed him. By mutual agreement, they didn't share quarters. While she bunked aboard *Freedom*, he made his home with the Erathians. The days were hectic and sped by, but the nights were long and lonely. Sleep came in snatches, if at all. Only her dreams gave her comfort, but she woke from them, arms and heart empty, tears soaking her pillow.

Occasionally she'd catch sight of him as he went about

his day. Once she saw him speaking with a young Erathian woman. When the woman tucked her arm in his, fierce and unwanted jealousy surged through Cora. She clenched her fists until her nails drew blood to keep from clawing the woman's eyes out.

After they found a piece of land, Cora used her MAT to fabricate the equipment and machinery the Erathians needed to build a community. Alex busied himself preparing them for life as Palian allies. Though Analyn and Nala now had translator chips and would eventually be ambassadors, they weren't yet fluent in the language or the customs, so Cora was forced to act as a temporary representative. To her surprise, as she came to know them as individuals, she found that the Palia ceased to repulse her. A working friendship developed between Hil-Rath and her. The Palia's innate curiosity about humans, their society and their customs, especially their sexual ones, kept their conversations interesting, if sometimes uncomfortable.

The dismantling of the compound where she and Alex had been held, and others involved in the same business, as expected, proved to be the most difficult; those Palia resisted the restructuring of their lives and livelihoods, but ultimately the Palia Ruling Council forced the issue. Cora wasn't exactly sure how they accomplished the goal, but day after day caravans consisting of dozens of naked, frightened and confused former captives arrived.

Cora also didn't miss the fact that none of the captives were males over the age of puberty. At some point the Erathians would have to deal with the issue of those missing males, but for now they were too busy helping the women and children assimilate into a strange new environment.

The arrival of so many women shook up the status quo of a society long dominated by men. The Erathian women quickly took over the details of caring for and housing the new arrivals. In order not to frighten the captives with even the minor surgery of implanting a TC, the Erathian women who knew herdspeak began language classes for the new arrivals. Because of the increased work and the need to move around freely, they shed the voluminous robes and veils that tended to frighten the newcomers. Cora grinned at the disgruntled yet appreciative looks the men wore as they went about their daily tasks.

She watched as Alex searched each group of captives. Though he said nothing and he dealt gently with the terrified people, she saw his disappointment when the one child he looked for didn't arrive. Part of her wanted him to find the son he sought; another part, a primitive, jealous female part she didn't care for wished it never to happen. Though she was leaving him behind, she jealously wanted to take his heart with her.

To counteract her twisted feelings, she asked the Palia council about the child. In response they claimed to have found no record of him, but did reluctantly admit that some records had been destroyed. In addition, she learned that rather than accept the council's decree, that compound's dominant male and several of his females had fled. The council wasn't sure, but they believed they'd taken some of the younger captives with them.

Two weeks passed before the Erathians began the long trek to their new land. Cora used *Freedom* to transport groups of workers to begin building. By ship the trip took mere hours, on foot and by dracas it would take the Erathians several weeks. By that time the first of the dwellings should be ready for them. She made several additional trips to bring supplies and items the Erathians couldn't transport through the mountains and the dangerous territory between them and their new home.

The deadline she'd set herself for leaving loomed close. With each day her heart grew heavier. As much as she longed to see Alex, to be with him again, she couldn't bring herself to change her mind, to either ask him to go with her or to give up her freedom and stay.

The last few weeks had proved that he belonged here. A natural leader, soon he'd form his own clan and sit on the Ruling Council. But this wasn't—couldn't be—her life. And though she wanted to deny it, his acceptance of her decision hurt. Was she so easy to let go? He'd left and forgotten her once before. When she left this time, would he forget her again?

And even though she'd begged him not to, why didn't he fight to keep her?

Alex searched the faces of each of the new arrivals. Like the others, this group consisted of women and children, but this time he recognized none of them. His son wasn't among them, nor had he been among the groups that came from the compound where he'd been kept. It occurred to Alex that he didn't even know his son's name. Now he might never know.

In the compound he hadn't thought of it. It hadn't mattered. Until Cora had arrived he hadn't considered himself a father or even a man, nor, despite his knowledge of biology, had he consciously grasped the fact that the child was his son and all that entailed. Though he'd felt a connection with the child, a need to protect and defend the boy, he'd never put a name to what he felt.

Now he knew. Love. Cora had opened his eyes to the true nature of man, the ability . . . the *need* to love and be loved in return.

After seeing to the newcomers' care, he turned and saw Cora watching him. Before she shuttered her face he caught a glimpse of her anguish, the same pain he felt. In a short time she'd be leaving. By her request there'd be no ceremony, no send-off to mark her departure. The night before, she'd said her good-byes to the Erathians and now they honored her by not gathering to wish her farewell. A few corridors away, *Freedom* sat ready to go.

Would she say good-bye to him, or leave without a word? Unaware that he held his breath, he waited.

Though over the past month they'd spent only minutes together and spoken few words, and of those none of importance, the thought of the emptiness he'd feel when she was truly gone from this world nearly drove him to his knees.

Instinct demanded that he scream out in rage and denial. That he grab her tight and never let go. That he bind her to his side by whatever means necessary. Beg, if that was what it took.

Instead he stood rigid, fists clenched against the need for her that was pounding in his veins. Stay or go, it no longer mattered to him. Whatever she wanted he'd give. And what she wanted was to choose. Though it might yet kill him, he'd honor her request. The choice had to be hers and hers alone. He couldn't interfere.

He closed his eyes briefly to block out the sight of her and regain control. When he opened them again she was gone. His breath escaped in a hiss of pain.

"Alex!" Ro'am's shout cut through his thoughts.

Letting his fingers uncurl, he released his tension, tamped down his regret and turned to the man who rushed toward him. "What has you so excited?"

"We've had a report of a small group of captives making their way up the mountain trail."

Alex laughed. "That's not unusual anymore."

"This is not a caravan; it's a group of three children and one lone Palia."

"I still don't understand the excitement."

"Not excitement. Concern. They're traveling through open country in Alavan territory. This is the time of year when the adults kick young Alavans out of their nests, to learn to fly . . . and hunt."

This painted an alarming picture. To encourage their off-spring to leave the nest, the adult Alavan would stop feeding them. For a ravenous Alavan, a young child would be tempting prey. Fresh from the nest, the immature Alavans would have no fear of humans. If hungry enough, even an adult Alavan would risk the danger of attacking a grown man. One lone Palia wouldn't be much of deterrent. Ro'am's next words froze Alex's heart.

"I think this is part of the group that ran away from the fighting compound."

"Get men and weapons." Alex dashed through the caves toward *Freedom*. On foot or even by dracas it could be hours before he reached them. If Cora hadn't left yet, he might have a chance to get to the group before any Alavans.

Inside the cavern he skidded to a halt. Empty. *Freedom* was gone. Pain threatened to send him to his knees. She was gone. Somehow deep inside, he hadn't believed she'd leave. But she had.

No time to grieve. He turned and ran toward the dracas stable. Nonetheless, though he doubted it would reach her, on his way past he stopped in the main hall and used the computer Cora had provided to send her a message. She'd attempted to set up a communication link between the planet and *Freedom*, but discovered that the base metals in the mountains caused intense interference. The main link was already in place at the new settlement, but even if he could get there to send a message it would only reach her as long as she was within orbital range of the planet.

They were on their own. And he was alone.

Dry-eyed and numb inside, Cora maneuvered *Freedom* out of the cavern. Pain and tears would come later. Once in the air she opened the viewscreen and, stomach lurching, forced herself to watch her ascent. Sparsely inhabited, untamed and dangerous, this planet had a wild beauty that called to her soul. As it fell away beneath her, the tree- and snow-capped mountains, rolling plains, and shimmering seas blurred to blue and green and white with touches of orange and red.

As much as she wanted to deny it, she understood Alex's decision to remain. Without his knowledge and guidance, the Erathians faced a dim future. The treaty between them and the Palia required a strong administrator. In a way she envied him his task, his calling. After he'd been reported killed, she'd thrown herself into Earth League Force and until she found him again it had filled the emptiness inside her. Now she doubted anything would. Would helping the Erathians fill the hole that her leaving left in his heart?

The com system crackled and squawked, then fell silent.

The higher she flew, the heavier her heart grew and the less free she felt. The chains that bound her to Alex stretched and pulled but didn't break. Nothing she did, no matter how far away or how fast she flew, she'd never be free of them, free of him. Even when she'd believed he was dead he'd lived on inside her.

Then why was she leaving him? To fly. To control her life. To be free. Free of what?

The answer hit her.

The pain of loss.

From the time she was a small child she'd struggled to be in charge, to be independent, not to need anyone or anything, to be free, because everyone she'd ever loved had abandoned her—her father when he died in a tragic accident, her mother to chase her own aspirations, and finally Alex when she'd attempted to control him. Since then, to protect her battered heart she'd refused to acknowledge her need to relinquish control, to fully give her heart without restraint into someone else's keeping.

Her search for freedom and control had imprisoned her more securely than the Flock's bars and cages. She'd thought if she held back that final bit of her heart she couldn't have it broken. But she was wrong. Her heart knew what it wanted and freedom ran a distant second. Her heart wanted Alex.

More than she needed to fly, more than she needed control, more than she needed freedom, she needed him. For her life to be complete, for it to have meaning and purpose, she needed to go back to make a life with him on this planet. The control she sought was an illusion. Love granted the only real freedom. Her decision broke the shackles constricting her heart, and for the first time in her life she felt truly free. Closing the viewscreen against reentry, she pointed *Freedom* back toward the planet.

As *Freedom* switched from space flight to air flight mode, the com crackled again. Cora tried adjusting the frequency.

"*. . . need help . . . refugees . . . Alavans . . . southern cliffs . . . rescue attempt underway.*"

The broken message chilled her. She'd seen the southern cliffs from a distance. Sheer, crumbling rock walls rose a thousand feet into the air; hundreds of Alavans nested in the crevices that the elements had worn from the rock. Even without the danger presented by the Alavans, the plateau above and the valley below those cliffs was unstable. During the rainy season or in the spring when the snow and ice melted, or sometimes without reason or warning, chunks of land broke away to crash down the steep cliff walls. Without hesitation she used her scanners to pinpoint the location and headed there.

As she approached the cliffs, she opened the viewscreen. Though her instruments could give her all the relevant information, she felt the need to see what was happening. An icy chill slid down her spine, and not from vertigo alone. Dozens of Alavans circled in the air above and around the edge of the cliff. Inside *Freedom* she couldn't hear them, but her imagination filled in the sounds of their piercing cries as they swooped and dove at the small group huddled on a ledge thirty feet below the cliff top. A dark streak of rock face with bits of stone and dirt still raining down showed where a piece of land had given way. Caught out in the open on the plateau, the group had fled down a trail to find shelter under an overhang on the cliff face. Once there the land had sheared away, trapping them on a narrow ledge.

The group consisted of three children, two girls and a toddler boy, and an adult Palia. Cora recognized both the Palia and the boy. The Palia was Ansal, from the compound, who'd given her sympathy, and the boy was Alex's son. With every swoop and dive, the birds knocked away a bit of rock from the ledge. If she didn't do something they'd soon be lunch.

Desperate for inspiration, she dove *Freedom* into the midst of the Alavans. Like water they flowed around her and then regrouped, seemingly unfazed by her presence. To them, *Freedom* was nothing more than a misplaced rock. She could fire the laser cannon, but at this range she feared hitting the cliffside and triggering another slide. She watched helplessly as the birds continued to swoop and dive at the terrified children huddled against the stone wall. There was nothing she could do without risking *Freedom*.

She pulled her eyes from the scene. Across the plateau, butted up against a wooded mountain slope, more Alavans circled a group of humans mounted on dracas. Every time one of the men attempted to move, the Alavans attacked. The men fought with swords and knives, but the birds swooped in, raking skin and muscle with razor-sharp talons, then soared out again unscathed. Though calm by nature and trained to stand fast, faced by so many Alavans, even the dracas pranced nervously and fought to flee. Alex, she could help.

Grateful for an excuse to abandon the children and the dizzying height, Cora took aim and fired the cannon at the birds. The shot burst through their midst, showering the men below with blood and burnt feathers. Though only a few birds fell from the sky, the rest scattered in panic. Taking advantage of the distraction, the men bent low over their dracas and raced across the plateau. Ravenous and determined to hunt and feed, the birds quickly regrouped to follow.

Unsure of what to do to help, Cora piloted *Freedom* above the men, providing a small shield for them. Enraged by her hindering presence, the birds dove against the ship's side. Though they could do no damage, the impacts rocked *Freedom* as it hovered mere feet above the men's heads. Each muffled thump and rasp of talon over metal made Cora cringe as she struggled to maintain control of her ship.

Alex came onto the viewscreen. His mouth moved as he shouted. Cora switched on the microphones.

"Drive the Alavans toward us. Get the children off the cliff."

Cora hesitated. Getting the children off the side of the cliff would require some tricky flying. She'd have to fly by sight and hover thousands of feet above nothingness. Fear sent an icy chill down her spine.

Was she willing to risk her life and *Freedom* to save them?

Out from under the protective shadow of *Freedom*, Alex held his seat on his nervous draca with his knees and clutched a sword in each hand. An Alavan dove at him from behind. Cora swung *Freedom* around. She lost sight of Alex, but felt the satisfying thunk as the ship hit the bird. She quickly righted *Freedom* and found Alex with the viewer again. The sight of him eased her fear and pain.

"Go!" he shouted again. "Get the children!" He swung his sword. The blade sliced through a bird's outstretched wing. The Alavan shrieked and whirled away. Blood splattered his head and shoulders.

"I can't leave you!"

"You have to! We can't get to them. You're their only hope. Go!"

"What about you?"

"We can hold them off!" He turned his draca and galloped out of view.

She turned the viewer to follow his progress. He and twenty other mounted men formed a circle near the edge of the cliff. The Alavans flew loops around them, searching for an opening, only to be driven away at the last moment. To keep them interested, every few minutes one man or another would break out of the circle and race away and back. Occasionally an Alavan managed to rake a talon across flesh, or a sword made contact with feathers, but it was a standoff that would end only when either the men or the Alavans gave up or dropped from exhaustion.

Alex was right. The men might be able to hold off the Alavans for a time, but they couldn't drive them away long enough to rescue the children. She and *Freedom* were their only hope.

Could she do it—face her fear to save another woman's son?

Alex's son.

There was no choice. Using every ounce of skill she possessed she piloted *Freedom* straight down the side of the cliff into the midst of the birds. The world dropped away beneath her. Her stomach lifted. Nausea rose in her throat. She gritted her teeth.

Feathered bodies thumped against *Freedom*'s sides. Several spiraled brokenly downward until they became nothing more than black specks. *Freedom* continued to plunge downward. Just before she hit bottom she turned *Freedom* up. Angry and confused, the Alavans followed.

For a few minutes she led the birds on a chase through steep cannons and twisting valleys. This precise flying required that she pilot the ship manually, so she swallowed her nausea at the sight of the ground hurtling by below. Several miles away, in a blind canyon, she looped *Freedom* over and behind them and opened fire. Soon the birds were either dead, wounded or had fled. Blood, gore and feathers splattered the canyon wall.

Hands shaking from an adrenaline rush, Cora headed *Freedom* back toward the cliffs. How long had she been gone? *Freedom*'s clock registered only minutes, but time had lost all meaning.

Though birds no longer threatened them, the children were unable to escape from the ledge, and they huddled against the wall. Cora eased *Freedom* up the side of the cliff. On the plateau the would-be rescuers performed a deadly ballet with the remaining Alavans. She could hear Alex and Ro'am shouting directions. Sweat and blood caked the men and dracas. Both men and mounts grew fatigued. The Alavans seemed tireless. They dipped and whirled, their shrill cries echoing through the mountains. Hunger and instinct drove them beyond fear, beyond reason. They'd fly until they dropped, and even then they'd claw and gouge with their last ounce of strength.

She started toward the men. Once the Alavans were gone, the men could rescue the children. The sound of rock cracking and the children's screams stopped her. The ledge was slipping. If she didn't help them now it would be too late. Her eyes locked on the small boy. If he died, a part of Alex would die as well—along with a piece of her own heart.

Cora positioned *Freedom* alongside the ledge. Locking the controls in hover mode, she opened the hatch. Ansal and the children crouched against the cliff face. She started to lower the gangway.

"No! Don't!" Ansal yelled. "The ledge will collapse."

Swallowing her fear, Cora gripped the edge of the hatch and peered down. Ansal was right. A fissure ran the width of the ledge, just inches in front of where she and the children crouched. The slightest touch would send it crashing down. A gust of wind buffeted the ship and bumped it against the ledge. With a creaking groan the outcropping shifted downward several inches. The two girls screamed in fear and buried their faces into Ansal's body. The boy stood straight, legs firm, back against the cliff and met Cora's gaze with confidence.

Shaken, she pulled back inside the ship. What options did she have? Alex, Ro'am and the others couldn't help her. They had all they could do to hold the Alavans at bay. They wouldn't flee; they wouldn't abandon the children to save themselves. To the last man they'd fight. Could she do any less?

She gathered her courage and looked out again. Her head spun and her vision blurred as her gaze plunged into the gaping void. Images of another cliff, of her father lying broken and still, made her heart race and her palms sweat. He'd fallen, and while she sat frozen in shock and fear, he'd died. Though the rangers who found her days later said he died instantly, she'd always felt she failed to save him. Her grip on the hatch frame slipped and she leaned into open air. *Freedom* swayed and dipped. She yanked her gaze up and focused her mind on the situation at hand: she wouldn't fail Alex's son or the others counting on her this time.

Could they jump the gap into the ship's hatch? Ansal's long muscular legs would make the leap easily, but the boy looked too small to manage the distance and fear paralyzed the girls. Ansal, like all Palia, lacked the upper body strength to throw them.

There was only one option; Cora had to get them. She needed rope, but when she started to the MAT unit the ledge gave another groan and broke away with a resounding crash. Pieces of it bounced against *Freedom*'s side and flew in through the open hatch. The impact rocked the ship and Cora fell backward. Her elbow connected sharply with the floor. Pain jolted through her arm. Dust and debris ballooned in the air, obscuring her vision.

Choking and coughing, she got to her knees and peered through the cloud of grit. Her heart thudded erratically. Had the ledge taken the children with it?

A breeze cleared the haze. Relief washed over her. They were still there. But not for long. The ledge they stood on was now only inches deep. One misstep and they'd fall. The girls clung to Ansal. The boy stood a few yards away. There was a break of about five feet in the ledge between him and the others.

The gap between the children and the ship was nearly ten feet, more than Cora could jump. Because of a small rock outcropping jutting above the ledge she couldn't maneuver *Freedom* any closer. Though risky, she had only one choice.

Cradling her injured arm, she climbed into the pilot's seat and repositioned the ship several feet farther out. Then she carefully lowered the gangway to span the gap with a flimsy bridge. To keep *Freedom* from bumping the crumbling ledge, she maintained a space of several feet. Locking the ship in position, she moved onto the gangway. Without the support of any ground, it bounced and swayed with every step.

Though over three feet wide, she felt as if the gangway was a narrow, swaying tightrope. She no longer heard the girl's muffled sobs, the men's shouts or the shrieking Alavans. The roaring of blood in her veins drowned out all sound. Cora stared straight ahead, attempting to focus on Ansal and the girls, but knew full well on either side of her the world fell into nothingness. The metallic taste and smell of blood in her mouth and nose told her she'd bit her lip. At the end of the gangway she stopped.

"Hand the girls to me one at a time," she told Ansal

The Palia didn't argue. She pried one child from her side

and, using all her strength, held her out. Pushing aside fear Cora grabbed the shaking child, rushed her up the gangway into the ship and ran back to repeat the process with the second girl. Once they were both safe, she held out her un-injured arm and told Ansal, "Give me your hand and jump."

Without hesitation, Ansal leaned forward, closed her fingers around Cora's and jumped. The impact of her body caused the gangway to bounce wildly. Though Cora braced herself, her knees buckled and she fell. Her injured elbow hit the metal. Pain sent shafts of lights sparking inside her head. Ansal landed beside her. The gangway dipped. Cora felt herself slid-ing broadside toward the edge and oblivion. Her hands scram-bled uselessly on the smooth metal . . . then warm fingers clamped around her upper arms and stopped her. Together, she and Ansal got to their feet and Ansal turned to the boy.

"See to the girls," Cora said. "I'll get him."

It surprised her when the Palia so readily followed orders from a human, but she didn't have time to think about it; the boy needed to be rescued. Blinking to clear the dust and tears of pain from her eyes, she took stock of the situation. The boy stood motionless against the wall, toes hanging over the ledge. One wrong move and he'd fall. When Cora looked at him, he met her gaze with his own steady one. It now held fear, but no panic. At the tender age of four he was already a man. And even if his dark hair and eyes, along with the stubborn jut of his jaw beneath its layer of baby fat, hadn't proclaimed him Alex's son, his strength and courage in the face of insurmountable odds did so.

There was a gap of nearly four feet between him and the edge of the gangway. At the corner of the gangway closest to the boy, Cora knelt down and stretched out her arms. "Jump. I catch," she told him in Herdspeak.

He didn't move.

"Jump!" she repeated in a stronger tone.

He searched her face, then gave a small nod. The absolute

trust in his eyes sent a shaft of emotion straight into her heart. She didn't know him. He was another woman's son, but in that moment she loved him.

She leaned toward him. The gangway dipped beneath her weight. She slid forward and for a moment her gaze dropped to the emptiness stretching between them. But suddenly she no longer feared falling or even dying. Only the thought of failing to save this boy, Alex's son, held any terror for her.

She smiled at the boy. His small body tensed. Pushing off the rock wall with all the strength in his arms, eyes locked on hers, he leaped.

Her heart stopped beating. He wasn't going to make it.

No! She wouldn't lose him. At the last second she threw herself forward until her upper body hung over the edge of the gangway. She reached out and clamped her fingers around his wrist. He cried out once in pain as his body jerked to a stop and dangled at the end of her arm. The world narrowed to the two of them.

Only Cora's lower body sprawled on the swaying end of the gangway kept them both from plunging into the void. The metal edge bit into her belly. She braced the toes of her space boots against the gangway and tried to inch her way backward, but the metal tips found no purchase. His weight dragged her forward.

She tried to grab him with her other arm, but pain blinded her. That arm was useless. She couldn't haul him up.

"I'll come help," Ansal said from the hatchway.

"No! Stay where you are," Cora shouted back. "Your weight could tip me off the edge."

The child would have to pull himself up onto the gangway. Once his weight was gone, maybe she could drag herself back to safety.

"Grab my arm. Climb up," she said.

He glanced down and shuddered. "We fall."

"Climb," she ordered.

With his free arm, he grabbed at her. His fingers bit into her flesh. She swallowed her scream as her arm tried to pull free of its socket. Then, like an agile little Earth monkey he clambered up and over her. The gangway dipped briefly, then rose until it jutted almost straight out from the ship. With his weight off her, she felt like she floated above the vast bottomless chasm. She lifted her upper body level with the gangway and tried to shift backward, but both her arms were numb. Without them she couldn't move. Soon her strength would fail, she'd sag and the downward momentum would cause her to slide off the edge. Pain and fatigue fogged her brain. Part of her wanted to close her eyes and give in to the blessed peace of oblivion.

But now wasn't the time to surrender control. Without her to fly *Freedom* to safety, the boy, the girls and Ansal would be no less trapped than before. The whole expedition would be a waste.

Summoning her strength Cora ignored the pain flaring in her body and inched her way backward. Finally, her whole body lay on the gangway. She rolled onto her back and stared up at the sky. The boy crouched near her feet, watching.

Dark specks floated in front of her eyes. Damn! Those weren't specks; they were Alavans. She scrambled to her feet, grabbed the boy's arm and, unmindful of the bouncing gangway, dashed for the hatch. As she shoved him inside and dove after him, an Alavan, talons poised, grazed the side of the ship. If she hadn't moved when she did, those talons would have sunk into her.

"Close. Abracadabra."

The smell of dust, blood and sweat burned Alex's nostrils and stung his eyes as he prepared to make his run. He tightened his grip on his swords. Leather creaked as he used his knees to urge his draca forward. Beneath him, the animal, lungs wheezing, trembled in fear and exhaustion but answered Alex's demand with a willing heart. They dashed forward.

Three Alavans followed, but maintained a safe distance from Alex's flashing swords. They'd learned quickly not to dive too close. This served both them and the men, as neither suffered further wounds in this macabre dance, but while the men and dracas grew weary, the birds' energy seemed inexhaustible. How long before they grew bored with this game and sought easier prey, perhaps the trapped and weaponless children? If they refocused their attack there'd be nothing he and the other men could do to stop them. The result would be the same when the men and dracas collapsed. Cora was the children's only hope.

As he started his run he searched the sky by the cliff edge for a sign of *Freedom* and Cora. She'd heard his call and come. Had she arrived in time? Were the children safe? Was she?

In his moment of inattention, his draca swerved to avoid a dead Alavan and stumbled. Caught off guard, Alex flew over the animal's head. Instinctively he tucked his body, hit the ground on his shoulder and rolled. Pain shot through him. The impact knocked the swords from his grip and the air from his lungs. Stunned, he lay flat on his back while his draca bolted toward the woods. Two Alavans chased the animal, but one still circled cautiously above Alex.

Alex remained motionless as he struggled to regain his breath. A sword lay several feet beyond his reach. Could he grab it in time to defend against the bird's attack? Or would its talons sink into him first?

Three men started to break away from the circle, to come to his aid, but Alex heard Ro'am call them back. The man was right. If they broke ranks, the Alavans would as well and it would only be a matter of time before they rediscovered the trapped children. And the odds were against the men, four to one. Alone they couldn't hold the birds off; together they had a small chance.

He was on his own. Muscles tightened as he gathered his strength to make his move. Timing was everything. Too soon and the Alavan wouldn't be within reach, too late and the bird would strike first. With a shriek of triumph, it flew upward then whirled and dove, wings spread, feet first, talons extended. Hand reaching for his sword, Alex rolled. Dust stirred by the big bird's wings clogged his throat. He wasn't going to make it. The sword lay out of reach as the bird's talons flexed open above his exposed belly.

Anger filled him. If he died, so be it, but the damned bird was going with him. He rolled again. Talons raked his side. His fingers found the tip of his sword. Ignoring the bite of blade, he swung it upward. The hilt struck the Alavan's wing, knocking it off balance and sending it upward squawking in protest. It shook its head. Alex scrambled to his feet and gripped his sword. One arm hung numb and useless at his side, probably broken. Blood pouring from the gaping wound in his side left him dizzy, and the blood from the cuts on his palm made his hold unsure. Still, he stood fast as the bird circled and prepared to attack again.

His head spun and his vision grew dim. The bird dived at him. Its shadow blocked the sun. Alex raised his sword.

Boom! Above him, the bird exploded. Feathers, blood and chunks of gore rained down on him. Before he could truly comprehend what was happening, the plateau echoed with noise, the shrill cries of wounded and dying Alavans and the cheers of men. He looked up and saw the Alavans being blasted out of the sky. With amazing speed and agility, Cora piloted her ship around and through the Alavans. Like a silver hawk, *Freedom* decimated the flock as if they were nothing but helpless sparrows.

The smell of blood and laser fire filled the crisp air. Feathers drifted in the breeze. Broken, bloody corpses of birds littered the plateau. Bloodlust and hunger replaced by the instinct for survival, a few of the wiser Alavans fled, and in minutes the fight was over.

Alex watched as *Freedom* landed several yards from him. Cora had come back. Hope exploded in his empty heart. Though she'd only been gone a few hours, in truth they'd parted weeks ago.

He took a step forward, then stopped. Would she stay? Could he stop himself from begging her to do so? If she did, could he live with the pain of watching her spirit shrivel and die? And if she refused, could he let her leave again without him? He saw no easy answer to their problem. To be together, one of them would have to give up a large piece of themselves. Was he strong enough to shoulder the cost of being that one? He had to be, because without her nothing else mattered.

The hatch opened and the gangway extended. With the sun behind the ship he couldn't see into the shadowy interior. He waited.

A familiar face peered out of the opening, then a small naked body exploded down the gangway. Alex dropped his sword, crouched and gathered the boy into his one good arm.

"Zan!" the child cried, wrapping his chubby arms around Alex's neck.

Joy and pain blurred together as the boy pressed his head against Alex's injured shoulder. Tears dripped down his back as the boy began to sob. Tears for what he'd found and what he'd soon lose again burned the back of Alex's eyes. He rubbed his hand over the boy's back in a soothing gesture. The feel of the child's smooth skin under his palm eased a tiny portion of the guilt in his soul. In moments the boy fell asleep.

Ro'am moved to his side. "How badly are you hurt?"

"I'll live. Will you take him?" Alex asked.

Ro'am lifted the boy from Alex and gasped. "Not if you

don't get that bleeding stopped." He called another man over and handed off the boy. "Let's get you aboard ship and back home to the healer."

Alex looked down at his side. Blood dripped from three deep gashes. He tried to rise, but his head spun and his legs wouldn't cooperate. "Cora? Where is she? Why hasn't she come to me?"

Ro'am's hesitation returned Alex to full consciousness. "She's hurt? Dead?" She couldn't be dead. No one else could fly *Freedom* that way. He stumbled to his feet and up the gangway.

"Cora!" he roared as he burst through the hatch. After the bright afternoon light, he could see little in the ship's dim interior.

"No need to shout. I'm here."

He followed her voice to the bridge. As his eyes adjusted he could see her sitting at the console. A Palia stood at her side, a hand on her shoulder. Two naked little girls attempted to hide behind her chair and the Palia's legs.

"Could we have a moment?" Alex asked the Palia.

The Palia looked at Cora. When Cora nodded, she coaxed the two girls from under the console and herded them into the ship's sleeping quarters.

Alex ran his gaze over Cora. Dirt and blood streaked her face, arms and clothing. Her golden hair was matted and stuck out from her head like straw. Still, she looked beautiful. "Are you hurt?"

She attempted to shrug but grimaced in pain. "Nothing serious. Some cuts and bruises. A swollen elbow and a wrenched shoulder. I'll live. You?"

"Same." He knew better than to try to shrug, but he had a question he had to ask. Its answer would decide everything. "You heard my call and came back. Why? You made it clear that the fate of these people didn't matter to you. That you were leaving and weren't going to come back.

That your freedom meant more to you than I did." Then he stepped back and waited for her answer.

Cora stared at Alex. "This isn't the time or place for this discussion." He looked dead on his feet. Blood dripped from his side. His arm hung from his shoulder at a strange angle and pain pinched his mouth into a tight line. She needed to explain, to make him understand what drove her, but not while he was swaying on his feet and not when she was feeling so weak, both physically and emotionally. Minutes ago she'd almost lost him again. Who knew what she might reveal in this vulnerable state? She swung her chair away from him. "Let's go see Maran, get cleaned up and then we'll talk."

With his good hand he grabbed the arm of her chair and yanked her around to face him, then held her there, his face and body looming inches over her. "The time and place is now. No more delays. You can't control this."

She sagged in her seat. "You're right. I can't." She looked up at him helplessly, unsure of where to start or how to explain.

His gaze softened. He reached out and stroked a strand of hair behind her ear. She shivered at his gentle touch. Seeming to make a decision, he smiled. "I'll go first. I love you. When you leave again, I'm going with you."

Shock held her speechless, then she burst out, "No! I won't let you make that sacrifice for me."

"It's not a sacrifice if it's what I *want* to do. Without you, nothing else I do matters."

She cupped his cheek in her palm. "You can lie to me, but how long can you lie to yourself? How long before the burden of guilt eats you up? You know you're needed here."

Sudden anger drove him to his feet. She watched as he paced the small bridge, a restless warrior without a foe to fight. "What about my needs? And yours? Must we give up our hearts and souls so that others can survive?" he asked. Then, as quickly as it had come, the fight drained out of him. He fell to his knees in front of her and laid his head in her lap.

Shame and remorse clogged her throat. Afraid to trust in their love, she'd brought him to this point. She stroked his hair.

"You begged me not to ask, but if I don't—"

She hushed him. "There's no need to ask. Even before I heard your call I was on my way back. I love you too."

He raised his head. Hope shone in his dark eyes. "You're willing to give up your freedom for me?"

"I finally figured out that being free had nothing to do with my decision to leave. Fear sent me running."

"Fear of what? Me?"

"Indirectly perhaps. More of losing control. Of losing myself. Of loving. Loving you made me feel vulnerable in so many ways it scared the stars out of me. My reaction to fear is to try to control it, and the only way I could do that was to deny it. But I discovered that loving you also makes me strong in ways I never guessed."

He stood and pulled her against his good side. With a sigh she rested her head against his chest.

"What about your position with Earth League Force?" he asked.

"My commission expired. And in five or so years when they finally send out a team, who knows—you and I may be ready to move on. And if we're not, they can get themselves another pilot. Wherever you are I'm going to be too."

"What about flying?"

She leaned back and grinned at him. "What do you call what I just did? Draca-riding?"

"Pretty fancy, but I had an altogether different type of flying in mind."

When his head came down and his lips closed over hers, Cora's heart finally knew true freedom. It soared.